THE BLIGHTED CLIFFS

EDWIN THOMAS

The Blighted Cliffs

Thomas Dunne Books
St. Martin's Press New York

THOMAS DUNNE BOOKS.
An imprint of St. Martin's Press.

www.stmartins.com

Library of Congress Cataloging-in-Publication Data

Thomas, Edwin, 1977–
The blighted cliffs / Edwin Thomas.—1st U.S. ed.
p. cm.
ISBN 0-312-32511-8
EAN 978-0312-32511-4
1. Great Britain—History, Naval—19th century—Fiction. 2. Great Britain. Royal Navy—Officers—Fiction. 3. Napoleonic Wars, 1800–1815—Fiction. 4. Dover (England)—Fiction. I. Title.

PR6120.H644B55 2004
823'.92—dc22 2004042825

First published in Great Britain by Bantam Press, a division of Transworld Publishers

First U.S. Edition: August 2004

10 9 8 7 6 5 4 3 2 1

for M
at bedtime

1

MOST MEN WILL TELL YOU – IN LATER LIFE, AT LEAST, WITH infirmity upon them – that what they truly regret is the drink. But looking back, what I regret most about that night is not having drunk more. Of course I'd had plenty: *more than the ration*, as they say, and enough to put me to bed, but not enough to knock me out until dawn. Which is a pity, because if I'd stayed in the tavern for a few more measures, I probably wouldn't have woken in the early hours with an artillery duel pounding in my head. And that would have saved me no end of trouble.

The first thing I noticed – after my head – was that I was not alone in my cot: something was huddled under the covers with me. This did not tally with any recollections I had of the night before, so I prodded it experimentally. My method was sound: the shape stirred, and a raven-haired girl appeared, the blanket held to her chest in curious propriety. I was relieved to see that from the neck up, at least, my judgement had not wholly deserted me.

'What the devil are you doing here?' I asked, rubbing my head. It was a largely rhetorical question – although I remembered nothing of her, I could certainly guess her trade – but it can be awkward starting these conversations.

'Don't you remember?' she asked flatly. 'The Crown an' Anchor?'

'Of course,' I replied, a white lie in the cause of gallantry. 'But did I engage you to stay the night?'

Her face hardened, and she stared with granite eyes. 'Nah,' she spat, 'I stayed cos it was warm.'

'Pity,' I said, although in truth I was in no state to discharge any outstanding obligations. 'Well, you've done your job, my little warming pan. Now you can go. Get your clothes on.'

She made no movement, but inclined her eyes downwards. Her cheeks darkened.

'Good God, girl,' I laughed. 'Nothing I haven't seen before – I can remember that much, certainly. You'll not get far in your profession if you come over all nunnish in the morning.' Still she did not move. 'Very well. I shall avert my sinful eyes. But don't go stealing anything, or I'll see you punished.'

I rolled over and burrowed my face in the pillow; it seemed to calm the pain slightly. I half hoped I would fall asleep again, but neither my head nor my churning stomach would allow that. I waited for what seemed a decent interval, then looked up. The room was empty.

'Silly whore,' I muttered, realizing I hadn't even taken her name. Still, I could presumably seek her at the tavern – the Crown and . . . something, she had said – if I needed her again. I anticipated a long, freezing winter in that godforsaken corner of Kent, and would need all the diversions I could find to survive it.

Left to myself, though, I could reflect on my immediate situation. I was in Dover, at the inn: I recognized the white-washed walls and the steep ceiling above me. This was certainly where the porter had brought me the previous evening. I was due to meet the *Orestes*, and place myself under the command of Captain Crawley. I was to be on my best behaviour, on this my uncle at the Admiralty had been very clear. 'This is your last chance, Martin,' he had thundered. 'I have little hope of your distinguishing yourself, but you will regret bringing any further shame upon the family.' By family, of course, he meant himself, although without relations in high places to embarrass I'd have been on the boat to India long ago, so I could hardly take exception. If I was not to lose the patronage of my uncle, I needed to work hard; I needed to behave; I needed to stay out of trouble. But what I needed most at that moment was a good, long piss.

I swung out of bed, alert enough not to crack my head on the steep roof, and fumbled around in search of a chamber pot. There did not appear to be one; perhaps the girl had stolen it in spite, or more likely it eluded my fuddled eyes in the dark. I looked to the window, but it was too high to be of use, so I pulled on my shoes – it seemed I had never removed my shirt and breeches – and descended to the privy in the stable yard. The morning air hit me as I opened the front door, and I flinched, but after a few seconds I started to find it agreeable. Whether it cleared my head or numbed it I could not tell, but at any rate the pain lessened and my belly seemed less mutinous. My slanting, stuffy garret lost its appeal, and having relieved my need I resolved to take a turn about the town. Borrowing a cloak from the hook in the stable, I let myself out by the gate.

I had seen little of Dover when I arrived, and saw little now: there would be at least another hour before sunrise, I guessed, and no lights showed anywhere (to avoid giving our enemies in the Channel a beacon, or a target, I later discovered). The streets were narrow and the houses crooked, but other than shadows I could see nothing save the line of the road, which I followed faithfully through the dark. It brought me presently to the shore; stars appeared, and although there was no moon I could see the shapes of masts and spars filling the sky to my right. The docks, I thought, and immediately turned left. I wanted to delay my reunion with the navy for as long as possible, and did not relish the thought of encountering Captain Crawley at this hour, dressed as I was and, I suspected, not wholly sober.

A beach ran along the sea-front, hugging the edge of the bay, and I let myself down the embankment onto it. I've never felt much love for the sea, my career notwithstanding, but it was good to get out of the cramped town and feel some space around me before boarding the tiny cutter that was to be my future. Besides, the air was sweeter here, the wind stronger; I could feel it blowing the evil vapours out of me as I tramped across the pebbles. I'm by no means a solitary man – I'd far rather the saloon with company than prayers in the attic – but there was something soothing in the silence, the emptiness of the shore that night. So much did I know.

Before I left, my uncle had commended me to introspection. 'Consider your wretched life,' he had roared, 'and see how base, how abandoned you are become.' Now his words returned to me, and I began to think on them. He certainly had a point. Not many men survived Trafalgar with no distinction whatsoever – it was one of those 'any man, be he ne'er so vile' occasions – but somehow I managed it. It was the drink, of course: while England was expecting every man to do his duty, I was buried in the *Téméraire*'s hold sleeping off a stinking hangover. How I got there, and why I hadn't, as was my habit, collapsed into my bunk, where someone could have roused me, I still don't know, but there I was. I didn't sleep through the battle of course – that much drink would have seen me dead without a shot being fired – but I knew nothing until I heard the first broadside thundering through the hull. If I'd gone on deck then, I might still have redeemed myself, for there was plenty of honour about that day, but the bastard French had upended a cannon onto the hatch above me, and there was no way of opening it. I spent the entire battle locked in the dark stench, terrified that at any moment a cannonball would come crashing through and finish it. Or worse, take my legs off and condemn me to the life of a crippled coward, beneath pity.

Obviously, my drunken luck saw off the French, and when the crew finally prised the gun off the hatch, I emerged as sound as my mother bore me. The midshipman who'd taken my place, meanwhile, was dead – a heroic death, apparently, sliced in half by French iron. He was given a hammock with two cannonballs sewn into the feet, the irony lost on the navy; I should have been court-martialled. But Trafalgar was a national triumph, sanctified by the good Lord Nelson's death, and trying officers for gross dereliction would have spoiled the mood. Much easier to send me to fight smugglers, far away from anyone of importance, and hope that a knife in the dark on a lonely beach would see justice done.

It was with this apposite thought that I noticed I had covered more ground than expected: I had come around the headland, and into the next bay. The stars were beginning to fade, and I thought I could see the horizon lightening. I was also aware that the breeze, which had done so much to restore me, now left me cold, even under the thick riding cloak. I decided to turn back.

Suddenly, a light flared at the head of the cliffs. A sentry, I thought, or perhaps someone from the castle hurrying home after a tumble with the farmer's daughter. But then a second light flashed, as if in answer, only this one from the beach, a few dozen yards ahead of me.

I froze. It could be soldiers, or fishermen, or any number of harmless possibilities, but the Kentish coast after dark was not renowned for its legitimate enterprise; that, after all, was what had brought me there. But I was supposed to face danger with a well-armed crew, not stumble upon it by accident. And I could hardly be more exposed, standing in the middle of open ground waiting for the sun to come up. I looked desperately for cover, but the beach was quite flat; only the broken rocks and shadows at the base of the cliff seemed to hold any safety. I glanced back in the direction of the light. It had gone out, or been hidden; at any rate, I couldn't see it, nor whoever had held it. But they must be there. I tiptoed to the cliff, holding my cloak against my body to keep it from flapping, and crouched in the dark.

And just as well: a moment later I heard footsteps crunching along the shingle. Not from where the lantern had been, though, but from Dover, from the same direction I had come. Had I been followed? The rock gouged into my back as I squeezed myself still tighter against it. I was thankful for the dark cloak over my light clothes, though it would be little enough protection if they had already seen me. But what were they doing? I lifted my head an inch and risked a quick look.

If I aspired to become an authority on the habits of the English smuggler – as, by my uncle's command, I suppose I did – then the scene before me could have been the frontispiece of my primer. A wide boat piled high with casks was drawn up on the beach, the tide coursing about its hull. It was extraordinary: I would swear it had not been there when I arrived a minute earlier, yet now there were a dozen men in action about her. Two held the bow, another pair stood on the bulwark rolling off great barrels, and the remainder manhandled them onto a bizarre contraption I can only describe as a long sled, for although harnessed to a pony, it sat on runners. A tall man in a dark coat, his hat pulled low over his face, supervised the action with what appeared to be a squat teapot, though from the thin beam of light it cast I guessed it to be some form of lantern. It was more reminiscent of a thriving dock than the actions of a gang of desperadoes, though they worked with an industry our tars would have struggled to match. Every so often I caught some impenetrable word – 'geneva', 'tubman', 'nanky' – but otherwise they worked in complete silence.

Had I been Ned of the Navy, or even the late Horatio, I would no doubt have burst from my hiding place there and then, stolen a cutlass and despatched those ruffians to their dismal fate with a dozen steely blows. Unfortunately for my country, I was Martin Jerrold: freezing, outnumbered and certainly not *that* drunk. And although I had no evidence, I suspected that they would kill as efficiently as they laboured. I stayed tight against the cliff, and prayed they came no nearer.

They must have unloaded about half their stock when suddenly a shot exploded into the night, the echo reverberating off the cliffs. I ducked instinctively, though it was clear almost immediately that it had come from the cliff-top. It was as well I did, for a narrow beam swept around the beach and passed straight over my head.

'Wassat?' someone hissed. From the general consternation, I guessed they were as surprised as I, though with my head down I could see nothing.

'Danny's up there,' came the reply – a deep, growling voice. 'Musta seen somethin' 'e didn't like.'

This was hardly reassuring, but then another shot sounded, again from above. My knees were pressed so tight into my belly I thought I would vomit. Only the terror prevented me.

'Danny's not answerin',' muttered the deep voice. 'Best stow it, an' quick. Meet at the bitch's head.'

I heard some movement: the soft rasping of wood on stone, and a few splashes in the surf. Then nothing. And then, just as I began to uncoil, a loud thud, as though something hard had hit the beach. A falling rock? Had I survived my encounter with the pirates only to be crushed under a landslide? But no more stones fell, and I dared not leave my refuge with the smugglers still abroad.

I stayed hedgehogged in my ball, listening for movement and trying to ignore the cramp in my legs, the ache in my gut and – *encore* – the throbbing in my temples. There was no sound save the waves, and eventually I convinced myself that the pirates had gone. Besides, the light had come up now, and I was hardly invisible. If they were there, they would certainly have seen me by now. I lifted my head.

The beach was empty, save for a shapeless bundle on the tidemark which I took to be some forgotten contraband. I was elated: I had survived the ordeal, and would not be found floating face down in Dover harbour. My powers of dissimulation, so odious to my uncle, had triumphed. I stood up, groaning at the pain in my thighs, and hobbled out. Every step was agony, but soon I would be back at the inn and in a steaming bath, looking forward to a stout breakfast and strong coffee. Then, suitably attired, I could stroll down to the docks and pay my respects to Captain Crawley. I might even be on time.

My reverie ended with the sound of shouts from around the next bend in the cliff. I started back for my hide, but my legs were too stiff. I had covered less than half the distance when the new arrivals burst into view, twenty of them at least. Cutlasses flashed in their hands, and it seemed I had merely swapped one gang of cutthroats for another until I saw their short jackets and trousers. *The navy.*

‘Get ’im,’ bellowed one, a huge man with a small whistle about his neck.

I turned to see whom he meant, before the pair of seamen sprinting for me clarified the meaning.

‘Oh no you don’t,’ I shouted, as dignified as I could manage. Not very, I suppose, but my commanding manner must have sown confusion among men expecting to apprehend a common pirate, for they paused. I pressed my advantage. ‘Allow me to introduce myself,’ I continued, pompous as George. ‘Lieutenant Martin Jerrold, of his Majesty’s cutter *Orestes*. At your service.’ I fear I might have given a small bow.

A shorter man, with close-cropped hair and a narrow face, pushed to the front. His dress was that of a gentleman, but there was no decoration on his blue coat.

‘What’s that?’ he asked. ‘Lieutenant Jerrold, you say?’

‘None other. But you have the advantage, sir. May I enquire . . . ?’

He raised a hand as a voice shouted from behind him. ‘Cap’n, sir! ’Ave a look at this.’

The men parted, and through the gap I could see a sailor standing by the bundle on the sand. My jaw sagged as I looked more closely: two unmistakable legs protruded from one end, and an arm flopped lifelessly at its side. It was a man, or had been. From the skewed angle of the neck, and the way the gulls picked at him, I judged him quite incontrovertibly dead. The officer wandered over and kicked him, but only the birds moved. Then he turned to face me, and I saw a wolfish grin.

‘So, Lieutenant Jerrold, it seems you have some explanations to give.’ He must have mistaken the horror on my face for offended gentility. ‘But of course, I’m forgetting myself. Jeremiah Crawley, Captain.’ He fixed his eyes hard on mine. ‘Also of his Majesty’s cutter *Orestes*.’

I retched.

2

THE HUGE MAN WITH THE WHISTLE – DUCKER, THEY CALLED HIM, the quartermaster – led me back to Dover; Crawley stayed to examine the body. The pebbles on the beach were slick from the tide and shifted treacherously with every step, giving me the miserable sensation of constantly tumbling forwards. Several times Ducker had to grip my arm to keep me upright. My legs bent and splayed like saplings, and there was a void in my stomach that screamed for wine – or better yet, brandy – to dampen my incessant shivering.

The footing improved as we reached the town, rounding the cliff under the famous castle and finding the road: here the shingle stones had been hammered into cobbles, but I felt no less wretched, for now there was an audience to witness my misery. The narrow street, as skewed in daylight as it had been in the dark, was thronged with people going about the trades of the town: bakers and coopers and fishwives and their custom, all staring as the quartermaster navigated us through.

I must have made quite an impression with my state of undress, my untied hair and the vomit spilled down my shirt front, for I soon caught the corners of many eyes flickering over me, and heard the rumours begin to grind. *Had there been a shipwreck?* people asked, wondering whether they might put to sea and earn some salvage, or *was it a dangerous lunatic apprehended on the shore?* Then someone said the words 'French spy', and a murmur passed through the crowd. I felt a tightening of breath all around; now they did not look away when I caught their gaze, but stared with unabashed hostility. Their voices rose, and their faces hardened. It recalled the mood at a hanging I'd once attended: not some gentleman-of-the-road or cutpurse, cheered even on the gallows, but a child killer, a notorious man of vile tastes whom the mob would have torn apart like furies had it not been for the militia. But I had no company of dragoons to protect me that morning, only Ducker, and he was finding it ever harder to push us through. Elbows and shoulders jabbed into me with careless antagonism, and I guessed that one overzealous shove from the quartermaster would be all the provocation they needed to far greater violence.

Ducker looked over his shoulder, and I could see the tension in his broad face. 'Not to worry, Lieutenant Jerrold, sir,' he called loudly. 'We'll soon 'ave you back at *Orestes*.'

I managed to nod my sagging head, desperately hoping that Crawley would not arrive with the corpse before we were through the crowd. But whether Ducker's little ploy had placated them, or whether they lost interest in my pathetic figure, our path became clearer, and our pace quickened. The business around us began to feel more purposeful, and the stevedores who manhandled their cargoes along the street seemed less inclined to break their work for the sake of a bedraggled stranger and his guardian. A file of soldiers marched past and I felt a sudden, insane flash of security, though whether they'd risk their lives firing into a riot on my account I very much doubted.

We came out onto the quay on the western side of the inner basin, a harbour choked with every manner of small craft. Their decks thrived with the labours of commerce, but I had little time to admire the scene for Ducker had opened the door to a lime-washed building next to a warehouse, and was ushering me into a square little room. Small windows were set high into its white walls, but the mournful light they admitted did little to cheer the air.

'You wait 'ere for the cap'n, sir,' Ducker told me, his voice giving nothing away. Then the door was shut and he was gone.

I slumped into a chair behind the empty desk in the middle of the room. I felt weak from my ordeal: the terror of the smugglers, the ghastly meeting with Crawley, and then the hostility of the townspeople. My wet shirt seemed colder than ever, and its constant stench under my nose only inclined me to spoil it further. Glancing down, I thought I could see a few lumps of the previous night's fish pie clinging to it; I looked about for a cloth or handkerchief to wipe it, but the stark room held nothing save a few pieces of plain wooden furniture, and I did not care to be found rifling through Crawley's desk when he arrived. God alone knew what he already thought of me.

Still, the disgust of my superiors had been something of a feature in my professional life, and as I reflected upon my predicament, my spirits rose. Meeting one's commander under such circumstances might be unfortunate and embarrassing, but as I'd not yet reported on board he could hardly have me up for indiscipline. True, I'd been in uncomfortable proximity to the smugglers, but nobody could think that I had managed to gain their employment after just a few hours in the town. And as for the unfortunate corpse, well, whether he was a victim of the smugglers, an inconveniently timed suicide, or simply a morning rambler who'd put a foot wrong, I knew nothing and cared less. I doubted I'd be commended for discovering him – those who find trouble never are – but I could hardly be blamed for his demise. And what of the danger to me, I realized, puffing with indignation. There were plenty of stories in the navy of men killed by their shipmates falling from the mastheads and striking them down on deck. If the idiot had decided to take his own life, I thought, he could at least have had the courtesy to examine the ground below, rather than risk taking an innocent soul to oblivion with him.

As if someone had been reading my uncharitable thoughts, the door suddenly banged open, and I looked up guiltily to see Crawley striding in. Since I had seen him on the beach he had donned a coarse wig, in the old style; it sat uncomfortably over a face that was lined with frustrations well in advance of his forty-odd years. In those rare moments when he relaxed his gaze, his eyes could seem almost kind; otherwise they would tense with an almost wounded suspicion. As he entered he was scowling, and his humour was not improved at the sight of me.

'Out of my chair, if you please, Mr Jerrold,' he snapped.

I banged my knee on the desk as I jerked upright, and shuffled around to sit in the chair opposite.

'And you'll sit when I ask you,' he added, equally sharply.

I rose again and stood there awkwardly, waiting for his invitation. Instead, he opened a drawer and shuffled through some papers inside, finally extracting one stamped with the large Admiralty seal. Holding it close to his face, he read it intently for several minutes while I shifted uncomfortably on my feet. It reminded me all too much of my school days; nor, from the unruly look in his eye, could I be confident that he was not about to reach for a cane.

He dropped the paper to the table and stared hard at me. 'Lieutenant Jerrold.' There was a contempt in the way he said my name that made me even less comfortable.

'I have my commission at the inn, with my belongings.'

'Hah,' he grunted. 'You certainly make a memorable arrival, Lieutenant. I take it you knew nothing of the corpse until we found him?'

I nodded my assent. 'I was taking a stroll to clear my head, sir, and had not even noticed the body when you found me.' I thought of mentioning my encounter with the smugglers as possibly relevant, but feeling no need to colour his perceptions of me yet further with tales of my cowardice, I kept quiet.

'I have left the body with the coroner,' Crawley told me. 'He may wish to question you, I suppose, though I did tell him that you would be thoroughly useless. In that regard.' He seemed bored by the whole business, but there was definitely an edge to his voice. 'I suppose you know why you are here in Dover?'

Only too well, but I refrained from an honest answer in the hope that my uncle might have exercised discretion in his orders to Crawley. Instead, I tried a tentative nod.

'Good,' barked Crawley. 'Because I have to tell you, Mr Jerrold, that it rather eludes *me*. Do you know how many officers one of his Majesty's cutters requires?'

Sensing that I could provide no satisfactory answer, I attempted a shrug of the shoulders.

'*One*, Mr Jerrold.' Crawley almost spat out the words. 'One. Her commanding officer. And tell me, Mr Jerrold, who might that be aboard *Orestes*?'

'You, sir?' I had meant it to be a firm reply, but it came out more like a question.

Crawley visibly flinched. 'Am I, Mr Jerrold? Do you question my authority, or are you possessed of some happy intelligence that I am not?' His face was flushed, and he was staring at me with a furious intensity.

My mind churned under his onslaught, and I struggled to grasp why I was being subjected to it. Had my uncle apprenticed me to a sadist? A dementate? But as I looked at his angry face I saw that there was a real puzzlement behind the glaring eyes, and suddenly the thought occurred to me: did he really not know why I was here? Could he believe that I might have been sent to relieve him of his command? It seemed laughable under the circumstances, but I could see no other reason for it, unless out of some unknown malice he was determined to drive me away.

'I was not even aware that there was the vaguest doubt as to your commanding *Orestes*,' I tried, as stiffly nonsensical as I could manage. I realized from his face that my words were still ambivalent, and dredged my brain for the wording of my commission. 'I am sent here, sir, to observe and execute what orders and, er, directions I shall receive from you. Sir.' I found myself nodding like a clown, willing him to accept my words.

His narrow face still burned with suspicion, but he relaxed an inch in his chair and rapped his fingers on the desk. 'Very well,' he allowed. 'But be mindful, Mr Jerrold: "The wise in heart will receive commandments, but a prating fool shall fall, and he that perverteth his ways shall be known." I shall not suffer you to be a prating fool.'

I think my mouth must have dropped a little at the sudden prospect of a sermon from this bizarre officer, but I managed to get out a few words about how much I looked forward to being under his command. He sniffed dismissively.

'Though for the moment,' he added, 'you shall stay ashore and carry out my orders here. I cannot have you confusing the men aboard my vessel, though it may be useful to have an extra sword in a fight.' He glanced at his paper again. 'I see you were at Trafalgar?'

'Yes, sir,' I said, keen to change the conversation, though I hardly wished to reminisce the occasion with him.

'You were a lucky man, Lieutenant, to have been present at our most glorious naval action since the Armada. Many officers would have given the use of a limb to be there. I do not know that you made the best of your luck, though I suppose you acquitted yourself honourably.' He looked at me shrewdly, and I tried to set a manly face. 'Certainly a *hero* of Trafalgar might expect better than a posting to this forsaken corner of the kingdom.'

I tried to protest my enthusiasm for the hunting down of villains who cheated the King's taxes, but he waved my words away.

'No-one comes to Dover, Lieutenant, unless his career is in the very greatest need of redemption. My predecessor on this station was relieved only because he enjoyed a great, indeed a unique, success against the smugglers. In the six months I have been here all I have endured is the enmity of the townspeople and the obstruction of the merchants, the sniping of the smugglers and the dangers of wind and tide. And the knowledge that every week hundreds of gallons of liquor, to say nothing of cloths and tobaccos and teas and the hundred other currencies of the smuggler, are being spirited past my petty blockade.' The vigour had left his voice, and his words were bitterly flat. 'If we pursue them, they throw their cargo overboard and become legitimate, or sail into one of the harbours the Corsican tyrant has kindly provided for them. Only last month we lost the *Ariadne* off Boulogne when she struck a reef chasing a lugger. And if we do ever enjoy a small success it is almost certain to be undone when we bring the culprits ashore. Men disappear from prisons, magistrates let them off with risible sentences, and impounded goods make their way into the shops. Dover is a festering wound on the face of England, Lieutenant,' he concluded grandiloquently, 'and we are but a tiny maggot trying to eat away at the rot.'

'And all to prevent people enjoying a few harmless pleasures,' I reflected, succumbing to the pessimism that had infused the room.

He stiffened. 'Even if you view tea and alcohol and tobacco as harmless pleasures, Mr Jerrold – and certainly *I* do not – you miss the point. It is the King's desire that all merchants should pay tax on their cargoes. Now you may believe that the King is the Lord's ordained instrument for the good governance of our sceptred isle, or you may believe that he is simply a feeble German well endowed by his parents, but if you wish to leave Dover for anywhere other than the churchyard or a life beyond the navy, you will dedicate yourself most sedulously to enforcing his wishes. That' – he jabbed a finger at me – 'is why we are here.'

I was so taken aback, by his bleak cynicism as much as his near treasonous talk, that I could think of nothing to say in reply, but simply stood dumbly before him while he glared up at me. The silence was broken by a rap on the door.

'Yes?'

I turned and saw the quartermaster standing squarely in the doorway.

'With your pardon, sir,' he began, talking straight through me. 'There's a gentleman 'ere to see the new lieutenant.'

I could not believe that this would be good news, and felt my heart begin to beat faster.

'From the Paving Commission.'

I tottered to the door, and saw Mr Stubb.

Mr Stubb was a great slab of a man, with a thick chin protruding from his shoulders, and a curiously compressed, anvil-like head. He did not carry much height, but his breadth was unshakeable and the girth of his limbs immense. He wore a look of unblinking purpose, and his voice grated with casual menace.

'Mr Jerrold.' It sounded as though he had perhaps swallowed some of the commission's paving stones. 'You'll come along with me.'

I could hardly think to disagree with this walking boulder, but suddenly Crawley's voice broke in. 'And where do you plan on taking my lieutenant, Mr Stubb?'

Stubb's narrow eyes swung slowly on to the captain. 'To the court'ouse, your 'onour. The magistrate wants a word with 'im. Regardin' 'is dead body.'

'What?' Crawley sounded irritable. 'I have already informed the coroner that Lieutenant Jerrold has no light to shed on that matter.'

'I couldn't say, your 'onour. But 'e does take against strange men found with strange bodies, does the magistrate.' Stubb's shoulders swelled slightly, stretching the seams of his tight coat to breaking.

'Lieutenant Jerrold may be a stranger to Sir Lawrence,' said Crawley icily, 'but I can certainly vouch for him as an officer of his Majesty.'

Stubb gave a toothless grin. 'Well, sir, then that's all's well that ends so. Sir Lawrence was wantin' you to come along too, so you can explain it to 'im yourself.'

Before Crawley could harangue him further, I felt a fat fist squeezing around my upper arm and was dragged into the street. The captain called that he would be along directly. It was scant comfort.

Stubb never relaxed his grip for a second, and I had to trot briskly after him to keep my arm from tearing off its shoulder. He said nothing, but led me quickly back along the harbour edge into the centre of the town. The tide was out now, and between the buildings I could see an oozy slope running down to the low water where dozens of small craft lay cock-eyed. From the stench, I guessed that not all the slime was mud: the harbour must double as the town's sewer.

We turned up yet another narrow street, though this was lined with shops of some refinement: ribbons and silks and fine waistcoats were their stock in trade, and the patrons correspondingly genteel. They had no shortage of curiosity, though, and turned from the well-stocked windows to stare at us, Stubb and his catch. It occurred to me, as I endured the hundredth prying little glance, that I was well on my way to becoming the most notorious stranger in Dover.

The road opened on to a small square, mostly covered by a large, colonnaded hall at its centre. I assumed this building was our destination, but Stubb pulled me behind it, past a pair of timbered inns, and across the face of a thin alley. I had barely time to see a pair of rusting manacles hanging down a thick stone wall before Stubb jerked on my shoulder again, and I stumbled after him through a looming gateway.

'Gibble!' Stubb bellowed. The word echoed around the dark room, though to little obvious effect.

I was thoroughly dizzied by my new surroundings, for in the gloom I could make out hardly anything. The floor was coarse under my feet, as if caked with sand or dried mud, and there was a mouldering flavour to the air. There were no lanterns or torches, and only after a few moments could I discern the vertical lines of some sort of gate ahead of us.

'Gibble!'

This time, after a pause, there did come a response: a slow, shuffling sound, as if an animal was limping out of its cave. A dim light appeared from my right, outlining a narrow passage and casting grotesque shadows across the wall behind. As the light came nearer the shadows rose, bending up the barrelled ceiling; now I could hear the huff of laboured breathing, the hollow slap of slow footsteps, and the cold clink of metal. I was gripped with a pounding fear. What horrors would Stubb and this Gibble inflict upon me in this forgotten dungeon? What could I have done to merit this fate? Where the devil was Crawley?

The man called Gibble hobbled into the room. His face bore the ravages of more diseases than I could imagine, and several greater disfigurements only his mother could have inflicted. The thin candle he held did little to soften his features, and he seemed impervious to the hot wax dribbling over his hand. His chest was bent almost to his stomach – an anchor back, as they called it – and what little hair he had jutted out in strange, craggy formations. If the aldermen of Dover had sought a turnkey to put the fear of hell into their prisoners, I doubt Lucifer himself could have supplied a better candidate.

'Was 'im?' slurred Gibble, lifting a fat finger in my direction.

'This is Mr Jerrold,' Stubb growled. Even he seemed repelled by the turnkey. ''Is Lordship'll want 'im soon. I'd watch out,' he added. ''E's a killer. Broke a man's neck.'

'Gyah,' gurgled Gibble inscrutably. He tugged at the large ring of keys on his belt and shuffled to the iron gate before us. After much fumbling and rasping, I heard the click of the lock and saw the gate open. It did not sound as though it had seen much use. 'Af'rou,' Gibble mumbled, crooking an arm in the direction of the open door. He might have attempted an ironic bow, but with the angle of his back it was hard to tell. Stubb however had no time for pleasantries, and without warning sent me staggering forward with a violent heave. I tumbled through the gate and went sprawling onto my face into a cold puddle of slime. The gate squeaked shut.

'I'll be back for 'im,' Stubb told Gibble, without any indication of when that happy hour might come.

I heard him stamp away and, looking up, saw the faint light of Gibble's candle retreating into his lair. Then I was alone, in the dark.

I pulled myself off my stomach and slumped against the dank wall. I felt myself shaking with spasms, involuntary and uncontrollable, and made no attempt to check them. My cheeks throbbed, and I ached to cry, but no tears came. A wave of horror and pity broke over me as I counted the injustices piled upon me since my arrival in Dover. I thought back on a lifetime of my father's sermons, my uncle's lectures, and the censures of the navy; wondering whether they had all been right: that I was doomed to fall into the Inferno. Would it matter that I was innocent of the death of the man on the beach? Were these the wages of sin my father had so coldly predicted for me only a week before, the whirlwind coming to reap me? Was I so completely forsaken?

The stink of shit filled my nose, and I tasted blood at the back of my mouth. I imagined myself beating and kicking Stubb until he begged for my mercy, or hurling Gibble into his own prison, but then I remembered falling in myself, felt the grazes on my hands and arms, and the tearless sobbing began again.

I raged and trembled, with all these thoughts and a hundred others burning through my head, until at last my mind was emptied and I fell into a broken sleep.

3

'OI.'

A whispering in my ear opened my eyes. I remembered dark tales of attacks and robberies, and worse besides, perpetrated upon hapless prisoners who dropped their guard. Was it too late for me already? I patted a hand down my side. No, I could feel the cloth of my shirt, and my breeches: at least they had left me the clothes on my back, soaked in filth though they were. And I was still lying in the position I remembered, so perhaps my virtue – I could almost hear a derisive *hah!* from my uncle at that word – remained intact. Beyond that, I had little worth the trouble of taking.

'Oi.'

The voice again, staying me on the brink of another round of self-pity. Something tugged at my sleeve, and I flinched in momentary terror, but there was no force behind it, no assault.

'Oi!'

This time, I had the wit to turn my head to seek the whisper's owner. The prison's gloom seemed to have lightened, or perhaps my eyes were grown accustomed to it, for I could now see the shape of a figure squatting next to me, his eyes very white as they peered at me.

'Who are you?' I mumbled through parched lips.

'Who's yerself?' he retorted, his teeth flashing in the darkness. His skin must be very dark, I thought, for I could see nothing of his face but the eyes and mouth.

'Jer . . . Jerrold,' I stammered. 'Martin Jerrold. Lieutenant Martin Jerrold. Sometimes.'

'Soldier, is yer?'

'Navy.'

The eyeballs widened. 'Yer don't say? What they do yer for then? Desertin'? 'Igh treason?' His voice dropped knowingly. 'The seaman's bent?' He must have seen me shiver, for he hurriedly added, 'Not that I goes fer that meself, see.'

'Murder.' If I was to swing for it, I could at least use my notoriety to keep the other prisoners at bay.

'Christ,' said my companion, clearly impressed. 'Who'd yer do?'

'I've no idea,' I had to admit. 'I was in the wrong place at an unfortunate time. What brought you here?'

There was some sort of movement by his face; possibly he was tapping his nose. 'Detained,' he said, 'at 'is Majesty's pleasure.'

Our conversation paused. I peered about me, trying to glimpse more of my surroundings, but there was nothing to see. Where were the other inmates? I wondered. Or was this a dungeon for particularly depraved criminals?

'Not a lot of custom at the moment,' agreed my fellow prisoner. 'Gets a bit lonely sometimes.'

'Is Dover really so honest a town?' If Stubb was any example, I had no reason to doubt the enthusiasm of its constabulary.

I heard a cackle of laughter.

'Don't you believe it, sir, whatever their lordships tries to tell yer. Just the wrong time o' year. They 'ad the assizes last week, cleared out the 'ole gaol to go afore the bench.' I heard a finger slide across his neck. 'Not a lot come back.' He chuckled wickedly. 'Though the truth of it is, they've not 'ad a lot to catch since old Cal Drake got scragged.'

I guessed he was about to launch into the story, though I was in little mood to hear a tale which ended with a hanging, but at that moment I heard a commotion at the far end of the prison and a familiar voice bawling for Gibble.

'They'll be comin' to take you to the judge,' offered my companion. 'Sir Lawrence.' I suspected he'd seen plenty of men make the journey.

'A merciful man?' I asked hopefully.

Again, that awful cackle. 'Sir Lawrence, 'e's one of 'em judges what thinks you can stop crime by 'angin' criminals.' He looked theatrically around the empty prison. 'Per'aps 'e's right. But you never know, 'e might be in a good 'umour this mornin'.' This, too, seemed a fine joke.

I heard the clamour of the gate, and the unmistakable tread of Stubb's boots.

'Mr Jerrold,' he called. 'Sir Lawrence'll 'ave you now.'

'See yer soon,' said the prisoner cheerfully.

Stubb marched me out through the gate, past Gibble's incoherent mutterings, and into the square outside. The light stung my eyes, and I screwed them shut; but no sooner had I done so than a great slap hit me full on the face. I recoiled at the shock and my eyes snapped open. It couldn't have been Stubb, for he had released his grip and was staring about, as surprised as I. Then other hands grabbed me, and I felt the cold steel of a blade against my back. *What was this?* Surely the death of a stranger on a beach could not have provoked such violence.

'Keep still, sir,' came a voice in my ear, and through the haze of fear and confusion I thought I recognized it.

Strong arms were holding me fast, but the knife was slicing up through my shirt, not into my ribs. The last remnant of cloth gave way, and I felt it being hauled off me. A small rivulet ran off my hair and into my eye, and I realized that the slap to my face had not been a blow, but a cascade of freezing water. I shook my head to clear it – like a wet dog, as Ducker said later – and shook it again when the unexpected figure of Captain Crawley appeared before me, holding what looked like a large bucket.

'Arms up now, sir.' The solid voice spoke again, and I

unthinkingly lifted my dripping arms into the air. Clean white cotton tumbled down over my head, and the hands behind me tugged it into place. 'Now, if you'll keep your 'ead there for just a moment.' A broad fist bunched my hair together and pulled it into a queue; I felt a ribbon frap it into place.

'Now the coat,' ordered Crawley quickly.

I meekly slipped my arms into the sleeves that were held up, and saw the white lapels and cuffs of my dress uniform coat. No, not *my* dress uniform coat, for it was a little short, but certainly an officer's coat.

'Is this a rescue?' I asked, managing at last to form some words.

'Sartorially, yes,' said Crawley. 'Had you gone in there as you were, they'd have hanged you on grounds of decency alone. And the public health. Justice may be blind, but I cannot think that she has no sense of smell.' He squinted at me. 'At least now you might pass for an officer.'

'Looks better from back aft,' said the voice behind me, which at last I identified as Ducker's.

But there was no more time to admire my appearance, for Stubb had regained himself and was advancing menacingly on Crawley.

'What the 'ell is you about?' he demanded. 'Does you want to be charged for assaulting a public constable?'

'If the Dover constabulary melt in the rain, Mr Stubb, then I must fear for the order of this town.' Crawley was at his most contemptuous. 'Was the shock of a bath so great?'

Stubb growled like a hound, but Crawley held his gaze unflinchingly. Ducker had stepped around to stand next to him, and he was at least the equal of the constable: not as broad, but with an advantage in height.

Stubb lifted his chin dismissively, then rounded on me, clapping his iron hand on my shoulder once more. 'You'll be late for Sir Lawrence,' he snarled. 'And 'e don't like to be kept waitin'.' He dragged me across the road, under the arches of the guildhall and up the staircase, with Crawley and Ducker in close pursuit.

'Remember, Lieutenant,' called Crawley encouragingly. 'The

magistrate will not hang you himself, only commit you to gaol until the assizes.'

Clearly he had not considered that that would condemn me to another six months of Gibble's hospitality.

The jurats of Dover had provided well for themselves when they built their hall, panelling it with dark wood and hanging laudatory self-portraits on the walls to watch over future generations. Windows all around kept the room no dimmer than the world outside, and the sputtering candles on a round chandelier made a feeble attempt at homeliness. Long tables and benches edged three sides of the room, but all were empty save the top table, where a trio of sombre figures sat together, all in black suits. The one on the left must be the clerk, for he scratched furiously at the paper on the desk with great flourishes of his quill, jabbing it into the inkwell periodically and spraying fountains of ink all about him. To the right sat the perfect reverse of this activity, a narrow man with a pronounced skull and sallow skin, perched very upright and quite still. And between them, wrapped in a thick black cloak which made him seem twice the size of his companions, the magistrate. He had a crooked back and a fleshy face that hung in folds off his cheeks. His eyes were deeply sunken, cast in shadow by the heavy lids about them, and he wore his hair powdered bone-white. His fingers, when they were not pressed together in front of his mouth, fiddled incessantly with a small ring of beads.

He tilted his head, and I felt those pitted eyes fix upon me. 'Lieutenant Martin Jerrold?' His voice was higher than I had expected from so large a man, and gratingly slow.

'Yes.'

'Lieutenant Jerrold, you are brought here under suspicion of murder. What have you to say?'

'Whom is he accused of murdering?' cut in a voice before I'd a chance to compose myself. I saw Crawley stepping forward on my right.

'You know that full well, Captain Crawley,' sneered the magistrate. 'The corpse found on the beach this morning.'

'Come, Sir Lawrence.' Crawley affected good humour. 'You and I both know that one cannot murder a corpse.'

'The name of the body is as yet unknown,' Sir Lawrence conceded. 'And he carried nothing on his person that hints at it. But it shall be unearthed.'

'And how is the lieutenant alleged to have killed this unknown victim?' Crawley was still smiling like a simpleton.

Sir Lawrence lazily flicked a hand towards the man on his left.

'The deceased died of a broken neck,' he croaked, almost whispering. I guessed him to be the coroner.

Sir Lawrence opened his mouth to add some comment, but Crawley was ahead of him. 'And is it not conceivable, your honour, that a man at the bottom of a three-hundred-foot cliff might not have needed Lieutenant Jerrold to break his neck for him? Or do you suggest that the lieutenant pushed him off the top and then raced down to admire his handiwork?'

'We do not believe,' retorted the coroner, 'that—'

Sir Lawrence cut him short. 'You yourself discovered Lieutenant Jerrold with the body, Captain Crawley.' There was something sinister in his tone, as though he were privy to some nasty joke. 'Tell the court – where did the corpse lie?'

'Near the water.' Crawley looked a little anxious now.

'And the tide was . . .?' Sir Lawrence tapped his fingertips together.

'On the ebb. Half out, perhaps.'

Sir Lawrence's lip curled upwards. 'Half out,' he repeated slowly. 'So at what distance from the foot of the cliff would that place the body?'

Crawley shrugged. 'Thirty, maybe forty feet. Why?'

'Because, Captain, unless the late victim had attempted a running jump from the cliff-top, and been of an athletic disposition at that, which I am assured he was not' – the coroner nodded his agreement – 'then I do not believe he could have propelled himself so far. Nor that any man, even one of Mr Stubb's physique, could have launched him there.'

'There was an offshore breeze that night,' tried Crawley, but Sir Lawrence swatted the objection aside.

'He was a man, Crawley, not a sail, and from my report of him he would have fallen like a stone. If he had fallen from the cliff. Which he did not.'

'It is my verdict,' confirmed the coroner, without emotion, 'that the deceased's neck was broken by a violent blow from a blunt object.'

'And it is my testimony,' retorted Crawley, his voice rising, 'that when I found Lieutenant Jerrold he had no such object about his person.'

I sensed Sir Lawrence's eyes roll back in mock horror under their hoods. 'And where indeed,' he asked with high rhetoric, 'might Lieutenant Jerrold have found such a weapon? Surely, Captain Crawley, even he could have contrived to do so on a beach covered with rocks of every size and weight? *And* found a convenient way of hiding it afterwards. I do not see that the facts admit of any other explanation.'

So that was it. They were going to hang me because I'd been found with an unknown body, and because they had not the energy to find out even who he'd been, let alone who might have killed him. I felt my legs begin to weaken, but Crawley had not yet surrendered.

'Pure circumstance,' he shouted, all quarterdeck thunder. 'Have you even a motive? No, sir, because you do not even know the victim, any more than Lieutenant Jerrold did when his stroll chanced to bring him to the place where the man had died. This is a judgement of convenience, Sir Lawrence, and it will not stand before a jury. You cannot hang a man because he is your only suspect.'

It seemed a poor time to mention the smugglers who had also been there.

The magistrate shrugged his hunched shoulders. 'The victim might well have been known to Lieutenant Jerrold, if not to us.' He spoke with deliberate carelessness, enjoying his victory over the raging captain. 'And I assure you, Crawley, that a jury will convict Lieutenant Jerrold on this evidence, if six months in the gaol do not wring a confession from him first.'

Crawley's face was very white; he seemed to be trembling with fury. I feared he might physically lash out and find himself condemned into my company; indeed, it seemed he would do just that, for he suddenly strode across the room, straight for Sir Lawrence. But there was no explosion. Instead, he bent his head close to the magistrate's ear and started whispering, his head jerking forcefully.

I looked about me. Ducker stood to my left, impassive as ever. The clerk still scribbled away in a mist of ink, and the coroner sat motionless as one of his cadavers. Outside the sky had darkened again, and beads of rain began to settle on the window panes. It made the candles seem suddenly brighter, though their light did little to warm the room. My ribs felt close about me, crushing my breath. I ached to be out of that miserable place, away from those three black fates, away from this horrid town.

Crawley straightened and walked back towards me, his face set hard. I could read nothing into it, but I presumed the worst. The magistrate rose, pulling himself to an imposing height under the mountainous cloak, and began to deliver his sentence.

'Lieutenant Jerrold,' he intoned soullessly, 'it is the finding of this court that the evidence against you, on the charges of having murdered a man not known in this parish, under the eastern cliffs, is purely circumstantial, and that you should not be committed for trial, nor detained any longer. Though I may add, Lieutenant, that should further evidence against you come to light, our justice will be swift, and severe.' I felt the bitter disappointment in his voice, and the cold anticipation of his final words. 'That is all.'

So completely had I written my own epitaph that it took several moments for the actual words to sink in. My blood raced, and I felt an enormous release, as though great boulders had been lifted off me. I could have cheered, or screamed out some gleeful gibberish, but in front of Sir Lawrence I made do with the idiotic smile that gripped my face. I saw Ducker nodding with a slow satisfaction, but

Crawley was already out of the door and down the stairs. We made no delay in following him.

When we caught him, on the far corner of the square, I was surprised to see him frowning in his triumph.

'What in heaven did you say to him, sir?' I asked, astonished at the turn of events he had manufactured. 'It must have been inspired.'

'I explained,' said Crawley, bringing me up by his stern tone, 'that if Sir Lawrence wished to maintain the benefits of the several lucrative contracts he enjoys with the navy, and for that matter with the army, he would stop this nonsense forthwith. It is not a threat I enjoyed making,' he added, though surely that could only have been half true, 'especially on behalf of your poltroonery, but if I had allowed one of his Majesty's officers to be thrown in gaol for murder, I doubt we should ever have caught another smuggler on these shores again.' Not, I assumed, from the loss of my own contributions. '"The reproaches of them that reproached thee fall on me", Lieutenant. We would have had corpses at our feet everywhere we looked, and a full wardroom in the gaol.'

In my current mood I could shrug off his gloom. 'Whatever your motives, sir, I am in your debt. And grateful beyond words.'

Crawley scowled still deeper. 'Then you can repay me, Lieutenant, by staying out of further mischief. And by devoting your time, and allowing me mine, to the task in hand.'

I nodded soberly. 'I shall indeed, sir.' I might have added more, but I already felt slightly ridiculous before his unforgiving stare.

'Then go back to your inn and give yourself a thorough scrubbing. I do not wish to find you giving my crew the gaol fever.' He looked at the clock on the church tower, which confirmed the settling gloom about us as the onset of evening. 'You may report to me in my rooms tomorrow morning at nine o'clock. Punctually.'

'Yes, sir,' I said, suddenly realizing how much I craved a warm bed. 'Nine o'clock, sir.' I turned to go.

'Lieutenant,' Crawley barked, and I looked back to see him with his arm outstretched. 'My coat, if you please.'

I returned to the inn, shouted for one of the servants to fetch me a bath, and climbed the twisting stairs to my garret. It seemed an age since I had descended them for that fateful call of nature. I would have to remember a chamber pot this time, I thought, fumbling with the door. Remembering again to duck my head, I stepped in, and almost immediately wondered whether I was in the wrong room. The chest at the foot of the bed looked like mine, as did the coat thrown over a footstool. The half-drunk bottle on the floor might well have been my unfinished business. But none of that explained the girl – unless, I thought vaguely, she was unfinished business too.

I tried surprise, for it came naturally. 'What the devil are you doing here?'

She looked up from where she was curled on the bed. 'You're always welcoming me like that.' Her voice was curiously mellow for one so young.

Those words brought me up short. So much had passed since the morning that I'd quite forgotten the events of the previous evening, but now they started to return. A hostelry, of dubious custom and worse refreshment, yet packed to the rafters, the sort of place where conversation is so completely impossible that drinking becomes the only diversion. A girl had approached me, or perhaps I had made the advance, and I believe we had negotiated a fee, though in the hubbub our contract might have been open to misconception. And then . . .

'You were in my bed this morning.' It sounded lame even as I said it, and I did little to redeem myself when I added, 'And you're in it again now.'

Her young eyes looked at me with concern. 'Do you . . . have trouble . . . remembering things?' she asked, slow and earnest. 'There was a man here once got dropped on his head, and he talked a bit like you. Soft Mick, they called him.'

I frowned testily. 'I am not the village idiot, if that's what you are asking. I was simply the worse for drink last night, and the worse for an exceptionally trying day now.'

I hardly expected sympathy from this creature, but I was a little put out that her immediate response was to giggle, before belatedly covering her mouth in a stab at decorum. 'Oh, you were the worse for drink,' she confirmed, obviously remembering it with greater amusement than I did. 'But don't worry, everyone that's new in Dover suffers with it. It's the way they let it down.'

I ignored her final comment, whose meaning I confess escaped me. 'Well, I might have been past sobriety, but I still have no recollection of asking you back this evening. I don't think I even know your name.'

'Isobel.'

'And did I request your company this evening?'

'You didn't,' she admitted, the laughter subsiding.

'And as I very definitely recall closing my eyes while you left, I assume you helped yourself to your fee, so that can hardly be outstanding. I never met a jade who'd short-change herself.'

'I suppose you didn't.' There was a brittle edge to her voice. 'Though if you'd counted the coins in your purse, you'd have seen I didn't take nothing! Perhaps if I'd known what you thought of me I would have done, but I didn't. Not,' she added spitefully, 'that there was much to pay for. A leer and a grope was all you were up to before you collapsed in your sleep.'

The passion of her outburst shook me almost as much as the words themselves. 'So you mean,' I began, treading carefully and trying not to be obtuse, though there was no delicate way of putting this, 'you're no whore?'

'Maybe to you,' she spat, 'but I never sold myself, no.' Moisture glistened in the corner of her eye.

I was saved the risk of further ingallantries by a knock at the door.

'Bath for Mr Jerrold,' called a voice outside.

'Blast!' I panicked. 'Quick, hide yourself.'

'Where?'

I looked around. There was no cupboard, and the curtains reached nowhere near the floor. 'Under the bed.'

There was another, more insistent knock. 'Mr Jerrold?'

'Why should I?' asked the girl. 'You ashamed to be seen with me?'

I shook my head irritably. 'My name in this town is, I suspect, already rather poor, but I would prefer to avoid any further allegations.' No doubt Stubb and Sir Lawrence could fashion a charge out of anything, and I knew the sort of tricks a girl could pull once she'd been found in a delicate situation.

She made no movement.

'Think of your own reputation then,' I begged. 'You would not want others to suffer from the same, unfortunate misapprehension as myself.'

That thought clearly made an impact, but still she hesitated.

'And I should be very grateful to you.'

Whatever form she thought my gratitude would take, it was clearly something that might be worth her while, for at that she slid off the bed and into the shadow beneath it, allowing me to pull open the door and only narrowly miss a punch in the nose from my impatient knocker.

'Bath for you, sir?' He was a pimply youth, about fourteen, with a rat-like face and gangly limbs. I stood aside to let him drag in the tub and fetch the jug of steaming water. 'You can 'ave another jug for tuppence,' he offered as he poured in the first, but I declined.

I thought this the end of the business, but he made no sign of leaving, and stood in the middle of the room shooting me suggestive little glances.

Of course. I pulled out my purse and found a ha'penny, which I pressed into his hand. 'There you go,' I told him. 'You can come and collect the tub in an hour.'

Still he stayed, his eyes fixed firmly on some high place over my shoulder. 'Was there someone else in 'ere?' he enquired loftily, rather more forward than his station allowed.

'Certainly not,' I retorted. I saw his eyes flickering about the room. 'And even if there were, what damned business would it be of yours?'

'Nothing,' he said, scratching his nose. 'Only the landlord do charge a shillin' if guests wants to bring company back to their rooms. "The wages of sin", 'e calls it.'

'I'll give you the wages of sin yourself if you don't disappear.' A mix of guilt and indignation put anger into my voice, and after a pause just long enough to be impertinent, the boy wisely retreated. I slammed the door after him.

The girl rolled out from under the bed, dust streaked over her thin white dress.

'Satisfied?' she asked coldly.

'Perfectly,' I answered, making a great effort at civility. 'Now, if you will excuse me, I should like to take my bath.'

'Good idea,' she agreed. 'You smell like filth.'

'That's because I've spent half the day rotting in the town gaol. The sooner I can wash it away, the better.'

'I'll scrub your back.'

I sighed, seeing where this was leading. 'Thank you for your kind offer, but I would prefer to bathe in privacy. Perhaps another time.'

'Please yourself.' She tossed her head. 'But I can't leave yet. The boy eats his dinner on the stairs about now, and if he sees me going down he'll be sure to peach you to the landlord. But don't mind about me. I'll just keep quiet in my corner.'

I glared at her. 'That's ridiculous. I can't bathe in front of you, it would be . . .'

'Embarrassing?'

'Indecent.'

She smiled sweetly, and affected a gruff voice. 'Good God, sir, nothing I haven't seen before, you know.' She dropped the mimicry. 'And your water's getting cold.'

I met her mocking gaze and held it, though within I was utterly bewildered. If I forced her out I'd seem an incorrigible puritan, and a hypocrite besides; if I didn't . . . But what could she really do – laugh? I could manage that, surely. And the challenge in her face was inescapable.

With a sigh of frustration, I pulled off my shirt, stockings and breeches and stood stark naked before her, staring rigidly ahead and refusing to catch her eye, all the while hoping that the dim room would hide my scarlet face. I noticed her mouth twitch, but she had the restraint to keep silent, and after a few more seconds in my classical pose – to prove that I was not the least abashed – I stepped into the tub and lowered myself into the water.

She watched me as I self-consciously splashed my face, then hopped off the bed.

'Glad you're cleaning yourself up, Mr Jerrold,' she said. 'I'd best leave you to it.'

'What?' Water flew over the side. 'What about the boy on the stairs?'

'I'll use the back steps,' she replied blithely, and was skipping out of the door before I could even hoist myself up. I had a momentary vision of myself tearing through the corridors after her, naked and dripping and screaming, and decided not to give chase. *Little bitch*, I thought, reclining back in my bath. She'd played me for a fool, though God knew what satisfaction she'd taken from it.

I lay in the bath, as the water got colder and my legs grew stiffer, glad that this horrible day was coming to a close. I'd lost count of the humiliations I'd suffered, but I had survived them, and a new day might bring new luck. Perhaps tomorrow I could set about restoring my reputation with Crawley, and avoid any more unhappy entanglements with the local judiciary. And that damned corpse from the beach, I thought with relief, could be left to Stubb, to Sir Lawrence, or to the Lord Chief Justice himself if he were so inclined. I was free of it.

I enjoyed that belief for a good ten hours, all through the night and into the following morning, right until the moment when I heard the pimply youth banging on my door, announcing that a letter had arrived for me.

4

'JERROLD!' THE LETTER BEGAN. PERHAPS THERE WAS NO exclamatory mark, but the force of its intention was certainly there. And without even looking at the signature, I knew immediately whence it came. Letters from my mother invariably start 'My Darling Martin'; my father and I rarely correspond. And the text I held left little room for doubt.

'You despicable, odious, ungrateful little toad. After all the considerable interest I have exercised on your miserable career, often against my wiser judgement, at the behest of my poor sister, your unfortunate mother, I have learned the most infamous news – of a depredation which, I confess, even I had thought beyond you. Not content with debasing the nobility of your birth and your commission at every juncture, it would seem you are now become a common criminal, or rather an uncommon one, for it is a most heinous and wicked crime that you are charged with. The resulting scandal, should it touch me, would be ruinous, both to my position and to the good name of our family.

'My patience with you is worn down by your prodigal dissipation of it, but these charges are weighty, and I know that my sister, in her innocence, would desire me to give you every chance of proving yourself. I shall therefore – with, I need not say, the deepest misgivings

– extend you one last indulgence. Clear your name within the fortnight, and no more shall be said. Otherwise, I shall not see you hanged as a murderer, but shall arrange forthwith a station in the Indies; there you can rot in obscurity until disease takes you. Do not think that you can escape this fate you have heaped down upon yourself by quitting the navy, for I shall not accept your resignation; to do so would be to acquiesce in your guilt. If you leave, you will be treated as a deserter.

'I fear you are immune to moral supplication, but you would do well to reflect upon the words of your commission: you may not fail, as you will answer the contrary at your peril.

'I remain, &c, your Affectionate Uncle . . .'

Trembling, I put the letter down. The sneering insults I could ignore: I had been hearing them for as long as I could remember. The threat, though, was stark, and terrifying. If the magistrate got me, I would hang. If I failed to exonerate myself, I would die of some poisonous fever on the far side of the world. And if I ran, I would be an outlaw, hunted by the authorities and navy alike as they vied for the privilege of my execution. What sort of choice was that?

At such a time, with such a dilemma, there was only one path open to me: I went downstairs and called for brandy. Perhaps, I thought bitterly, it would achieve the end that all around me so clearly anticipated.

The taproom was empty so early in the morning, but after a few shouts and thumps the boy, the bringer of baths and letters, appeared from the kitchens.

'No brandy,' he announced in a superior tone. 'S illegal, ain't it. Frog. Unless,' he added surreptitiously, 'you're on the wink?'

'What?' I asked, too distracted to pay him much notice. 'Well, if you've no brandy, perhaps some gin.'

He pulled a near-empty bottle from under the counter and splashed the liquid into a cup. I grabbed at it eagerly, and tipped it into my mouth.

'Jesus!' There was a searing pain in my throat, and I could feel the evil spirit trickling down my gullet. 'You could kill a man with that.'

If alcohol was to be the death of me, I did not want it to be a half measure of cheap gin.

'Sorry, sir,' said the boy diffidently. 'I forgot you was foreign. Not from about 'ere,' he explained, before I could protest my English birth. 'Best let it down a bit.' He scooped some water from an open cask and poured it with my gin. 'That'll do you, sir.'

I tried another sip. It was no longer immediately lethal, though it reminded me why I'd never had much taste for it.

'Is all the drink so strong here?' I asked. If I was to be spending much time in Dover, this would be important intelligence.

He scratched the side of his head. 'Reckon so. Not been nowhere else, of course, but they says it gets weaker the further you goes inland. Per'aps it don't travel well.' He nodded thoughtfully. 'Must be an expensive business, gettin' boused up in them parts.'

Doubtless I could have spent a happy morning enquiring into the local spirit market with the boy, with plenty by way of illustration; perhaps I would have done just that after a few more sips of the gin, but at that moment the sound of a tolling bell drifted through the open window. I counted the strokes out of habit, but it was only as they hit seven, passed eight and touched nine that with a great shock I remembered my meeting with Crawley. All other thoughts vanished from my head, for I knew I could ill afford to provoke him further. Without his protection, I would be utterly at Sir Lawrence's mercy.

I left my unfinished drink for the boy to drain – doubtless he would still charge it to my account – and rushed outside, ran for the gate, then thought of Crawley's concern for appearance and bolted back to my room to snatch my dress coat. I saw my uncle's letter lying on the bed and stuffed that into my pocket, then was galloping back down the stairs three at a time.

I ran all the way to the harbour, as fast as I could, but the first bells were still chiming the quarter hour as I arrived outside Crawley's front door. Ducker showed me in wordlessly.

'Is it ordained, Lieutenant, that no man shall know the hour of your coming?' Crawley did not look up from his desk. 'Or are you unacquainted with the laws of time?'

'My apologies, sir,' I stammered hoarsely: the combination of gin and running had left my throat in agony. I tried to think of the best light to cast on my excuse. 'I was delayed by a letter from the Admiralty.'

Crawley looked up sharply. 'Were you, by God?' he asked. Suspicion consumed his face, firming its creases to stone. 'And what, pray, did their lordships have to communicate to you that they felt unworthy of my attention?'

I saw immediately my mistake. 'Not an official message, sir, not at all. Merely a personal communication.'

His face darkened still further. 'A *personal communication*? What a fine relationship you must enjoy with their lordships, Lieutenant, that they should see fit to write *personally* to a junior officer, behind the back of his superior.'

This was going disastrously awry. 'My uncle—'

Crawley cut me off. 'Do you have this *personal communication* with you, Lieutenant?'

I nodded the affirmative.

'Do you believe that a captain should be in full command of all facts pertaining to his subordinates, particularly those concerning Admiralty matters?'

What could I do but nod again?

'Then, Lieutenant,' he concluded dangerously, 'I suggest you show me this *personal communication*, that I might judge its significance for myself.'

I pulled out the paper and handed it to him. My cheeks stung, as much from what he had said as what he was about to read, and I could hardly bear to watch his eyes flickering silently over the page. Simply standing there became an ordeal, and I desperately wished myself anywhere but in that cramped, spartan little room.

Crawley looked up, and to my surprise I saw that the hard set of his mouth had softened, and that there was a hint of scarlet under the lines of his face. He cleared his throat awkwardly. 'Well,

Lieutenant.' The bite was quite gone from his voice, and he sounded almost sheepish. 'This is, ah, not what I had anticipated. I must apologize for my presumption.'

I thought it might have been the realization of my uncle's position that had so transformed him, but surely no-one reading that letter could believe that he offered me any protection, nor that I had any access to his favour. I could only assume that he must truly have been shamed by the bile he had found, having expected something quite specifically different.

'Still, this does make your predicament very clear, eh, Lieutenant?' Crawley looked at me intently. 'You maintain your innocence, I take it?'

'As a vir— As a baby.'

'Then what do you intend to do?'

The question hung in the air; I found myself again confronted full-on with my impossible alternatives. But in my confusion, I began to see that I really had little choice. I could hardly announce to Crawley my intention of deserting, even if I fancied my chances, which I did not. Sir Lawrence he could keep at arm's length. Which left only one path. What did I have to lose?

'Naturally, sir, I am intent on clearing my name of this vile slur.' And if my name could not be saved, then perhaps at least my neck.

'Of course.' Crawley was all business now. 'And as you have a mere fortnight to do so – or rather less, as I see the letter is dated yesterday – I suggest you begin immediately. You cannot prove your own innocence until the real villains are brought to justice.'

'Yes, sir.'

'The Lord alone knows how one begins to untangle such a crime,' continued Crawley. 'But I suspect that you will find rather more enthusiasm for the task than Constable Stubb. Possibly more intellect as well. And it seems entirely likely that this foul event may have a more than passing bearing on our real business of hunting down the smugglers. Which reminds me: there is a meeting up at the castle this evening to discuss the smuggling question, and how we and the soldiery are to co-ordinate our efforts. It may provide you with some clues to the murderer, if we are fighting the same enemy. Regardless, you remain under my command and I shall expect you to continue to execute your duties as my subordinate officer – or rather, to begin to execute those duties – in addition to making your personal enquiries. Six o'clock, and please show a little more regard for the hour this time.'

'Yes, sir.' I was quite overwhelmed by his rattling speech, and could think of nothing better to say.

'You had better take Ducker with you,' he added. 'I fear you have a knack of attracting untoward attentions in this town, against which he may be some protection.'

Keeping a close eye on me all the while, I thought, though I was in no position to argue.

'Remember the words of our Saviour,' Crawley concluded sternly. ' "Ye shall know the truth, and the truth shall make you free." Salvation lies in truth, Lieutenant.'

And what is truth? I might have asked, but decided against playing Pilate to his proselytizer. With a hasty mutter of thanks, I fled the room.

'Well, sir,' said Ducker in the corridor. Clearly he had heard everything. 'Looks like we'd best be findin' the killer.' He sounded implausibly optimistic.

'If we're extremely lucky,' I told him sourly, 'we might even discover the name of the victim.'

Ducker reckoned there was little to be done in town: no-one had come forward to identify the body, let alone his murderer, and it seemed unlikely there would be any better response to a pair of naval officers banging down doors. So I decided to make for the cliffs, in the hope that they might yield some secrets, or that someone living nearby might have heard something.

Ducker was not convinced. 'Could be a bad choice, sir,' he cautioned.

'Why?' I did not like being second-guessed already.

'The killer always returns to the scene of the crime, so they says.'

'Does he? Then perhaps we will catch him there.'

'Not quite my meanin', sir.' I sensed he was about to argue further, but he must have thought better of it, for he restricted himself to a dubious look and kept quiet.

The tide was rising, so rather than splash along the shoreline, I opted for the cliff-top. Whatever the coroner might say, I had heard the gunshot up there, and the thud of something falling from a height: I was convinced that there the crime had been committed. Besides, I did not think that the smugglers had seen the corpse before they left, and after that I had been the only man on the beach. Which was of course the magistrate's reasoning, I remembered, and hastily turned my thoughts elsewhere.

'Ducker?' I asked, panting as we climbed the steep hill towards the castle. 'You're *Orestes*' quartermaster, and I her lieutenant, and Crawley her captain. Where's *Orestes* herself?'

'At anchor. There.' He pointed an arm back towards the harbour, though from this distance I had no hope of making her out among the forest of masts. 'The cap'n's got ideas,' he added, half disapprovingly, as though they might be dangerous.

'Ideas?'

'Cap'n Crawley reckons there's no gain fightin' smugglers at sea if there's no-one to catch 'em when they unloads on land. Thought of it one night after we chased a lugger into shore. By the time we 'ad the boats away an' boarded 'er, she'd cleared 'er 'old an' was clean as salt.'

'But there must be dragoons patrolling the shore?'

'Ridin' officers,' said Ducker scornfully. 'Drunk. Or ancient. Or in the smugglers' pockets. An' if they does see somethin' rotten, they 'as to ride away an' find the dragoons. If they doesn't go runnin' off the opposite way.'

'And this scheme is actually designed to *catch* the smugglers?' It sounded as though the criminals could hardly have devised it better themselves.

Ducker sniffed. 'Cap'n Crawley don't think so. Gets us workin' in shore parties, or in the boats, most o' the time. Could o' joined the army if I wanted all that.'

'And what does the admiral think of him abandoning his command so often?' I did not imagine that in such desperate times, with the French menace never far from our shores, he would applaud such profligate use of his fleet.

But Ducker had no comment, and lapsed into silence.

We passed the mighty bulwarks of the castle, where dozens of men laboured at the walls, and moved into farmland beyond. The empty fields were flecked white with the chalk that had been ploughed into them, and rolled away to the horizon across the gently curving landscape. It felt very high, and very open, though a few small copses broke the horizon. The castle quickly disappeared behind a rise, and we walked on in solitude.

'There,' I said at length, gesturing towards the shore. A low building could be seen behind a clump of trees, a few hundred yards from the cliff and near to where I guessed the shot had been fired. 'They must have heard something.'

'If you says so.' Ducker showed little enthusiasm. I suspected the task of chaperoning me was already becoming tedious.

'I do.'

We crossed the field, let ourselves through the gate and approached the building. Or rather the buildings, I saw as we drew nearer, for there were several: a low brick farmhouse, and half a dozen barns and sheds in various states of repair forming a rough, open courtyard in front of it. A vicious reaping hook lay rusting in a patch of weeds, and hay covered the ground. From somewhere out of sight came the sound of hens chattering, but the only living thing visible was a dappled shire pony, his bridle hitched to a ring in the stable wall.

I crossed the yard, taking care to step around the keepsakes other animals had left, and banged on the thick front door. It sounded muffled in the chill February air.

'They must be out in the fields,' I suggested after a minute had passed in silence. I banged again, but a snort from the pony was my only answer.

I heard a squeak of hinges to my left, and turned to see the door to one of the sheds standing open. A thin man, with a weathered face and bright eyes, had emerged and was leaning on a tall pitchfork, surveying us in silence. His shirt was unbuttoned to the waist and rolled up to the elbows; despite a lean build, there was no mistaking the strength in his arms.

'Do you live here?' I asked.

He nodded slowly.

'I am Lieutenant Martin Jerrold of his Majesty's cutter *Orestes*.' I noticed Ducker stiffen beside me, as if he did not think I should have said so. 'This is Mr Ducker.'

The farmer took this impassively. 'Hamble,' he said at length, with obvious reluctance. He did not offer his hand.

'Farmer Hamble, we are investigating the death – which is to say, suspected murder – of a man at the foot of those cliffs over there.' I waved my arm in the general direction. 'Yesterday morning, shortly before dawn. Did you hear anything untoward?'

'No.'

'Oh.' I regathered myself. 'But I heard – that is to say, I heard reports that a shot was fired, hardly any distance from this very place. Surely you must have heard it.'

'No.' Hamble's face tightened, and I fancied I saw the prongs of his pitchfork incline ever so slightly towards me.

'Nothing at all?' I did not hide my disbelief.

'No.'

'Had you seen anyone pass by here earlier, perhaps heading towards the cliffs?'

'No.'

'So to recapitulate,' I struggled on, 'you neither saw nor heard anything.'

Hamble paused, weighing the words for some hidden trap, then nodded his grudging agreement. He looked at me in silent expectation of the next question, and I stared back, trying to muster a grave dignity, for in truth I could think of little more to ask.

'Hamble!' A shrill voice called from an open window, where a woman's head had appeared above us. 'Dinner.'

'Mrs Hamble?' I asked, lifting my hat to her.

A pinched face craned a little further out of the window, its gaze equal parts curiosity and suspicion, and I saw her eyes turn fractionally to her husband before she answered in the affirmative.

'Lieutenant Jerrold,' I shouted up. 'Investigating a murder.' If my words held any shock for her, it was well hidden. 'Tell me, Mrs Hamble, did you happen to notice anything unusual here early yesterday morning?'

Again I caught a quick glance between her and her husband. 'No.' She shook her head emphatically. I was almost resigned to another series of fruitless exchanges, but she saved me the effort. 'Didn't hear nothin', didn't see nothin', don't know nothin'.' Her tone admitted to no challenge.

'Nothing at all?' I tried to sound surprised. 'Not even a gunshot?'

'Nothin'.' She was firmer than ever. 'We was asleep.'

'You must sleep very soundly, Mrs Hamble.'

She considered that carefully. 'We does,' she said at last. 'About here, them what sleeps like the grave don't go rushin' into it.' I think it was the longest sentence I ever got from either of them, nonsense though it was. 'Your dinner's goin' cold,' she added, turning her attention back to Hamble. The window slammed shut.

'Far be it from me to keep you from your dinner,' I told the farmer, who was clearly champing to be inside. 'But, tell me, is there anyone else near here who might have heard something? Our enquiries have some urgency.'

Even the thought of a cooling meal could not hurry the man. 'John,' he decided eventually. 'Fisherman. On the beach.'

'Excellent.' This sounded far more promising – indeed, the only useful fact I'd had from the pair of them. 'How might I find him?'

Hamble pointed across the field behind him. 'Through there, an' down the next cove.'

'Marvellous.'

I was all primed to stride off when Ducker's hand clapped down on my shoulder. The sensation was becoming tiresome.

'Beggin' your pardon, Mr 'amble,' he said, and I bridled that he should not be begging *my* pardon. 'But you've a bull in that field.'

A funny look crossed Hamble's face. 'Forgot that,' he said. 'Go by the south field, then. Cliff'll take you down.'

I nervously scanned the field he'd indicated. Lumbering beasts have always worried me, unless on a plate with potatoes and gravy, and the thought of a near miss with the bull was most unsettling. This way, however, seemed clear enough.

'Thank you for your consideration, Mr Hamble,' I told him, pompous and completely insincere. 'You've been most helpful.'

It took us but a few minutes to cross the southerly field. Here the breeze whipped about us, and I had to hold down my hat to keep from losing it. The ground sloped towards the cliff, and the long grass was thick with rainwater, but I was determined to be thorough in my investigation. Dropping to my knees I crawled right to the very brink, pushed my head over the edge and stared down.

I hardly make a habit of peering over precipices, but even I could tell that this was uncommonly sheer: the chalk face dropped almost plumb to the shore. At its foot a few white boulders lay broken on the grey shingle beach, and I realized with a start that they must once have formed the very cliff-top where I now lay. A seagull's cry echoed mournfully off the rock and cautiously I edged my way back a little.

'What do you reckon?' I shouted over the wind to Ducker.

He nodded. 'That's the place we found you, sir. An' the body.'

I looked around, but I could see nothing to belie the coroner's view. Any man who fell, or jumped, or got pushed off this place would fall as straight as the cliff behind him. The tide was in well past where it had been the previous morning, yet I doubted whether even now a falling object could reach the water's edge. *So who broke his neck?* However much I puzzled at it, I could think of no answer save the smugglers.

I looked back over my shoulder at the Hambles' farmhouse: it was no distance at all. I could see the buildings perfectly, see where Hamble had left his pitchfork leaning against the front door, even make out a hen clucking its way across the yard.

'They must have heard the shot,' I mumbled to myself. 'And there was at least one of their lookouts up here.'

'Whose lookouts, sir?' Ducker was in with his question before I'd realized I had spoken aloud. 'An' what was the shot you was tellin' the farmer about?'

Damn! I'd completely forgotten that I had not yet mentioned my encounter with the smugglers to Ducker, nor to Crawley nor to anyone, in fact. I cursed myself for an idiot and tried to invent a plausible lie, but Ducker's unyielding stare confounded me and I could think of nothing that would do. Besides, I rationalized, the truth, inglorious though it was, might as well come out. I could hardly afford to be seen acting suspiciously, nor to have been concealing facts pertinent to the murder. And I was sure that whatever Ducker saw would be relayed immediately to Crawley.

As best I remembered it, and as briefly as possible, I told the story. Ducker listened without comment, though he must have inferred most of it from what I had let slip already. Only after I had finished with a lame explanation for my reticence did he offer any comment.

'So the owlers *was* about that night.'

'Owlers?'

'Smugglers. We'd been given the nod that they was makin' a landin' – that's why we was there where we found you. Spent all night runnin' about in the dark, an' all we caught was shadows. Though it sounds like we'd 'ave 'ad 'em clinked if it wasn't for your body.'

'*My* body? Why, if you had arrived in time there might never have been a body.' We glared angrily at each other, but he knew he could go no further without risking charges of insubordination, and I had little stomach for the quarrel. 'It would appear,' I offered by way of conciliation, 'that we were both dislocated that night.'

'That we was,' he agreed.

There was nothing more to be learned from the cliff, and I did not like the look of the heavy clouds massing behind us, so we pressed on along the path, following where it swung sharply inland and descended rapidly towards the shore. The noise of the surf grew as we clambered down the thickly wooded hillside, until we emerged on the shoreline to see rollers breaking over a shallow bay. It must have been a well-protected spot, for the cliffs that cupped it were thick with green vegetation, and a coarse sand was mixed in with the stones on the beach. But apart from one tumbledown stone cottage, which could not have been inhabited for fifty years at least, there were no signs of life.

'He'll be a wet man if he lives in that,' I observed, looking at the roofless building and cursing Hamble for sending us on a fool's errand.

I was just steeling myself for the unhappy prospect of climbing back up the slope when something caught Ducker's eye.

'There, sir.'

For several seconds I could not see what he was pointing at, but then it became clearer: a tiny, slanted shack perched against the cliff face, right in the crook of the bay, almost invisible from the main beach. A small rowing boat was moored near it.

'He'll be a wet man if he lives there, too.'

The sea reached to within a few yards of the hut, and it would not take much of an onshore wind to send the waves crashing about it. Even now, with the great headland behind providing shelter from the blowing westerly, spray spattered it, and the narrow path that led there looked dangerous going. In bad weather it would be completely impassable.

I began to doubt Ducker's wisdom ever more as we slipped and tripped our way towards the shack, grabbing at the creeper on the cliff to support ourselves. Who but the worst misanthrope could want to live somewhere so inaccessible – and if he were such a misanthrope, should we really be risking our lives to meet him? And then there was the building itself: barely four feet long, and projecting some distance above the ground, it would barely serve for a privy in any normal house. Yet its dimensions were not constant, I noticed, when an unusually benign stretch of ground gave me the chance to take my eyes off my footing. It bent inwards, not skewed by bad construction, as I had thought before, but by design, almost like the curves on a ship's stern.

At that thought I paused, for I suddenly saw how close to the truth my fancy had been. The hut was not shaped *like* a ship's stern, it *was* a ship's stern, the rear end of some fishing smack that looked for all the world as if it had been run at the cliff with such force that the greater part of its hull had buried itself in the chalk, to such a depth that only the aft section still protruded. It seemed impossible, yet the nearer we came the more it appeared that the structure was not propped against the cliff, as reason told me it surely must be, but was indeed sunk into the rock. Now we were close enough to see the rotting hull, complete with barnacles still encrusted on the bottom, and there was no doubt that it must extend well into the cliff wall.

A new mystery presented itself: where was the entrance? I thought I could make out a scar in the timbers where a door had been cut through, but it was above our heads, and there were no stairs. I looked to the cliff, but did not care to risk my life on its slippery, crumbling surface.

'John?' I shouted, raising my voice over the crashing surf. And then, feeling somewhat presumptuous, I essayed the alternative. 'Mr John?'

One of the salutations must have sufficed, for without preamble the door I had seen swung open. I could discern nothing within, but a second later a rope ladder came tumbling out, almost striking my head. Choosing to read nothing malicious into that, I grasped the rungs firmly and hoisted myself up.

The memory of Dover gaol swamped me as I entered the gloom, and had my body not already cleared the threshold I might well have fallen back onto the rocks below. The darkness, save for a small area by the door, was complete, the stench, though this time of fish, equally overpowering. Somewhere, further in, I could hear a scraping and rattling, and with mounting apprehension I remembered my misgivings about the sort of man who would live in a place like this.

A spark flashed, and the light of an oil lamp flared before settling at a more moderated pitch. Its yellow light illuminated an extraordinary room, long and thin, extending many feet into the cliff, with the bowed walls of the vessel it had once been. It was packed with all manner of queer things, many of them the ordinary tackle of a fisherman, but many others that could only have been scavenged from the beach: an empty birdcage, several china dogs, and what appeared to be a small swivel cannon.

'Is it too bright for ye?' asked an unexpectedly soft voice.

I took my eyes from the surroundings to focus on the figure who sat at the table in the centre of the room, twisting carefully at the knob on the lamp. His hair was unkempt, matted into grey curls and a long tangled beard, and his blue eyes stared with a wide intensity, but there was no threat in his open face. He wore a faded woollen jersey, so holed it seemed the mice must be eating it off his body, but despite the lack of a fire – there was no chimney – he did not seem unduly cold.

'I usually keeps it off,' he explained, still fiddling at the lamp, 'to save the waste of oil.'

I realized I had yet to introduce myself. 'Lieutenant Martin Jerrold,' I said awkwardly. 'This is Mr Ducker.' I gestured to where the quartermaster had scrambled in behind me.

Our host seemed unworried by our identities, and waved us over to sit at the table with him.

I took a stool, and was surprised it did not feel damp. 'I should have thought, in a position so close to the sea, you'd have been very wet in here,' I remarked.

'Aye, a wet soul, that's me,' he chuckled. 'So where are my manners, ye'll be askin' me next.'

Before I could protest, he had risen from his chair and was rummaging in a locker by the wall. I heard the chinking of glass within, and saw him return with a bottle and three mismatched though indisputably well-crafted crystal glasses. He poured us each a measure of the spirit.

'Your health.' I raised my glass apprehensively, fearing that it would make the gin of the morning seem wholesome by comparison, but, *mirabile dictu*, it seemed to be a rather fine French brandy.

I drained it, and looked hopefully at what remained in the bottle.

'I finds it on the beach, sometimes,' the fisherman explained. He pushed the bottle across the table. 'Help yourselves.'

I needed no encouragement, and a stern look from Ducker could not deter me from a second, even a third draught.

'Who did you say you was again?' asked the fisherman, wonderfully tolerant of my extravagance.

'Lieutenant Jerrold,' I repeated. 'But I do not think I have the pleasure, Mr . . .'

'Strange,' said the man, cocking his head, 'I thought I heard ye call it earlier. Simon John, I am.'

He showed a perfect indifference to whatever our business might be; so, without a prompt, I was forced to make the start myself. 'Mr John,' I began, the brandy raising my voice perhaps a little louder than it might have been, 'did you witness anything unusual early yesterday morning, shortly before dawn?'

'Unusual?' He twisted the woollen jersey in his fingers. 'The gulls was quiet.' He thought a little more. 'I was out in the boat then. Fishin'.'

This was more promising. 'Fishing. Off the coast here?'

'Aye. I doesn't go far.'

'And did you see any other craft? A lugger, perhaps, or something smaller, somewhere round the next bay?'

The fisherman gave a small smile. 'No, sir. I doesn't see much, ye know.'

Perhaps it was something in his voice that caught me, or Ducker's fierce scowl, or maybe at last I saw that those staring blue eyes were in fact staring at nothing at all, but suddenly it struck me with all the force of my father's strap: the man was blind. My cheeks flushed red, and my only consolation was that he could not see my shame – until I realized how churlish a thought that was too, and banished it.

'Mr John,' I said miserably. 'My apologies for disturbing you, and my thanks for your hospitality. I think we had better be making our way back.'

I had embarrassed myself and learned nothing; my sole consolation was the brandy. And, as I slithered down the swaying ladder and stumbled back across the rocks, even that seemed an intemperate indulgence.

5

'STILL,' I SAID, ONCE WE WERE ATOP THE CLIFF AGAIN HEADING BACK to Dover, 'it's not been a complete waste of a day.' With thirteen left to save my neck, I could hardly countenance lost time.

'No, sir?' Ducker's tone suggested he might be humouring me.

'No.' I held my ground. 'If nothing else, we've discovered that the locals possess a curious, which is to say downright suspicious, immunity to strange events on their doorstep. I find that very significant.'

'If you'd wanted to know the locals'd be no use,' said Ducker wearily, 'I could o' saved us a journey.'

'Did you know the fisherman would be blind?'

''E could've 'ad a pair o' telescopes for eyes an' I'll wager 'e'd still not 'ave seen a thing. No-one sees nothin' round 'ere. Look at that farmer.'

'Are you saying that he's involved in the business?' It seemed unlikely, but a desperate need for a culprit spurred my hopes.

'Depends what business,' said Ducker, unhelpfully. 'In the business o' your murder, likely not, though you'll never be sure. In the owlin' business? 'E's probably not landin' kegs o' geneva on the beach every night, but that don't mean 'e don't know to keep 'is nose out o' whoever's business it is.'

'And whose business is it?'

'Couldn't say.' Once again Ducker was proving entirely useless. 'But 'e's probably not livin' in a broken boat shoved in a cave.'

I growled, for although what Ducker said rang true, it did not give me much comfort, and his manner bordered on insult. It irked me too that he had managed to unsettle my good mood, forced though it had been. When he quickened his stride, I did not bother to keep pace.

It was not just Ducker bringing on gloom, though: the black clouds I had noticed earlier now covered the sky, advancing the afternoon and placing us in deep shadow. The pitch of the wind rose, blowing shrill into our faces, and I was forced to clutch my hat under my coat. A drop of rain stung my hand, then two more on my cheek, and I guessed the full onslaught was about to break.

'Best head away from the cliff,' bawled Ducker, who had paused for me to catch up. 'Nasty gusts hereabouts.'

I hardly needed convincing. Although the result might be fascinating, I had no desire to prove Crawley's hypothesis as to how far the wind might carry a man off the cliff-top. And the path was already barely visible; in a few minutes, with darkness rushing in, it would be lost completely.

'Over there.' I pointed to where a narrow, wooded valley sank away to our right. 'It should provide some shelter.'

No sooner had I spoken than a peal of thunder rolled across the sky. I saw doubt on Ducker's face, but I held to my decision: if lightning was to strike, it seemed better to offer a choice of targets and take our chances. Though from what Ducker had seen of my luck, I realized, that might seem a poor idea.

The quickening tempo of the rain, and the way the wind whipped it against my skin, decided me, and without further consultation I started running across the field. My shoes grew heavy from the mud that clumped onto them, and my shirt was soon clasped tight to my skin, but I carried on, bent on reaching the sanctuary of the woods. A quick glance over my shoulder sent me sliding down on one knee, but I recovered my balance even as a gust of wind tried to toss me in yet another direction. Now I could see the edge of the trees, hear the wind hissing through their branches only a few yards on.

I reached the valley's rim. The trees dropped away before me, and I was about to plunge into whatever shelter they might offer when I saw an orange light glowing on my left. The water running off my sodden hair had half blinded me, and I needed a moment to clear my eyes; even then I could hardly be sure, peering through my fingers into the whirl of rain and cloud, but it seemed that at the head of the shallow valley, hidden until now by the slope, stood a house. I could see only the vaguest outline of the building itself, but light shone from its windows like a beacon.

'There,' I shouted, though I had no idea if Ducker had heard me; then I was stumbling across the hillside, making as straight as I could for that inviting light. My feet slid constantly away from me, and though the slope provided some protection against the wind, the rain beat down heavier than ever.

As I neared the house, I began to see its size: with its two storeys, crenellated rooftop and miniature turrets, it seemed more the home of a squire than a farmer. Its gardens too were fashionable rather than practical, I noticed, gouging my way across the lawns. There was no obvious entrance in the façade ahead of me, but a gravel path around the side brought me out to the front, where a large portico, like some Grecian temple, announced the door.

'This'll do,' acknowledged Ducker as we came under the roof. 'We can wait 'ere till it clears.'

'Certainly not,' I retorted. 'A fine pair of ruffians we'd make, loitering on these good people's doorstep.'

I heard a muttered reply, something about a pair of ruffians loitering in the parlour instead, but I was learning to ignore his naysaying. Besides, rain was still driving between the columns, and I was freezing in my soaking uniform. Without further argument, I tugged on the chain that hung by the door and heard the tinkling of a bell within.

After some moments, a servant in black livery, with a powdered wig sitting crookedly on his young face, opened the door.

'My apologies for the intrusion,' I announced grandly, 'but we are two travellers in need of shelter. Will you convey my compliments to the gentleman of the house, and tell him that Lieutenant Jerrold desires his acquaintance.'

The boy looked surprised, but vanished promptly enough, leaving the door standing open. Inside I could see a wide staircase, small paintings of hunting scenes on the wall, and several doors leading off in different directions. Were it not for the flickering light of the chandelier, which rocked in the breeze, it would have seemed perfectly welcoming.

The servant returned. 'This way,' he told me, too shy to meet my gaze. He showed us across the hall and through another door into a dim room.

'What an agreeable surprise.' The voice, low and gentle, came before I had accustomed myself to my surroundings. 'I had not expected the pleasure of company.'

Staring across the room, I took in the woman who had spoken. She reclined on a divan opposite me, and in her languid pose needed only a bunch of grapes to look the complete Roman maiden. Auburn hair drooped in ringlets about her face, framing delicate cheeks and full, slightly pouting lips. Her dress was in the old French style, with a neckline nearer the waist than the neck – a suckling dress, some call it, though I've yet to meet a mother who wore one. It clung to the curves of her figure almost as close as my wet clothes on me. A glass, half full, sat on the table beside her.

'Lieutenant Jerrold,' she murmured, raising her head slightly to peer at me. 'You're dripping mud on my carpet.'

Embarrassed, I looked down to see the truth of what she had said. Though it was ridiculous, I could think of nothing better than to remove my shoes and stockings.

'I must apologize,' I stammered, standing there barefoot. 'We did not set out thinking to pay a social call, but were caught in the storm.'

She lifted a hand, then let it fall back across her chest. 'No matter, Lieutenant Jerrold.' Her voice was slow, and somehow distant. 'Your company is . . . a pleasure.' I noticed a slurred edge to her words, as if she could not quite keep hold of them.

'You are most kind.' I was trying to keep from staring at her, but the rise of her bosom tugged constantly at my gaze, tantalizing me with a little flush of rose on the line of her dress. 'May I request the honour, Mrs . . . ?'

'Lady.' She invested the title with unfeigned *ennui*. 'Lady Cunningham.' She paused, distracted by some hidden thought. 'My husband is away.'

This was all a little fantastic, standing without shoes in this blandly tasteful drawing room as a half-dressed Delilah tempted me, without the least enthusiasm, from the couch.

A thought struck me. 'I wonder, Lady Cunningham, could I enquire, without seeming forward: did you happen to notice anything unusual outside the night before last?'

Her dull eyes fixed on me. 'The night before last,' she repeated, sipping at her drink. She jerked her head. 'But I forget my hospitality. Please sit down. Would you care for a drink?'

'A glass of wine would warm me nicely,' I admitted, surprised at her sudden change of conversation. Her manner was so vague I could hardly tell whether she had forgotten her thought midway, or intended to divert me from my question.

She called for the boy – Samuel was his name – and ordered him to fetch wine, while I took the chair opposite her. Ducker remained standing against the wall behind me.

'Your health, Lady Cunningham.' I took a sip, and coughed in surprise as, for the second time that day, I tasted a rather fine French refreshment. 'You must have a well-stocked cellar to still be serving this after so many years of war.'

She shrugged carelessly. 'The butler buys it in Dover, I think. I usually keep to my tincture.' She tapped a long nail against the side of her glass.

'Concerning the other night,' I pressed. 'Do you recall anything out of the ordinary?'

'Lieutenant,' she said, sitting upright and quite oblivious to my question. 'You're watering my furniture.'

I looked down and saw a patch of damp spreading across my seat. 'I do apologize,' I said, jumping to my feet. 'My uniform, I fear, is the worse for the weather.'

'Poor Lieutenant,' she cooed. 'How remiss of me. You must change at once, or I fear you will catch your death. My husband has some clothes which should do.'

'There is no need . . .'

But she would have none of it. A sudden energy had possessed her, and she was all bustle. As she stood, I noticed with a start that her dress was not all of a piece, but opened down the middle, tied over her petticoat with thin ribbons. None of it served her modesty particularly well, and I felt my breeches tightening.

'Will your man want dry clothes?' she asked.

Unfortunately, I could not see Ducker's face, but I guessed he would be livid at being called my man. I thought it hilarious.

'I'll do fine, thank you, ma'am,' he answered evenly. 'Sailors dry easy.'

'As you please.' She turned back to me. 'Samuel will find something for you.'

Samuel led me up the broad stairs and opened the door to a darkened room.

''Ere,' he said, putting a candle down on the dresser.

I looked around as he rummaged in the wardrobe, taking in the solid wooden bed, the heavy curtains, and the thick carpet beneath my toes. Two strongboxes were stacked against the wall, and a small ivory mirror lay on the dresser next to the candle; otherwise there were few clues to the owner's tastes. Even the paintings, I saw, were near duplicates of the ones downstairs.

Samuel pulled out a shirt and a dark suit and laid them on the bed. 'Might do,' he muttered, leaving the room.

It took some effort to prise off my clothes, for they were stuck fast against my skin, and no small amount of tugging would move them. I felt uneasy, and not a little vulnerable, standing exposed in a stranger's room, and I was in haste to dress when a creak at the door rent the stifled silence.

Already unnerved by the mournful house, I spun around. The door was hanging loosely ajar, and to my shock, as I looked through the crack, I saw Lady Cunningham standing on the landing. The light from the chandelier shone through her dress, silhouetting her figure with a golden haze; she stood perfectly still, and showed no recognition or embarrassment, yet seemed to be watching me.

I snatched the shirt and hauled it on, grateful that it hung low enough to cover my dignity. Still the watching Argus did not avert her gaze, nor yet show the least acknowledgement of an impropriety.

'Lieutenant, sir?' I felt a surge of relief to hear Ducker's voice from the foot of the stairs. 'Rain's let up. Time we was going.'

Turning my back on Lady Cunningham, I pulled on her husband's suit and bundled my own wet garments together. Fastening the buttons as swiftly as I could, I stepped out of the room and made for the stairs, passing Lady Cunningham rather self-consciously.

'You may leave those here,' she said, waving at the sodden clothes I carried. 'The maid will wash them.'

I had no time to argue. Nodding my thanks, I dropped them where I stood.

'My husband was away,' she added, talking as much to the empty air as to me, and at first I thought she was just repeating an excuse. 'I sleep badly, you see. I was trying to find my bottle when I saw it out of the window.' I realized that my question on the night before last might finally have registered in her mind. 'Burning, down in the valley.'

'You saw a fire in the valley?' I asked, and she nodded earnestly. Though it might easily have been a gamekeeper eating his dinner, it was the first report I had heard of anything unusual on the heights that evening, and I was determined to investigate it. Later.

'My thanks for your hospitality, milady,' I said quickly. 'And for the loan of the suit. I hope to have the honour again soon, but I fear I may be late for an appointment. At the castle,' I added, in a cheap attempt at insinuating my dignity.

She looked up. 'The castle?' She gave a little laugh. 'Then you may see my husband.'

I froze.

'I beg your pardon?' I said.

'My husband,' she repeated. 'Sir Lawrence Cunningham. His duties often take him to the castle. Why, Lieutenant, are you acquainted?'

Ducker kept us moving at a brisk pace, for there was still some distance to cover, but it was hard work when I fervently wished every step were taking me backwards. My legs grew heavier with each passing minute, and there was a familiar clench in my stomach; I began to regret my generous helping of the fisherman's brandy. It did not help that my breeches – or rather Sir Lawrence Cunningham's breeches, I thought miserably – kept falling down, forcing me to walk with one hand permanently clasped to my waist. Nor did it help to think what his wife's rambling conversation might make of our encounter, or to worry about what other injuries he might soon impute to me.

Far sooner than I wanted, though doubtless too late for Crawley, we came to the castle gate. My mood hardly inclined me to close observation, but I had the impression of great angular towers and flint-pitted walls looming all around. The sentry needed some persuading of my rank, for doubtless most officers did not appear at the gate in sagging funeral garb, but after some words from Ducker he let us pass. Through heavy doors, up several flights of stairs, and past two plainly dubious soldiers, I at last found my way to the appointed place.

'Better never than late, Lieutenant.'

Crawley berated me almost immediately, though I sensed from the mood of the room that they had barely begun their business. There were five of them around a broad oak table: two in red coats, two in blue, and one dressed in a black that looked horribly familiar.

'I see you have dispensed with your uniform as well as your watch.'

'I beg your indulgence,' I apologized, for what seemed the fiftieth time that day. 'My uniform was soaked through by the storm, and I had no opportunity to make repairs. These clothes were borrowed from a house where I found shelter.' I tried desperately to keep from looking at Cunningham, but there was no avoiding the stare burning into me from under that bone-white hair.

'It seems Lieutenant Jerrold has yet to master the Dover weather,' observed a voice from the head of the table, and laughter broke the tension as I took the remaining seat. To my great dismay it was opposite Cunningham, and next to Crawley.

The man who had spoken, a colonel, wine-faced and with hair that no longer needed powdering, made the introductions. He, it seemed, was named Copthorne, and he held a high position at the castle which necessitated his supervision of the measures against smuggling.

'Captain Crawley you know,' he continued, 'but I do not think you will have met Captain Davenant, though doubtless you have encountered his reputation. He commands the *Lancelot* out in the Downs, and is here to offer us the benefit of his experience.'

A proud head inclined stiffly at the compliment, though Crawley blocked any fuller view. I had heard of Davenant, though I would never have given him the satisfaction of saying so. Even if, like me, you never pored over the *Gazette* or the *Chronicle*, you could hardly escape the fame this dashing frigate captain, 'our Nelsonic hope', had won for himself. I suspected he would be insufferable.

'Beside him sits Captain Bingham.'

An army captain, this one, I surmised from the scarlet uniform. He seemed much the same age as me, and must have had some income to have bought his commission so young. The face was possessed of a lazy confidence, but seemed friendly enough under its untended shock of red hair.

'Captain Bingham's company is routinely detached to act against the smugglers onshore,' Copthorne was explaining. 'For all that Crawley tries to take it into his own hands.' There were chuckles around the table. 'And Sir Lawrence Cunningham—'

'I have had the pleasure,' I interrupted, before Cunningham could get a gibe in.

'I am aware,' said Copthorne sharply, and I groaned silently, for his tone made it clear exactly what he knew. 'Sir Lawrence is here to advise us on the judicial aspects of our war against the smugglers. A most vital function,' he reminded me sternly. 'And he is also able to use his position in the town to provide much-valued intelligence.'

'Which brings me here this evening, Colonel.' Cunningham's voice had lost none of its reptilian grate since last we spoke. 'I am told, by one of my informants, that a cargo is to be landed tomorrow night, somewhere down the coast towards Folkestone. I am also told that it may be the work of the largest gang we have seen since the days of Drake.'

This seemed very significant to the others, but meant nothing to me. 'Sir Francis Drake?' I asked innocently.

Half the table erupted into great hilarity, while the other half, notably Crawley and Cunningham, stared with open scorn. Bingham repeated my question with some mirth, but Crawley seemed to have taken my evident mistake as a personal slight, and was at pains to correct me.

'If you had the least interest in performing your duty, Lieutenant, you might well have troubled yourself to learn a little relevant history. Had you done so, it is highly likely that you would have noticed the prominent role played by the notorious, late and very much unlamented Caleb Drake.'

The name sounded familiar, though not from any particular acquaintance. Perhaps I had heard it spoken in a tavern.

The room fell into an awkward silence. The soldiers studied their cuffs intently, while Captain Davenant simply seemed bored. I deliberately avoided Cunningham's gaze.

'Well,' said Copthorne with a discreet cough. 'I believe Sir Lawrence was speaking.'

Cunningham looked up. 'I am given to believe that we should expect two luggers and a shore party. Perhaps fifty men in all.'

'I take it, then, that a pair of riding officers will not suffice.'

Copthorne's joke drew laughter. 'But a company of infantry could teach them a lesson, I'll wager.'

'If we find them,' said Crawley sourly. 'Your informant has given us at least half a dozen reports in the last few weeks, Sir Lawrence, and I confess I have yet to find truth in any of them.'

'My agent,' retorted Cunningham, 'has provided half a dozen reports and you have yet to make use of any of them. If you will insist on scampering about the shore playing constables rather than exercising the command appointed to you, it is hardly surprising that my hard-won intelligence is squandered.'

Crawley was unrepentant. 'Sir Lawrence, how often have I argued that smugglers must be caught onshore? Otherwise it wants the wisdom of Solomon and the patience of Job to prove to the courts where their cargo was bound.'

I guessed from the surrounding expressions that this was not a new debate.

'Absolutely, Captain Crawley,' Colonel Copthorne agreed. 'But Bingham's company will see to that. *Orestes* will be needed to cut off the smugglers' escape to seaward.'

'Good Lord.' Captain Davenant affected shock. 'You'll have to take your boat out, you know, Crawley, and do some inshore work as well. Think you're up to that, Lieutenant? Shallow waters near the coast, you know.'

The combination of a sneering tone and the word 'lieutenant' had given me to think that he addressed me, but from the direction of his words, and Crawley's white-hot face, it seemed that for once I was not the object of contempt. I had grown so used to Crawley's courtesy title of captain, and his obvious superiority, that I had forgotten he was merely a fellow lieutenant. I found the thought relieving, though I had not the least idea what Davenant was driving at.

'If there's to be a pair of the smugglers,' said Crawley, trying to maintain his calm, 'then *Orestes* will be outgunned. I shall need support, Captain Davenant.'

Davenant sighed. 'Chasing after smugglers is hardly the best use of a man-of-war, Lieutenant, and I doubt the admiral would happily sanction it. Certainly not while a whole French fleet remains out of harbour and unaccounted for. But . . .' He lifted a hand theatrically. 'I may be able to "turn a blind eye", as they say, to the admiral's instructions. I suspect he will indulge me a little measured disregard.'

This, I presumed sourly, must be the 'devil-take-'em' spirit so applauded by the press.

'We shall rely on you, then,' said Colonel Copthorne. I don't believe he was taken in by the posturing for a moment, but he had what he wanted.

'I shall endeavour to be there.' Davenant straightened his lapels. 'And if I fail, Crawley, you'll just have to take them on at two to one. It's been done before, you know.'

'Excellent.' Copthorne rose from his chair. 'Captain Bingham's company will seal off the beach, *Orestes* and *Lancelot* will block the seaward route, and Sir Lawrence can send them off to the colonies. A fine plan.'

'And we can all pray that the French don't plan their invasion for tomorrow night,' finished Bingham.

'With Mr Fox and his Whiggish friends now in Whitehall,' said Cunningham stonily, 'I should have thought that Buonaparte could happily leave his entire army in Austria. It can hardly be long before the little Jacobin leading our government signs us up to whatever peace the Corsican tyrant offers him.'

His rant silenced the conversation instantly; as soldiers of his Majesty, none of us could acquiesce in such a scathing slander of the government. I wondered that Cunningham was boor enough to put us in so awkward a position.

Once again, it was Colonel Copthorne who found a tactful retreat. 'Buonaparte must be cursing himself,' he said. 'If he'd waited six months before abandoning his invasion camps, his two greatest obstacles, Pitt and Nelson, would have been removed.'

This was too much for the noble Captain Davenant. 'Come, Colonel. His greatest obstacle was the navy. We didn't all die with Nelson, you know.'

'Well, if peace does come,' said Copthorne, pouring from a decanter, 'the first article of the treaty had best be for the full restoration of good brandy. I've had a devil of a time getting this.'

In the midst of the discussion I saw Crawley preparing to leave. As he had had nothing to drink, and evidently little to say, I was hardly surprised. I was inclined to follow him, for I had no desire to spend any longer in Sir Lawrence's company, but before I could move I felt a tugging on my sleeve, and turned to see Captain Davenant standing by me.

'Just joined *Orestes*, have you?' he asked quietly.

'That's right, sir.'

'How do you find Lieutenant Crawley?'

'Well enough, sir.' I was on my guard – pealing officers to their superiors was ever a sure way to find trouble. 'Are you acquainted?'

'We are,' he said, arching his eyebrows significantly. 'We were prisoners together, at Verdun, a year or so back.'

'I had no idea . . .'

'I only mention it,' continued Davenant, 'because during our time there, before we were both exchanged, there were rumours.' He shot me a sideways glance.

'Do you mean . . .?'

'Nothing was ever discovered, of course,' he said smoothly. 'But . . . Has Captain Crawley ever explained to you how he came to be stationed here in Dover?'

I shook my head.

'I shall say no more, then.' He straightened. 'A pleasure to make your acquaintance, Lieutenant Jerrold. I trust that I shall be seeing, and hearing, much more of you.'

'The honour will be mine,' I said gravely, for I can match any man's humbug. But I was intrigued by his words, for there must be something to them. Surely he did not abuse his junior out of pure malice.

I saw Crawley exiting the door and, making my excuses to the company, I joined him on the stairs. We walked in silence, he lost in thought, I too confused to say anything after Davenant's mysterious confidence. The night was cold, and the storm seemed to have blown itself away, for a few stars shone dimly above us.

'Heading back to your inn, are you?' asked Crawley as we passed the gate. It was as well I was with him, for I would never have found it on my own.

'Actually, sir, I have a few more enquiries to make.'

'Hmm.' Crawley considered it. 'Well, Lieutenant, as long as you make the quay by half past eight o'clock tomorrow morning. It will be a long day, and a long night, too. Particularly if Sir Lawrence's intelligence proves to be of its habitual standard.'

'Yes, sir.'

'So you had better go and find out what you can about your dead body while you have the chance.'

Of course, I hadn't the least intention of investigating 'my' dead body, not at that hour. I had done enough for the day, and besides, where could I have gone? I doubted the coroner would thank me for arriving at his door for a discussion of the man's injuries. No; I did have enquiries to make, but they were of an entirely personal nature that was no concern of Crawley's. Mad though she had been, the image of Lady Cunningham in her gauzy dress had fixed itself in my thoughts and aroused a hunger I was determined to satisfy before the night was done. Returning to finish my business at Sir Lawrence's house was out of the question, of course, so instead I made my way down the steep hill and into the town where, after a few mis-steps, I found myself outside the Crown and Anchor.

It seemed quieter than the last time I had been there, though that was only an impression: my memory of the occasion was far from perfect. But I was able to push my way to the bar without too much jostling, and needed only a couple of minutes to snare the landlord's attention.

'Excuse me,' I shouted over the din, 'I'm looking for a girl called Isobel.'

He cupped his hand behind a hairy ear. 'Wassat? Don't sell no drink called Isobel.'

'Not a drink, a girl,' I bellowed, before I caught his meaning. 'Ah, I see. A brandy.'

He looked at me suspiciously. 'You that navy man?' he asked.

With my instant notoriety in a town the size of Dover, a lie would have been futile. 'Yes, I am.'

'No brandy.'

'Wine?'

He considered it. 'All right. Portuguese, though.'

It might have been Portuguese, or it might have been Chinese for all I knew; certainly it was barely drinkable. But with my coin across the counter, I could resume my enquiry.

'She ain't here. Sometimes she is, but not now.'

Somehow I managed to drain my glass and bang it on the counter. He refilled it, and again I paid his exorbitant fee. Much more of this, I thought, and I would be in no state to enjoy Isobel's company. Again.

'So where can I find her?' I tried to keep my voice sober, for if the landlord thought I was losing my senses he would prevaricate all night, until I was well into my cups.

He squinted at me. I had finished my drink, but this time I held the empty glass and stared calmly back. *You'll get no more from me tonight*, my expression said. Even the pleasures of Isobel could hardly be worth a third serving of his rot.

'She lives with the 'ores, down on the woolcombers' street, off the castle road,' he said, giving up. 'Though she ain't what you think.'

'My thoughts are my own business,' I retorted stiffly, though his words had surprised me after her vehement denials. I threw him a final coin. 'No, thank you – you can have that for nothing.'

I knew where the castle road was for I had just come down it, though it took me longer to retrace my steps when I had to pause at every turning and alleyway to see if it might be the woolcombers' street. None was, or at least none was announced as such, and at length I found myself at the very end of the road, where the path began to wind up to the castle. Ahead of me loomed an imposing stone church, of which I could see little beyond its gaping arches.

But there seemed to be a figure with a light in its yard and so, letting myself through the iron gate, I approached.

'Hallo?' I hailed him, but no answer came. I tried again, but again silence. Nor did he even move. I grew suspicious, and moved around to see his face better, weaving my way between the slanting headstones with mounting apprehension.

'Idiot,' I chided myself, for I saw instantly my mistake, and stepped forward to look closer. From the front it was obvious: this was no man, but a statue, made to a full size and with a lit lantern in his left hand. He stood, carved in white marble atop a low plinth, his back slightly bent and his arms spread open, reaching forward over me. Doubtless it was intended to be benevolent, but in the dark, and looming from his pedestal, it gave the unsettling impression that he was about to swoop down and grab me about the neck. It was the only such monument in the churchyard – the rest were far more modest – and it was clearly new, for it had yet to be disfigured by moss or weather. I leaned closer to read the inscription, to see who this exalted, conceited paragon had been.

'Caleb Drake.'

At the shock of hearing the words spoken suddenly aloud I shuddered; for a fleeting instant I thought the statue had come to life and would indeed fall upon me with the terrible vengeance of the dead. Then I realized that the voice had come from behind me and, still trembling, I turned.

'Did I startle ye?'

Even if he hadn't, his appearance was hardly reassuring. The long black robe of a priest hung off his gaunt figure, and thin white hair grew wild around his bald head. He carried a lantern, but it did little to illuminate the hollows of his face. He spoke in a high-pitched whisper.

'Yes,' I said, ill-temperedly, my blood still pounding. 'You did.'

'I apologize,' he croaked. 'I'd only come to trim his wick.'

I looked up to where the lamp glowed over my head. 'It must be a troublesome memorial to need such maintenance.'

The priest shrugged a bony shoulder. 'The estate provides for a candle to be lit every night.'

'Why the candle?' Despite my anger with the man, I was intrigued.

'After the fashion of Saint Christopher,' explained the priest. 'In remembrance of all the ships he helped ashore.'

My mind was clearing from the shock, and remembering what Crawley had said about this Caleb Drake I guessed he had not been the town's pilot.

'I heard Caleb Drake was a notorious criminal.'

The priest lifted a finger to his lips. 'It is unwise to spcak ill of the dead,' he admonished me. 'Particularly on holy ground, and when they are but a few months in their grave.'

'Still, a rather fine grave for a criminal.'

'For all his wickedness, he was a much loved man. You see?' He pointed to the lettering on the tomb. Underneath the name were the words: 'Dedicated to his memory by his loving brother, and all who knew him. MDCCCV.'

'He had a brother?'

'Indeed. But he has not been to Dover these many years. He lives in the Indies.'

I wondered whether he lived there of his own accord, or at the King's pleasure. 'But he returned to erect the memorial?'

'He sent the money through his banker. Mr Mazard made all the arrangements.'

'Still,' I pressed, 'I marvel that he was given a place in the churchyard.'

'Where better? Was not our Lord himself hanged as a criminal, among criminals? And did he not come into the world to save sinners? "Joy shall be in heaven over one sinner that repenteth, more than over ninety and nine just persons." And Drake was repentant, before they hanged him.'

No doubt: the noose must have made more converts in its time than ever the cross did. But this was becoming rather more relevant to my own predicament than I found comfortable. I returned to my original purpose.

'I wonder if you might help me. I am trying to reach the woolcombers' street.'

'If ye leave by the gate and turn left, ye'll find it the first road on your right.'

'Thank you.' A fresh thought struck me. 'And I wonder, do you know . . . which is to say, are you aware . . .' I tried to phrase this without causing offence. 'Do you know of a girl named Isobel who lives on that street?'

'Indeed I do,' he said, with unexpected vigour. 'I attend there often myself. A very worthy establishment. The things those fallen women do are quite remarkable.'

If his attitude to Caleb Drake had puzzled me, this positively stunned me. Not that I'd never heard of a priest who strayed, far from it, but one who was so shameless in his debauchery? He must have had a martyr's faith in God's enduring mercy.

He clearly read the look on my face. 'Some in my congregation think me odd, you know, but I draw my strength from the Bible.' A hitherto undiscovered chapter, I could only presume. 'After all, did not Christ himself consort with the harlot?'

I was sorry I could not stay for a sermon, for this brand of religion obviously had much to offer a man like me, but the night was drawing on and the cemetery was not where I hoped to spend it. Having obtained more precise directions – 'five houses along, the sign is unmistakable' – I gave my thanks and left him fiddling with Caleb Drake's lamp.

I found the street and the house easily enough, though my mind was more than half distracted with the encounter I'd just had, and anticipation of the encounter I was about to enjoy. 'Home of the Lady Magdalene', read the sign over the door, though the building itself was prim enough. I mounted the steps, and was further confused to see a line from the Psalms inscribed on the lintel: 'Wash me throughly from mine iniquity, and cleanse me from my sin; for I acknowledge my faults, and my sin is ever before me.'

With my sins very much before me, I lifted the heavy knocker and let it drop against the door. The sound echoed around the deserted street, but to no effect. I tried again, though my desire was seeping away rapidly on that cold doorstep.

A small hatch in the door shot open with a bang, and a square of yellow light shone onto my chest. I stooped to look in, and saw a solitary eye gazing sternly upon me.

'We are closed.' It was a woman's voice, but hardly the inviting tones I had expected. 'You may come tomorrow.'

'But—'

'No, sir, we are very strict. We take no custom after four o'clock.'

'But madam—'

'Miss!'

'Miss, I only seek a few words with Isobel.'

'Isobel is abed. As all good Christians should be at this hour.' The hatch snapped shut, the eye vanished.

I surrendered to my fate and returned to the inn, wondering all the way whether I was losing my senses, or whether Dover really was the most impossible town in England. Unsurprisingly, I found no answers.

6

MY THIRD MORNING IN DOVER BEGAN IN EXACTLY THE MANNER OF the first two, with a pounding and bad news. The pounding was again the boy on my door, the bad news the men awaiting me in the courtyard: Sir Lawrence Cunningham the magistrate and the mountainous Constable Stubb, both charmingly matched in long black cloaks and wide-brimmed hats, like something out of a puritan tailor's shop window. Their breath steamed in the blue half-light.

'Mr Jerrold.' Cunningham's voice did nothing to warm the morning air. 'My apologies for disturbing you so early.'

'Not at all, Sir Lawrence. It preserves the rest of my day for matters of importance.'

Cunningham's eyes narrowed. 'You may not enjoy the liberty. Some new facts have reached me which cast you in a most inauspicious light.' My bravado vanished at the menace in his words. 'I wonder, where were you last night?'

'You know full well,' I answered. 'At the castle with you.'

'You left early with Crawley. Where did you go afterwards?'

Was he trying to indict me for being turned away from a brothel? I thought back. 'To a tavern. Then to a church, and then to bed.'

'And Crawley was with you?'

'Captain Crawley and I parted outside the castle gate.' So far I was on strong ground, but there was a lazy edge to his questions that worried me.

'What was the name of the tavern, Lieutenant?'

'The Crown and Anchor,' I said truthfully.

A knowing look flashed between Cunningham and Stubb.

'What took you there?'

'I wanted a drink. Why else?'

'Had you been there before?'

I was about to answer in the affirmative, but something in his manner checked me. He'd been rattling off his questions fairly sharply, but with this last one he had seemed to tense, like a trapper watching a fox as it poised its foot over the jaws. Stubb was leaning forward too, as if waiting for my next words to condemn me. It would be madness to lie, for doubtless they could produce witnesses; indeed, from the trend of their questions, they probably already had them. Catching me in deceit would only seal my guilt in Cunningham's mind. But I could not escape the conviction that he *wanted* me to admit my presence in the Crown and Anchor the night before the death, and if that had brought him calling at this hour then he must assign it a great significance. And though I could not imagine what that might be, it could only be to one purpose.

'No.'

My heart thumped faster, for now I had strayed from the bounds of fact, and was vulnerable. But I doubted that the truth would have served me any better. *What did Cunningham know?*

The triumph on Cunningham's face told me he was not deceived. 'You had never been to the Crown and Anchor before?' he repeated.

'No.'

'So how, Lieutenant, do you explain a witness who saw you there the night before the corpse was discovered on the beach?'

'I do not know that I have to explain it. What does it matter?'

'It matters because I demand to know.' My obstinacy was evidently beginning to irritate him, for his thin voice was rising yet higher.

'Is the refreshment so much better elsewhere?' I remained

flippant. 'I have a mind to try the Dolphin tonight. Would that be a more appropriate choice?'

'Can you deny that you were at the Crown and Anchor three nights ago?' Now his face was hot with anger, and the words screeched forth like the call of some carrion bird.

'I have denied it, twice. And will continue to do so until you accept it. Your witness is probably mistaken. He must have seen me in another tavern.'

'That I very much doubt,' Cunningham sneered. 'He is the Crown and Anchor's landlord.'

'The . . . then he is mistaken.' I was tripping on my words now, for Sir Lawrence clearly knew my lie. But I'd long ago learned that flat rejection, if maintained long enough, can stall the most damning evidence simply by wearing down a man's patience.

And Stubb was not the most patient of men. 'Keep on denyin' it, Mr Jerrold,' he growled. 'We knows you was in there, and we knows who else was there. And we knowed you'd go back, too: the killer always returns to the scenes of 'is crime.'

That article of faith seemed so common that I suspected the killer would be the last man back on the scene. But there was much to puzzle me in Stubb's words, and I had little time to consider them.

'So am I now supposed to have committed a crime at the tavern as well?' That seemed to be his meaning. Perhaps he and Cunningham were bent on tarring me with every crime in the parish, until one or another stuck. 'Or do you propose that I thumped the man over the head while he waited for his drink, then dragged him unseen through Dover onto the beach?'

'So you did see 'im there!' Triumph shone in Stubb's face.

'Who?'

'You knows who. You just said: you saw 'im there waiting for 'is drink.' His square chin dropped in a grotesque leer. 'We knowed you'd give it up with time.'

'Forgive me, Constable, for being a little slow.' There was not a straight thought in my head at that moment. 'You are telling me that the body I discovered on the beach had been seen in the Crown and Anchor the night before?' I paused. 'With me?'

'Got the shillin' 'eads up,' he agreed.

'Was I seen talking with him?' Surely I could not have been so unlucky as to have been drinking in the same room as that wretched corpse.

'No,' allowed Stubb.

That was something, at least. My confidence began to swell.

'Was I seen consorting with him at all?'

'No.' Stubb shifted on his feet. 'But that don't mean—'

'And why not, Constable? Because I was not there. It was . . .' I stopped, within an ace of hanging myself. 'It would have been a busy room filled with men and noise, and I doubt whether the landlord could in all truth remember one out of a hundred customers, let alone, as you suppose, two.'

'But we need not rely on the landlord.' Cunningham had kept silent during Stubb's attack, watching with a vague air of disapproval from under the shadow of his hat. 'Or at the least, we can verify his story. He says you were seen with a girl.'

I had forgotten Isobel. If the landlord remembered her, then she could demolish my defence with two words.

'The widow Dawson.' Cunningham wiped a dewdrop from the rim of his hat. 'I imagine she can unravel this matter.'

I imagined she could, and prayed it would be in my favour. It might yet prove to be the landlord's mistake, for surely no-one could confuse a young waif like Isobel with any widow.

Cunningham and I stood in that freezing courtyard staring silently at each other, while Stubb went to fetch the Dawson woman. I suggested retreating inside for a drink and some breakfast, but Cunningham waved the idea away impatiently. The grooms shovelled piles of steaming dung from the stables, and the morning light slowly took on the greyness of the day as my legs stiffened and my clothes grew damp.

Stubb returned; instantly I saw that I was ruined. God knew what her conjugal history had been at such an early age, for she did not look much more than seventeen, but there was no mistaking the girl at Stubb's side, complaining loudly at the force of his grip. Isobel wore a modest blue dress, and her hair was tied back in a way that accentuated her thin little neck, but her dark eyes flashed with anger.

'If you have to drag me out of the laundry,' she hissed at Sir Lawrence, 'there's no cause to do it like I was a common thief.'

'No,' he agreed. 'Stubb, let her go.'

Reluctantly, Stubb released her arm, though he stayed standing uncomfortably close, licking at his lips.

I saw my one chance. 'Sir Lawrence believes we met in the Crown and Anchor three nights ago,' I said quickly. 'I have assured him that you will disprove—'

'Silence!' snapped Cunningham. 'Mrs Dawson, I apologize for the need to trouble you, but I must establish certain facts. The landlord at the Crown and Anchor claims to have seen you talking to, and leaving with, Mr Jerrold here, three nights back. I do not wish to impugn your virtue, Mrs Dawson, for I am all too aware of the esteem in which you are held.' Through my confusion, I noticed the sarcastic bite in his words. 'But I must know the answer.'

We all stared in silence, waiting for her judgement; the only sound in that courtyard was the rasping of a spade on the stones. Isobel looked between us, anger plain on her gaunt face, and I could guess that after my boorish behaviour she would have few regrets in condemning me. Every second that passed was, I felt certain, only postponing my fate, and the waiting was like a slow-burning fuse in my gut. If she was to convict me, why could she not deliver the blow swiftly?

'No,' she said, her voice quiet even in the silence. 'I was in the home all night. Miss Hoare can tell you so. Is that all?'

The relief that flooded my face almost matched the fury in Cunningham's. 'You are quite sure?' he asked dangerously.

His anger seemed to give her strength. 'I'm sure,' she said with a shrug. 'What would I want to be doing with a man like him?'

'What indeed?' From the twitch in Cunningham's face, I guessed even his cold mind could imagine something. Possibly something quite exotic, I thought, remembering his wife. 'Thank you, Mrs Dawson. We will no doubt be calling if we have a further use for you.'

'You can save your bulldog next time,' she spat. 'You might find nicer questions get nicer answers.' Avoiding my grateful eye, she turned, and marched stiffly out through the gate.

'I do not know what you did to her,' said Cunningham, 'but you clearly managed to break her in well enough.' Stubb made a crude gesture with his fingers. 'Though I suppose there never was a girl who couldn't be tamed if you pricked hard enough at her thighs.'

If he hoped to goad me into an indiscretion protecting Isobel's honour, he had misread me badly, but I could not leave his smug leer unchecked. 'Does that include your wife, I wonder?' I asked politely.

I fancied I saw his body jerk under the cloak. 'My wife?' Menace filled his voice. 'What do you know of my wife?'

There were many answers I could have given, from the bland to the slanderous. 'I know that she is a most hospitable lady.'

Perhaps he would have taken my words at their literal meaning and had done with me, or perhaps not, to judge from what came later, but at that moment a scrawny boy, in a hat that was at least a size too large, walked into the courtyard. He held a bundle of blue and white cloth before him, and marched straight towards me, tilting back his hat to peer at me as he approached.

'Lieutenant Jerrold?' he asked, and with a shock I recognized him as Samuel, the servant boy. 'Lady Cunningham said to give you back your clothes that you left with her last night.'

Had he announced that Lady Cunningham was in the stables waiting to pleasure each of the grooms in turn, I doubt the reaction could have been fiercer. Even as I dumbly took my laundered uniform, I heard a strangled roar from my right. Without warning, Cunningham crossed the yard and with a vicious kick sent the boy sprawling across the stones. He lay there, whimpering, while the magistrate bent his face very close to mine.

'Your little band of whores and traitors may have protected you again, Jerrold,' he hissed, spittle spraying over my cheeks, 'but you cannot defer justice for ever. You find it amusing to trifle with me now, but you will not make me look the fool.'

There were several obvious retorts to that, but this time I wisely left them unsaid.

Cunningham departed, dragging Samuel by the collar and trailing Stubb in his wake. I pitied the boy his misfortune, both in his employment and his timing, and wondered whether his mistress would fare any better at Cunningham's hands. I could not say I had any great feeling for her after her games the evening before, but I would not have wished Sir Lawrence's vengeance on anyone. Particularly when it seemed only a matter of time before he meted it out on me.

For all that, I did not want that punishment forestalled by Crawley's. I had little idea of the time, but little hope that it was in my favour. I set out for the harbour with all speed, praying that I did not encounter Cunningham on the way.

To my relief, I reached the quay without incident; to my greater relief, Crawley was not on hand to castigate my time-keeping. Instead, Ducker was there, leaning against a piling and sucking his pipe.

'Mornin', sir,' he greeted me. 'Expectin' the smugglers to surrender at the sight o' you?' He gestured to my side, and I realized with embarrassment that I had forgotten my sword.

'Where's the captain?' I asked, avoiding the question.

'In there.' Ducker jerked a thumb at the white-washed building. 'Goin' over the plans with Cap'n Bingham from the army. Just as well,' he added thoughtfully. 'Said if you wasn't 'ere afore 'e was done, 'e'd sail without you an' court-martial you 'imself later.'

Wonderful. Between Crawley and Cunningham, I marvelled I was still alive at all, let alone at liberty.

'I was making investigations,' I told Ducker huffily. 'I have discovered that our corpse was seen drinking at the Crown and Anchor the night before we found him.'

Ducker nodded. 'No wonder 'e washed up dead, then.'

'Lieutenant.' Crawley had emerged from the building. 'You honour us with your presence.' He checked his watch, and I braced myself for another assessment of my punctuality, but he clearly had higher things on his mind. Or had given up. 'We had best be off – the tide waits for no man.'

I sat stiffly in the stern of the boat while the coxswain guided her through the jumble of craft filling the basin. There was little hope, in that narrow space, of the sort of sharp rowing that had been expected from the *Téméraire*'s boats, but the men worked cheerfully enough. I recognized a few faces from the party that had found me on the beach, and caught several sidling glances aimed in my direction. Clearly a fresh start aboard *Orestes* would be impossible.

With that thought, the cutter herself swung into sight. I had seen some of her sort before, of course, around the harbours at Portsmouth and Gibraltar, but never this close, and I was startled to see how small she appeared. A single, improbably tall mast rose out of the flat line of her deck some way in front of the centre, with a long boom jutting back well over her stern and a bowsprit protruding almost as far forward, like some ancient narwhal. Those spars would support an enormous sail area, giving her the speed and agility for which her type was famed, but they utterly dwarfed the deck beneath.

The crew raised their oars as our boat glided alongside her black hull. I could hear a whistling and banging from the deck as Crawley made his entrance; then it was my turn to mount the rungs in her side and scramble over the gunwale. It did not feel very dignified, still less so with two-score men lined up to watch me, but I managed to keep hold of my hat and offer Crawley a half-hearted salute.

'No time to lose.' Crawley was all action. 'If we are to use this tide, we had best get the anchor up. Put the men on the capstan, Lieutenant.'

'Yes, sir.'

There were barely fifty men aboard *Orestes*, against the seven hundred-odd there had been aboard the *Téméraire*, but the cutter's size made her deck seem twice as crowded, and I had a devil of a time finding her petty officers to get the men to work. I was dazed by the bustle, the constant shouting and creaking, the smell of tar and salt, the myriad diverse tasks needed to put a ship to sea, all forgotten in my time ashore. The pitching that began as we passed the pier heads and the shelter of the headland weakened my legs, and I had to dive below for a nip of rum to steady myself. Crawley showed no such failings: he stood by the tiller – for *Orestes* had no wheel to steer by, but a long handle ideally placed to knock a man's knees out in heavy seas – and barked orders to the crew, the wind streaming his grey queue behind him. For all that he had us running around onshore so much of the time, clearly this was his element.

We spent the day beating westwards down the Channel, for it was Crawley's plan that we should come back on the smugglers with the wind behind us. He had let it be known in Dover that we were headed for Portsmouth with dispatches, and we maintained that course all through the day until nightfall, pausing only once in the afternoon to exercise the guns. Five on each side, I noticed glumly, and while they might give the smugglers a scare, they'd hardly raise a splinter against a real ship.

'Best 'ope the wind don't drop,' Ducker observed, as *Orestes*' bow swung back into her wake. 'Otherwise they'll have a clear run inshore.' He had a chart in front of him, weighted down on the deck with a lantern. Otherwise we carried no light.

'What's our position?' Crawley, who had been in his cabin, was back on deck and looking anxious. The carelessness he had shown as we left harbour was gone.

Ducker tapped the chart. ''Ere, sir.' He had had men measuring our speed with the log line since sundown, and with frequent glances at the compass he was plotting our course in intricate detail. 'Still some ways to go. Should get there about midnight.'

'Too soon,' muttered Crawley. 'And too dangerous. It'll be low tide then – best take in a reef.'

He seemed jittery, and I remembered Davenant's gibe about shallow waters. None but an idiot ever liked to sail close to land at night, but even here, a mile out, Crawley looked unduly worried. Before I could broach the subject with him, though, he was away again, giving orders to shorten sail. Which might eventually bring us upon the smugglers in deeper water, I thought, but would in the interval simply prolong our journey through the darkness, with all its attendant hazards.

Like so many dangerous situations, though, the majority of the trip passed uneventfully: however close you may be to a rock, there will be no excitement until you actually strike it, and we struck none that night. At three bells, on Crawley's suggestion, I went below to my hammock – itself something of a rebuke, for I was used to having a cot – and tossed my way through a few hours of restless half-sleep. I had felt much relaxed since coming on board, for despite the unfamiliarity of the vessel and her unknown crew, the routine of the navy was unmistakable, and strangely comforting after the constant disorientations of Dover. Here my rank conferred immediate authority, and the tasks, though straightforward, demanded my full attention. But in my hammock my mind was at liberty to wander, and it returned always to the unsettling sights of the last three days: the gulls pecking at the body, the filth in the gaol, the statue in the cemetery and a furious Sir Lawrence Cunningham raging at me in the dawn mist.

I must have fallen asleep somewhere in those memories, for I awoke to the soft thud of men sliding from their hammocks and climbing the ladder. It must be midnight, I realized, the start of the middle watch: I had best go up.

The air on deck was fresh, and very cold. I could just see a hazy moon through shreds of cloud; otherwise, the only light was the dim circle from Ducker's lantern. Picking my way around the cannons and over piles of coiled rope, I went aft, where the quartermaster sat cross-legged in front of his map, like some Persian mystic communing with his gods. Crawley stood next to him, leaning against the gunwale, his face very pale in the grey light. He wore his sword.

'Good morning, Lieutenant,' he said quietly as I approached. He seemed unusually subdued. 'Did you sleep?'

'A little.' I waited awkwardly to see if he would give me the watch and retire to his cabin, but he showed no sign of moving. 'How much further?'

Ducker looked up. 'A ways yet, sir.' He tapped a finger on the chart. 'We're 'ere. And the smugglers . . . who knows? There's one good bay between Dover and Folkestone, but whether they'll go east or west, I couldn't say.'

'They're building fortifications on the west side,' said Crawley. 'Saw them this morning. I guess they'll go east.'

'They ain't buildin' forts at this time o' night, sir,' retorted Ducker. 'An' I never knowed a builder as couldn't look the other way if there was a barrel o' rum for 'im to see. Nor a soldier neither.'

That sparked a thought. 'If we're unsure where they're landing,' I asked, 'how will we ensure that we rendezvous with the soldiers? They might end up facing them on their own.' Worse yet, *we* might end up facing them on *our* own.

'If the infantry find them first, they will set off a false fire from the beach. If we find them, we wait until they land their cargo, and then fire the guns.'

'And what of *Lancelot*?'

'Davenant should be over there.' Crawley gestured out to sea, where somewhere in the darkness lay the coast of France. 'With the tide as it is, he will wait there, so if one of the smugglers makes a run for it he can intercept her.'

For the next three hours we saw precious little. Occasionally a light would flare on the shore, but there were no other boats visible, and Crawley refused to let us alter course to investigate without a signal from the soldiers or a clear sighting of a ship. And so we sailed on, with no sound but the pull of the ropes and the slapping of the sea on the prow. I began to yawn, for my turn in the hammock barely counted as a nap, and anticipation soon became boredom when nothing happened. About half past three – seven bells, though in our secrecy we did not strike them – we cleared for action. All the crew were on deck now, crouching by their guns, and despite the order for silence there was a low, excited murmuring among them. Clearly they looked forward to the battle far more than I, who was not altogether unhappy that there had been no sign of the enemy.

'There, sir.'

Ducker, with his keen eyes, had seen it first: another light, towards the shore but clearly at sea, flashing with a deliberate rhythm that must be some sort of signal. I turned my telescope on to the land, but there was no reply to be seen.

'Probably behind a rock,' muttered Crawley.

I took the glass from my eye and looked back at the light. It still flashed in the same pattern, and was definitely moving towards the coast.

'Alter course two points to larboard,' Crawley ordered, and I had to step smartly out of the way as the tiller went over.

The lantern was put out, and two men went to the fo'c'sle with leads, for the tide was still only half in and our new course was taking us into ever shallower waters. Their soundings were relayed back along the deck in whispers, and I thought back to childhood games of Gossips, hoping that the message would not become too garbled in transmission.

'Eight fathoms.'

We were close enough now to see the land, a lumpy darkness between the greys of sea and sky. Still there were no lights there.

'Bring in the mainsail.'

Crawley's face looked drawn; his eyes flicked between the land and the mast with a frantic intensity. There was a flapping of canvas, and a hollow rattling from the beaded collar of the boom. It sounded horribly loud in the silence of the night, but better that, I thought, than the cracking of the hull on the seabed.

We had slowed almost to nothing, with only the jib to drive us forward. The men at the guns were looking about anxiously, and I could feel an unspoken terror at the invisible hazards all around us, the rocks and enemy we could not see.

'Four fathoms.'

'Drop the anchor.'

There was a splash from for'ard. Crawley was scanning the shoreline for any sign of movement, but against the black of the land we could see nothing.

'Lieutenant.' Crawley beckoned me over. 'Take the jollyboat inshore and see what you find. If the smugglers are there already, set off a musket. Otherwise, stay silent and observe them.'

'Yes, sir.'

A cold panic gripped me, for in an open boat we would be terribly exposed when the cannons started firing. Nor was I reassured when Crawley gave me only four men, none of them looking any more grateful than I at the assignment.

''Ere, sir.' Ducker found me just as I was about to go over the side. 'In case they don't run when they sees you.' He handed me a cutlass. It was no officer's blade, but the smugglers would hardly make a distinction. Though if it came to that, I doubted any sword would be much help.

I took the weapon. 'Thank you.' I must have looked quite the pirate, with a musket over my shoulder and a cutlass in my belt. All I needed was a dagger in my teeth and a parrot by my ear.

We cast off. 'Slowly and quietly,' I ordered, but the impending danger must have put the wind up them, for I never heard so many splashed strokes and jumped locks. Every noise only heightened the tension, and soon our little crew was in a proper funk. It didn't help that they had their backs to the land, and constantly craned their heads about despite my orders to keep shipshape.

A harsh creak tore the night air, very loud, and very close off our starboard side. All five of us turned instinctively to see its origin. With a splash and a clang and a thump, one of my men dropped his oar and fell off his thwart.

'Silence,' I hissed. I thought I could see the shadow of a hull, but in the darkness, and with more than enough nerves to colour my imagination, I couldn't be sure. 'Pull harder,' I whispered, 'but *quietly* this time.'

I pushed the tiller over, and watched the shadow slowly draw away from us. If it was a boat she must have had an unusually shallow draught, for almost immediately I noticed that the noise of the waves had grown louder: we were close in on the beach. I peered intently at the pale strip of surf that glowed before us. There seemed to be a dark shape breaking the line, but it could as easily have been a rock as a boat. I tried my glass, but in the darkness it gave me no firmer impression. We needed to go closer, but we were already within range of a musket, and I remembered Cunningham's prediction of fifty ruffians gathered onshore. There were, I knew, plenty of revenue officers whose devotion to duty had taken them straight to the hospital, or the cemetery.

'Can any of you swim?'

There was a vigorous shaking of heads. I was at an impasse: I dared not fire my musket without proof that the men were on the beach, but equally I dared not go in closer to make sure. But what if they were on the beach, and then left? Crawley would be livid if they stole off from under our noses, for even if he intercepted their boat at sea, all evidence of their illicit commerce would be long gone.

With a hiss and bang, a white light flared in the sky, illuminating the beach like a sheet of lightning. In a flash, I saw a boat piled with barrels on the sand, and dark figures unloading it; I took my musket, and, holding it well away from me, fired into the air. The sound was lost, though, for even as I pulled the trigger a broadside exploded out of the darkness behind us, five great tongues of flame. With a whimper I flung myself into the bottom of the boat, and felt others piling in on top of me. But there was no scream of iron overhead, no splashes, and mercifully no sign of the jollyboat splintering into matchwood. After a safe interval, I jabbed an elbow into the body above me, and felt him reluctantly lift himself off.

I pulled myself up, chilled by the bilgewater that had soaked into my side, and looked about. We were surrounded by lights: lanterns showed in at least two places out to sea, while on the beach there flickered a chain of torches. A double line of bayonets glinted in the orange glow, and behind them I could see the white crossbelts and trousers of our soldiers, their red coats turned brown by the firelight.

Before them, as I had seen, a small boat lay at the water's edge, the two men standing near it silhouetted against the torches.

'At 'em, lads.' Apart from those two lonely figures, there did not appear to be any danger on the beach, but there remained the real possibility of a sea-battle between *Orestes* and the ship the smugglers had come from, and I was determined to be well clear of it. My crew were obviously of much the same mind, for they pulled several mighty strokes until our hull ground into the sand and we could leap ashore.

I heard the rattle of muskets, and stopped cold at the sight of a dozen steely barrels trained on my chest. 'Don't shoot,' I called weakly. 'It's Lieutenant Jerrold.'

'Jerrold?' It was Captain Bingham, the red-headed officer who'd been at the meeting in the castle, striding out from behind his line of men. 'What the devil are you up to, sneaking around here and waving that bloody great cutlass like One-Eyed Jack the pirate? You're supposed to be cutting off their retreat.'

'Captain Crawley was impatient for your signal,' I explained, letting the sword droop by my side. 'He sent us in to reconnoitre. And to join the action,' I added defensively. '*Orestes* is still out there.'

'I gathered that,' said Bingham drily. 'And it seems she's found the lugger these two came from.' He gestured out to sea. *Orestes*' crew had struck a lantern, and by its light I could see her second boat against the hull of a small lugger. The rough shouts of our boarding party drifted over the waves. 'Doesn't sound like they're putting up much of a fight,' Bingham continued, cocking an ear. 'Much like these two ruffians.'

'Not exactly your army of fifty bloodthirsty villains with enough spirits to render every man, woman and child in England insensible.' The disappointment in my voice was genuine enough, though not at the missed battle.

'No,' Bingham agreed. 'Still, we must work with what the good Lord and Sir Lawrence give us. Let's see what these scoundrels were about.'

We walked down to the boat. It looked smaller than the one I had seen on my first night in Dover, and although it was loaded with casks, it seemed there was plenty of room for more.

'Did we interrupt them in the middle of their task?' I wondered.

'No.' Bingham was definite. 'I watched the lugger from the moment she started signalling, and set off our fire the moment her boat landed. There were only these two with it, and they hadn't a chance to do anything.' He kicked a barrel that lay on the sand. 'This was the first one off.'

'Please, sir.' One of the smugglers, his arms pinned behind his back by a burly corporal, began to plead in a high-pitched voice. 'We ain't done nothin' wrong.'

'Really?' Bingham looked at him disdainfully. 'And this?' He kicked the cask again.

'Ballast, sir. Our ship 'ad a leak, an' we 'ad to offload it.'

'Ballast, you say? We shall see. Sergeant!'

Another of the redcoats came forward, pulling a worm-iron from a pouch on his belt. He stepped across the barrel so that he straddled it, twisted the iron into the bung, then heaved backward, popping it out like a cork.

Bingham held a pewter cup to the edge of the hole, and rolled the cask over so that liquid splashed out. 'Let's see what sort of vintage ballast your ship carried,' he said, raising the cup. 'Your very good health.'

He took a gulp, choked, and almost immediately spewed it straight back out, covering the impassive sergeant in a fine spray.

'Too strong for you?' I asked jovially.

'You may taste for yourself,' retorted Bingham, wiping his mouth on his sleeve.

He handed me the cup, and I sniffed it warily: I knew from experience that the spirits in Dover's hostelries were strong enough, and could imagine in what concentration they must be shipped. But this clear liquid did not smell of alcohol, it smelled – salty? And it tasted . . .

I saw Bingham grinning as I too spat out the foul liquid. 'Sea-water,' I gasped.

‘Precisely.’ The humour was gone from his voice again.

‘Why would anyone risk their lives trying to land salt water in the dark?’ It seemed the height of lunacy – unless our exalted new government had put a tax on the oceans themselves.

‘It were ballast,’ our prisoner repeated. ‘We ’ad to offload it.’

‘We’ll see about that,’ muttered Bingham grimly. ‘I wonder what we’ll find in the hold of your ship.’

A sentry’s challenge interrupted him, and I looked out to see another boat floating a little way off beach. ‘Ahoy,’ called a voice I recognized as Ducker’s. ‘We searched their lugger – nothin’ aboard. Must’ve got it all ashore.’

‘Damn!’ Bingham’s face was red with anger. ‘All they brought here was sea-water. We’ve been had, Jerrold – a proper fool’s errand. We’ll have to let go the entire crew, ashore and afloat.’

‘What about the other men on the beach?’ I asked, growing ever more confused.

Bingham frowned. ‘Which men? There was no-one here but my company, until these two bastards turned up.’

‘Oh.’ I struggled with my thoughts. ‘But before they brought the salt water ashore, they were signalling to someone from the lugger.’

Bingham considered this. ‘Well?’ he snapped, turning to the prisoners. ‘Who were you signalling to?’

One of them still hung his head and seemed too petrified to speak; the other looked up with big, round eyes. ‘Signallin’, sir? We wasn’t signallin’ no-one. Just tryin’ to get the ballast up, we was. We ’ad to offload it, see?’

That more or less ended the affair; with no evidence and no crime, what else could we do? Under a cloud of invective, Bingham let the two captives return to their freed lugger, then began the long march back to Dover. I guessed it would be a cold and bitter plod. Ducker took the news back to Crawley, which was as well, for I later discovered he took some persuading that I was not at fault in this debacle. I followed in my own jollyboat, whose crew, I noted, had watched the whole business crouched safely behind her hull. Dawn was lining the horizon before we were ready to weigh anchor again.

'Back to port, sir?' I asked Crawley, as our sails cracked taut in the wind. The night's excitement had kept me well awake, but now I felt a painful shortage of sleep, and I did not think a hammock would be sufficient cure.

'No.' Crawley still fumed at the waste of the night's work: no prisoners, no prizes, no glory – *nothing but a laughing stock when we sail back into Dover*. 'We will stay on patrol for a few days. If Cunningham was right, there may yet be some action to be had. If not, then at least it might keep *you* out of trouble, Lieutenant.'

'Yes, sir.'

Anything that would keep me out of Cunningham's path was bound to be a benefit, but I was conscious that the days before my uncle's ultimatum were beginning to slip past all too rapidly. And I had a curious – and quite unexpected – yearning to see Isobel again.

'Get below and get some sleep.' Crawley looked at the edge of the sail. 'We'll follow this wind a few miles further, on to the Downs. Let the admiral see that I do not squander my command all the time.' He paused. 'Tomorrow, perhaps, I will send you to do some Swiss fishing.'

7

'WHY SWISS? SURELY THERE CANNOT BE MUCH FISHING IN THE cantons?'

I let my hand dangle over the side of the jollyboat, enjoying the remove from *Orestes*. We had come back up the coast that morning, after the futility of the night's adventures, and had now passed east of Dover. The great bulk of the South Foreland rose on our left, while ahead of us lay the busy Downs anchorage, where scores of sails of all sizes waited for a fair wind to speed them off. Behind us, in open water, *Orestes* was spending the afternoon exercising her guns.

Ducker looked at me from the opposite side of the boat, one arm gently guiding the tiller. 'Swiss cos we're fishing for geneva.'

'Gin?'

'Aye, sir. When the owlers reckons they might get caught, they ropes their kegs together an' drops 'em overboard. Got a weight at either end, so they stays there 'til the coast's clear, when they comes back an' fetches 'em up.'

'Extraordinary. But how can they be sure of finding them?'

'Easy.' Ducker grinned. 'Same as us. You takes one o' these' – he held up a long arrowhead with two rows of broad flukes sticking from its shaft, and a rope spliced around the ring in its end – 'an' drags it behind while you rows over the spot 'til it catches on the casks; then you hauls in your catch.' He dropped the hook over the stern of the boat and began paying out the line behind it.

'Marvellous. But surely the seabed is hardly littered with tubs of gin waiting to be found. We must have some idea of where we're looking.'

'Sometimes. If we're lucky, an' if we seen 'em dropping it.'

'But have we seen anyone acting suspiciously near here?'

'No. But the cap'n reckoned the owlers you saw a few nights back might 'ave left somethin'.'

I stared back at the land, at the sepulchral cliffs looming in the hazy sunlight, and shivered. They might be the great rampart of our island, or whatever other nonsense that poet had written, but to me they were horribly forbidding. I turned back to Ducker.

'So have you ever caught anything in this fashion?'

It seemed improbable, though I supposed no more futile than anything else I'd seen of the war on smuggling. We might as well have asked for voluntary contributions to the customs fund and left a box on the quay for all the good we were doing.

'Once, sir. 'Bout a year back.'

'And how many years have you spent trying?'

Ducker scratched his chin. 'Four, I reckon. Came 'ere recoverin' from a wound I took in the Indies, an' never got ordered to move on.' He nodded slowly. 'Four years, four cap'ns. Cap'n 'uckle – 'e died quick; then there was Cap'n Beattie: married an earl's daughter an' never came back; then Cap'n Ramsay, who nabbed Cal Drake; an' now Cap'n Crawley.'

'Who would doubtless very much like to have something other than seabirds to shoot at.' Another cannon fired from *Orestes*' deck. They had been at it all afternoon, a constant rumble in the background. 'How did he come to be sent here?'

Ducker stiffened. 'I reckon that's 'is business, if 'e wants to tell you or no.'

'Of course.' I thought back to his list – something else had tugged at my attention. 'But Captain Ramsay, you say he caught Cal Drake?'

'Aye, sir.'

It must have been the fifth time I had heard that name, and I determined to get at the story behind it.

'Who was Cal Drake, Ducker?'

The quartermaster was temporarily distracted with the line: it had jerked taut, and must have snagged something down below. He gave it a firm heave, and my expectation receded as quickly as it had risen when the line went loose again.

'Seaweed,' said Ducker. 'Just strong enough to keep you guessin'.'

'But about Cal Drake . . .'

Ducker let out the line again. 'Not a lot to say. 'E was a local lad. Started out a fisherman, an' realized 'e could catch a lot bigger fish on the other side o' the Channel, smugglin' brandy to England an' news to France. Some say 'e met Boney 'imself, back when 'e was bent on invasion an' wanted pilots for 'is fleet. But whatever the truth o' that, Drake 'ad 'is own fleet – two-score luggers at least, runnin' a regular ferry every night. 'Ad the 'ole town o' Dover in 'is pocket. Near to 'alf the men you'd see 'ad scars on their cheeks where Drake cut 'em for talkin' what they shouldn't, and there wasn't a man you could say "Cal Drake" to that wouldn't run a mile less 'e wound up face down in the tide.'

That set me thinking, for I had my own interest in people who wound up face down in the tide – or close to it, at least.

'But Ramsay hunted him down?'

'Aye. Drove 'is ship inshore an' wrecked 'im one night.' There was a distant look in Ducker's eyes now. 'We followed 'em in with the boats, fought 'em all over the rocks, through the surf an' up the cliff. Cut down 'alf the crew, but Drake reached the top an' started inland. Took the dragoons three days to corner 'im, but they finally found 'im stashed up in the Queen Anne's Head, an' dragged 'im back to Dover. Where Cunningham 'anged 'im. Best thing 'e ever did.'

'And his fleet?'

'Some of 'em we caught, an' a few got wrecked up on the coast, abandoned cos of a rumour that Drake was nailin' all 'is crew to the magistrate. Some went to France, an' I'll wager some of 'em are still making the voyage today.' He chuckled. 'Tell you one thing, though: I never seen the price o' rum so 'igh as the night they brought Drake in.'

So that was the sort of heroic action needed to win a reprieve from Dover.

'And since then?' I asked. 'Has there been much trouble with the smugglers?'

'Calmed right down after Drake swung. Cap'n Ramsay 'ad a bit of a name for 'imself, though 'e didn't stick 'ere long. But they reckons it's gettin' worse again now – not that we've seen none of it.'

'And what of Caleb Drake's brother?'

But Ducker was distracted. The line was tight again, and this time, I saw, it did not break free when he yanked at it.

'Boat your oars,' he called, sweat beading on his forehead as he kept hold of the line. 'Get your 'ands on.'

I passed the rope-end back to the crew so they could heave from their benches. I feared a sudden snap would send them all tumbling backwards over one another, but there was still no give in the line that, hand over hand, slowly came inboard.

'Looks like you're a lucky man, Lieutenant,' said Ducker. 'Either that or someone that's lost an anchor'll be pleased.'

Still the rope kept coming, dripping a thin trail of water down the centre of the boat; surely it must almost be done. Excitement gripped me: this would be something to show Crawley.

There was a thump and a shudder as something knocked against the bottom. Ducker took a boat-hook and pushed the line clear so that the burden would not catch on our hull.

'Ready, lads – *heave*!'

With a great splash, and a foam of bubbles, our prize burst free of the water, bumped over the stern and landed on the deck at my feet. I stared; behind me, I heard at least one man vomiting. As Ducker had predicted, there was indeed a rope tied to it, hanging over the side where the weight that had kept it down dangled. But, although he might have been Swiss, this was no keg of gin. For the second time in a week, and only a few cables from where I had found the last one, I stared at a corpse.

After a wave of disgust, I confess my second thought was one of insane relief. 'You've all seen me this time,' I said, looking wildly around the gaping faces of the crew. 'I didn't kill him.'

Ducker gave me a queer look. 'What exactly does you mean, sir?' he asked slowly. '*This time* you didn't kill 'im?'

I had little mind to correct him; I could not take my eyes from the body. The corpse on the beach I had seen only from a distance, and in enough distress that I had not paid it much notice; this one, lying on its back on the deck before me, I could hardly escape. I'd seen enough dead men in the charnel after Trafalgar, of course, when there was barely a full set of limbs to share between a dozen men, but the body in front of me, I think, was worse than any of those. Its skin was bloated, puffed up like dough and turned a strange, bruising purple where dye from the man's coat had leached into it. Weed had wrapped itself up one of the legs and become tangled with the hair, though thankfully the fish had yet to begin their feasting. But it was the face that really fixed me, contorted into a perpetual, silent scream, with blue eyes staring wide into the fate that had taken him.

Ducker turned the body over. It landed on my foot, and with a stifled shriek I jerked it away, jolting the boat violently. The motion upset the corpse, and it began to roll in the bilge, side to side like a clock pendulum. We all looked on in silent horror, unwilling to touch the thing until the rocking eased and it came to rest.

Ducker lifted it again, this time more cautiously. 'Reckon 'e drowned,' he said, having peeled off the coat and waistcoat to reveal the shirt underneath. 'No blood nor nothin'.'

In my brittle state, I was about to snap some acid comment about the cause of death hardly being a matter for dispute, but thankfully I checked myself: the last thing we needed was recrimination added to the black atmosphere on our little boat. And Ducker had a point. If the man at the bottom of the cliff had not, contrary to all reason, fallen off it, then what was to say that the man at the bottom of the sea had drowned?

'An' not by accident, neither.'

Ducker hauled in the rope tied around the man's ankle; on its end was a sack – small, but surprisingly heavy. Taking his knife, he sliced through the canvas. Wet sand squeezed out through the slit.

'Is that . . . is that a smuggler's weight?' I struggled to form any sort of sentence while the face stared at me.

'Maybe.' Ducker was frowning. 'Like I said, only ever found one o' these before. That were weighted with stones. Not so much sand in these parts.'

'But if the smugglers had come over from France . . .'

'Aye.' He did not appear to be concentrating fully on my words. 'But there's somethin' wrong with this.'

'Something very wrong,' I agreed. 'I'm no coroner, but from the state of him he can't have been down there very long. And he must be barely half a mile from the other body – possibly killed on the very same night.'

'Aye.' Still Ducker sounded distracted. 'But that ain't the real sticker.'

'What, then?'

'Well, it's this, sir.' Ducker was shaking his head. 'See, I knows 'im.'

It took a second for his meaning to sink in; even then, it still seemed ludicrous.

'You know – knew – this man?'

'Aye, sir.'

'A smuggler?' Even with the horror lying before me, and the preservative effects of the sea-water on his flesh beginning to wear off, I dared to think that this might yet prove some sort of an opening.

But Ducker was shaking his head. 'That's the thing, sir,' he said slowly. ''E ain't a smuggler. 'E's Mr Webb.'

'Mr Webb?' It seemed grotesque to give this foul thing a name.

'Customs officer. Worked up the coast in Deal, but 'e'd come down to Dover sometimes to visit Cap'n Ramsay.'

In my agitated state I could barely make sense of this.

'That is Deal's revenue officer?'

'Was, sir. Went missin' about six months back. Not been seen since.' He looked down at the body again. ''Til now.'

We rowed back to *Orestes*, our progress jarred by the desire, plain in every face, to be rid of our cargo as soon as possible, set against the gruesome spell of the corpse, which continually drew our sickened eyes. The bitter smell of gunpowder was still in the air as we approached the cutter, though the drill had finished some time earlier, and someone aboard must have seen what we carried for one by one I saw the men come to the side until it seemed the whole crew must be lined along the gunwale. Even Crawley's cocked hat was there, up near the stern. Soon I could hear the chattering among them, but it tailed into silence as we came under her bows.

'Leave it down there,' shouted Crawley. 'I'll not have that festering aboard my ship. Mr Palmer, find some canvas to stitch it up. You may do it in the boat.'

I saw the sailmaker head for his stores, and relief on the faces above me. They'd rather have slaughtered a flock of albatrosses than hoist a dead body aboard, and I had no doubt that once the jollyboat had been swabbed out and scrubbed down, a little grog would find its way onto her planking to avert the evil omen.

'In my cabin, Lieutenant,' Crawley ordered as I gained the deck.

I followed him down the ladder and through into a tiny hutch of a room scarcely larger than my own quarters on the *Téméraire* had been, and certainly nothing against the splendour of *her* captain's apartments. Crawley squeezed himself onto the bench that ran along the stern – there were no windows – and gestured me to take the seat opposite. He was not smiling, though he seemed more irritated than angry.

'It seems I cannot let you alone for half an hour but you manage to entangle yourself in some mischief. Every time I look about, you seem to be dragging in dead bodies – like a faithful cat, I don't wonder.

I sometimes think I ought to clap you in irons simply for the preservation of humanity.'

'I have been—'

'And when you are not digging up corpses,' he continued, 'it is merely because you are in the midst of some other misadventure. Antagonizing Sir Lawrence; playing the fool with your superiors; ruining naval operations.'

'But this is significant, sir,' I pleaded. 'It may be a nuisance, but it is hardly inconsequential when a revenue officer is found drowned.' I repeated what Ducker had told me of Webb.

There was a pause as Crawley considered this.

'I've heard the name – vanished before I arrived, though, so never met him. You think it important, do you?'

'Who else but a smuggler would want to kill a revenue officer?'

'It could as easily have been a jealous husband.' Crawley gave what I feared was a significant glance. 'But I agree, the smugglers would appear more obvious.' He tapped the table in front of him. 'Anyway, the body must be disposed of, and I have no intention of wasting good victuals pickling him so he can accompany us up and down the coast. When Mr Palmer has finished wrapping him, you may take the jollyboat into Dover and deposit him with the coroner. Or rather, you had better take Ducker. He can go to the coroner, for the less your name appears in this business the better. I may think it tiresome that you persist in finding these inconveniences, but to Sir Lawrence it would doubtless be perfectly damning.'

It would be a hard pull into the harbour, and I doubted the boat's crew would thank me for a prolonged journey with the corpse. But Crawley was not finished.

'You may stay in Dover, Lieutenant, although I will need Ducker and the jollyboat back. I confess that the meaning of all these events escapes me—'

'And me, sir.'

'No doubt.' He did not take my interruption kindly. 'But I am beginning to think that your brace of corpses may not be entirely unrelated to the increase in smuggling that we are seeing – or at least, that Sir Lawrence assures me we are seeing. It may even be something significant, Lieutenant.' He stared hard at me. 'Something we both might profit from.'

'Yes, sir.' If he was pinning his hopes on me, I thought, he must truly be desperate.

'You will investigate this business ashore, while I chase my tail out here. Make such enquiries as you see fit, but I suggest you first travel to Deal to ask Webb's successor for any intelligence he may have. The man can't have vanished completely for six months, and he certainly wasn't underwater that long. I shall send word to the inn if I require you aboard again.'

'Thank you, sir.'

I guessed Crawley had few regrets about sending me away from his command. For all the evidence I had given to the contrary, he had never quite dismissed his suspicion that I was sent to undermine him. But the chance to pursue my enquiries, fruitless though they had been thus far, was a lifeline, particularly with four days of my fortnight already spent to such little gain.

The journey to the harbour was as sullen as I had predicted, and although the breeze carried the stink of the body away behind us, it gave the men a devil of a job to row against it. With obvious revulsion, their glances returned again and again to the bundle on the boat, and had it not been for Ducker's calming influence I think I would have feared for their discipline. As it was, I was glad to be away from them when at last we nosed up against the jetty and I had clambered out. I left a good five minutes before they followed so as to disguise the connection between us. I could imagine the sort of looks their long parcel would attract as they paraded it through the streets, and did not delay in returning to the inn.

It was far too late to set out for Deal; in fact, I wondered whether Ducker would have time to make the trip back to *Orestes*, for already darkness was falling. I would go the following morning. In the interim, I thought, I would recover some of the sleep I had lost the night before. I lay down on my bed, pulled the rough blanket over me and closed my eyes.

Immediately I saw that this would not do. Tired I might have been, but the moment my eyes closed all I could see was the gaping, empty face of Webb, staring up at me from the bottom of the boat. I shuddered, and reached instinctively for the half-started bottle of wine on the floor. That was no good either, for I remembered its provenance half a second before it touched my tongue. Mine may not be the most discerning of palates, but the Crown and Anchor's wine had a bouquet all its own, which was hard to forget if once tasted sober.

I had many lines of thought to consider, from the resurgence of the smugglers to the hundred new questions raised by Webb's body, but the taste of that bile reminded me of my encounter the previous morning. If I could not sleep easy, I resolved, I might as well make good my time by returning to that forsaken tavern and enquiring after the men who had been drinking there. It was not without its risks, of course: how would it seem to Sir Lawrence Cunningham, who doubtless would get wind of it? And could I afford, either financially or physically, to buy the landlord's co-operation again? But the closeness of the bedroom and the prospect of a long evening in the ghoulish company of Webb's apparition convinced me that it would be best.

Though it was dark outside it was not yet supper time, and the tavern was uncommonly quiet when I entered. A quartet of villainous-looking regulars were clustered in an adjoining room, but a single glance on my entry clearly sufficed them, for they returned almost immediately to their mutterings. Otherwise, it seemed empty.

The landlord greeted me with a genial grin. 'Well, if it ain't the navy lieutenant what's so generous with 'is brass. Back for more wine, is you, sir?'

I ignored the pleasantries. 'You pegged me to the magistrate,' I said boldly, trying to sound more menacing than plaintive. 'And after all my custom.'

He affected a wounded look. 'Peg you, sir? Never. Asides, what's an 'onest man to do when 'e's asked to co-operate with unravellin' a murder? 'Specially by a man like that Constable Stubb. Awful fearsome, 'e is.'

He had my sympathy there, but I remained adamant. 'What did you tell Constable Stubb, landlord, that made him come knocking on my door the next morning?'

The landlord looked deeply shocked. 'Knockin' on your door? Why sir, I never said nothin' that could make 'im think that a gentleman like you could be doin' no 'arm.'

'What was it that you *did* tell him?'

'Only that you'd been in 'ere a few nights back, an' I seen you chattin' with that Isobel Dawson.'

'But you didn't.'

'Beggin' yer pardon, sir, but I—'

I threw him a guinea. 'You did not. Put that towards my next bottle of wine.'

'Well, it were dark, sir, an' very busy. You knows 'ow busy it gets in 'ere. Might be that I mistook meself, it bein' so dark. An' busy.' He thought hard. 'An' I might – I say *might*, mind – might've been a little too sure tellin' Constable Stubb what I thought I seen.'

'If he asks again you will doubtless be more circumspect.'

''Spect I will,' he agreed, pleasingly docile.

'And what else did you tell Constable Stubb? About the dead man?'

His eyes widened. 'That man they found under the cliff? Terrible that were.'

'I know. I found him.'

'Bless you – did you, sir?' He nodded energetically. 'So the constable might've got the wrong end o' the bottle.'

'He said you'd seen the dead man drinking here that night.'

'Did I?'

'Yes.'

'So I did, then.' He was looking at me anxiously, trying to decipher my intentions. 'That's right, I did. Sittin' over there, 'e was, deep in the corner. I wouldn't o' recognized 'im when the coroner showed me if 'e'd not come up to get 'is drinks.'

'Did he drink much?' It seemed unlikely that this would resolve itself as the simple case of a drunkard who staggered over a cliff, but I meant to be thorough.

'Not so much, no. Few glasses o' brandy.'

'And did he drink alone?'

'No, sir.' The landlord leaned over the bar, setting his face uncomfortably close to my own. 'There was two others with 'im.'

Now this might be useful. 'Did you recognize any of them?'

'No, sir.'

'What did they look like?'

'Couldn't say, sir.' My frustration must have been evident. 'It were dark in 'ere, sir, an' awful busy.'

'So it was. Did you ever meet a revenue officer called Webb?'

'Webb, sir?' He scratched his ear. 'No, sir. There's Mr Nealy down at the customs 'ouse.'

'Mr Webb worked in Deal, until some six months ago.' I did not reveal where Mr Webb was now. My guinea had bought the man's co-operation, not his silence, and I did not want Stubb linking me with yet another mysterious death.

'That'd explain it. Don't never go to Deal much.'

'So you know nothing about any of those men, other than that they had a few glasses of brandy?' I suppose I ought to have been getting used to such disappointments from my enquiries.

But the landlord was shaking his head. 'Not at all, sir, not at all. I knows they was foreign.'

'What?' I stared at him in disbelief. 'You saw nothing of them, and never knew them, yet you know they were foreign?'

'Well, two of 'em was.' He sounded wounded at my scepticism.

'And how do you know that?'

''Eard it from Mrs Pring. They was lodgin' at 'er boardin' 'ouse.'

'Mr Vitos, one of them was called; the other . . . Laminak, I think he said.'

Mrs Pring stood before me in her apron, her arms folded across her prim bosom. Her house looked respectable enough too, although the fact that it was down the alley by the gaol would have deterred me from staying there. I doubt I'd have slept well knowing Gibble lay behind the cherry-striped wallpaper.

'And how long were they here?'

She looked at me cautiously, but my dress uniform, into which I'd had the foresight to change after leaving the Crown and Anchor, obviously reassured her, as it had when I'd knocked on her door. 'They were here just the one night. Arrived very late on Saturday, left the next morning.'

'And can you describe them to me?'

'Mr Vitos, he was quite large, to put it plain, sir. Mr Laminak was taller, and thinner too, with a great black beard. They both had dark hair, of course, being they were foreign.'

'Of course. And they'd never stayed here before, or since?'

'Never. But then, the constable said they found Mr Vitos dead the next day.' A thought crossed her tight face. 'Could you not get this from Mr Stubb? He was very thorough when he came.'

No doubt.

'We like to make our own enquiries in the navy, ma'am,' I said bluffly. 'Saves us getting our signals awry.'

Her eyes narrowed. 'He asked about a navy officer too, the constable did. Asked if a Mr Jerrold had come to see the foreign gentlemen.' She considered this a moment. 'What did you say your name was again?'

'Crawley. Captain aboard his Majesty's cutter *Orestes*. Tell me, Mrs Pring, did you chance to overhear any of their conversation?'

'Of course not.' She looked most indignant. 'My guests have their privacy, you know. I don't go eavesdropping all about them.'

'I never meant the least injury. But I should be deeply in your debt for anything you may remember. Particularly in light of Mr Vitos's sad fate.'

She pressed her thin lips together. 'Well, I didn't see much of them, you know, what with them arriving so late. But I did hear them say they were leaving to go to the bank in the morning.'

'To the bank? On a Sunday?'

My hopes of getting any sense from the woman sank, but the disbelief in my tone had clearly affronted her for she drew herself taller and declared: 'Certainly on a Sunday. That was why it stayed stuck with me. Foreigners, I thought to myself, blaspheming the Sabbath with their greedy ways. I was glad to see the back of them.'

This was useful information, though hardly ideal: if getting news out of a tavern keeper and a landlady had been a struggle, I could not imagine trying to break down the reserve of a bank clerk. And it would take far more than a guinea to bribe him. 'I wonder, Mrs Pring, did they mention which bank?'

With a great show of reluctance, she told me. 'Mazard's Bank.'

Having expressed my gratitude to the informative Mrs Pring, I decided my final task for the evening – for it was too late to visit Isobel, unless I fancied the pleasure of her guardian's conversation again – would be to examine the bank. I don't know what I anticipated finding, for it was unlikely that a strongbox marked 'Vitos' would be sitting by the front door with a key in its lock, and I did not intend to see Sir Lawrence add bank robbery to his list of charges against me. But I had hit upon this unexpectedly productive seam of enquiry, and I was determined to follow it until it dried up. And the name 'Mazard' chimed with something I had heard before, though at that moment it evaded me.

Unsurprisingly, my run of luck ended before the sombre frontage of Mazard's Bank. It was a squat structure by the quay, looking on to the mercantile street behind it and standing next to a large warehouse which, from the lettering on its side, seemed also to belong to the Mazard company. No lights showed in either building, nor in fact in any of the houses on that road, and I was forced to acknowledge that I could go no further that evening. Still, I at last had a name to the body – to both bodies, in fact – and that was good, for I was convinced I would not discover the killer until I understood more fully the circumstances of the victims. I still had several avenues of enquiry open, I was free of Crawley's biting sarcasm for a few days, and if I could keep clear of Sir Lawrence and his minions, I might well make some real progress.

None of which happy thoughts, I discovered when I had climbed into bed and shut my eyes, could prevent that ghastly image of Webb's distended face from looming before me all night.

8

DESPITE THE UNSETTLING DREAMS, NONE OF WHICH I COULD properly remember afterwards, I awoke feeling surprisingly well rested, and my mood was further enhanced when I was able to climb out of my bed at leisure and dress at my own pace, without interruption. Only when I had completed my toilet to my satisfaction did I descend the stairs.

The boy was there, mopping half-heartedly at the bar counter. Isaac was his name, I had discovered the previous evening. He wore his habitual look of nervous suspicion, as if an invisible hand were ever poised above to strike him, but he managed a quick smile when I tossed him a couple of pennies.

'As we agreed,' I said cheerfully. 'The price of a good night's sleep. Did anyone call for me?'

'Nah,' he said, taking one last swipe at the bar with his oozing cloth. 'But they might tomorrow,' he added swiftly. 'Can't be too careful.'

'Indeed not.' I was quite happy to keep paying the fee to deter unwanted morning visitors.

As I waited for Isaac to bring my breakfast, I enjoyed the contemplation of my first day in Dover entirely at my own command. With Crawley at sea, and Ducker no longer vigilant over my every move, I was free to go as I pleased, and that pleased me mightily. Not, of course, that I could while away the day in diversions and entertainments, for I was much aware of the need for action if I was to satisfy my uncle, and my modest success the previous evening had only stiffened my desire to prevail. And I doubted Dover's hostelries and their rough custom would admit to an agreeable day's drinking.

Still revelling in my freedom, I began to consider what I would do. Although I was keen to learn more of Messrs Laminak and Vitos, I was mindful of Crawley's suggestion that I should investigate the late Mr Webb a little further. On the one hand, it seemed perverse to investigate another death when I had made so little progress on the one on which my life depended, but I did not believe that two fresh bodies so close to each other could be wholly unrelated. It was even conceivable that Webb could have been the third member of the party at the Crown and Anchor on that fateful night. Besides, the sun was shining – as much as it ever did in Dover – and my spirits were high. A walk along the open cliff seemed far more attractive than a morning spent interviewing bank clerks.

My breakfast digested, I left the inn. The Deal road was up past the castle, and as I reached the end of the street that led there I saw again the church which marked the last resting place of Caleb Drake. It had been dark when I was last there; now I could see the church in its fullness, a stolid building with a square tower and jagged, tooth-like arches framing the door. The parson was gathering flowers in the cemetery, and he gave a sprightly wave as I passed.

The sight of him reminded me of our last encounter, and that Isobel's home lay just past the corner. I had not seen her since the business with Sir Lawrence in the stable yard two mornings back, and I owed her thanks for that at least. But I did not intend to try that door again without advance preparation. Crossing to the spiked fence bounding the churchyard, I gestured the priest to come over.

'A fine day,' he answered my greeting.

'Indeed.' There was definitely a blue tint to the grey of the sky today, and that, I supposed, merited excitement. 'Tell me, Father, what is the nature of the employment at the Magdalene Home on the woolcombers' street?'

He squinted at me. 'I know what ye think, and there's many a man who thought likewise.' I squirmed under his gaze. 'But although they live by the statutes of Christ, under the direction of Miss Hoare, they take no holy orders. They merely reside there until they have the spiritual means to make their return into society. Until then, they go about the Lord's business.'

'And that is?'

'They purge their souls in works of ablution, finding salvation through cleanliness. Their work is much prized in the town for, as it is written, "wash me and I shall be whiter than snow".'

'Do you mean,' I asked, after a pause, 'that they run a laundry?'

The old priest nodded. So that explained why my efforts at courting Isobel's custom had been received so unfavourably, and why, though I had thought it queer at the time, they received no business after dark. I thanked my luck that I had not been more direct with Miss Hoare, if she it had been.

To my pleasant surprise, I was spared the hazard of further indiscretions at the Home of the Lady Magdalene when I called: instead of a nun berating me through the hatch, I found Isobel.

'Is Miss Hoare about?' I asked, peering around the door.

Isobel shook her head. 'Gone to Canterbury. Shall I tell her you asked after her?'

'No,' I corrected her hurriedly. 'In truth, I had come to see you.'

She looked gratified by the admission, and cocked her head to hear more.

'I wanted to thank you for lying about – that is to say, er, misremembering certain events in front of the magistrate the other morning.'

'Misremembering?' she asked coyly. 'I was in bed all night that night I met you. Miss Hoare'd give me a right dunking if she thought I'd not been.'

'A dunking?'

'Her way of seeing to us – dunks us in the laundry vats when we misbehave.'

'Well, Mrs Dawson—'

'Isobel. Sir Lawrence Cunningham's the only one who calls me Mrs Dawson.' A look of revulsion crossed her face.

'Isobel, then. I'd like to thank you for being in your bed that night. And I apologize if I was uncouth the last time we spoke at the inn. I meant no insult.'

'That's all right, Mr Jerrold.'

I could not have her addressing me as though I were her husband. 'Martin.'

'I can see you could get confused, meeting a girl who didn't ask for money to sleep with you. Don't suppose you get it often.'

I bridled at the suggestion, and was about to offer a sharp retort when I saw the laughter in her eyes, the gently mocking curve of her lip. 'Certainly none so pretty as you,' I answered, in a stab at gallantry. For she was pretty, in a slightly scrawny fashion: dark hair fell straight down behind her bony shoulders, and she had a pert face and a small nose and eyes that brimmed with mischief. Her skin was a smooth, milky white, save on her arms, where it was furrowed red from the laundry.

She laughed again. 'Well, if you think you can pay me off with kind words, you're likely right.'

'If I had more to offer . . . In fact, if I *have* more to offer, if there is anything I can do to confirm my gratitude, I am eager to show it.'

I saw something spark in her eyes, and remembered that it was the promise of my gratitude which had coaxed her under the bed at the inn. Clearly there was something she wanted of me. But for the moment, she kept it to herself.

There was a pause.

'Well,' I said awkwardly. 'As I say, my thanks for your good offices. But if they are not to have been in vain, I fear I must take my leave.'

'Where're you going?'

'Deal. I have enquiries to make there concerning a dead revenue officer.'

'I'll come with you.' My astonishment at her presumption, and at her forthright tone, must have shown, for she added, 'I'd be so very grateful if you took me for a walk.'

I took her meaning at once, and felt the freedom of my own destiny falling away around me.

'What about Miss Hoare?' I asked lamely.

'She's in Canterbury, remember? And the scrubbing can wait for tomorrow. I'll get my bonnet.'

Isobel vanished behind the door, leaving me quite perplexed. Out of instinct, I resented anyone who would thrust herself upon me uninvited, but out of honour, with my protestations of gratitude still ringing about me, I could hardly refuse. And although it would not do to arrive at the gates of the customs house with an urchin on my arm, some company on the long road to Deal might be welcome.

I am told that on a clear day one can see all the way to France from the cliffs; indeed, that the previous summer the locals entertained their fears watching the massed armies of invasion parading on the foreshore, until the moment of relief and anticlimax when they saw them march away to Austria. It is sufficient comment on the climate I enjoyed during my time in Dover that I never had the least indication that another continent might lie beyond the horizon, but that day with Isobel, when occasional openings in the high cloud admitted blue sky and shafts of sunlight, was perhaps the closest I came.

We walked up around the castle, retracing the path I had taken with Ducker, but instead of following the Deal road, which took an inland route along a ridge, Isobel insisted we take the cliff path.

'It'll take longer,' I objected.

'It'll be nicer,' she answered. 'And I'm the one who should worry myself, walking too near the cliff edge with a man of your reputation.'

Before I could deny the slander, she was skipping off across the field towards the sea. Another of her jokes, I supposed; at least *I* only offered her insult inadvertently.

'I never murdered anyone up here, nor down on the rocks either for that matter,' I protested, when at last I caught her up.

'I'm sure you didn't.' She stopped, looking at me with a firm gaze. 'I know what you were like when I left, and I should think you didn't get much better after that.'

'Thank you,' I muttered. It was exoneration – of a sort. 'Although I doubt your opinion will convince a jury, if it comes to that. Especially as it's well known you were in bed at Miss Hoare's establishment all night.' A thought occurred to me. 'You didn't chance to notice three men sitting at a table in the Crown and Anchor that evening – two foreigners, Vitos and Laminak, and another man no-one saw properly?'

Isobel wrinkled her nose in thought. 'Don't think so. It was very busy there, though. And of course, I only had eyes for you.'

'Did you?' After her run of insult and innuendo, I took any compliment with some suspicion.

'Of course. Isn't every day a handsome lieutenant walks into a place like the Crown and Anchor.'

I was surprised my fellow officers had such scruples. 'I chose the first tavern I found,' I explained. 'What took a good Christian washer-woman like you there? Fetching some black strap for Miss Hoare?'

She giggled. 'Miss Hoare doesn't drink – at least, not in front of us.' I had a brief vision of Miss Hoare and Captain Crawley together forming a holy union for abstinence and cleanliness. 'I went, out the window and over the roof, cos I'd had enough of Miss Hoare's dunkings and Fat Bess trying to pinch my fingers in the tub. I wanted some nonsense.'

'And you decided on the Crown and Anchor?'

She shrugged. 'It needed to be where word wouldn't get back to Miss Hoare.'

It certainly seemed unlikely that many of Miss Hoare's acquaintances would frequent that place.

'So how long have you been living in the laundry?'

'How long've I been in gaol, more like. Three months, since my husband died.'

I had forgotten this particular little mystery. 'Your husband – Mr Dawson, I imagine?'

'Corporal Dawson, he was. Passed through on his way to Hanover. Liked the look of me, I liked the look of him, and I was . . .' She paused. 'Tired of living in the poorhouse. Been in and out of it for as long as I can think – "a leech on the good will of the parish", as the magistrate was kind enough to say once. I thought I'd escape it. Even living with a bad man'd be better than living with a score of 'em, an' I'd not have got anything from him I didn't get from them.' She laughed, with a shocking bitterness for a girl so young. 'Not that he had time to do anything, good or bad. The day after we married, he was on the boat to Hanover. Two months later they told me he'd died of a fever on the march, and it was back off to the workhouse for me.'

I felt suddenly numbed by her bleak voice as much as the misery in her story. As a child I had several times followed my father around while he ministered to the poor, and seen plenty of the condition in which they lived, but it had never seemed real, more like an exhibit or an illustration, with as much life in those mute, grimy faces as in my regiment of wooden soldiers. I could not comprehend the truths behind Isobel's words, only try to mumble something inarticulately sympathetic.

'It happened,' she cut me short. 'And that's it. I cried when I heard, but I didn't know him. I think he was a good man, but they'll not write that on his tombstone.'

An idea began to grow in me, and although it seemed hideous to be thinking selfishly in the face of such misfortune, I could not help wondering what Isobel intended with me.

'Don't worry,' she said, perhaps anticipating my thought. 'I didn't fix on you in the tavern for my next husband.' Considering the brief tenure of the previous incumbent, this was something of a relief. 'Like I said, I just wanted some nonsense.'

Under the circumstances, I could hardly resent being merely nonsensical, but for the moment I was trying to be serious.

'Could you not have found employment elsewhere?'

'There were none who'd take me. Sir Lawrence and his banker friends had just set up the laundry, and they wanted girls in it who could work cheap. Once they'd made sure everyone in town knew that, you couldn't get work for begging.'

'It seems we both have reason to dislike Sir Lawrence, then.' There certainly seemed to be few enterprises in Dover that did not have his fingers somehow sunk into them.

'More than you'd think,' agreed Isobel. 'I lived four years as a maid to him. Terrible, that was. When he was in a mood, he'd rage about the house with a poker, beating the walls and anyone who crossed his path. And even when he wasn't in a mood, he'd still snarl at you if you even dared to look at him. I was so glad when he went away to London and wouldn't take me. A real beast, he is.'

'Did he . . . ?' Whether out of concern for Isobel, or an urge to rake through Sir Lawrence's character, I found the indelicate question emerging even as I formed it.

'Did he have me?' She snorted. 'No. Not that he didn't try, of course, but you learn tricks in the poorhouse, and after I'd seen what he did with Lady Cunningham I made sure to stay clear. Probably gave him more reason to throw me in with Miss Hoare when he got the chance.'

There was a silence, save for the breeze snapping at her skirts. Her story had a horrible fascination, and though she clearly had few qualms telling it I felt uncomfortable hearing it told. And I could not in decency probe any further into Sir Lawrence's debauches.

Isobel must have wearied of the tale herself. 'Anyway, now you know about me, what about yourself? Have you got a better story to fit a day like this?'

If the day was considered to be rather dull, then my story matched it well, but Isobel had granted me an intimacy and I wanted to reciprocate. So, as we walked, I told her what little of my life seemed relevant: my childhood in Hampshire, and my upbringing as the only grown son of a vicar, a meek and ineffectual man who had easily succumbed to his brother-in-law's insistence that the navy offered the only hope for his son's improvement. I recalled how I had crawled and puked my way through five years as a midshipman until, after three failed examinations, I found a board which cared less for my manifest unsuitability than for my uncle's influence. I talked about the boredom of being at sea, and the rare bouts of terror when an unknown sail was sighted. I even told her the truth about Trafalgar, for when someone has seen you standing naked in the bath tub there is precious little dignity left to protect. I told her all this, and doubtless a hundred other insignificant details, but she listened without interruption, save the occasional question, and seemed as happy to be hearing these irrelevancies – nonsense, perhaps – as I was to speak them.

We passed the bay where the fisherman's hut stood, and carried on up the coast, and at some point I felt a jostling against my side and saw with surprise, and no little pleasure, that she had linked her arm through mine. Thus we came into Deal.

I had not visited Deal before, and what I saw now from the heights above did little to spur regret. It looked a sober sort of town, inescapably formed around the square barracks and hospitals that accounted for so much of its area, and a world removed from the pinching, crooked jumble of Dover. But where Dover was formed like a wedge driven between the two headlands that buttressed it, and so could only grow inwards and upwards, Deal, with no such constraints of geography, ran as a thin ribbon along the sea-front, indulging in a dignified distance between each of its well-tempered buildings. And while Dover's chaos thrived on the energy of private commerce – the only port in England, I believe, where even the navy's supplies were carried by local boatmen – Deal was a thoroughly garrisoned town.

'You'll look better if you arrive at the door without me,' said Isobel.

We were descending from the cliffs. In the distance, out to sea, the masts of the Downs squadron rode gently at anchor, while hoys and galleys thronged the water in between.

'I'll look incomparably uglier if I arrive without you,' I argued, glad that she had saved me from having to broach the topic. 'But the officials may find it more decorous, and it might be deemed seditious to have you distracting the guards.'

She laughed, her long hair blowing forward around her face, and as she squeezed my arm tighter I found myself smiling with more sincere happiness than I'd felt in weeks.

My high spirits did not impress the sentry at the customs house, but at the mention of the names Crawley and Webb he let me through into an anteroom. It had much the same official austerity as Crawley's office in Dover, with white walls and small windows, but the occupant here had clearly felt the need to add a touch of warmth, for a few paintings of ships and storms hung on the walls and a thick rug covered the floorboards.

'Lieutenant Jerrold, eh?' I rose to greet the stout, ruddy-cheeked man who entered. 'Camberwell. How do you do, sir? Don't stand on ceremony, for God's sake, sit down and have a drink.' He took a decanter from a cabinet. 'Brandy? One of the perks of the job, eh, confiscating the contraband.' He winked obviously. 'After all, only way to tell if it's the real thing they're importing or just imitation Cornish rot.' He swilled the liquor in his glass. 'This, I think, is rather good.'

I could only agree. Clearly the Revenue had engaged an expert.

'Now, the man tells me you're here about my unhappy predecessor, Mr Webb. Turned up, has he?'

'After a fashion.' I described the circumstances of Webb's reappearance. 'Captain Crawley believed that you might know something of his movements.'

'Know something?' Camberwell laughed. 'I fear you've wasted your journey, Mr Jerrold, if you've come to find out what I know. Never met the man. Only came here because he'd gone.'

'But there must have been something, surely? He can't have vanished completely for six months.'

'He could if he was strapped down to the seabed.'

Camberwell refilled my glass.

'His condition suggested he had only been underwater a few days.'

'Hah! Then it's a mystery, Lieutenant. He walked out of this very office one afternoon and went to ground completely. We tried to find him, of course – can't have a King's official disappearing like that. Asked at every house and farm in the area, and every boatman in Deal, but none of them had seen a thing.'

I remembered my own experience making enquiries of the locals, and discounted that fact accordingly.

Camberwell was not yet finished. 'Of course, it all got a bit lost in the Drake business.'

'The Drake business?' My mind was suddenly alive to all manner of possibilities.

'Caleb Drake, the smuggler – you must have heard of him? It was two days after Webb vanished that Ramsay and his men smashed Drake's gang. After that, no-one much cared for a missing revenue officer.'

'Was there any hint of a connection between the two events?'

I was struggling to find a pattern: Webb vanishing just before Drake was caught, and then turning up dead at a similar time, and in a similar area, to the mysterious Mr Vitos. Did that add up to a link between Vitos and Drake, or was it just exaggerated fancy?

But Camberwell was, for the first time, looking slightly reticent. 'No,' he said hesitantly. 'No real connection at all. Pure coincidence, I should think. More brandy?'

'Thank you. No *real* connection, you said? A vague connection, perhaps?'

Camberwell filled my glass rather fuller than was necessary, though if he hoped to addle me with spirits he had underestimated the quantity required. Indeed, quite the contrary: the warmth of the drink was beginning to break down my sensibilities and give me an uncharacteristic swagger.

'Mr Camberwell,' I lectured. 'Two good men lie dead. Now you hint to me that the most nefarious villain to have cursed these shores in recent times may have played some part in the matter. Can you, sir, in good conscience withhold the full story?'

'Drake was hanged six months ago,' retorted Camberwell, his face redder than ever. 'I very much doubt even he could reach from beyond the grave to kill Webb, or the other fellow.'

'But I believe that Webb's disappearance then, and his reappearance now, cannot be unrelated. If there was a hint of Drake's involvement when he vanished, it may shed vital light on what has happened since then.'

Camberwell's fat lips were pursed together in silence, his cheeks puffed up behind them. I drained my glass, and he did not offer more.

I tried some idle speculation. 'Perhaps Webb had been instrumental in uncovering Drake's whereabouts for Captain Ramsay, and feared reprisals when he knew Drake would be caught.'

'Hah! Perhaps indeed.'

'Or perhaps,' I continued, trying to read his stony face, 'Webb was in league with Drake, and feared he'd be found out. Especially if he had wind that Ramsay was closing in on Drake.' Camberwell's eyes narrowed; I carried on with my thought.'Perhaps Webb was known to be a little closer to the smugglers than he should have been. After all, why try landing your cargo on a beach at night when for a few pounds' worth of French goods you can sail it into harbour right under the officer's nose? It wouldn't be the first time a revenue officer had dabbled in the trade, or the last.' I stared pointedly at the decanter on his desk.

I find it remarkable how often the urge to correct an upstart's ignorance overcomes men's better judgement.

'I should have thought, Lieutenant, that you would have the courtesy not to impugn my hospitality under my own roof.'

'Not in the least – the brandy is delicious.'

'Perhaps there *are* revenue officers who take a small pinch from the cargoes they inspect and impound.' Camberwell was talking slowly now, measuring his words with caution. 'But if there were, they would remain perfect innocents when set against Mr Webb and his activities. There reportedly never was a lugger that crossed the Channel without a full report as to where our cutters and riding officers would be, or what time Webb's personal attentions in the harbour could be assured. Of course, such services were hardly rendered out of charity, and they say that Webb, when he went, was as rich as any venturer. In fact, Lieutenant, I would go so far as to say that when he disappeared, he saved the service a great embarrassment, and that whoever threw him overboard merely anticipated the work a jury and a hangman would have done had he ever been found alive. Now, good day to you.'

With Camberwell's hospitality exhausted, there was little else to do in Deal. I entertained the idea of asking around the town about Webb, but accosting strangers has never been my style, and I had not the least idea where I should begin. Besides, although it was but a little past the lunch hour, the walk back would take us almost until dusk.

I found Isobel where we had agreed, happily gazing into shop windows; taking her on my arm, I set us on the path back to Dover. It had been a long journey, but well worth it. Not that the riddle had become any clearer – quite the reverse – but after days of knowing nothing, I would far rather a surfeit of facts which might at some stage admit to a narrative, than the contrary. Webb's story was clear enough, of course: clearly he had ceased to be of use to the smugglers with whom he had cast his lot, or perhaps he had been suspected of some treachery in the matter of Cal Drake and they had decided to be rid of him. The only mystery was the intervening six months, for if he had become a fugitive it was unlikely he would have remained in the area all that time. And how did his death relate to Mr Vitos's? If Vitos had been another smugglers' informant, then surely someone would have known him?

I scratched away at these thoughts as we trod our way down the coast, letting Isobel's chatter wash over them. She must have endured a harsh upbringing, between living in the poorhouse and being sold into domestic employment, but if it had put a certain weariness on her young shoulders, it had not crushed her humour, nor her liveliness, and she made for pleasant company as she talked of childhood games, of the places that were dear to her, and of the ridiculous eccentricities of the families she had worked for. The air around us grew hazy, and colder too as the light began to fade; I wrapped my arm tighter around her thin waist and cupped my hand over her hip.

She stopped on a low rise. 'But they were the worst,' she said, pointing to where the jagged rooftop of Sir Lawrence's house pricked up above the rim of the valley. 'Some of the families were cruel without meaning it, and some because they didn't care, but him, he was cruel because he didn't have it in him to be kind.'

'Then don't look at his house.'

I pulled her round. The movement brought her up against me, and out of instinct I moved forward so that she pressed yet closer. She did not pull away. The sun was sinking before us – the only sunset, I think, I ever saw in Dover – and its last beams reflected off the clouds above, suffusing the air with a warm, copper light that coloured Isobel's skin perfectly. A profound silence surrounded us, and it seemed for that instant that we existed in perfect solitude.

I inclined my head, and saw her mouth rising to meet mine. There was a sharp breath as my cold nose grazed her cheek; then our lips brushed against each other, hesitated, and met. I felt her hands against my shoulders, pressing me forward, and was conscious that I did likewise. For a long, tender moment, we held the embrace, letting the warmth pass between us.

'We'd be more respectable over there,' she whispered as we paused for breath. She nodded her head towards the wooded valley where I had thought to seek refuge from the storm.

'Respectable? How does one do this respectably?' I gave her another long, unrespectable kiss.

'By going where no-one can see us, of course.'

She pulled free from my embrace, though keeping hold of my hand, and began running across the field. The earth crunched under our feet, and the chill air rushed past us as we spread our arms like sails and swooped down into the pines, laughing and whooping, letting go to pass around trees and then touching again, until we stumbled into a clearing on the valley floor. I swung Isobel in towards me, clasped her tight and kissed her some more. Disappointment surged when she pushed me back, but it was only to bring her arms forward so she could start fumbling at my breeches.

'Are you sure?' I asked, startled. Suddenly everything seemed to be happening very swiftly.

She giggled. 'Course I'm sure. And you've been wanting this since you met me, haven't you?'

'Well, yes. But that was when I didn't know—'

'When you didn't know me?' There was a sparkle in her eyes. 'Are my manners so revolting? Or do you think it's improper to carry on with a washerwoman?'

'I'll show you improper,' I answered, although my timing was unfortunate, for she had just undone the last button on my breeches and pulled them down to my knees.

Nothing she hasn't seen before, I thought.

'Lie down,' she commanded me, and I obeyed.

The ground was cold, particularly against the exposed portions of my skin, but the carpet of pine needles was soft enough. Isobel was hitching up her skirts.

'You'd better hurry,' I called, looking up at her. 'I can't wait for ever in this blasted cold.'

'You'll be warm enough soon,' she retorted, lowering herself onto her knees astride me. I felt her hands moving deftly about under her petticoats. 'You can't imagine how you could want this after living locked up with six girls for three months.'

Having spent months at a time locked up with seven hundred men in a floating prison, I could imagine it all too well; not for nothing are the girls in Portsmouth the most expensive in the country. But all that was far from my thoughts at that moment, for Isobel, true to her promise, was warming me quickly. I could feel my desire stiffening as she wriggled herself into position above me, and—

'Aaah-tchoo!'

A sneeze from behind a cluster of ferns exploded into the hushed twilight air like cannon fire. Isobel started back, damn near maiming me, and stood up. Her skirts fell into place and she was instantly the model of propriety, while I lay sprawled on my back for all the world to admire. Cursing, I struggled to my feet and tugged at my breeches.

'Who the devil was that?'

My face was scarlet, though not solely from anger, as I stared about; Isobel, looking more irritated than alarmed, did likewise. It was hard to see anything in the gloom, but as I stepped towards the place whence the noise had come, I heard a scuffling. It sounded as though it was retreating, and with a shout of vengeance I plunged in after it. A shadowy figure was on the ground before me, crawling away on his hands and knees, but I grabbed at his shoulder and held him back, eliciting a yelp. He squirmed, but I was strong in my rage, and he unusually light, and with a firm grip I hauled him into the clearing.

'Samuel?'

Isobel recognized him first under the dirt-streaked face, but I knew him well enough too. It was Sir Lawrence Cunningham's servant.

'I didn't mean nothing by it, Miss Isobel,' he pleaded. 'I didn't know you was going to be there, until you *was* there. I wasn't out to spy on you.'

I snorted, for it was not so very long since I had been his age, and I knew full well what I, and any boy of my acquaintance, would have done if granted such a spectacle. But Isobel was talking gently to him, with the indulgent tone of a mother, though I saw with a shock that she was nearer in age to being his sister.

'It's all right, Samuel, you weren't to know,' she said soothingly. 'Did you come here to escape Mr Cunningham?'

Samuel wiped an arm across his dripping nose. 'He's been in a terrible fury with me since I took back Mr Jerrold's clothes.'

He glared at me, wounded accusation filling his face, and though I was not yet minded to pity him, I tried for a little conciliation.

'Do you come here often, then, Samuel?' I fear it came out gruffer than I could help.

'We all did.' Isobel answered for him. 'When he raged, he'd sometimes go into the servants' rooms looking for someone to beat, so we'd come here to hide.'

A thought sprang into my mind. 'So tell me, Samuel, was Sir Lawrence in a bad mood five or six days ago?' I could hardly imagine he was ever in a good mood.

Samuel looked at his knees, avoiding my question.

'You can tell Mr Jerrold,' said Isobel, crouching beside him and putting an arm around his shoulders. 'He's a friend.'

Doubtless Samuel had seen enough to guess that, but my curiosity was overcoming my frustration.

'I apologize if I have caused you unwonted trouble, Samuel. But if you saw anything suspicious or unusual six days back, I must know.' Still he did not look at me. 'If you can help me, it may even serve as a kick in the belly for Sir Lawrence.'

Samuel sniffed loudly, and I offered him my handkerchief. 'There was three of them,' he said quietly.

'When did you see them?' I tried to keep my tone gentle.

'Saturday. Sir Lawrence was having lunch with the banker, and once I'd served out the food he let me go. I come down here.'

'And you saw them?'

'Smelled them first. They had a fire going and it was smoking, being so wet. I crawled up on them.'

'And you saw them?' I prompted again.

'Only through the branches. Can't see hardly nothing through the branches,' he added, glancing at Isobel and blushing hard.

'I'm sure you couldn't. But you saw something?'

'Yes. All in black, they was, one of them with a black beard. He had dark skin, too – and another one. One of 'em was fat, and the other tall, like you. And they talked funny.'

'Funny?'

'Foreign.'

'Could it have been French?' If the smugglers were bound up in this, then surely their associates would likely be French.

'Don't know, sir – never been to France. But the third one was English.'

'How could you tell that?'

'Cos he was Mr Webb.'

'Webb!' The boy's tale had set me stewing with anticipation, but his latest words transfixed me utterly. 'Webb was here, last Saturday? How did you know him?'

Samuel trembled silently, and I saw that my voice, sharpened by a keen hope, had brought him to the edge of tears.

'He'd come to dinner sometimes with Sir Lawrence. I seen him once or twice, that's all.'

'Not to worry, Sam,' said Isobel. She stroked his arm. 'It wasn't your fault you came on them.'

Though I was grateful for Isobel's calming influence, I could not help but plunge on with my questioning. 'And did you hear the others' names?' Never had I felt so close to the answer.

But Samuel was looking unhappy. 'I don't know, sir. They all spoke foreign, and names and words and all, they all sounds the same foreign.'

Slightly to my embarrassment, I found that I was pacing a line back and forth across the clearing, like some martinet. I stopped, and thrust my hands into my pockets.

'And after they'd finished talking, what did they do then?'

Samuel dropped his eyes. 'The two of them, the foreign ones, they left. Mr Webb stayed here.'

'The two foreign ones left.' Already in my thoughts they were confidently named Laminak and Vitos, but I did not want to confuse the boy further. 'What did Mr Webb do then?'

'Don't know. The others'd walked too close to my hiding and frighted me, so as soon as they was gone I snucked off.' He sniffed again. 'It were terrible, sir. If they knowed I'd seen them they'd have killed me, and if Sir Lawrence knowed I'd seen them then he'd have killed me. Hates the smugglers, he does.'

'What makes you think they were smugglers?'

'Who else'd they be? Had a big bundle stashed in the trees over there, and they looked like they didn't want it found.'

'And did you come back later to see if they were still here?'

But Samuel merely shook his head and hunched himself over, avoiding my gaze.

'We'd better get you back to the house,' said Isobel gently, rising to her feet and pulling him after her.

I was reluctant to let him go, for here at last was the one person who'd witnessed something significant and was prepared to tell of it, and I wanted to be sure I had got everything I could from him. But he looked in no mood to talk further, and I knew where to find him if he was needed again.

The last hints of sunlight were playing over the western sky as we emerged from the woods, and looking over my shoulder I could see the hemisphere of the moon climbing into the night. Isobel had Samuel by the hand, and we walked him to the edge of the Cunninghams' property. Orange light spilled onto the lawn.

Isobel took my arm as Samuel vanished around the side of the house. 'He saw the dead man, didn't he?'

'A brace of them, I should think. Webb, of course, and I believe Vitos, the man at the foot of the cliff, was one of the foreigners.'

All the way there my mind had been puzzling at the mystery, trying to fit Samuel's story into what I knew already. Webb had vanished for six months, only to turn up encamped in the woods with a pair of foreign smugglers. A few days later, two of the trio were dead.

'I'd dearly love to find this Mr Laminak,' I reflected aloud, 'and hear what tale he's got to tell.' I considered this. 'If, of course, he's had better luck than his companions.'

I left Isobel at the laundry; despite my pleas, she refused to go back to the inn with me.

'The girls might forgive me shirking a day, but if they thought I was out all night with a man they'd have a galloper off to Canterbury in a second. Some things can't be forgiven. And besides, it'll save you paying the boy there for our sinning.'

'That's not what I meant,' I objected, and it was true: although I'd happily have returned to the unfinished business of the afternoon, I'd have been as comfortable simply enjoying her company.

'How shall I see you next, then?' I asked, somewhat peevishly.

She reached into my pocket and pulled out my handkerchief. 'I'll get this washed for you, and send it back to the inn with a note.'

That seemed unnecessarily sly, but if it saved me another encounter with Miss Hoare, or the jealous attentions of Isobel's colleagues, then I could accept it.

'Goodbye, then,' she said, and lifting herself onto her toes she placed a soft kiss on my cheek. 'And thank you for the day. It was . . . unusual.'

I stooped to kiss her lips, but to my frustration she turned her head so that I caught her somewhere near the ear.

'Not here, Mr Jerrold,' she said primly. 'It would be improper.' And before I could damn her impudence, she had slipped off my arm and through the door. I heard the bolt shoot home after her.

My thwarted desire for Isobel and my confused attempts to make sense of what I had learned that day meant the short journey back to the inn passed in something of a daze, and it was as well that Stubb and Cunningham were not abroad or I should have walked straight into them. But I was not so lost in my thoughts that I missed the bulky figure in the shadows of the stable yard as I passed through the gate. I tensed, and for a wild moment wondered if it was the mysterious Mr Laminak.

'There's some luck, sir – I was about to be on my way. Cap'n Crawley said to give you fifteen minutes, and they was just comin' up.'

Ducker stepped into the lamplight.

'What's this?' I asked. 'I thought Crawley wouldn't send for me unless he needed me.'

Ducker flashed a grin. 'An' so 'e does, sir. Leastways, 'e said 'e'd take you if 'e could get you.' He escaped with the impertinence by attributing it to Crawley. '*Lancelot*'s signalled. There's two sail been seen off the Froggy coast, an' they want us to come an' help corner 'em.' He paused. 'You might be wantin' to bring your sword this time, sir.'

9

WITH NIGHT UPON US AS WE ROWED OUT OF THE HARBOUR, THE boat's oars were loud in the water. A few cables ahead I could see *Orestes*, her lines silhouetted against the half-moon that shone behind. Although a soft breeze blew us on, everything seemed unnaturally still, frozen in the biting air. I huddled deeper inside my boat cloak.

'I thought you were meant to have returned to *Orestes* last night.'

Ducker's presence on land had made me instantly suspicious, for I had no illusions as to the extent to which Crawley trusted me.

'Coroner weren't too 'appy 'bout bein' sent another body,' Ducker explained, easing off on the boat's tiller. Clearly the coroner should have discovered the duties of his office before acceding to it. 'Kicked up a fuss, an' kept us there all night. Then 'e wouldn't let us go today until the cap'n come in to clear it up.'

The jollyboat slapped into an oncoming wave.

'A lucky thing I wasn't there,' I thought aloud.

'Your name did get said.' Ducker looked at me inscrutably. 'But the cap'n got 'em to thinking you 'ad nothing to do with it.'

'As well he should.'

The moon disappeared as we came under *Orestes*' shadow, and I heard the grating of Ducker's boat-hook on the hull – the same hook, I thought with a shiver, that had helped hoist poor Webb inboard the day before. Ice was forming on the ladder, chilling my fingers and undoing my footing: the sword at my waist clattered into the hull, but I managed to gain the deck without mishap.

Crawley was against the far gunwale, peering to the southwest where, far off, three small lights pricked the darkness. Straightening my hat and sword, I crossed to stand behind him and coughed discreetly.

'Lieutenant Jerrold.' Crawley's face was taut, but he remained civil. 'Ducker found you, then.'

'Yes, sir. After I had made some significant discoveries in the matter of—'

'Doubtless they are fascinating.' Crawley cut me off sharply, then reconsidered his tone. 'Of course, these things are of great importance to you. But there are more immediate matters to hand. Captain Davenant believes he has had news of a pair of luggers making sail from Boulogne – had it off a fisherman, apparently.' There was no hiding the doubt in his voice. 'His design is that *Orestes* will meet them and drive them back towards the coast of France, where he will be waiting to intercept and engage them.'

'Playing the hounds to his huntsman,' I said.

Crawley's face twitched. 'Curiously, Lieutenant, those were his words exactly.' Instantly I regretted them. 'Perhaps they will even make it into the *Gazette*, when it reports on this glorious action.'

'If they've anything to write of.'

Although success would doubtless be lauded as doughty Davenant defying the odds, the chances seemed far higher that we'd manage little more than a night sailing up and down the Channel, playing blind man's buff over an area of too many square leagues.

'Precisely, Lieutenant.' The edge came off Crawley's words as he saw I shared his misgivings. 'And if we fail to bring the luggers to account, it will all be down to *Orestes*. *Lancelot* will have been on station and in position throughout.'

What's a man to do if his pups can't run, eh? I could almost hear

Davenant explaining the situation to his friends. But I didn't share Crawley's fear that we might be denied our share of glory. Far more worrying to me was the thought that the luggers might not be acting from the same script; might, instead of running at the sight of us, decide that the pair of them against a small cutter made for alluring odds.

The wind was off the beam, coming straight over the starboard side, and although it lacked power it was steady enough to put us on course. We headed west, and a little south, our decks cleared for action and every spare eye trained on the sea to leeward. The night was clear, and we followed the broad, silver road rippling before us with ease, while our deck and sails shone in the moonlight.

'Be a bold smuggler to risk a run on a night like this,' muttered Ducker. 'Usually they prefers the new moon.'

'After our recent run of form, I doubt they apprehend us to be much risk.' Crawley's gaze never left the horizon. 'Sometimes I feel they must know our movements before we ourselves do.'

'Hoop-eyed, the smugglers is, sir,' said Ducker sagely. 'An' if we can see 'em, then they'll not have the height o' difficulty seein' us back.'

'Though that problem may soon cease.'

I gestured forward, where wisps of fog were beginning to blow over the bow. Already the seas about us were becoming hazy, and the horizon was closing in fast. One by one the crew on deck began to vanish; the mist enveloped the mast, blocked out the moon, then surrounded us until I could see little more than Crawley, Ducker, and the half-dozen men immediately to hand. Even the sounds of the ship's movement seemed curiously distant. We were marooned in the fog; it seemed that nothing else could exist beyond our close circle. And it was bitterly cold.

'Strike a lantern,' ordered Crawley. 'Even if there are enemies about, they'll never see it through this.'

One of the seamen fetched the light. It cast a sickly, yellow glow, and although we could now see one another better, it reflected off the mist to make the walls about us seem more solid than ever.

I heard a thud from for'ard, and a second later a sailor emerged from the gloom.

'What is it, Harvey?' asked Crawley.

'I were in the shrouds, sir,' said Harvey. His voice had a soft, country drawl. 'Just afore the fog came down, sir. I thought I saw a shadow out to larboard.'

'You think?' As a rule, and unlike most of the officers I'd known, Crawley believed in addressing the men courteously when he could, but now there was a clipped sarcasm in his words. 'I cannot be chasing shadows, Harvey.'

'Sorry, Cap'n Crawley, I couldn't get a good eye on her. The more I were lookin', the more she went.'

Crawley bit his lip. 'To larboard, you say. Towards France.'

'Aye, sir.' Harvey looked most uncomfortable. 'Like I say, sir, beggin' your pardon, it were too hazy to be sure.'

'Very well, Harvey, thank you.' Crawley waved a dismissal, and the seaman vanished gratefully into the mist. 'What would you do? Mr Jerrold?'

My head snapped up at the sound of my name; although I had heard his question, I had assumed it to be directed at Ducker. But the quartermaster was now a blurry shape standing aft by the tiller, and Crawley's gaze was very much on me.

'Well, Mr Jerrold?'

'We . . .' I tried to piece together a response, for I have ever found myself vacant when asked for an opinion. 'We seem unlikely to have much chance of getting a better sight of anything while this fog's about. We may as well test his story. One course'll be much the same as another when everything's near invisible. And it ought to be safer heading out to sea: the tide'll be on the ebb now, and we don't want to be too close inshore.'

Crawley frowned, then nodded. 'True enough. Although in this weather, we could skin the cathead from another ship and still not notice.'

I kept silent. Crawley could take my advice or not as he would; I cared not, for I had no better guess. Still, I was quietly gratified, and a little apprehensive, when I saw that he did order *Orestes* around on to a more southerly heading. He might even have entertained some hopes of success, for he ordered the lantern doused and put the seaman back in the shrouds lest the mist fade.

For my part, I began to regret my suggestion almost as soon as the tiller had turned us on to our new course. Davenant had been sharp enough to place the burden of this fool's errand on Crawley; now it was my judgement that would be held to account if, as I suspected, we encountered nothing more dangerous than fog all night. Not, I thought with grim consolation, that Crawley was then safe, for ultimately the decision to take my advice was all his own. And from what I knew of his position, I doubted he would be allowed any more failures than I.

But even if I could shift some of the blame on to Crawley, that still left me on this freezing, fog-bound ship sailing blindly towards what was probably a superior force, with a treacherous and implacably hostile coast beyond. My shoulders became tight, my breathing was sharpened, and my breeches came to feel very snug about my waist. Occasionally one of the men would pad silently past, heading aft to confer with Ducker or forward to attend to the sails, but otherwise we moved in silence. It began to seem that we inhabited a ghost world, that we were no more real than the mist that wraithed us, and I had to lay a palm against the cold iron of a cannon to reassure myself that there was yet substance about me.

'What was that?' Crawley, hunched over the rail, looked up. 'Jerrold, Ducker – did you hear it?'

I had been so lost in my thoughts that I had not, but I saw Ducker beside me nodding his agreement, and so hastily did likewise.

'Somewhere to larboard,' Ducker whispered. 'Some bangin', and voices.'

I strained my ears, hearing nothing save the roll of the waves. But the breeze was stiffening, I noticed, and the circle of fog about us seemed less oppressive. There was even the faintest hint of grey light in the air.

'There again, sir.'

Ducker was leaning over the gunwale, peering out; he must have heard something, though try as I might I still could not be sure that I made out anything other than the sounds of *Orestes*. My imagination needed little enough prompting to amplify even those familiar noises.

'If the owlers is out there, they'll be slipping past while we're talking. Should we come about, sir?'

'It could as easily be *Lancelot*,' I countered. We had enough chance of getting lost in the fog as we were, without needing some damn-fool manoeuvring to disorient us further on the slight chance that another ship, friendly or otherwise, might be somewhere in the darkness.

Ducker ignored me. 'If it's an enemy, we'll want to come round an' get upwind of 'em. Otherwise we'll be drivin' 'em the wrong way, an' they'll never run into *Lancelot*.'

'Bring the ship about and lay her on the larboard tack.'

Crawley's cheeks glistened with the moisture that had settled on them, and I realized as I saw it that the moon must be strengthening.

Men stood from where they had crouched by their guns and, following Ducker's whispered instructions, took their places on the rigging. I saw the helmsman put the tiller over, and felt the timbers stiffen as the wind caught the boat on her beam. A cannonball rolled free of its position by the gun captain and spun across the heeling deck, almost taking off a man's foot before it thumped harmlessly into the bulwark. The rumble seemed very loud, and was joined by a staggered squeaking as the stays took the strain of our new course. I could make out the mast now, see our bow coming round, and I looked anxiously ahead of it to see if Ducker's and Crawley's ears had really heard any more than the sounds of their imaginations. Still there was no sign of any vessel, friend or foe, but I could see an ever-widening expanse of water about our hull; the fog was drifting in ever more feeble shreds. The men must have felt as relieved as I that we no longer sailed blind, for they began to smile again, and to whisper to one another.

'Deck there.' The voice from the shrouds was thunderous in the night. 'Ship, near off the starboard bow.'

It seemed there was not a man in the crew who did not rush to the rail and stare. I had to duck myself under the boom to get there, for the mainsail had been obscuring my view. I had just enough time to see the silvered edges of a hull, some rigging and the corner of a sail, barely two lengths away, before they melted into the night again. I rubbed my eyes. Beside me I could hear at least one sailor swearing it must be some ghoulish spectre. But I had something far more real to worry about.

'Mr Ducker,' I called urgently. 'Did you see her?'

'Aye, sir.' His drawn face told me he had reached the same conclusion. 'And her sail.'

'Precisely – a *square* sail.' I might not have been the consummate sailor, but I knew enough to know that any ship carrying a square sail would outsize us. 'Perhaps it was *Lancelot*.'

'Looked too small for *Lancelot*,' said Ducker. 'More like a brig.'

A brig was better than a frigate, and a frigate better than a hundred-gun first-rate, but if she was an enemy and was armed then, whatever her rating, we would have a devil of a job if we engaged her. But for now there was no knowing: whatever she might be, she had vanished into the night and fog leaving not a trace. Perhaps, I thought irrationally, she *had* been a ghost.

'She was on the opposite tack,' broke in Crawley. 'And she'll be moving away from us now. Bring her about and give chase.'

'Aye, sir,' said the helmsman.

The crew began to pull again as our bow turned through the wind; the sails flapped and luffed, and the boom hovered dangerously overhead, lolling backward and forward. We had come directly into the wind, and our motion was slowed to almost nothing.

'Sweet Jesus!'

Ducker's shout stunned us all – not by its volume, though that was jarring enough, but by the profound shock in a voice that was usually so solid. I followed his gaze, and heard similar cries break out as we all saw the sight that had seized him. The fog had parted again, and sailing out of it, now no distance away at all, there thrust the huge bow of a man-of-war. A frigate, I guessed, and though she would have looked dinky enough next to a ship of the line, she towered over us with an awesome, looming bulk, her timbers gleaming black and evil. The thought of what her heavy cannon could do against our few popguns froze me with terror. I could hear calls and shouting coming from her deck, see shadowy figures moving about her side, but had not the strength to move.

'Haul in the mainsail!' Crawley bellowed, all stealth now forgotten. 'Tighter now, tighter! Grape shot in thc guns!'

His commands snapped the men from their horrified thrall, and they began to haul in the sail, so close that it seemed impossible for it to drive us forward at all. An ominous rumbling came from over the water, and I saw a dozen snouts appear in the frigate's side; we were close enough to hear her guns run out. The men looked anxiously around, but Ducker and his mate moved ferociously among them, barking and striking at any man who neglected his task.

The edge of our sail, which had been flapping lifelessly, straightened and went taut. Crawley had it so far in that it had caught the wind at last and given us a little more headway. But the frigate was crossing our bows; in seconds she would be able to rake us from stem to stern while at once blocking our wind. And at this range, her gunners would not be lost for targets.

'Give way to starboard!' I shouted wildly. 'Try and sail behind her – it's our only chance!' I could not shift my eyes from her guns, from the knowledge that at any moment they would hurl fire and death at us.

'Silence!' thundered Crawley. 'Keep your course, steersman!'

'But that'll take us straight into her!' Our guns would be pointed at the open sea, while our enemy would have all the leisure she needed to pour shot after shot down our length. It was madness.

But still she had not fired. Her cannon were implacably trained on us, and I fancied I could see the glow of a match through at least one of the open gunports, but those awful, gaping muzzles remained silent.

'Qui va?'

A metallic voice hailed us through a speaking trumpet, and I felt a fresh surge of fear as my last doubts were dispelled: it was a Frenchman. But clearly they were not so sure of us; perhaps Crawley's peculiar tactics had indeed confused them. And with every second that they hesitated, we were inching closer.

'Weapons, Mr Ducker,' whispered Crawley. Then, putting his own trumpet to his mouth, '*Ami, ami!*'

He made no endeavour to disguise his accent: he must have hoped they would think us to be English smugglers and allow us alongside. I looked to the sail, and then to the length of black water between our two ships. We were in an impossible position, and moving horribly slowly, but if there was to be a fight I would rather take it on to her deck, outnumbered though we'd be, than sit under her guns and be casually blasted to the seabed. Crawley had clearly made the same calculation, dangerous gamble though it was. We were barely two lengths from her now.

But it was not to be. Whether they saw the facings on his coat or noticed the pile of arms being pulled through the hatch, or whether they simply realized that we showed no intention of deviating from our course, they lost patience. I saw a figure on her quarterdeck raise his sword and, without preamble, slice it down in the clean swoop of an executioner.

We were right under her guns, and they could not miss. Nothing on earth can compare with having to face a broadside from so low and exposed a position, and no cutter was ever built to take it. We had no protection, no bulwarks to take the blow, to serve as a shield; nothing but a short distance of cold air between us and uncompromising death.

They all fired at once, which, even in my terror, surprised me: they would have done better to take aim at us gun by gun, for we were a narrow target coming in head on. Most of that first broadside flew harmlessly wide. The sight it made, though, was something indescribable: a wall of smoke and fire that exploded before us, the roar hammering into our ears and the heat scalding our faces red.

Bitter smoke swamped the air; it was like being back in the fog, only with a thicker, choking smell filling our lungs and mouths and clothes. Then there was another crash: the topmast plunged to the deck, dragging a great swathe of the mainsail and a tangle of rigging down with it, while the larboard shrouds collapsed like a whip onto the men who stood beneath.

But amid all this carnage, our crew was surprisingly intact. A few were trapped under fallen rigging, and one was screaming where a spar was crushing his contorted back, but the majority seemed unhurt, as surprised as I was that we had survived that lethal broadside. We must have been too close, and too low, for the balls to have struck properly, I thought jubilantly.

'Hard about!'

Crawley was coughing violently, but otherwise seemed safe. *Orestes* began to turn, putting her side towards the enemy, and I saw with a start that we were so close that our long bowsprit scraped her hull.

An uneven volley of musket fire crackled out from the frigate's deck, and my relief at having survived the broadside vanished as I fell to my knees. Frantically I patted my arms and chest, but I seemed unharmed; then, just as I had reassured myself, a heavy weight thumped into me and I was knocked sprawling backwards. For a second I thought a falling spar had pinned me, that I would now suffer a slow, crushing death rather than the merciful swiftness of a musket ball. But it was not timber on top of me, but a man, and I remembered with horror as I saw the blood spreading over his shirt that there was nothing the least merciful about musket fire. His face hung slack from the neck, shock frozen into it. He was dead already, I think, for there was no life in the body that flopped over me like a blanket, and it took a terrible effort to roll him off into the scupper. Shaking, I stumbled to my feet.

'Take the men for'ard and prepare to board,' Crawley shouted at me. 'I shall be with you directly. Go on, Lieutenant,' he added angrily, seeing my witless look of shock. 'This may be our only chance!'

'Yes, sir.'

I was bewildered, dazed by the noise and smoke and chaos, by the dead man's embrace. I might have stood there like a statue had Ducker not pulled my sword from its scabbard and set it into my hand.

'Come on, sir!' he bellowed in my ringing ear. 'No time for it!'

Nor was there, for the French, seeing our desperate plan, were massing by the rail, and I could hear the continuing crack of musket fire. If they could pour too much of that down on us, we would be slaughtered to a man.

Staggering like a drunkard I tottered forward, picking my way over the wreckage until I came amidships. The crew lay low against the deck, cowering behind the gunwale, though that was little enough protection against fire from above. But how could we mount the hull to get at them when they were crammed in up there ready to resist us?

'Get low, sir!'

Ducker's hand reached around my neck and pulled me down. My legs buckled and I fell hard on my knees.

'Fire!'

Crawley roared the command, and more explosions rocked *Orestes*. Somehow the gun captains had managed to get matches to all five of our starboard cannon, though debris now covered half of them, and the men cheered at the noise of our broadside ripping into the enemy. I remembered how tiny those guns had seemed when I first saw them, but in such close confines they gave a sound like something out of the line of battle. How much damage they did I could not see, but a cloud of splinters erupted into the air, and it was as well we were all huddled behind our barricade.

'Through the ports!' Ducker was shouting. 'Take 'em where they're not expecting it!' He helped me to my feet. 'Come on, sir, give the lads a cheer.'

'At 'em, boys!' I yelled, or some such nonsense, for words become instinctive and meaningless in such moments.

It sufficed, though: the men surged forward, and grappling irons rattled against the frigate's hull while desperate hands pulled themselves up onto the gunports. I saw the ghastly sight of a head dissolving in crimson spray as one of the enemy cannon fired point-blank into him, but then the man behind him got through the gap and I heard the sounds of battle starting within. I was almost too terrified to move, but Crawley was behind me, and I would not be left on our deck for him to find me alone; moreover, several of the crew were still hesitating, looking to me of all people for a lead, God help them. And if I stayed behind, the marksmen above would not have to look too hard for a target.

Grabbing a pistol from the deck, I took hold of a rope and leaped into the darkness. My fingers were numb with cold and fear, and I dreaded that at any moment I might slip and fall into the icy water, or get crushed between the two hulls, but I managed to claw my way up the side. Then I had to countenance the possibility that, like the poor seaman before me, I might be climbing through a gunport with a loaded cannon to greet me. But hanging off the side of the ship was doing me no good. My blood churning with panic, I heaved myself up and tumbled over onto the hard wooden deck. To my left and right I could see others of our crew slithering through the holes, but the bulk of our men were battling near the companion ladder, knotted together in a hard-pressed circle. With another shout of false courage I ran towards them, discharging my pistol into the choking smoke beyond and then laying in with my sword.

It was desperate work, though with so many men in so small a space, and no room to swing or cut, it was hard to land decisive blows; instead, our two sides heaved against each other as if in some vast wrestling bout, while sword-blades stabbed blindly between the gaps. Looking behind I saw that another group of Frenchmen were coming down the forward ladder to try to break us from the rear, but Crawley was now aboard and mustering a second file of our men to resist them. They protected us, but became increasingly outnumbered as French reinforcements flooded down; we were squeezed closer and closer until at last we fought almost back to back. A blade hissed past my face; soon they would have us pinioned so close together they could hack us apart at will. Had there not been such a press of bodies about me, I might have collapsed.

Somewhere in all that shouting and clamour, I thought I heard a distant banging; then the deck seemed to shudder, and a succession of powerful thuds pounded the deck over our heads. The crowd around me began to lessen. We were moving again, driving forward with lunging blades, while our enemies were in an unmistakable retreat. I pressed home the advantage, letting a week's accumulated frustration batter down my safer instincts so that I cut and slashed with a fury I had never known. Too much fury, I saw too late, for although the enemy were retreating before me – before *us*, to be accurate – my excitement had taken me beyond the safety of our ranks and I stood exposed in the space between the two sides.

'Watch yer 'ead, Lieutenant!' called someone from behind.

I swung about, and saw a snarling French officer coming at me across the deck. I lifted my sword to check him and he stopped, but the strength I gained from seeing him falter melted away as he pulled a pistol from his coat. I froze, petrified between the twin impulses of either charging him before he could fire or hurling myself down out of his way. The gun came up. I saw him closing an eye and squinting down the barrel, a look of intense concentration fixed on his face.

There was an explosion, a burst of smoke, and a crack. Then nothing.

I remember little enough of that fight, and nothing at all after that moment, but I do recall the strange sensation when I regained my senses. I was lying propped against the bulwark next to a cannon, my head resting on a bundled hammock, and for several minutes the images I saw mingled freely with half-recollected scenes from my awakening after Trafalgar. There was little to choose between the two: the stink of blood and powder was everywhere, and shirtless men ambled back and forth across my field of view, shapeless bundles dragging behind them. A sheep was bleating somewhere in the distance, and I could hear sharp orders being rattled off from on high. Was this the afterlife – sitting in a bloody coffin while the sounds of the Lord almighty drifted in through the skylight? But that did not seem right. I had never heard the Almighty myself, but I doubted He spoke with the voice of Captain Davenant.

I chuckled at that, wondering whether the comparison would please him, but the shaking of my head induced a terrible ache in my temples. Had I been shot? With a start I remembered seeing the ball – or at any rate, the pistol – coming for me. But when I raised a hand to my forehead it came away clean, and definitely touching skin, not bandage.

Gingerly, I got to my feet. It set my head pounding again, but I steadied myself with a hand against the beams and managed to shuffle across to the ladder. A stiff man in a red coat – a demon, I thought vaguely, or maybe a marine – bustled past me, paying me no notice. There were fewer bodies than I remembered. And there was light coming through the hatch above, as well as cool, pleasant air. Screwing up my eyes – they were tender – I gripped the rungs of the ladder and carefully lifted myself up.

'Alive, Lieutenant?' Crawley's voice. Perhaps I had not ascended to heaven.

'Don't know, sir,' I replied honestly. 'Was I shot?'

He snorted. 'I shouldn't think so, Lieutenant. Apparently you dived out of the way just as your opponent fired. I fear your instincts may need a little adjustment, though: you jumped headlong into the edge of the companionway and knocked yourself cold. Ducker had to run the villain through for you. Ah, here comes Boyes.'

I turned, and began to notice the activity about me on deck. A squad of marines – *Lancelot*'s, maybe? – were herding prisoners below, pricking none too tenderly with their bayonets if any faltered, while those sailors who could still stand were trying to drag the wreckage off the main deck. Smoke and fog still filled the air, but I saw an officer – also from the *Lancelot*, I guessed – making his way towards us. Another man, not in uniform but surprisingly well-kempt, followed.

'*Lancelot* arrived?' I asked Crawley.

'None too soon.' *Lancelot*'s newly arrived officer answered for Crawley, speaking brusquely over him. He was tall and thin, with an arrogant face that made no secret of his own self-regard. 'A few more minutes and you'd have been ground down to nothing. *Lancelot* put a broadside through her rigging and a company of boarders on her deck and swept them up nicely.'

'I could hardly forget, Lieutenant Boyes.' Even among the ruins of battle, neither officer affected any warmth. 'Has the prize yielded anything to your search?'

'Sadly, we failed to find anything of value.' I suspected the frigate would have been looted quite thoroughly before any official inspection was made. 'But we did turn up this little curio.' He pulled the second man forward. 'This is Mr Nevell, an Englishman discovered without explanation in the hold of a French man-of-war.'

'Mr Nevell?' Crawley's eyes swivelled on to him. 'What have you to say?'

The man gave a shrug, and a surprisingly careless smile for a man in his predicament. 'I was trying to find a passage home, after being wrecked in the *Ariadne*.'

'And did you misplace your uniform then, Mr Nevell?' Boyes showed no sympathy.

Nevell smiled again. 'I see your confusion, Lieutenant,' he said. 'But no, I'm not with the navy.' He paused. 'I work for the Post Office.'

10

BOYES WAS THE FIRST TO REACT TO NEVELL'S UNEXPECTED WORDS, and did nothing to mask his incredulity.

'Queer place to be delivering a letter. Would a packet ship not have served you as well, without the added hazards of being mistaken for a Frenchman or hanged as a traitor?'

'Sadly, I had no choice in the matter.' Nevell remained studiously polite. 'After the *Ariadne* was wrecked I managed to swim ashore and evade the *gens d'armes* for a week, but they grabbed me while I was trying to haggle a journey home aboard an English free-trader in Calais. They too wanted to shoot me for not being in uniform.' He smiled at Lieutenant Boyes. 'Fortunately I convinced them I was a civilian, and they decided to imprison me instead. I never had much ambition to spend the war in a French gaol – too many nasty stories surround them – so I slipped out when they weren't looking and stowed away on the first ship I could find, thinking to get some distance away from the inevitable search parties. I was hardly in a position to negotiate my passage.'

It was quite a tale, rendered even more incongruous by his well-tended attire and the calmly bemused set of his youthful face. His brown hair was neatly tied back with a length of French ribbon, and only a tar stain on his thigh suggested he had not stepped straight from a fashionable assembly. Perhaps for this reason, or perhaps simply out of spite, Boyes stared at him with outright disbelief, as if he had just announced that he had flown down from the moon. Crawley, however, was giving him an appraising look.

'Tell me, Mr Nevell,' said Crawley. 'What became of Captain Smith and his crew after the *Ariadne* foundered?'

Nevell frowned. 'Captain Stowecroft, was it not?' he asked earnestly. Then, catching Crawley's eye, he began to smile. 'Was that your gambit, Captain? Did you expect to catch me as a spy?'

Crawley shrugged.

'Captain Stowecroft and his crew and I became separated in the surf, and I could not wait for them on the beach as I feared we had been seen by a shore patrol. Sadly, when I was caught, my interrogators made no mention of any other survivors, although that may be because they evaded detection better than I.'

'The only man left from the crew – how marvellously convenient,' Boyes remarked with a sneer.

Nevell looked pained. 'Please, Lieutenant. After my extraordinary good fortune in finding a rescue from my predicament, do not tell me that I have merely swapped the captivity of my enemies for that of my own countrymen.'

'That depends on who your true countrymen are.' The arrogance in Boyes' thin face was unyielding. 'Perhaps we could ask the Frenchy captain what he knows.'

'I'm sure a meeting with him could be arranged,' said Nevell.

There was an awkward silence.

'Of course,' said Crawley, choosing his words carefully, 'the frigate's captain is dead.'

As Boyes grasped Nevell's insult, his face began to flush; it seemed momentarily he would be moved to an act of some violence. Much as I appreciated Nevell's wit, and much as I would have enjoyed seeing him lay into that prig – for despite Nevell's slight build and unassuming manner, there was definitely a hint of steel within him – I felt that an officers' brawl on the quarterdeck of a

French prize would not be looked upon kindly by their lordships at the Admiralty. Particularly if I became involved.

'On the topic of the dead,' I broke in, 'I fear I have lost my sense of the action since I, ah, lost my senses.' It was a pathetic joke, the sort that might have caused endless mirth at one of my parents' dinners, but it served well enough to break the mood. I pressed on. 'For all the valiant fighting I saw, and of course partook in, it seems incredible that some fifty of us, in our scrap of a cutter, could overwhelm and capture so large a prize.'

This last comment did little to placate Boyes, and he turned his ire on me. 'You did not. For all your *valiant fighting*' – from his tone, we might have been playing in the bath rather than battling for our lives – 'you were within scant inches of becoming Buonaparte's prisoners yourselves, and giving him your little dinghy as a prize. Fortunately for you, having first successfully engaged and defeated her companion brig, we of the *Lancelot* were then able to come up on them and force their surrender.'

'Indeed we did.' A new voice joined our conversation: Davenant, springing from the hatchway and advancing upon us with a great, cocksure smile lighting up his face. 'Of course, it was good of you to bring them to bay, Crawley, and I shall record your presence at the action in my report.' He slapped him jovially on the back. 'You'll get your prize money, never fear. But we've more important matters than dividing the laurels to see to.' He gestured behind him, where a pair of marines were escorting forward a French officer. 'This is Monsieur Giscard, the *Thermidor*'s first lieutenant. Until this morning.' He chuckled; Boyes dutifully followed suit. 'Monsieur Giscard informs me that they were escorting the brig to the Texel, carrying men bound for the Austrian front. *N'est-ce pas, monsieur?*'

Giscard, a short, stout man with a drooping face and unkempt hair that sat ill above his new uniform, nodded glumly.

'They burned the charts of course,' continued Davenant off-hand. 'And I'd never trust more than half a word a Frenchy says, but it seems likely enough. They'd lightened her quite substantially to get her into the estuary, taken out some guns and lost a few score of her crew. Lucky for you, eh, Crawley? At full complement she'd have sunk you faster than a Breton rock.'

'And were there soldiers on the brig you captured?' enquired Crawley icily.

Davenant waved the question away. 'Didn't have time to examine her myself, left that to the boarding party. My abilities were needed elsewhere at the time, you may recall.'

'Of course.'

'Anyway, there's little sense in waiting here for them to send a fleet to punish us. Not unless you fancy another crack at glory, Crawley?'

Crawley shook his head, his neck trembling.

'Boyes will take command of the *Thermidor*. He can take her back to Sheerness and get her repaired. Your popguns made quite a dent in her side, you know; you can tell your men to be proud of themselves. As for me, I shall return to Deal and make my report to the admiral.' He peered over the side at *Orestes*. 'I suppose you'll be able to hobble back to Dover, Lieutenant? I can have Boyes give you the tow if you require it.'

'We may,' said Crawley tightly, 'be able to manage without you. Sir.'

We did, but it was a devil of an effort. It took half the morning to jury-rig a sail, and even then it made a feeble job of the light wind we were given. My head still ached from its misadventure the night before, and I almost collapsed again when I tried to look up at the fractured masthead to supervise the rigging work.

Thankfully, Crawley saw my predicament, or at least the futility of my contribution, and put me on a party clearing debris from the fo'c'sle, while he set himself wholeheartedly to the work of repair. I think if he had not busied himself mending the ship he would have been brought to doing it greater damage, for there was no disguising his rage that the prize he had almost taken was now snatched from him, and would be appended to that famous list of ships gloriously defeated by Captain Davenant.

Thermidor was under way long before *Orestes*; we stood on deck and watched her square sails drawing away, leaving us alone in the sea. All traces of the night's fog had cleared, and once we no longer had the French frigate against our gunwale, we could see *Lancelot* and her second prize, the small brig, tacking slowly back towards the English coast. The sky was overcast, threatening rain – a *mackerel sky*, as Ducker put it – but, as if intent on frustrating Crawley at every turn, or perhaps to keep him isolated until the head of his anger had passed, the wind remained faint and variable. In view of the scant, frail canvas we had been able to mount, that proved something of a blessing.

It was long past the early winter sunset when we finally drew close to the land.

'We'll not risk entering the harbour tonight,' said Crawley, his voice now showing nothing but exhaustion. 'We'll anchor in the roadstead, make our way in at first light. Mr Jerrold, you may have the first watch. I shall be in my cabin.'

It was a sharp night, and very dark. Occasionally a sliver of moonlight would pry its way through the clouds, but otherwise I was left in an icy void. I tried stamping my feet and striding purposefully up and down the deck, but anonymous complaints from below put an end to that, and I could only huddle my boat cloak closer about me, pull my hat down over my frosty ears and entertain myself by tapping out familiar melodies between chattering teeth. And try to ignore the clarity the cold gave to the ache in my head.

I don't believe I drowsed off, but the noise, when it came, certainly startled me more than it should have. My chin snapped up, and my eyes were suddenly very wide open. It had been a splash, some way out in the darkness, and my first thought was that it could be a cutting-out party: smugglers, or Frenchmen, come to take their vengeance on us. Should I sound the alarm? If I was wrong, the crew would not be quick to forgive me; the earlier misdemeanour of my thumping footsteps would be minor in comparison. But, I told myself, the sea was unlikely to be crawling with brigands and villains at this hour; far more likely the splash had been entirely natural, a wave falling over itself or some such thing. Or was that how the watchman aboard the *Thermidor* had deceived himself the night before, as *Orestes* crept up on him? I peered more intently than ever over the side, willing the darkness to part; I think I would almost have preferred a boatload of pirates armed to the teeth, if only I could have seen them, than having to contend with the unyielding anxiety of blindness. As it was, I had nothing to give me confidence either way, only gnawing doubt.

So keenly did I scan the space before me that I did not hear the grate of the companion hatch, nor the footsteps approaching me across the deck. Nor even the voice in my ear. Only when a hand tugged at my arm did I notice the presence, and spin about in pure, sudden terror.

It was not One-Eyed Jack, nor Blackface Bill, nor any of the other demons I had imagined. To my surprise, it was Nevell, the postman we'd found aboard *Thermidor*, who had elected to return to Dover with us rather than take the faster route to Deal aboard the prize. After his encounter with Lieutenant Boyes, I could quite understand his decision.

'Did I startle you?' he asked, a wry grin on his face. 'I hope you were not asleep.'

'Certainly not. I merely thought I had heard a noise out there, and was trying to discern its source.'

'They do say that concentrating on silence is the surest way for a lookout to miss the real danger.'

'They teach you that in the Post Office, do they?' Crawley had seemed happy enough with Nevell's tale of derring-do under the noses of the enemy, but I'd not yet satisfied all my suspicions.

'I've pursued various professions.'

'And what brings you on deck?' My fraught conjectures still played out in my mind, and I wondered whether this mysterious passenger might not have come out to signal his evil cohorts aboard.

'I couldn't sleep. Although not because of the sound of your footfall,' he added hastily.

'If I've learned one thing since I came to Dover,' I told him, 'it's that one should never leave the comfort of a warm bed in the middle of the night. Lands you in all sorts of trouble.'

'The famous body on the beach? I've heard all about it.'

'Don't tell me it's the talk of France now.'

Nevell laughed quietly. 'No. I had it from the crew. They view you as some sort of talisman, you know.'

'You mean a curse, I presume.' It had not escaped my notice that few of the men would catch my eye, and that when they obeyed an order it was usually to take themselves away from me.

'I wouldn't put it that way,' said Nevell earnestly. 'I believe they think you some sort of a magnet for bad luck. As long as it attaches itself to you, it stays away from them.'

'Until I attract a particularly vicious typhoon or a razor-sharp reef while we're out at sea.' I'd never known sailors want any contact with bad luck other than to throw it overboard.

Nevell shrugged. 'Perhaps I misunderstood them. But they do talk of the bodies you've found.'

I wondered whether they saw my influence in the death of the man who had fallen into my arms the night before, and, if so, how much longer they would tolerate me. But Nevell, heedless of my discomfort at his line of conversation, was continuing.

'In fact, I'm told that you discovered poor Hal Webb.'

There was more in his voice than just a man fishing for a yarn, and I stared hard at him through the gloom. Between the darkness and his naturally innocent face, though, he was as impossible to make out as the waters around us.

'Did you know Webb, then?' I asked. 'I thought he was a customs man.'

Nevell nodded. 'Indeed he was. But as I say, I've pursued various occupations. And it's one of the great satisfactions of working for the Post Office, you know, the broad sweep of people you meet.'

'I'm glad my postage pays for such entertainment.' I trusted the man ever less. 'Yes, I did find Webb, though it was Ducker, the quartermaster, who hauled him in. You can visit his grave in Dover.'

'I shall. But tell me, Lieutenant, was there anything suspicious about the corpse?'

'Besides the fact that he was five fathoms down with a sandbag round his leg?'

He could have had all this from Ducker, or from any of the men who'd been there; he could even have got it from me, with much less trouble, if he hadn't accosted me in the middle of the night. My concern over the splashes in the distance – I had heard several more while we talked, each stiffening my nerves more than the last – did not incline me to conversation.

'He had no personal effects on his person, Mr Nevell, and no paper conveniently inscribed with the name of his murderer. He was drowned, deliberately, probably by someone else but equally possibly by himself. Perhaps his conscience caught up with him.'

'His conscience?' prompted Nevell.

'Please, Mr Nevell.' I paused mid-sentence, for I had heard another sound off to my left, somewhere ahead of the bow. 'Did you hear that?'

'I confess I did not.' He cocked his head and affected to listen for a few seconds. 'No. But you were expounding on Mr Webb's conscience.'

'If you knew him at all,' I said shortly, 'you'll have known him better than I ever will. And you'll perhaps know that he vanished from Deal under something of a cloud.'

'I do. But I also know that men sometimes take themselves into clouds to get lost.' Nevell sounded more cautious now, and stared at me significantly.

'Maybe they do, but it's no concern of mine. I need to discover the provenance of the first body, Mr Vitos, not the enigmatic Mr Webb. Fascinating though he may be.'

'Do you really think the two unconnected?' Nevell's tone spoke his own answer to the question.

'No,' I admitted. 'Indeed, I know they are not.'

Overcoming my misgivings, I told him Samuel's story in brief words, how Webb and Vitos and Laminak had been together on the cliff-top the day before I found Vitos. Almost exactly one week back, I realized with a shock; it seemed an aeon.

Nevell listened intently. Laminak was clearly new intelligence to him, and he asked several questions about the man, until I realized I had confided in him everything I knew. Which seemed little enough when I remembered I had about a week to turn it into proof of my innocence, but it seemed to please Nevell.

'Well,' he said, when I had finished and turned my attention back to the dark waters. 'You've been most generous with your knowledge.'

'I have,' I agreed. 'And now, Mr Nevell, if you still lack the urge for sleep, you might do me the kindness of sharing yours. If Webb is implicated in Vitos's death, what do you know of him?'

Nevell pursed his lips. 'What do you know of a man named François de Barbé-Marbuis?'

'What do you know of the baker's boy? As much as he concerns me, which is to say, not at all. I asked about Webb.'

'De Barbé-Marbuis,' continued Nevell, ignoring me completely, 'is Buonaparte's Minister of the Treasury.'

'He must be a rich man.' I was only half listening.

Nevell shook his head. 'Quite the reverse: he's a bankrupt. Took the French treasury and invested it recklessly. Now his friends are rich as lords, and he's got nothing but promissory notes and receipts – paper.'

'No doubt the Corsican ogre has been sympathetic.'

'The Corsican ogre will probably send him off to the Indies to rot in oblivion. But for the moment, he has the overwhelming concern of trying to govern, and subdue, half the continent with little more than whatever coin he can find behind the divan.'

'He certainly keeps his frigates undermanned.'

'But that's the mystery of it,' explained Nevell. '*Thermidor* may have been shorthanded, but his army's as strong as ever it was, and strung out across Europe keeping his grip on power clenched tight. Still clothed, still armed, still fed and still paid.'

He looked at me expectantly.

'Then he's obviously not half so near bankrupted as you supposed.'

'He is, and he isn't. He survives by grace of a stream of cash, thousands of pounds a week in gold coin pouring into Paris. And can you hazard a guess where that gold comes from?'

'Citizens of a grateful Europe?'

I sensed some climax was coming, but though Nevell's sense of theatre was obviously acute, his denouement was niggardly.

'Possibly. For now, your guesses are as good as any we can manage at the Post Office. It's a curious thing, nonetheless: the kingdoms of the continent are up to their crowned heads in debt, and it would take a rich country to provide Buonaparte with the funds he needs.' He glanced at me to see if I followed him. 'The sort of country that could afford to lavish its expenditure on luxuries. Tea. Brandy. Calicoes. Tobacco.'

I looked at him in confusion. 'You infer that the satisfaction of our appetites is somehow also feeding the French?'

'I infer nothing,' said Nevell coolly, though beneath that implacable voice I thought I sensed a note of passion. 'But there are facts. If you wander about the country near Calais and Boulogne, as I recently have, you will find two enormous depots – small towns, almost – vast smugglers' markets with every facility the English free-trader could want. All carefully ordered and maintained by the grace of the French government.'

'So Buonaparte supports the smuggling trade?' I asked, incredulous. I would no more have expected to find Lord Grenville opening the taps at the local alehouse. 'But why should he do that?'

'Perhaps because he does not wish us to want for comfort while he tries to pummel us into submission. Or because he hopes we will drink and smoke and dress ourselves to death.' Nevell snorted. 'Or perhaps because somewhere in all that commerce there is enough of a profit to be made to keep his throne solvent.' He looked at me shrewdly. 'Smuggled goods don't mysteriously appear in the middle of the Channel, you know – they must come from somewhere. And there, wherever it may be, you can be certain that someone will be making a profit.'

'But can the proceeds of our vices be so vast as to sustain an empire?' For all that I contributed to the national debauch, surely we would needs be a nation beyond the wildest depravity to pay for quite so much sin and tea.

Mercifully for the moral standing of our country, Nevell was shaking his head. 'There's certainly money enough to be made in the smuggling trade, though they hardly publish their accounts, of course. But no, not so much that Buonaparte could survive off it, I think. Yet I am convinced that there is some link between the smugglers on these shores and Buonaparte's coffers. Which is why your work interests me, Lieutenant, and why I would dearly love to have talked to Hal Webb before he found his way onto the sea floor. He might have had an interesting tale or two to tell.'

And perhaps he could also have told an interesting tale or two about how Mr Vitos came to be at the foot of a cliff with a broken neck. But that was just one question among the many that flooded my mind at every word Nevell spoke. To begin with: 'And how does a humble employee of the Post Office come to know all this?'

But the inscrutable Mr Nevell, who it appeared talked only on matters and at times of his choosing, murmured a goodnight and retreated to his hammock.

Leaving me as cold, confused and skittish as ever.

11

WE ENTERED THE HARBOUR THE FOLLOWING MORNING, SUNDAY, using the boats to tow us in, for our makeshift sail had come unstuck in the night. Thankfully, that was the worst that befell us: whatever the cause of the noises and splashes I'd heard, or imagined, no-one had come into sight.

Once we were moored by the boatyards, on the seaward side of the basin, I discovered the benefit of a devout commander, for Crawley let all but the barest of skeleton crews off the boat on a day's leave to observe the Sabbath as we saw fit. It certainly made a change from the sort of zealot who remembered nothing of the Bible beyond the line about sparing the rod and spoiling the crew. But although I for once had an empty day stretching before me, the prospect of some unaccustomed leisure did not lift my spirits in the least; indeed, it weighed upon me. The dirty light of the day seemed to tarnish everything it touched, including my spirits, which were drab enough to begin with. And the ever-present rain was getting heavier.

It was the sort of day I might often have spent in a tavern, but I had no-one to drink with and I doubted many of the locals would welcome a naval officer to their table. If I went back to my room at the inn, I would likely be lunatic by nightfall. So I walked through the town, and knocked on Miss Hoare's door.

A young girl answered, a scrawny thing, with wide blue eyes and red hair tied in pig-tails. I doubted she was much younger than Isobel, but her figure was not yet womanly – or perhaps she was just underfed – and she lacked Isobel's more thoughtful demeanour.

I lifted my hat. 'Is Miss Hoare at home?' I asked stoutly. The first law of sneaking is to be as forthright as possible.

She giggled behind a cupped hand. 'No, sir,' she said, wobbling into a low curtsy. 'She ain't.'

This was excellent news. 'How about Mrs . . .' I searched my memory for Isobel's married name. 'Mrs, um, Isobel?'

The blue eyes opened wider still. 'Isobel's 'ere, yes, sir.' She bobbed again, leaning forward ever so slightly. 'Was you wantin' to see 'er? We doesn't normally take visitors. 'Specially on a Sunday.'

'Doubtless you can make an exception.' I was in no mood to be thwarted by this puck of a gatekeeper.

'Sure I can,' said the girl, winking heavily. 'For a shillin'.'

Her opportunism was astounding. 'You'll have tuppence and not a ha'penny more,' I told her, loath to set her in bad habits.

She pondered this, chewing on a braid. 'I could do it for a sixpence. An' that's only a penny for every stripe I'll get if Miss 'oare finds me out.'

I wondered where she had learned these bartering skills, and what future career they might open for her. Clearly they were squandered on washing.

'Sixpence, then.' I was reluctant to linger much longer on the doorstep.

A well-scrubbed palm shot out under my nose, and the coin vanished into her tiny fist.

'Now don't spend it all on gin.'

She smiled innocently. 'Never. Save it for brandy, I do. Come on.' Grabbing my hand, she pulled me over the threshold and into a narrow, dimly lit hallway. 'Is Isobel expectin' you?' she asked, tugging me up a curling flight of stairs. None of the other inmates was to be seen, thankfully, but the cloy of soap was heavy in the air.

'Not exactly,' I admitted. 'Why?'

'Nothin'.' The girl giggled, her braids swinging around her face. 'Sometimes people likes surprises, I s'pose.'

We had reached a thin, low-roofed corridor at the top of the house, lined with doors on either side and hung with liberally embroidered quotations from the Psalms.

'Incline not my heart to any evil thing, to practise wicked works with men that work iniquity,' I read.

My guide raised a slim finger to her lips. 'Shhh,' she whispered theatrically. 'Don't want to wake no-one. Isobel's—'

But I needed no more help finding Isobel, for at that moment a door at the far end of the corridor opened, and she stepped out, wearing nothing more than a simple white shift, with her dark hair loose about her shoulders. She saw me and started. A queer look crossed her face before she came swiftly down the hall to meet me.

'What are you doing here?' she hissed. 'Don't you know what would happen if you were found here? And what are you doing with him, Sally?'

''E fought 'is way in,' said Sally dreamily. 'Like Sir Galahad storming the Castle Perilous.'

'Well, it'll be perilous enough for sure if Miss Hoare finds out. Come on.' Isobel pushed open the nearest door. 'In here, and you stay clear, Sally.'

Blowing me an impertinent kiss, Sally skipped off down the stairs. Isobel followed me into the tiny room and shut the door behind her. I sat down expectantly on the low bed.

'You shouldn't have come,' she told me. 'I said I'd send your handkerchief when we could meet.'

'But Miss Hoare's away.'

'She'll come back,' said Isobel darkly. 'And not all the girls here are as devilish as that Sally. There's some who'd fork anyone they thought had been breaking the rules. 'Specially if it was with a man. And Sally's got a wild enough tongue herself – she'd say anything for mischief.'

'Well, I apologize.' Isobel's attitude was beginning to grate upon my temper. 'I've had a miserable few days at sea, soaking up French broadsides and seeing men die on top of me; I merely hoped for a little diverting company. Some nonsense, as you might say. But it would seem that you own the monopoly for arriving unexpected in other people's rooms.'

I stood up, glaring at her. She put a hand on my arm.

'Sit down. I didn't mean to scold you. It's just if they bang me out of here, that's it. And you surprised me.' She sat next to me on the coverlet, and squeezed her knee against mine. 'I am glad to see you. Now what's that about the bodies? You haven't found another one, have you?'

I gave a bitter laugh, and slumped back against the rose-painted wall. I felt suddenly terribly weary, drained, and it must have shown, for Isobel pulled me around so that my head was in her lap. I stared up at her smooth, white throat, and the worried little face above it.

'No wickedness,' she warned me, though there was a flush in her cheeks. 'Not here.'

'No wickedness,' I agreed, not really disappointed: there was no devilment in me at that moment, and the cradle of Isobel's thighs, the absent-minded way she stroked at my hair, was all I desired.

I began to speak, and quickly found myself drawn into the tale of the battle, the frigate coming out of the fog, Crawley's mad assault, the terror of facing that broadside and then climbing into the cannon's mouth. I feared I was boring her, but the dark eyes looking down on me never dulled; indeed, whenever I tried to pass over a particularly gruesome episode she would insist on drawing the details out of me. It was warm in the sloping room, and though there was but a single lamp it cast a kindly light. For the first time in as long as I could remember, I felt very much at peace, as though the stains and grime of the past days were being scrubbed off me. I also felt an increasing regret that I had agreed to abstain from wickedness. As I had suspected, I was not made for playing Sir Galahad.

'And what of you?' I asked, when I had at last spoken my fill. 'How have you amused yourself since Friday?'

'Badly,' she said shortly, her hand pausing over my temple. 'Sir

Lawrence Cunningham came to inspect us yesterday, see how his precious investment was going.'

I had forgotten that Cunningham was a part-owner of this establishment. There was a real anger in her voice, which in turn sparked some inexplicable tension within me.

'Did he abuse you?'

'Nothing above a few sharp words and a threat or two. Kind enough, by his custom.'

'We seem alike in that respect,' I mused. 'Neither of us seems able to avoid him.'

She nodded. 'I've worked for him since I was twelve – it was a terrible place to grow up. I cry when I think Samuel's still there. And I was lucky. After two years he got himself elected to Parliament and spent half the year in London with his important friends. Now he's always here.'

'Sir Lawrence was at Westminster?' My opinion of the electors of Dover fathomed new depths. No wonder the country was in such turmoil.

'It didn't work, though. He made the wrong friends, or said the wrong thing, or did something wrong.' I could quite imagine that Sir Lawrence might have been a little intense for the back-slapping club at Westminster if my fat-faced cousin, who held a seat, was at all representative. 'He came back spitting mad and cursing everyone you could name. After that none of us could avoid his rages.'

It certainly explained his perpetual temper.

'Anyhow,' said Isobel, stretching her back and pulling her dress straight, 'Miss Hoare's a bulldog, but she's not half so evil as him. And some day I'll be rid of him completely.'

'Me too,' I murmured fervently. 'Me too.'

We chatted longer, about what I cannot recall, and at some time my eyes began to close, and I started catching only the ends of sentences, asking her to repeat herself, losing myself in the middle of my own words. Her body was warm through the cotton shift, soothing and comforting; in those moments I felt stripped of my cares, my concerns and trials forgotten. For all I was an interloper in

Miss Hoare's fiercely guarded fortress, so long as I lay swaddled there I felt safe.

The unexpected sound of a baby crying opened my eyes.

'Is that . . . in here?' I asked drowsily.

'He's Nell's,' said Isobel. 'She got in a bit of trouble with a fisherman before Miss Hoare took her in.'

The thought of Miss Hoare seemed to stir Isobel; she lifted my head off her, and stood up. Outside the gabled window, the sky was now dark.

'You'd best go,' she said. 'You've been here too long already, and you never know when Miss Hoare'll be back. She may be better than Sir Lawrence Cunningham, but you'd not want her finding us here. Least of all on the Sabbath. Come on.'

She pulled me, unwilling, to my feet. I was reluctant to leave that gentle room, but she was already at the door, peering cautiously into the corridor. I could hear nothing save the gusting of the wind against the roof, and the baby still wailing in the distance. Isobel waved me forward.

'Let yourself out, and make sure you shut the door properly. Miss Hoare needed reviving last time it was left unlatched. And next time you want to pay a call, let me make sure it's safe before we meet. I'll not have you getting me thrown into the street.'

That seemed abrupt, and I was poised to protest, but at that moment she stopped my mouth by putting her lips firmly over it. My eyes widened; I was so surprised I almost resisted her. But already she was drawing back.

'And thank you, Martin.'

I came into the street. In the doorway of the facing house there glowed the soft haze of a pipe, but before I could discern its owner I was distracted by an unexpected and wholly unwelcome new arrival: Crawley. He did not seem particularly well humoured, and the sight of me did little to cheer him.

'Are you cleansed from your wickedness, Mr Jerrold?' he asked, gazing sceptically at the sign over the door behind me. From his stern manner, I found it hard to tell whether he spoke in jest or in earnest enquiry after my soul; I replied with some indistinct comment about my sins being ever before me.

He harumphed in response. 'And mine too, it seems,' he said with quiet anger. 'I am just escaped from a meeting with the army and the riding officers.'

'Surely a proud occasion,' I tried, walking the line between compliment and obsequy. 'After our triumph over the frigate.'

Crawley's deep-set scowl suggested otherwise. 'Captain Davenant's triumph, I believe you will find, Lieutenant. The riding officer reports that he witnessed several score smugglers assembled on the beach last night, but due to his lack of resources – or resourcefulness, one might say – he felt unable to apprehend them. Apparently, he avers, this is *my* failure, mitigated only by the fact that for all the assembled throng of villains, no ships arrived, so no illicit business was transacted.'

'Then it can hardly be deemed a failure.'

'To hear Sir Lawrence Cunningham tell it you would think otherwise. It hardly matters that an enemy frigate is worth a thousand local vagabonds in gaol; the responsibility for French ships in the Channel was Davenant's, so the glory for their capture is his also. My duty was to apprehend the smugglers, and in that, it seems, I have failed.'

Although the weariness in his voice touched me, I confess that the first thought in my mind was relief, that for once where there was blame to be affixed I was not its object. A more sober second thought reminded me that blame was ever a fluid element, that it could easily slide from a commander onto the shoulders of his subordinates. But by then, I fear, my face had already betrayed me, for Crawley's head was suddenly thrust very close against mine, his skin unsettlingly luminous in the lamplight.

'Do not think, Lieutenant, that you will profit from this episode. There will be no repercussions for now, and if there are, then you are as bound to *Orestes*' fate as any of us.'

Clearly he had misjudged my ambition, which would more than satisfy itself by simply escaping censure for any length of time. But I could hardly say as much to Crawley with dignity, not least because he was already speaking again.

'Also, Lieutenant, there is to be an assembly tomorrow evening. Some dismal local affair, I believe, but the good gentlefolk organizing it have chosen to dedicate it to celebrating Captain Davenant's glorious victory. No doubt they feel that thus they will draw a broader attendance of grateful Englishmen. As subordinate officers in the action, our attendance will naturally be expected.'

At that moment, I almost felt sorry for the old puritan. Drinking, dancing, gambling, not to mention, I hoped, the window-dressed daughters of the local gentry, and all to the self-appropriated glory of Captain Davenant. No wonder Crawley looked so grim as he jammed his hat low over his head and stalked off.

12

I WAS EATING A SOLITARY BREAKFAST THE NEXT MORNING, LAMENTing the inn's unfortunate pretence at coffee and trying to drown the taste with marmalade, when Isaac reappeared.

'None of that,' I snapped, fending off his advances with the coffee pot.

''T ain't that,' he sniffed. 'It's this.'

He pulled out a sealed, folded paper that seemed to have become unaccountably grubby in the short journey from the courtyard to the breakfast room. I took it, and suddenly the quaking in my stomach was no longer merely caused by the coffee, for the imprint of an anchor wound with rope, stamped into the red wax which spilled across the paper, left me in little doubt as to its provenance. Trembling, I cracked it open.

'Jerrold!' The salutation had lost none of its accusatory force, though he had thoughtfully included another sentence of the usual opprobrium to allow no mistaking his meaning. Then: 'It is a week now since I learned of your ignominy, and if in that time you have not stirred yourself so much as to write an acknowledgement of my concerns, I have not sat so idle. The *Centurion* sails from the Downs for Port Royal, Jamaica, this Tuesday next, and I have arranged with her captain, a man with the sternest commitment to discipline, that you shall take passage with him as supernumerary. Once in Jamaica, the port admiral shall dispense with you as he sees most fitting, weighing your merits and punishing your offences.

'If you are minded to escape this doom, do not think that you may appeal to your mother's credulous goodwill this time. The only path of salvation open to you is to cleanse your name – which, though I do not carry, I feel I bear like a martyr his cross – of the stink and opprobrium you have drawn down upon it.

'I remain, &c . . .'

Such was my shock at this onslaught that it was some moments before I realized I had, unthinkingly, taken another deep gulp of the execrable coffee.

A brisk walk along the sea-front to the docks and several doses of chill air forced down my throat by a blustering wind restored my spirits a little. Only a few figures straggled about the streets, most of them moving at a strange, oblique angle to counter the gusting breeze. It was too late for the fishermen, I supposed, and too early for many others to be out.

Not aboard *Orestes*, though: her decks swarmed with activity, and already they were lifting out the fractured stump of the mast in a tangle of lines and rigging. Crawley, as usual, was in the thick of it.

'Keep clear, Mr Jerrold,' he bellowed as I approached. 'You'll find more than a headache if you fell yourself with this.'

As if to illustrate his words, the men on the tackle let the mast-head drop several feet closer. It jerked in the breeze, bucking like an animal on its tether.

'Am I required here, sir?'

Between the rattle of commands and the pulse of the wind, it was hard to hold any conversation at all.

'What's that?'

Crawley was scowling, but I was immediately forgotten as the mast suddenly lurched around, sending the men around it tumbling to the deck.

'Belay that, belay that!' Crawley shouted frantically. 'Mr Ducker, get men on the lines *now*!'

When it seemed the rogue spar had been tamed, I tried again. 'Excuse me, sir, am I—'

Crawley spun around, his face creased with anger. 'Blast it, Mr Jerrold, but if you are to be nothing but a damned nuisance then kindly remove yourself from interrupting our labours.' Without further comment, he turned his back on me.

I was shocked, as much by the fact that he had been moved to such language as by the fact that he had directed it at me. In front of the men, too. Clearly the insults he had suffered at the meeting the previous night, and the prospect of an evening toasting Davenant's health, still weighed on him. At least, I hoped so. I could not but wonder whether I had committed some grievous, unwitting sin that had given offence.

Across the harbour a large white belfry surmounted the tall walls of Mazard's Bank. I had seen it only from the landward side before, on the evening when Mrs Pring's recollection had taken me there; now I could see six-foot-high letters painted on the brickwork proclaiming the name with commercial enthusiasm. It reminded me that the trail of Laminak's and Vitos's last movements had ended there; it also reminded me of Nevell's tales on *Orestes*' deck. If vast profits were being amassed from the trade in contraband, then the smugglers would need a reliable banker. And they could hardly have failed to consider Mazard, such, I reflected as I looked up at those giant letters, was the power of his advertising.

Leaving Crawley thrashing about on the deck, I wandered round the harbour, crossed the little bridge over the stinking pent, and came up against the bank's stern frontage. At first I thought it was closed again, for my initial push on the door yielded nothing; it was only when I essayed a second heave, uncharitable thoughts about bankers' hours uppermost in my mind, that the heavy oak reluctantly swung inwards, admitting me to the gloom of the sanctum.

A doorman stopped me almost immediately. Why he did not stand outside, where he might have been of some aid opening that lump of a door, I did not enquire, for his build did not invite an examination of his methods.

'May I assist you, sir?' he asked with solicitous menace. 'Do you have business with the bank?'

'Lieutenant Martin Jerrold of his Majesty's navy,' I told him curtly, my sharpness pricked by his vague resemblance to Stubb the constable. 'And my business here is his Majesty's business.' After a fashion.

The doorman's bulk curtained off everything behind him, but there must have been someone within for I heard an irritable voice calling over his shoulder, 'Show the man in, Belson.'

He stepped back, admitting me to the room beyond. It was small, much smaller than the façade of the building would have suggested, and possessed of none of the gilded indulgences common in such institutions. It was a wise economy, for ornamental flourishes would have been thoroughly wasted on a room with no windows and only a quartet of stuttering oil lamps hanging on chains from the ceiling. By their meagre light I could see a long table set opposite me; behind it I fancied there sat a stiff figure, the only other living creature there. He might have had spindly fingers, a beaked nose and calculating eyes, but such a description would rest more on my conception of how a bank clerk should look than on any features I actually observed through the murk. His voice, though, would have fitted such a portrait handsomely.

'Lieutenant Jerrold? George Fichet. How may I be of service? If you wish to deposit your prize money – perhaps from *le Thermidor*? – I am afraid that we deal only with agents.' He spoke deliberately, and terribly slowly; so much so that listening became a trial, and I soon longed to close his sentences for him.

'My seven pounds a month sadly leave me without the capital to make a deposit,' I said, trying to affect good cheer. 'I have come, on the King's business, to make enquiries of those who do. In particular—'

But Fichet was holding up a hand in protest. 'Mr Jerrold,' he reproved me. 'We are a bank, not a newspaper. The business of our clients is always in the strictest confidence.'

'Even when they're dead?'

The stiff back flinched not at all. 'Even when they are dead. There are wills. Estates. Descendants. Widows. All must be protected.'

'Of course. But if the client was murdered, then it may be in the interests of his estate to uncover the truth behind his death. Even if it requires sifting through his financial records.'

Fichet tutted. 'Perhaps. Upon a personal instruction from the client.'

'He's dead,' I repeated, swallowing my exasperation.

'His descendants, then, or his executors.' He was implacable.

'But if there were no descendants,' I pressed, 'and if there were implications, strong implications, that he had been involved in illegal activities, then you would naturally be keen to seek out the truth of the matter.'

I exaggerated, of course: no banker ever wants to find out exactly how his customers earn the riches to make their deposits, for it might tarnish his reputation. Worse, he could be forced to give the money back. I guessed that just such considerations exercised Fichet's grinding thoughts during the ensuing pause.

'Naturally,' he said at last. 'And naturally we take great care whom we choose to have bank with us.' I wondered if by 'great care' he meant the ogre on the door. 'But without permission from the man's descendants – or, at the very extreme, a request from the magistrate – we can do nothing for you. You, after all, are not known here. You yourself could be a criminal.' He blew air through his nose – I think it was an attempt at laughter.

I wondered whether he was alluding to the accusations against me. Probably, I decided. He had after all known all about the *Thermidor*.

'I could be a criminal, but I am not. I am an officer of his Majesty and—'

'The two are not mutually exclusive, you know.' Again the snort.

'And I demand you extend me your co-operation.' He had me riled now. 'Beginning with any information you may hold on two gentlemen named Messrs Vitos and Laminak.'

I believe I could have spent the rest of the day grappling with his obstructions, and with no window to mark the passing hours perhaps I would have stayed all night as well, but at that moment there came the tinkling of a bell from within the woodwork behind him, bright tones like warm sunlight in that sombre room.

They made far more of an impact on Mr Fichet than anything I had yet said. With a hasty apology, he leaped to his feet and retreated to the far wall where an unseen door swung silently open, casting a slab of yellow light over the floor. Whether it had been deliberately concealed in the woodwork, or merely masked by the gloom, I could not tell, but Fichet vanished through it into a corridor beyond. A cough behind me, a sly reminder of the doorman's continued presence, discouraged me from following him on my own initiative. Instead I stood there, wondering what new intrigues this presaged.

I was not long with my thoughts, for Fichet quickly reappeared.

'Mr Mazard delivers his compliments,' he said, his eyes raised like a schoolboy reciting his text. 'In a matter so important as assisting the King's officer, he feels it would be remiss of him to do otherwise than pay you his personal, most assiduous attention. He requests your presence in his private office, where he may speak plainly without agitating our other clients.'

Who those other clients might be I could not guess; certainly they were nowhere in evidence in that room. But Fichet, clearly agitated himself, had already placed a bony hand on my shoulder and was steering me around his desk and towards the open doorway. I moved hastily, for there was something dead in his touch that I was suddenly anxious to escape.

'You will find his office at the head of the stairs on your right,' Fichet added as I stepped into the passage.

The walls were painted in a rich, glossy cream, reflecting back the light of the candles that lined its alcoves and filling the space with a warm, mellifluous light which dizzied me after the murk of the main room. Following Fichet's instructions, I made for the stairs, which rose in a steeply curving spiral a little way down the corridor. Moving through this silent, inner sanctum, I felt my breath begin to quicken; the beating of my heart seemed unusually prominent. Nor were my apprehensions eased when I heard the sturdy click of the door closing behind me. Looking back, I could only just discern the two grooves in the smooth wall where it had been. There did not appear to be any handle on my side.

'Jesus,' I muttered quietly, for I did not have the courage to break the stillness surrounding me. But what did I have to fear? This man was one of the premier financiers in Dover, a bastion of society and a valued voice in the town's counsels. Even if that spoke more of his wealth than his morality, surely it lifted him above the sort of man who would do injury to a naval officer.

Still unconvinced, I mounted the twisting stairs, trying to shrink from the loud creak of my every footstep. They led higher than I had expected, two storeys at least, and ended not on a landing or at a door, but by emerging suddenly into a bright, exposed room. I blinked, and looked around as my head rose into it, for it seemed I had entered the summit of a lighthouse rather than a banker's office: the room was round, and constructed entirely of large glass panels set in a thin white frame. There was an uninterrupted view through these windows, of the thickly clustered roofs and smoking chimneys of the town in some directions, of the jumbled masts and spars of the harbour in another. It was like some hothouse, or orangery, and despite the coolness of the day outside, all was warmth within. This, I realized, must be what I had taken for a belfry atop the building.

Bringing my gaze back within the confines of the glass room, I saw the twin mahogany pillars of a large desk to my left, and a pair of daintily shod feet crossed between them. As I mounted the final steps and raised myself into the chamber, my eyes followed the line of the legs, up over silken calves, carefully tailored white breeches, and then, above the desk, to a slender, almost feminine body dressed in the lace cuffs and angular coat of the French style.

'Mr Jerrold.' His voice was deeper than I'd expected, and quite thick. 'Henry Mazard.' He did not rise, nor did he offer me a chair.

I looked into the face: a broad oval, with features that seemed almost flat against the smooth expanse of skin. His eyes were wide and lazy, with a bored emptiness that could in no way be mistaken for dullness. I thought I detected a trace of a foreign declension in his words, as well as hauteur. I returned his cool stare with what I hoped was a nonchalance of my own.

'I am grateful to you for receiving me so promptly.'

'My clerk tells me you have come on a matter of importance.'

'Indeed.' I tried to arrange myself into a more commanding posture. 'A matter of the greatest importance. It concerns—'

'The dead man you found at the cliff? Mr Vitos?'

Mazard widened his eyes into a look of artificial concern. I tried not to display my irritation at his interruption.

'Mr Vitos, exactly. And his companion, a Mr Laminak. Laminak,' I repeated, my words garbling themselves as I found myself unable to reciprocate the composure that met me. 'Did you know him?'

Mazard's teeth flashed like knives. 'I did not. My good friend Sir Lawrence Cunningham apprised me of the details of his misfortune. And your part in it.'

'They are alleged to have been your customers.'

He twitched his head. 'Sadly, Mr Jerrold, I can only repeat what my clerk has already told you. We have no customers by those names.'

'They said they were coming here,' I persisted. 'Last Sunday. Their landlady remembers them saying—'

'On a Sunday?' Mazard gave an amused giggle. 'Please, Mr Jerrold, we are not Jews here. I was in church, naturally. Your landlady is mistaken.'

'Which church?' His words were too well oiled for me to credit them; I would not let him glide away from my enquiries without some attempt to pin him down.

'I have a private chapel at my home.' He lifted his hands an inch off the table, and seemed to study his knuckles.

'I may have mistaken the date,' I allowed, retreating a little to give myself room. 'Or the landlady herself may have misremembered.' Though I suspected Mrs Pring's memory would be quite as tight as her bodice.

'Unless you have also mistaken their names, the date is of little consequence. We pride ourselves on the intimate service we provide our clients, Mr Jerrold – they are all well known to us. And yet . . .' He held up an indulgent hand to stem my inevitable contradiction. 'If it will satisfy your curiosity, Mr Jerrold, as an officer of the navy which we all hold in such irreproachable esteem, I will do my utmost to put your fears to rest.'

I did not see where his hand went, but from down below I heard the delicate chimes of the little bell. Almost immediately, Fichet's head appeared by my foot, staring up from the stairwell.

'The ledger, Mr Fichet,' said Mazard. He folded his hands together as the obedient head vanished. 'I shall open my books to you, Mr Jerrold. As you may know, a banker may as well open his soul.'

'Which yields the higher return?'

A tolerably awkward silence ensued, during which Mazard's flat face showed not a twitch of emotion, while I dropped my hands into my pockets and looked self-consciously out through the surrounding windows. A large frigate, not unlike *Lancelot* – though at this distance it really could have been any frigate – was beating slowly down the Channel; nearer to shore, dozens of light vessels – snows, pinks, sloops, hoys – swarmed across the fractured waves, tossing precipitously in the squally conditions. Many of them, I guessed, would be heading round the headlands and up to provision the squadron at Deal.

'It is an indisputable advantage being able to survey my little fleet from this eyrie,' said Mazard, breaking the silence. 'My crews know that they are always watched by a higher authority.'

I turned my gaze on to the docks below us, where a handsome new brigantine was taking on a sizeable cargo.

'Your merchantman?' I asked, pointing.

'Indeed, her too,' said Mazard. 'But equally the lighter vessels over there, carrying beer and bread to your fellow sailors in the Downs.' My face must have registered its confusion openly. 'The navy has granted me the contract to transport their local supplies. In partnership with the noble Sir Lawrence Cunningham, of course.'

I would have been curious to learn what other businesses he and Cunningham had contrived together, but before I could form any more questions a dusty Mr Fichet re-emerged from below, staggering under the weight of the enormous book he carried. I was impressed he had managed to negotiate the stairs with it, for even Mazard's stout desk shuddered as he put it down. As he stepped aside, I saw him gingerly sucking on a finger that had been under the book.

With some effort, Mazard turned the ledger around so that it faced me, and prised open the leather-bound cover. The paper was very thin, and it took him some while to flick through the pages and find the place he sought.

'*Voilà*,' he said with a broad, inviting smile. 'Our transactions for the last week but one. Naturally, you will find none on the Sunday. And I do not think your Mr Vitos was in a condition to be banking after that, as you will appreciate. But if it will satisfy you, you may inspect our records as your conscience demands.'

I bent forward and squinted at the narrow writing, the cascading columns of times and dates and names and amounts. Naturally, I did not expect to find anything pertaining to Vitos or Laminak – I quite believed that Mazard knew his customers well enough not to reveal it if they had banked there – but I was willing to play along with this charade of co-operation. And I was intrigued by the sums of money which seemed to run through his hands as a matter of course. Many of the entries were for amounts in excess of a hundred pounds, and a few even required a fourth figure to be squeezed into the confines of the credit column, though most of the names meant nothing to me. With a single, notable exception.

'Caleb Drake?' I read the name aloud. 'An extraordinary man indeed, if he is in a position to be taking eighteen pounds a month so long after his death.'

'The estate of Caleb Drake. The upkeep of his memorial, which requires some care.' Mazard's face resumed its habitual set. 'But if you have nothing more to do than idly pry into the business of my honest customers, whose privacy and discretion are their greatest assets, then I will ask you to finish your examination of the book.'

'I see you have many customers abroad.' I ignored his invitation to leave. 'None of them in France, I trust?'

'These are turbulent times for the citizens of the continent, particularly those of wealth and position. A sound bank is to them the gravest necessity. I doubt they would be amused if they knew an upstart officer, one with the most slanderous stains on his reputation, had tried to involve himself in their private affairs.'

I lifted the book's cover and let it drop shut. I took satisfaction from seeing the glass walls shiver with the bang it made.

Much though I enjoyed irritating Mazard, I was relieved to escape his high nest unscathed. For all his smiles and courtesy, there was an uncomfortable chill about him that made me uneasy, made me feel glad to have passed the door without having my limbs ripped off for my impertinence. He was that sort of man.

He was also the sort of man to whom dissembling would come easy, I guessed, although with such a skill it was inevitable that I would be unable to tell. Certainly it was entirely possible that Vitos had been trailing a herring across his tracks when he mentioned Mazard's Bank, but if he *had* gone on the Sunday morning then he ought to be the sort of customer Mazard, or at the very least his clerk, would know. The ledger was an irrelevance: although I presumed that every transaction would be entered somewhere, I had no illusions that the book he had shown me had been exhaustive. Of course, he might have been an honest citizen extending me complete co-operation – that too would have explained his every action, and in a flawless light. But that would make him unique among my acquaintances in Dover, and I very much doubted a banker would take that honour. None of which inclined me to trust him for a second, but short of trying to break into that miniature fortress when he was away, I had little prospect of proving my suspicions well founded or otherwise.

It was still well before noon when I regained the street, and I doubted that there had yet been time for Crawley's temper to cool. Rather than risk returning to *Orestes*, I loitered among the shops and stalls of the town, enquiring where I could whether anyone had seen Vitos or Laminak the previous Sunday. It was something I had thus far resisted doing, on the principle that it was unlikely to turn up anything novel, and my prediction proved depressingly accurate. The shops, of course, had all been shut, and could tell me nothing, though few let me escape without bombarding me instead with endorsements for their produce, their prices, their 'what-I-could-do-for-a-naval-gentleman-like-yourself' offers. Once I saw Stubb walking along the far side of the street – not nearly far enough, in a town like Dover – but he ostentatiously ignored me. Perhaps he had some urgent paving to attend to. And so, after a fruitless hour and the dozenth offer of a pair of patent mittens, I ambled back to the harbour.

Snargate Street seemed busier as I reached its western end. Perhaps it was just the bustle of midday business, but I felt a definite current in the crowd that seemed to be pulling towards the docks. My impression was confirmed as I emerged onto the wharf where *Orestes* was moored: here there were scores of people, hemmed around the walls of the battery and spilling over onto the shingle beach; others lined the rope walk beyond. All had their backs to the town, and stared intently out to sea. From their appearance I could see that although their ranks were peppered with tars and stevedores, many of them were the ordinary folk of the town. What spectacle could have drawn them here?

I pushed my way to the upper edge of the beach, where the slope of the pebbles kept those in front of me from blocking my view. It was a precarious position, for the crowd behind me jostled for a similar advantage, but I managed, through unscrupulous use of my elbows, to maintain my place.

'Careful,' said a voice beside me.

I tried to ignore it, lest an exchange with the man turn violent, but as a hand grabbed my arm I instinctively turned to see who had reproached me. To my great surprise, it was the postman from the French frigate, Nevell.

'Carrying a letter for me, are you?' I asked, unsure where I stood with him.

He grinned. 'No letters, I'm afraid. Actually, I'm due to return to London this afternoon on the mail coach. But I heard that the invasion was happening, and thought it would be a shame to miss it.'

I wondered if I'd heard him right, but following his arm, and the gaze of the assembled throng, I saw his meaning. Half a league or so out to sea, her sails taut in the snapping breeze, a small coastal lugger was tacking her way towards us. Doubtless a dozen such vessels beat the same path every day, but few of them, I'd have wagered, would have had a French *tricouleur* jacked to their mastheads. No wonder the crowds were out in force.

'If it's an invasion, he's hidden the rest of his fleet well,' Nevell observed.

'She'll be under our guns soon enough, too.'

In fact, she was probably in range already, for the Dover shoreline had batteries every few hundred yards between the bluffs, as well as the guns in the castle and on the heights to the west.

But that was merely the introduction to the spectacle, for now, from behind the headland, there slowly emerged the bow of a man-of-war, her sails set to the royals and all her guns run out. Water foamed against her prow; above it the gilded sword and shield of her figurehead shone even at this distance. *Lancelot.*

A cheer went up from the crowd as they recognized their champion, the hero of a hundred battles and the scourge of the French.

'Is this genuine?' I asked Nevell, more confused than ever. 'Or does Davenant intend to re-enact his triumph over the perfidious French for the entertainment of the people of Dover?'

'I've a notion he's not come to fight this time,' replied Nevell.

As if in confirmation, the next act of the drama now presented itself: the lugger's *tricouleur* fell to the deck, and a plain white pennant was run up in its place.

'A surrender?' I asked, mesmerized by the scene.

'A parley, I think.'

Whichever it was, Davenant responded almost immediately – so immediately, in fact, that it seemed he must have anticipated it. Tiny figures could be seen racing along *Lancelot*'s yards; with admirable precision her sails were hauled in and furled until her sticks were bare and her headway ceased. There was a plume of spray by the cathead as her anchor plunged into the waves.

'We are fortunate to have Captain Davenant, really,' said Nevell, his face as straight as a beam. 'Who knows what peril he rescues us from? And now it seems he prepares to board.'

An enterprising hawker was, for a penny, offering a half-minute's gaze through his telescope, but I could see well enough with my naked eye. *Lancelot*'s pinnace had come out from under her far side and was pulling for the French ship, which had followed suit in striking her canvas. She bobbed in the swell while *Lancelot*'s boat approached. I fancied I could see Davenant's cocked hat in her stern.

'The intrepid captain takes his hard-won prize.'

Nevell intoned it solemnly, but I could see the mischief in his face. Though no doubt the caption would appear as fact in the papers tomorrow, for Davenant, if he it was, had climbed the ladder now and disappeared into the blur of the lugger's deck.

'Perhaps he's defecting to the French,' I said hopefully. That would be something for the *Gazette* to explain, and for Crawley to cheer.

'If he's passing on our secrets, he could certainly do it with greater subtlety.'

Nevell had a broad grin on his face as though it amused him tremendously. I too found the whole scene so improbable that I could not but enjoy it, and wait to see its outcome.

Davenant did not stay long aboard the lugger: within minutes, while the attention of the crowd was still rapt, he could be seen descending back into his boat. A large chest was hoisted down after him.

'Replenishing his wardrobe with the latest French fashions?' offered Nevell.

'He'll have to pay duty on them then when he comes ashore. Maybe it's a gift from Buonaparte – a crate of champagne for the King, with his respects, and apologies for being an impertinent tyrant.'

'And a notice of surrender, and his solemn declaration to present himself at Newgate in a month?'

'Unless, of course, it's a decoration from an admiring French nation, to the gallant captain who has so marvellously and single-handedly thwarted them.'

'Or maybe,' said Nevell, more soberly now, 'it has more to do with having a peacemonger in the government now. With Pitt out and Fox in, I'll wager a great deal more than you can afford that that lugger is passing on correspondence to negotiate a truce, maybe an end to the war.'

I looked at him. 'For a man who's spent the last fortnight in a French gaol, Nevell, you've a remarkable knowledge of what the new ministry's up to.'

'Of course,' he said simply. 'I'm the one who delivers their letters.'

Lancelot's boat had disappeared into her lee now, while the lugger had hoisted her sails and put about, the blank pennant still streaming above her. The spectators, concluding that the entertainment was over, thinned; the man with the telescope now advertised the meat pies he had in his satchel.

Nevell clapped me on the shoulder.

'Goodbye,' he said, genuine warmth in his voice. 'And good luck. I shall follow your story with interest, especially if it does prove to bear on my own concerns.'

'Which reminds me,' I said. 'I paid a visit to Mr Mazard this morning, the banker.' I pointed Nevell's attention to the brick building across the harbour. With the sun reflected off the dazzling glass turret, it was impossible to know if Mazard was still within, but I suddenly had the uncomfortable feeling that he must be up there, watching. 'He was kind enough to show me his ledger. Naturally everything was most discreet, but I think I can tell you, without infringing a confidence, that he may well know a great deal about large sums of money passing through Dover. I believe that was your concern.'

Nevell frowned. 'Indeed it was. Although a small bank in Dover oughtn't to have the capital . . .' He shook his head. 'You may well have served me a useful turn, Jerrold, and I shall enquire further. Much further, perhaps. But now I must be making for London, and I fear I may already be delaying the coach. I should be glad to hear of anything further you apprehend on the matter, though.'

'I shall write if I discover anything. I assume the post will find you?'

He laughed. 'Indeed. Though be careful what you write – you never know who might be reading it.'

He shook my hand, then slipped into the crowd and vanished.

I crossed back to where *Orestes* was berthed. Crawley was standing on a bollard, a telescope still trained on *Lancelot*, and I had to cough several times before he opened his free eye and noticed me.

'Back, are you?' he grunted. 'Well, I suppose there is a limit to the mischief you can do now.' A shining new mainmast had been stepped aboard *Orestes*, its novelty all the more obvious in the absence of any rigging to clutter it. 'I had thought to send you with the boat to examine the beach where the riding officer claims to have seen the smugglers,' he continued, 'but I fear there is now not the time before nightfall, before this *assembly*.' His voice managed to imply that its organization was somehow my doing. 'However, you may be of some use on board. There's still work enough to be done. Such as we may complete before Davenant's little triumph.'

13

THE ASSEMBLY, TO WHICH CRAWLEY INSISTED I GO, MAY HAVE BEEN IN honour of Davenant – 'and those intrepid men who aided him', as the handbill said – but the noble fellow had graciously agreed that the proceeds from the evening should be donated to the Soup Society who, in anticipation of a good night's takings, had requisitioned rooms at the Bull, an inn not far from my own.

'Course they would,' sniffed Isaac, when I told him where I was bound.

I was dressed in my full regalia, white cuffs and lapels gleaming with pipeclay, and a ridiculous hanger by my side. I was not sure whether taking it into a room with Sir Lawrence would be a good idea, but I held out hope that it would look heroic enough for the company to stand me a few drinks. Isaac certainly seemed impressed, but he had an adolescent's fascination with all things violent and dangerous and was not to be relied on. Though he was more critical of my destination.

'Bull's owned by that Mr Mazard, ain't it,' he explained when I quizzed him. 'An' 'e's the one what's in charge of the Soup Society.'

It seemed I was fated to cross paths with Mazard again that day. Still, for all Isaac's cynicism, the rooms seemed to suit well enough when I arrived – late. They backed on to the house's public bar, but there was a private door for those whose gentility would quaver at the prospect of walking through a tavern, and from the cut of the ladies' gowns I surmised there were few problems with the draught. The decorations were less to my taste: several suits of armour had been hauled out of some dungeon, possibly the castle's, and the refreshments were laid out on a round table with a large red shield painted on it. A miniature of a man-of-war floated in a silver bowl, heeling over against its rim; it looked as though it was shipping soup through its gunports, and might soon sink. Scores of candles lined the walls and hung in the chandeliers, but nothing gleamed so bright as Davenant's twin epaulettes in the middle of the room, surrounded by a lesser constellation of admiring diamonds, pearls, jewels and gold. I avoided him, and made instead for the card room in the far corner. No-one brought me a drink.

Although the green-topped tables were all in place, the card room was empty when I looked in. The whist players were still loitering around the dim edges of the ballroom, trying to make up their rubbers without allowing in any of the sharpers who were doubtless present. I've never had much of a hand for cards myself – my luck generally disallows it – so it's always been one vice I've kept free of (*pace* my uncle, who maintains my disreputation is complete). And I was in little mood for conversation, which I feared would inevitably draw itself to the hero of the hour.

I had just asked a girl to dance and been rebuffed – the gentility of course had their daughters pinned onto their dance-cards like butterflies to protect them from rakes like me – when I heard a voice calling me. I turned, and for a moment did not recognize her in her high-throated gown, as modest as her previous dress had been scandalous. Though curiously, this was the more alluring.

'Lady Cunningham.' I bowed. 'An honour and a pleasure.' Though the thought that her husband must be near was less pleasurable.

'Lieutenant. Lieutenant.' Her carriage was very stiff, a far cry from her previous languor, but her voice remained carelessly loose. 'Samuel tells me you got your clothes back.'

'Yes, thank you, milady.' I remembered the rage it had provoked, and wondered whether Sir Lawrence treated her any better. 'Is your husband here tonight?'

She snapped up a hand, and let it fall limply back. 'Somewhere, I think. We are not . . .' She hiccuped. 'Do you find me beautiful?'

A courteous answer was as impossible as the question was unexpected. 'I, ah, find you . . .' I tried again. 'I find you most . . .' Her eyes were fixed deep into me, addling my thoughts further. 'Which is to say, I find you most admirable.'

Her head nodded off its stiff perch. 'Admirable,' she repeated. 'Abmiradle. The admiral finds me admirable. Do you, admirable?'

'You know so.' Edging backwards, I bumped into the man behind me and felt a wetness trickling down the back of my breeches. 'I do beg your forgiveness,' I began, though it was I who would be sitting in a pool of punch for the rest of the evening. But my apology faltered on my lips as I saw the tall, black-suited mass of Sir Lawrence louring over me.

'This is admirable Jerrold,' giggled his wife, heedless of the pink liquid dripping off his cuff. 'He finds me admiral.'

I had hoped that Cunningham would have grown accustomed to such *bêtises*, would laugh them off with the carelessness they deserved, but instead his sunken face, perilously close to the chandelier above, flushed crimson.

'The devil you do,' he growled. 'You not only spill my drink, but also abuse my wife? What sort of gentleman do you take yourself for?' He paused. 'As if I need ask.'

That was unfair; I could have said far worse about his wife, and accurately too. But this was a time for retreat, not combat, though I still had my hanger if he did turn lunatic. The vein on the side of his neck was throbbing most alarmingly.

'The room is noisy and misunderstandings are easy. If Lady Cunningham found me uncouth, it cannot have been intentional.'

'What?' demanded Cunningham. 'You forget, sir, that I am still the magistrate of this town, and I can have you cast back in gaol for Gibble to paw at my pleasure.'

And pleasure it would be, I had no doubt: he was visibly salivating at the threat.

'If I have given offence, I can only apologize, and assure you of my honourable intentions.'

I could see that he enjoyed my squirming, and for a time I would do so to keep the peace, but my patience was not boundless. Sir Lawrence, though, seemed in no mood for moderation.

'And if I don't hang you for murder, I have no doubt I shall soon see you swinging for treason. I've a good idea why my hard-won intelligence is so often squandered: it has been perfectly obvious since you arrived. Even without the bodies.' My fingers were now playing over the hilt of my sword, but it did not curb Sir Lawrence's temper. Quite the contrary: he laughed openly. 'If you so much as show an inch of steel in this building, I'll have you in court for a breach of the peace.'

His wife had been thankfully muted through much of our exchange, but she chose that moment to re-enter the conversation.

'You'd better not get on the wrong side of Admiral Jerrold's sword, Sir Lawrence,' she taunted him. 'A mighty weapon, is it not?'

Another moment and I believe I would have found myself plaintiff in a case of upsetting the peace, but Sir Lawrence was slow to react, and in the seconds while his chest swelled, a light tinkling spread from the centre of the room to silence the assembled company. Cunningham was frozen in his rage, but even he could not erupt in front of an attentive audience. Very deliberately, I turned my back on him – it took some courage – to see the cause of my deliverance.

'My ladies and gentlemen,' began a stuffy voice from between two suits of armour. Quite unexpectedly, I had been rescued by Mazard, who stood there eyeing the crowd with his usual cold reserve. 'On behalf of the Soup Society, I welcome you to our little ball, and thank you for your presence here.'

A few of the ladies, doubtless those who thought this the pinnacle of social occasion, tapped their gloved hands together.

'And of course, we must thank Captain Davenant, the "Lion of England", as the papers style him this morning.'

The paper in question was the *Kentish Gazette*, the sort of rag even I could get a favourable notice in if I had a mind to.

'He honours us with his presence here, and we are delighted that he has generously agreed to bestow his favour – for which, need I say, there are many suitors – on our gathering this evening.'

Fine words, though there was no warmth in the delivery; indeed, to my ear, the whole speech seemed spiked with irony, though I admit I might have chosen to hear it so. But the crowd liked it well enough, and offered Davenant a sustained burst of applause which he took with a raised eyebrow and a modest bow. I imagined the india-rubbers would be out on more than a few dance-cards.

'As will be known to many of you,' continued Mazard, 'the Soup Society was established to allow its members to subscribe to the feeding of the deserving poor. For five shillings, a member can nominate a worthy pauper to receive our weekly offering.'

I wondered why all this would appeal to Mazard: surely he would rather turn five shillings into a crown than into a full-bellied beggar.

'You will know also that we at Mazard & Company administer the Soup Society at the behest of its late founder. I am sure that he would appreciate most greatly having Captain Davenant as a fellow patron, and so I ask you to raise your glasses to our two great benefactors, Captain Davenant and Caleb Drake.'

It was neatly done, with a cattish smile and a jaunty cock of the glass which left Davenant speechless, while the rest of the room erupted in appreciative laughter and applause. Davenant was blushing furiously; he looked as though he wanted to say something to extricate himself from such infamous company, but the attention of the room had subsided back into a general hubbub and he was left stranded. He also looked as though he might need a drink, so being a charitable soul I made my way over to him.

The adoring crowd of provincial princesses had temporarily abated, perhaps because he himself no longer seemed such good company: his chin was down, and his whole uniform appeared to have lost some of its habitual starch.

'Cheer up, Captain Davenant,' I said jovially, filling a glass with punch for him. 'Drake's dead, so at least you won't have to shake him by the hand.'

'It was a base duplicity,' he complained. 'Surely they must know that any association with that villain Drake could be most unhelpful to my reputation.'

'Perhaps they cannot conceive that anything could tarnish your glory, sir.' My delivery was not completely sincere, but he was too fretted to notice.

'Sometimes I wonder what we fight for, you know, Lieutenant. A rabble of merchants and their fat daughters who cannot see goodness but they sink their claws in. Grasping, vulgar, insatiable.'

I wondered if these were the same people who had subscribed to that well-gilded sword he wore at his belt, or who wrote earnest letters to the newspapers wondering how a noble warrior like Captain Davenant could have been overlooked for higher command when so many lesser men flew their own pennant.

'Doubtless it is the burden of fame,' I said, offering him my full support. And another glass.

'It is, you know,' Davenant replied seriously. 'Now, take a man like Lieutenant Crawley. There's a man nobody would ever trouble to trouble. And why? Because he hangs on to the scraps of his commission by his fingertips. If anyone hears of him it is bound to be for one reason only, and one they'd sooner forget.'

'That being?'

Davenant took another long draught from his glass and handed it back to me. '*Glorious*, of course.'

For a moment I was thrown. If this was his true opinion of Crawley, he had kept it well concealed.

'Anyone who scuppers his ship like that merits all the derision he finds, to my mind, and if it doesn't do to kick a dog when he's down, then it doesn't do to keep him under the table either.'

At last, through a haze of punch, I began to understand many things. 'He was aboard the *Glorious*?' I asked in wonder. It certainly made my own transgressions seem positively benign.

'Had the watch,' confirmed Davenant, who should probably have been more discreet. 'Stories differ, of course, but you can't escape the facts. Cracked her open like a walnut on a rock off Brest. More than eighty men dead or captured. That, of course, is how I met him, in that blighted hole at Verdun where they took him.'

This was news. Even I knew the story of the *Glorious*, the most infamous casualty of our blockade of the French ports. The thought of her fate had given me no end of sleepless nights on my own station off the enemy coast. But that Crawley had been mixed up in it – almost at the helm, if Davenant was to be believed – was quite another matter. I was astonished he had been gifted any command at all after that. No wonder he had had such suspicions of my appointment.

'That's what people remember about Crawley,' continued Davenant, evidently mistaking my shock for rapt attention. 'But what fewer know, and perhaps more should, is what went on at Verdun.'

'And what was that?' I felt like a spectator at a street brawl: disgusted, but compelled to know more.

'Well, it was all rumour, of course.' By now Davenant's diction rivalled Lady Cunningham's. 'But he was queer out there, stayed away from the usual society, you understand?' I could understand perfectly why Crawley might prefer his privacy, recently shipwrecked and with only men like Davenant for company. 'So naturally, when it was whispered that one of our officers was offering his services to the French, all eyes were on Crawley.'

This sounded like malicious tattle to me – not that I mind it as a rule, but I needed little imagination to see that Crawley, in a distressed state, would not have fitted well with Davenant's circle. Davenant, however, seemed to place great store by it.

'That is why I find myself in agreement with the old toad over there.' He jerked a finger to where Sir Lawrence and Mazard were in intent conversation. 'I'd say that there is a rat in our defences, you know, but it's not you. You've not got the spirit for it, I think. I'd bet a filly to a farthing that it's Crawley.'

It sounded like a gallon of pure nonsense to me. Crawley might have some curious habits, but he seemed the least likely traitor I could imagine. Not that that made me any happier to sail with him, knowing what he'd done to the *Glorious*. Perhaps it was just as well that *Orestes* was laid up in harbour. But as I've said before, pealing my superiors to their superiors is too dangerous a game for me. I tried to change the subject.

'What, if I may enquire, sir, was that business with the French lugger this afternoon?'

Davenant looked at me crookedly, then raised his nose and tapped it significantly. 'Navy business. Highest urgency. Sealed dispatches, and from Whitehall, not just the Admiralty. All the way down from on high. Secret mission, you know – can't say more.' He was slurring fast. I doubted he could have said more – coherently, at least – even if he'd not been bound to secrecy.

'They say it's the prisoners, of course,' he continued, finding the strength to ramble on somehow. 'Transport board, exchange of officers, that sort of thing. But you and I know different.' He winked, but had difficulty reopening the eye. 'Frenchy handed over documents, secret documents, went straight on the coach to London. It's peace, of course. That weasel of a minister Fox'll have it at any price.' He put an arm around me. 'And where does that leave us, the warriors? No prizes. No promotions. No glory. Just endless ghastly balls, with jumped-up bankers sticking their teeth in you. Peace. Ghastly.'

He put down his glass, more loudly than was polite, muttered something about his breeches being too tight, and stumbled away.

'I tell you, Cunningham, you worry too much.'

Just as I was wondering where to amuse myself next, I heard the name of my antagonist close over my shoulder. Fortunately, when I turned, I found that a suit of armour shielded me from his view. He and Mazard were talking in low voices.

'If that pimp Fox negotiates a peace, you'll say I was right to worry, Mazard,' Sir Lawrence was saying. Speaking quietly did not come easy to him, particularly when he was agitated. 'You may be able to stomach the loss, but I'll feel it hard enough.'

'Of course I do not want to lose so much,' said Mazard, with the air of someone trying to calm a petulant child. 'But peace brings its own opportunities.'

'Nothing half as neat as what we have now.'

'But what will stop that? Governments can exchange pieces of paper, but paper is cheap, and words are easily forgotten. Britain desires greatness, France desires greatness; they cannot both be great, and neither will choose to be humble. Britain cannot be defeated at sea, nor France on land, so I assure you, Cunningham, this war will still be being fought by our grandsons when we are long retired.'

Sir Lawrence grunted. 'You had better be right, Mazard. Too much depends on it.'

'I am right,' said Mazard simply. 'And even if I were not, I never make a loan without security. Nothing will change, I guarantee it. Will you drink with me to that?'

'It hardly seems decent to have a drink on Drake's account.' Sir Lawrence gave a grim laugh. 'Not after I hanged him.'

Mazard was philosophical. 'We all reap as we deserve. And we, you can be sure, will most certainly continue to do so.'

They moved towards the punchbowl while I watched from the dark corner where I had retreated, wondering whether I would have gained any more sense from that conversation had I not indulged so freely in the refreshments. I saw Mazard looking about, and shrank further back. He did not seem the sort of man to welcome being overheard, however nonsensical his words.

Back in the card room the sets had got themselves together; eager to keep well out of Sir Lawrence's path, I joined them, taking the place of a recently ruined young sprat who'd departed in tears. The seat was conveniently close to the punchbowl, which might have contributed to his downfall, but I found myself on a run which even an increasingly merry disposition could not halt. From this I deduced it owed more to luck – for once – than skill. I had the feeling that I was not matched against the worthiest opponents – the play seemed louder, and more expensive, at the other tables – but I collected a useful enough pile of pennies and half-crowns before at last my bladder compelled me to give up my chair.

I made my way out through a small door that led on to the stable yard. There was much laughter and merriment here, almost more than inside, and shadowy figures milled everywhere: men, mostly, but some women, knotted together in small groups, or leaning against the walls in solitude, or on their knees puking into a corner. Across by the stables, a line of men stood over a pile of hay, their legs open, and I joined them. From one of the stalls in front of us there came bestial noises of a peculiarly human variety.

'Ah, Jerrold. Enjoying yourself are you?'

It was Colonel Copthorne, the jovial officer who had chaired our meeting at the castle, standing next to me pissing into the straw. Steam rose in the cold night.

'Most entertaining.' My form at the card table had improved my humour, as had the attentions of the several young ladies it had won me.

'Funny how we gorge ourselves like this in the name of feeding the hungry,' Copthorne reflected. 'All a sham, of course.'

'Is it?' I felt little surprise that a society run by Mazard should evade its charitable mission.

'Absolutely, Lieutenant. What, after all, would you expect of a benevolent society founded by a smuggler?'

'Charity for the bibulous?'

'Almost.' Copthorne buttoned himself. 'But no. Drake established the whole thing for men with no other means of support. No other legal means of support, you follow? Meant the smugglers could eat when their ships didn't come in, and eat a damn sight better when they did. And the good folk of Dover could satisfy themselves that they had a clear conscience, one that wouldn't attract the attentions of Drakc and his gang.'

'A neat little scheme. Where do all those five shillings go now?'

'Couldn't say. The society's been quiet since Drake danced the gallows. Good fun, though. Wouldn't you say, General?'

Looking up, I saw that I had not been promoted: Copthorne had switched his conversation to the man on his other side, a new arrival. I could see little enough of him with Copthorne in the way, and the circumstances did not permit a gentleman to stare too closely, but I reckoned he was at least as tall as I, with a slight stoop and an obvious nose.

'It passes,' was his icy verdict. 'I have little patience with these provincial affairs. Too many shopkeepers trying to auction off their daughters.'

He finished his business and tidied himself away, then retrieved his drink from a mounting block. Although our breath made clouds in the cold, he showed no intention of returning inside. I was all of a mind to tempt my rare luck at the cards again, but Copthorne was already making an introduction.

'General Wellesley, allow me to present to you Lieutenant Jerrold. Lieutenant, this is General Sir Arthur Wellesley, lately returned from Hanover.'

We batted through the ritual pleasantries, each as scrupulously hollow as the other, establishing along the way that indeed he was an army officer and I in the navy; that we were both in rude health; and that we had little else in common beyond the fact that we pissed in the same pot.

'And did you trounce the Corsican harlequin in Hanover, sir?' I enquired, less respectfully than I might have. This stable yard cum pissoir cum drawing room cum brothel lacked much by way of formality.

'I did not,' Wellesley responded. 'Damn fool errand, sending an army to Hanover when it needs to march through Prussia to get anywhere. Prussians wouldn't let us through – Buonaparte's apparently promised Hanover to them, as soon as he conquers it – so we came back, empty-handed and seasick.'

'Perhaps Lieutenant Jerrold, being a navy man, cannot imagine having to seek out the enemy,' said Copthorne smoothly. 'It seems all they need do is sail out of harbour to find them.'

Wellesley grunted, boredom evident across his hawk-billed face.

'And what brings you to Dover now?' I asked. I could not turn my back and cut a major-general, however pompous, and it was too cold to keep quiet.

‘I am travelling back to London, and then on to my next command. In Hastings.’

I almost laughed. ‘That’s a poor turn, sir. You must have truly wrecked matters in Hanover to find yourself stationed there.’ Hastings, as I understood it, had all the stigmas of Dover without the excitement.

Wellesley did not look happy at the prospect either, but he looked even less happy with my impertinent talk. ‘Hastings, need I remind you, is where the French last successfully invaded, seven hundred and forty years ago. Some would count it an honour to command the first line of defence if they came again, to win the battle King Harold so infamously lost. Particularly if the navy fails to stop Buonaparte getting there.’

‘And you have surely heard of General Wellesley’s heroic exploits in India?’ added Copthorne, looking none too pleased with me. He was glancing meaningfully towards the door.

‘India?’ I echoed, with reckless hilarity. ‘India, and then Hanover, and then Hastings. What a miserable run of it you’ve had, sir. Nothing on earth could entice me to India.’ Although I knew well my uncle might soon be trying.

‘My brother is the governor-general,’ said Wellesley contemptuously. I think he was unaccustomed to being gibed at by his juniors.

‘All the worse. So much interest at his disposal, and the best he can manage is those dungheaps. I fear you’ve played your cards damn poorly, sir.’

‘I fear, sir, that the same could be said of you.’ There was poison on his tongue now, and having since read of the man’s notorious duels, I am relieved he took no further exception to me.

I shook my head vigorously. ‘Not at all, sir, not at all. I’ve played my cards damn well. Think I’ll play them again, actually, if you’ll excuse me. Goodnight.’

I walked off, less steadily than was respectable, leaving a fuming general and a horrified colonel to their pleasures.

14

'DID YOU ENJOY THE NIGHT'S FESTIVITIES?' ASKED CRAWLEY.

It was an uncharitable question. My red eyes and grey face were answer enough, and it was only because of a wretched hangover that after a mere four hours of sleep I had returned to *Orestes*. It seemed a safer way of seeking fresh air than another stroll along the beach.

'They entertained well enough.' I was desperate for a drink. 'Did you attend, sir? I did not see you there.'

'I left early.'

'I arrived late.'

'I am hardly surprised,' said Crawley. 'What does surprise me, though I confess perhaps it should not, is the note I received from Colonel Copthorne this morning.'

'Yes, sir?'

'A curious request. He tells me he has a distinguished guest he wishes to show over our ship. I am happy to oblige, though we are hardly rigged for visitors.' He glanced over the half-strung mast. 'However, he suggests that you, Lieutenant Jerrold, should be sent on some errand that takes you well away from the vessel.' He stared at me sharply. 'He also conveys his hope that your head is recovered – a reference to the *Thermidor* action, I take it.'

'I cannot imagine to what the colonel alludes,' I said carefully. 'But I had been thinking: it may be well for me to take the jollyboat over to the beach and have a look where that riding officer saw the smugglers. Maybe they, er, left something behind.'

Crawley was not deceived by my bluff for a second, but he had insufficient facts at his command to do anything other than scowl. 'An estimable project, Lieutenant,' he allowed. 'But I require all hands for the rigging work this morning. Maybe this afternoon they can be spared.'

'I see, sir.'

I remained impassive. Talking was too much effort, and I was not about to let Crawley prise any more details of the previous night from me.

He rapped his knuckles on the gunwale, and frowned deeper. 'I suppose, Lieutenant, I might send you to the victualling yard. On the London road – do you know it?'

I nodded. Although I had never been there, I knew it by reputation: it was the navy's local brewery and bakery. Nor could I have missed the flotilla of small boats which flocked to the harbour daily, ferrying supplies up the coast to the fleet at Deal. Mazard and Cunningham's boats, I remembered.

'You may pay my respects to the agent victualler, and pass on my request for the next month's supply of beer and biscuit.' It was a delivery errand, unvarnished and quite unworthy of my rank, but I accepted it with due humility. Anything to escape. 'And if you should encounter any persons of rank along the road, Lieutenant,' finished Crawley, 'please be sure to pay them due deference.'

I did not know exactly where the yard was situated, so I had little alternative but to wander up the London road until I encountered it, hoping that it would be obvious, and that I would not have arrived in Southwark before finding myself gone too far. The town stretched for about a quarter of a mile out of the market square, the houses generously built for the most part, but it was something of a façade, for very quickly I could see stretches of meadow and green field through the gaps in the buildings. Birds were calling, and I thought I heard the sound of a stream to my right.

Eventually, just past where the houses ceased and the open countryside began, I found the victualling yard. I could hardly have missed it, for the rich smells of hops and malt and baking dough steamed from its chimneys, a sickly mix which turned over my frail stomach. I wondered whether Crawley had deliberately sent me to a brewery in my enfeebled state, for I could quite imagine the old abstinent playing me such a trick.

It was as well I had the odour to guide me, though, for without it I could easily have mistaken the building for a church – which, I guessed from its square tower and arched doorway, it must once have been. What the good Lord would have thought of His house being commandeered for the navy's purposes I did not presume to guess, but I doubted that their ephemeral lordships at the Admiralty had asked His opinion. Besides, it had obviously been built in a time when religion was a far more dangerous pursuit, and it suited the navy perfectly: its walls reached far up the tower, and were everywhere studded with sharp outcrops of flint. To this charm the navy had added, bricking up the thin windows in its side so that the complete effect was one of a monstrous, overblown mausoleum which even the jumble of thatched outbuildings against its far wall could not dispel. It seemed exactly the place where, as the rumour had it, a man might have fallen into a boiling copper and been brewed through into the fleet's beer supply.

A small wall encircled the compound, though it was hardly necessary: the narrow gate was not even guarded. I lifted the latch and let myself through. Pack animals grazed in the yard, while behind them loomed great stacks of casks with cabbalistic numbers chalked upon them. A squat man in seaman's dress, with two arms' worth of muscle bulging from the one that remained, crossed over and enquired my business.

'I have a supply order from Captain Crawley of the *Orestes* to give to the agent victualler,' I told him.

He stuck out a fist, in a way that might have given offence were it not so large. Instead, I could do nothing but pass over the paper. He grunted.

'Is anything more required?'

He shook his head.

The errand had taken me less than half an hour; I could hardly return already.

'Could I perhaps look into the brewery, or the bakehouse? I have often wondered at the provenance of our supplies.' Usually with a few choice words for the purser thrown in.

The seaman's bullish neck turned a fraction. 'Can't do that, sir,' he said with a leer. His teeth numbered more than his limbs, but it was a narrow victory. 'Nasty things 'appens in there.' I wondered whether he was referring to the reputed accidents, or merely to the produce.

'I see.' I shifted on my feet. 'Well, go about your work then, seaman.'

'Reckon I will,' he said, and scratching the stump on his shoulder he wandered away.

He left me at a loss. It would be several hours before I could safely return to *Orestes*, and in the interim I did not care to be in town lest I encounter Copthorne and his general, or anyone else who bore me a grudge. But I well knew the perils of wandering the countryside alone. And I hardly wished to spend hours in contemplation of the brooding edifice before me.

The clatter of a drum brought the answer. At first I thought it simply the rattle of casks being shifted inside the depot, but a glance down the road revealed twin columns of infantry emerging from between the houses. Captain Bingham, whom I'd last seen on the beach near Folkestone cursing the salt-water smugglers, was at their head.

'France is that way, you know,' I told him, pointing back towards Dover. 'Or are you bound for London to overthrow the government?'

He grinned down from his mare, his unruly red hair squeezing out from under his hat. 'Perhaps I'm hunting down suspicious villains seen lurking on the public highway. Deserters, probably.'

'Scum,' I agreed cheerfully. 'A peril to society. I shall inform you if you see any.'

He laughed. 'Actually, we're due to block the road about half a mile up there. See if we can intercept any contraband bound for London.'

'If it's a drink you're after, the Crown and Anchor can supply you quite readily, I'm sure. But I'll accompany you, if I may – ensure that none of your seizures gets misappropriated.'

'From what I'm told,' said Bingham drily, 'they'd be safer with Caleb Drake.'

I looked up at him, sensitive to any injury he insinuated, but there was malice in neither his voice nor his face, and I let it pass. Clearly he had referred to my reputation as a sot rather than to Cunningham's allegations of treachery, and I'm honest enough not to stand on a dignity I don't possess.

The next half mile was pleasant enough as we walked the edge of the meadow that descended to the placid river on our right. A chalk escarpment rose steeply beyond it, the towers of the castle just visible over the brow, while to our left a valley stretched back beyond old abbey buildings. The air was sharp, tinged with a hint of woodsmoke, and a few hardy birds chirruped from the leafless boughs by the roadside.

As we reached a weatherbeaten finger of upright stone, Bingham called a halt.

'Boundary of the Corporation,' he told me. 'Allows us a choice of magistrates. If we catch anyone, we just make sure we arrest them on the right side of the line. Over here and they'll be taken back to Dover, a few more paces and we can send them elsewhere. Wherever we've the best chance of convicting them.'

'And where is that?'

'Dover,' he said unhesitatingly. 'Certainly while Cunningham's in charge.' He must have seen the loathing in my face. 'Oh, I agree he's an ogre, but there's not been a judge to touch him for putting away the rogues we catch. Most of the rest are so well in with the smugglers they have their own accounts at the Calais markets.'

Bingham arrayed his men in a loose cordon across the road, with pickets spread out across the fields to catch anyone trying to circumvent the blockade. Then we waited. Bingham and I swapped accounts of our careers – the superiors we'd toadied, the pranks we'd played, the girls we'd conquered, or tried to – but otherwise little interrupted the hazy peace of the morning.

Bingham had just finished a lengthy tale concerning a drummer boy and a Spanish whore when a whistle from the sergeant drew our attention. A hay cart had rounded the turn in the road behind us and stopped, its driver looking anxiously at the line of scarlet coats that blocked his progress. There was nothing he could do without drawing unfavourable attention, however – the width of the road did not even allow for the cart to turn – so, reluctantly, he shook his reins and ordered the horse forward to where we waited.

'I thought you might be gen'lemen of the road,' he explained, when Bingham enquired the reason for his hesitation.

'A pearl of wisdom for you,' Bingham told him. 'Highwaymen and thieves rarely parade around in bright red coats and crossbelts.'

'Some does. I knowed a man got robbed by a colonel of dragoons once.'

Suspicion and concern had added even more lines to the carter's face, and the hand holding the reins trembled.

'And what is your business?'

Bingham stroked the horse's flank. It was a handsome beast, its coat far glossier than its driver's.

'Takin' 'ay from the priory down to Mr Thanney's farm. 'E's bought 'isself a new cow.'

'Marvellous,' said Bingham, with profound indifference. 'Anything else under that hay, carter?' Lazily, he pulled out his sword.

A pair of narrow eyes looked worriedly at the blade. 'No, sir.'

'Really?'

Bingham slashed a couple of strokes through the air, the steel humming; then, reaching up, he ran his sword over the cart's edge and straight into the pile of hay. The carter watched, horrified. It came out clean, but Bingham took a step forward and again sank the blade in up to its hilt. Again, nothing. He moved on around the side of the cart, tried again, and this time I heard a thud, saw the few projecting inches of steel quiver with the impact.

'Carrying firewood as well, are you?' asked Bingham, bracing himself against the cart to pull the sword free.

The carter nodded, his eyes tight with fear, but Bingham was ignoring him.

'Sergeant, uncover this.'

Two of the soldiers pulled themselves onto the cart and began throwing the hay onto the ground. If the carter felt injured by the cavalier way in which his load was dispersed, he made no comment, but kept his back turned and his eyes downcast. I wondered whether that was in part due to the two bayoneted muskets held close by his side.

'Look at this, sir.'

I looked to the voice that had spoken: it was one of the soldiers on the cart. Straw and chaff clung to his scarlet coat, but he looked triumphant as he held up a short length of rope, each end knotted onto a small, stout barrel.

'What's in those, carter?' Bingham's tone was mild but unbending, like a schoolmaster with an errant pupil. 'I can hammer them open perfectly easily, so you've nothing but a few seconds to gain by lying.'

The carter whispered something inaudible. Only after three promptings from Bingham could I finally discern the solitary syllable: 'gin'.

'Gin,' repeated Bingham. 'And of course, you've paid the duty on it.'

The old man shuffled his head up and down.

'There's four more pairs o' tubs in 'ere,' reported the soldier on the cart. 'Ten in all.'

'Naturally you will have a receipt from the customs agent, or at least from the merchant you bought them off,' prompted Bingham.

The carter's head trembled from side to side. 'Left it in town,' he whispered.

'In town?' Bingham was unsurprised. 'That is a pity. You know what we must do with unaccustomed liquor, I suppose?'

'Yes.' His voice was slowly returning, though the eyes remained fixed on the ground.

'We shall take them to the customs house. You may reclaim them there on production of a receipt within the ensuing week. If not, they may be confiscated.'

The soldiers had jumped down from the cart and were now busily tossing the hay back onto it, though a fair portion of the load was lost to the breeze, or stayed stuck in the muddy road.

'Where did you get them?' asked Bingham, keeping his attention on the carter.

'Don't know. They ain't mine. They wasn't there when I loaded the hay on.'

'Come now, you surely cannot tell me that you were unaware of your hidden cargo?' Bingham was abrupt. 'Where did you get them?'

The carter shook his head silently.

With an impatient shrug, Bingham took the flat of his sword and swatted it against the horse's rump. It bounded forward, jolting the cart into motion and bouncing the driver near off his seat. For a taciturn fellow, I discovered, he certainly had a voice for cursing. We watched him rattle into the distance, his ten barrels still lying on the roadside.

'You let him escape,' I said, surprised.

'Of course.' Bingham wiped the strands of hay off his sword. 'I doubt a jury would have convicted him for owning a few tubs of geneva whose provenance we could not prove.'

'But he was a smuggler,' I protested. It was the first time I had seen one face to face, and although he had hardly been the cut-throat villain I expected, it seemed outrageous that he should go free.

'He was nothing of the sort,' said Bingham airily. 'He was an errand-boy. He may have been carrying the gin for himself, or for a friend, or for one of the gangs or for his poor sick mother's chill, but I'll wager he's no more met the man who brought it into the country than you or I will have met King George in a Chatham tavern.'

I had met some intriguing characters in Chatham taverns, but never, I had to confess, our esteemed monarch.

'Had we arrested him, whether the court sent him home to his wife or off to Botany Bay, it would have made not an ounce of difference to the problem of the smugglers.' Bingham was quite exerted now. 'They would have found someone else to carry their cargo, some gull who fancied earning more in a day than he could in a month of honest labouring, and barely noticed the trouble. No, the men we want are the venturers, those who finance the enterprise; failing that, the gangs that bring it ashore. Once they've had done, there's not a man who can stop it making its way inland.'

'We stopped it,' I pointed out.

'We stopped ten tubs – forty gallons. There's probably a hundred times as much passing through even as we speak. What do the smugglers care?' Bingham waved his hand. 'They know perfectly well that some of their cargo, some very small fraction, will be intercepted. They allow for it, part of the costs of the business. Natural seepage, if you like.'

'So why bother with the roadblock?' My voice was sharp, for his bitterness had riled me and I did not care to be informed that my every effort was futile.

'Maybe we'll catch someone important one day. But more to the point, it makes it harder for them to get their cargoes through. They have to be cleverer, which means spending more time and money. With any luck, eventually they'll tire of the effort and either do something foolish or retire from the business. But at the moment, we're like a man trying to stem a flood with a mop.'

Bingham's words affected me greatly. I suppose I had always had a notion, somewhere in my head, that although I rarely seemed to accomplish anything, much of that must be down to my own incompetence and failings. I had never considered that even the unlikely habit of executing my duties perfectly might still be fated to fail. I suppose I ought to have felt vindicated in my idleness, but strangely I felt only a tugging sadness.

'Still,' I said positively. 'At least we have those forty gallons of gin. What happens to them?'

'On the assumption that the carter does not defy expectation and return with a letter from the customs collector, it will be taken away and destroyed.' Bingham smiled. 'Probably by the regimental mess.'

There was surprisingly infrequent traffic on the road that morning, and what little we did meet proved entirely honest.

'The word must be out. I reckon we'll not find anyone carrying contraband now,' said Bingham. 'Unless he's a particularly fine specimen of fool.'

His prediction proved gloomily accurate, and my belly was already signalling that the lunch hour was drawing near before our next excitement. This did not come from Dover, though, but from the opposite direction, from London. It was a coach and pair, with two well-matched white horses in the traces and little more than a single journey's mud to spoil the gleaming paint, and the coat of arms emblazoned on it. A squat figure in a very upright hat drove it, while a liveried footman stood behind the compartment. It was, by some distance, the most respectable vehicle we'd encountered that morning. We were instantly suspicious.

So, it seemed, was the driver. Although we were in plain sight across the road, he did not spare his whip until he was almost upon us; then, when it became apparent that the file of soldiers would not give way (I was safe by the roadside), he pulled his reins up short and brought the beasts and the carriage slithering to a halt directly before us. Steam puffed from the horses' nostrils; their flanks heaved. Behind them, I saw the coachman had one hand under his cloak.

'Name yourselves,' he snarled. 'I've orders to stop for no-one, least of all vagabonds who block the public highway.'

'Well, you now have orders to hold your damn tongue,' said

Bingham. 'Most particularly when you address one of his Majesty's officers. Where are you bound?'

The coachman leered silently, pointing to his mouth in an insolent gesture of holding his tongue. I saw his right hand was still hidden.

'What the devil's going on?' A sallow face was poking out of the coach's window, its powdered wig knocked askew by the frame. 'Thought I told you not to stop.' His piggish eyes caught sight of Bingham and his company. 'And who the deuce are you?'

'Captain Bingham. We had a report that smugglers were using this road.'

The man gave a braying laugh. 'Smugglers? Smugglers, my dear, d'ye hear that?' He spoke into the coach, then rapped a weak-looking fist on the crest that was painted under his window. 'D'ye see that, Captain, eh? Does that not tell you all you need know?'

'Unfortunately not.'

'Arlington.' He spoke it like an incantation, and looked keenly at Bingham, as if expecting the word to work some magic on him. 'Arlington – does the name mean nothing to you?'

'Unfortunately not.'

'Well, damn me, Captain, you ought to pay more attention to your betters. I am Lord Arlington, and Lady Arlington is inside with me. You are distressing her, and insulting me. I propose you remove yourself from my path immediately.' His cheeks were quite puffed up now; it made his face seem uncannily like a scone.

'Sadly, Lord Arlington, it is not unknown for smugglers and villains to pretend at being nobility,' said Bingham evenly. 'I would be grateful if you would dismount your carriage – and Lady Arlington, too.'

'Certainly not.' Lord Arlington's cheeks coloured. 'You are the villain here, sir. I do not *pretend* at being nobility, I *am* nobility.'

'Then would you kindly – nobly – dismount?'

Bingham maintained his composure, but even as he spoke one of his men stepped forward and pulled the carriage door open over Arlington's head. It banged the back of his skull and almost pitched him into the mud; he had to leap out with a yelp to keep his balance. Ooze covered the gold buckle on his shoe.

'Thank you,' said Bingham politely. 'And Lady Arlington, too.'

'Lady Arlington will not be accosted and forced to dirty her skirts on the common highway.'

Lord Arlington patted the back of his head gingerly, as if expecting his palm to come away caked with matted hair and blood, though I suspect he found only a bruise.

'I should no sooner besmirch Lady Arlington's dress than her reputation.'

With these words, Bingham leaped onto the step and pulled himself into the carriage, to the sound of a horrified shriek from within. Arlington started forward but only doubled himself over the musket barrel that was thrust before his belly.

Bingham's cheerful face reappeared in the doorway. 'Have no fear,' he called, oblivious to Arlington's contortions. 'Your lady's honour is safe – I merely startled her. Sergeant! There is a box in here that would feel the benefit of some air.'

I heard the sound of fresh protestations inside, matched by Arlington's struggles before me, but he was capably restrained by the men around him and was impotent to stop the chest being manhandled onto the ground. Even without his complaints, though, I would have guessed he did not want it opened, for it was built from thick teak and bound with half a dozen stout iron hoops. A yawning keyhole was the only chink in its formidable armour.

'What's inside?' asked Bingham.

'Devil take you,' spat Arlington.

The men had moved away from him slightly, so he was not forcibly restrained – we were not, after all, brigands – but there was no question of his moving anywhere.

Bingham repeated his question.

'Why don't you see for yourself?' Arlington pulled away his neckcloth and opened his shirt. Fumbling inside it, he took out a large key on a cord, pulled it over his head and handed it malevolently to

Bingham. It turned in the lock with a heavy click. 'Do you think me an impostor at nobility now?' he sneered.

'I never heard that wealth equated to nobility,' replied Bingham, though we all knew that to be a lie. And, in as much as the one can buy the other, Arlington was noble. Even the soldiers ordered to watch him craned their necks over to see inside the strongbox, while I forgot my upbringing and stared like a peasant. Inside, piled all the way to the brim, scattered one over the other like a pirate's treasure, lay hundreds upon hundreds of gleaming golden guineas.

For a man presented with more money than he will feasibly own in a lifetime, Bingham remained remarkably cool. Though even he could not prevent a certain obsequious note creeping into his voice.

'And what do you propose to do with that, sir?' he asked.

'That's my own business, damn you,' said Arlington, but with less malice than before. Whether he felt a miser's cheer at seeing his hoard, or whether he enjoyed impressing his rank upon us, there was a mirthless smile curling at the edge of his mouth. 'Unless Mr Fox has now made it a crime for an Englishman to prosper. But as I am always eager to assist my country, I will tell you: I am taking it to my banker for safe-keeping. I had feared to meet with thieves on the road; I had not expected they would take the guise of the King's soldiers.'

Bingham nodded. 'I apologize, sir, if we have caused you distress. Sometimes we can be over-zealous in the pursuit of our duty.' He managed to sound passably contrite. 'But you are wise to think to your safety, so I shall give you a squadron of my men to accompany you to your bank.' He lifted a hand to still Arlington's protest. 'No, I am happy to spare them, and I would rest easier knowing that your eminent person – to say nothing of your fortune, and of course your estimable wife – was safe. Lieutenant Jerrold will accompany you.'

Naturally, Arlington resisted; naturally, Bingham prevailed. I was put at the head of ten men – six in front of the carriage, four behind it – and off we marched, a fine procession of pomp which, if it insulted Lord Arlington's liberty, must certainly have flattered his dignity. I felt uneasy in my place at the front, partly because, as a naval officer, marching with ceremony was not a skill I had needed to master – there is only so far one can travel on even the biggest ship of the line – and partly because the clopping of the horses' hooves was ever close behind me, and I could not convince myself that the driver might not suddenly lay on the whip and skittle us all out of his way.

Soon, though, we came into Dover, and simply steering through those crooked streets must have taken all the coachman's wits. There were several times when my little platoon had to pause and wait, and once when only a stout heave from the men behind got the carriage round a tight corner, at the expense of a deep scar across one of the wheels. Only when we turned on to the waterfront did the road become wide enough to admit the coach with ease again.

'You may leave now, Lieutenant,' said Arlington, popping his head carefully out of the window. 'I dare say we have weathered the storm, and your protection would be better used elsewhere.'

'Doubtless it would,' I agreed sincerely. 'But it's the last mile is most treacherous, as they say, particularly when it runs near a harbour. I could not conscience it if misfortune befell you now.'

Arlington grunted, but under the sarcasm there was a truth in my words, and he knew it. 'Very well,' he allowed. 'But Lady Arlington wishes to dismount here.'

'Certainly.'

Pre-empting the coachman, I pulled open the door and took the hand that was extended to help her down. Lady Arlington had stayed hidden in the carriage all this time and I was curious to get a sight of her, though now that I did she seemed little more than what I would have expected: far younger than her husband, fair haired, with pale skin, fine posture and bored eyes. The fashioning of her dress and spencer were as predictably immaculate as her complexion, but all this perfection served only to give her the sheen of a varnished doll. And probably the character to match, I thought, as she moved disdainfully past me.

I was little concerned with her, though. Nor did I much care about

Arlington and his strongbox. Had a highwayman accosted us and robbed him at gunpoint, I would as soon have given the rogue a shilling for the entertainment as discharged my pistol in his face. But I did want to know where Arlington banked, for I had a notion I could guess, and my hunch became a certainty as we led the carriage around the inner edge of the harbour and drew up outside the brick frontage of Mazard's Bank. I directed two of the men to unload the chest, but almost immediately Mazard's Goliath of a doorman emerged and, with a respectful salute to Lord Arlington and a menacing glare at me, lifted the box into his arms and carried it within. No doubt the sight of its contents would warm the cold embers of Mazard's heart.

We were on the opposite side of the harbour to *Orestes* here, and as Arlington disappeared with a final scowl I peered around the side of the building to get a look at her. A tall red uniform was standing stiffly at her stern; I could also see Copthorne gesticulating animatedly, and Crawley on the side looking awkward. Clearly it was not a propitious time for me to make my return so, feeling a bit like the Duke of York, I marched my little contingent back to the roadblock.

I was glad of the time to think, for I had the beginnings of an idea forming in my head. Just before we had left the harbour, I had turned to look back. On a cloudy day, with no hint of a sun, the walls of Mazard's glass room were perfectly clear. And there, for all to see, were Mazard and Arlington, deep in conversation.

'Did I miss anything?' I asked Bingham. It seemed unlikely: his men were mostly sitting by the roadside now, chattering away and looking more like a church picnic than an army.

'Only lunch,' said Bingham, sucking on a chicken leg. 'And, of course, a thrilling battle with a horde of barbarous villains whom we battled to a bloody victory.'

'I'm more distressed about the lunch,' I told him, truthfully. 'But I've discovered where Lord Arlington banks.'

'And?'

Bingham tossed away his chicken bone. It bounced off a tree and ricocheted into a group of his men.

'Mazard's.' Lowering my voice, I explained my concerns. 'Why would anyone from London want to bank in Dover, want to bring a fortune in gold all the way down a dangerous highway to an unknown provincial banker?'

'Perhaps the service is more courteous down here?'

'Perhaps. Or perhaps Mazard can make him a return that's a damn sight handsomer than anything he could get in London.' Briefly, I repeated what Nevell had told me that night aboard *Orestes*. 'Who would be better positioned to get his hands on enough gold to fund the smugglers than Dover's most eminent banker? And what richer profit could he turn with it?'

'Perhaps he collects for the children's hospital.' Bingham was frowning. 'You make an argument, Jerrold, I grant you, but you'll need to be more circumspect when accusing a man such as Mazard of crimes like that. He's one of Dover's most respected citizens.'

The competition for that honour was hardly rigorous.

'And also one of the most powerful,' continued Bingham. 'He doesn't just have his finger in all the pies in town, he owns most of them outright. He and your friend Sir Lawrence Cunningham exercise a complete hegemony in Dover. Tight as breeches. Do everything together. Mazard, as I understand it, finds the money, and Cunningham, as alderman, ensures the necessary permissions and privileges are granted. You've seen the work being done on the defences up at the castle? All contracted to Mazard & Company, in partnership with Cunningham. They supply the fleet at Deal. They own shops, chandlers, laundries, public houses, anything they can turn a profit on, and all manned by grateful poorhouse workers thanks to that illustrious Commissioner for the Poor, Sir Lawrence Cunningham.'

I suppose this ought not to have been surprising intelligence: I had seen them conspiring together at the ball, after all, and had enough evidence of the long reach of their interests to draw my own conclusions. But Bingham's stark assessment still took me aback, not least because of the implications it threw on Sir Lawrence's role in the scheme I was imputing to Mazard. I confess there was a certain shameless joy in the thought that he might end up a prisoner in his own gaol, though of course at the moment that was merely the most libellous speculation.

My thought must have shown in my face, for Bingham was smiling slyly. 'Perhaps I ought not to have said that. I can imagine it might not be the thing to deter you from your idea of an eminent conspiracy.'

'No,' I admitted. 'And it would certainly explain much that's happened.' The failings of Sir Lawrence's intelligence, to begin with, and his insistence on there being a spy in our ranks. How better to disguise his own guilt than by trying to lay the blame elsewhere? And on me, at that.

But Bingham was shaking his head. 'Enough, Jerrold.' He spoke lightly, but with a measure of seriousness under it. 'Someone must bank the smugglers' gold – well enough. Mazard has an ample collection of golden guineas – true too, but he is a banker, and golden guineas are his trade. Mazard and Cunningham work often in partnership – again true, but that does not make Cunningham a smuggler, any more than the fact that he has taken a disliking to you. These coincidences admit to many explanations, Jerrold, and most of them are far more innocent, and far safer, than what you propose.' He turned away. 'Sergeant, get the men back on their feet. They look like a herd of cattle there.'

Little happened that afternoon. Although Bingham did not avoid my conversation for more than half an hour, his easiness was gone, and it seemed he spoke to me only with reluctance. Few travellers passed on the road, and soon the light began to fade. The trees took on a dusky, purple hue, and the air over the fields grew misty. A dog was barking somewhere in the valley, but otherwise all was still, silent. There was now no banter among the men, nor officers: I was thoroughly distracted with my turbulent thoughts of Cunningham and Mazard, while I imagined Bingham was wondering how far I would take these lunatic allegations, and how he could avoid having any part of them. Of the two of us, I feared he was probably the wiser, but he had a full stomach to anchor his thoughts, while I felt the absence in my belly ever more keenly.

Just on the cusp of evening we heard a rumbling in the distance towards Dover. Bingham, who had been poised to order his men home, looked up.

'It appears to be our esteemed acquaintance Lord Arlington,' he said, peering into the gathering shadows. 'I doubt there's another coach like that in Dover.'

'Let's hope there's still light enough for his coachman to see us,' I muttered.

But this time the driver did not charge our line; instead, he slowed his horses to the gentlest of walks from the moment we came into sight. It seemed an interminable wait for them to cover the ground between us, and every second the day grew darker and the air chiller. At long last, the carriage rolled to a gentle stop before us.

'Still here, are you?' said Lord Arlington from the carriage. He sounded disappointed.

'Still here,' confirmed Bingham. 'And still obliged to search all passing traffic.'

'Still obliged to be a damned nuisance, you mean?' grumbled Arlington, but he was obviously playing for form. 'Do as you must, Captain. Not going to get out, though – too damn cold.'

I looked through the doorway as Bingham climbed in. The strong-box was gone, but a wooden crate had taken its place at Arlington's feet. Perhaps in anticipation of our encounter, it had not been sealed.

'A fine selection,' Bingham complimented him as he lifted the lid and looked at the array of bottles inside. 'You must have a great familiarity with spirituous liquors. You have a receipt, of course.'

'Of course. Why the devil wouldn't I?' Arlington kicked the box dismissively. 'Nailed to the top.'

Bingham held the lid close to his nose. 'Of course. And in there?' He gestured towards a small leather case on the bench beside Lady Arlington. 'Another purchase?'

'Devil take you, Captain, that is my wife's. I will not have you insulting her dignity by prying into her personal effects.'

But Bingham ignored the outburst and deftly lifted the case, snapping it open.

He laughed. 'See this, Jerrold – a poppet.' He held it into the light of the carriage lantern. It was a cloth doll, perhaps a foot tall, its white linen skin stretched over a surprisingly detailed woman's body, swelling in all the right places, and in profile remarkably like Lady Arlington. It even shared her fair hair. 'And a wardrobe for it as well.' Bingham picked a dainty doll's dress out of the case. It too was exquisitely made, more like the miniature of a real garment than a crude toy. 'The latest French fashion, if I recall my wife's magazine correctly,' he said. 'Tell me, Lady Arlington, who is your dressmaker?'

'My dressmaker?' she asked coldly. 'Sir, my dressmaker is in London. What you hold is merely a fancy I found in Dover.'

'Of course.'

Bingham handed back the doll to Lady Arlington, who bundled it swiftly into the case.

'Have you quite exhausted your duty now, Captain?' Arlington was biting his knuckle. 'We have many miles yet to travel, and the road can be dangerous after dark. I do not care to be assaulted by brigands on it. Again.'

'I wish you a pleasant journey.'

Bingham stepped backwards out of the door and hopped onto the ground. The driver lashed his whip, and we watched the lantern pass down the road and out of sight.

'What was your purpose with the doll?' I asked, intrigued by Bingham's words. 'And why ask of her dressmaker?'

'Because I have seen the poppet before, and not in a toy-shop window. On a smuggler we captured some months back, carrying a load of calicoes and silks, together with several dolls of near identical appearance.'

'Have we banned French toys?'

'It isn't a toy,' Bingham explained. 'It's a model, a dressmaker's doll. Shows off the latest styles from Paris without the need for a travelling wardrobe. The good ladies of society choose their dresses, then buy the cloth for it from the same smuggler who brought the doll.' He looked up at my uncomprehending face. 'France may be our sworn enemy, Jerrold, but she is still the height of fashion.'

Bingham led his men back to the castle; I made my way to the docks to rendezvous with Crawley. I feared he would barrack me for returning nearer to the supper hour than lunch, but he seemed careless of my apology and sent me back to the inn.

'Get a good night's sleep, Lieutenant,' he ordered me. 'I hope to have *Orestes* ready for sea tomorrow, and thereafter we must double our efforts to hunt down the smugglers. Neither of us can long afford continued failure.'

With my uncle's letter of the day before still exercising my thoughts, I could hardly disagree. I thought of proposing my idea of Cunningham and Mazard's involvement, but the doubts Bingham had voiced, and Crawley's unpredictable, combustious temperament, dissuaded me. Perhaps I would try when I was feeling bolder, and when I was not standing almost in the shadow of Mazard's building. On whose roof, I noticed, a lamp still glowed orange.

15

ISAAC WAS AT THE BAR WHEN I ARRIVED BACK AT THE INN.

'There's an 'andkerchief for you,' he said when he saw me.

'Damn the handkerchief, and fetch me some pork and a large glass of claret. What do you mean, a handkerchief?'

My thoughts on the short walk back had been occupied with ever more elaborate constructions of what Cunningham and Mazard might purpose together, and those had quickly given way to even more fanciful imaginings of what they would do to me if they knew I suspected them. I had little patience for enigmatic bar-boys.

'I means this.'

Isaac began pulling out his pockets, producing all manner of disreputable objects, most of them filthy, until, with the flourish of a travelling magician, he extracted a balled-up handkerchief. I took it gingerly by the corner.

'This is mine, you little thief.' I just about recognized it, although a nasty black stain had leached into one of its edges. 'Where did you get it?'

'Laundry girl left it for you,' said Isaac defensively. 'Said to tell you to blow yer nose on it.'

'I shall certainly do no such thing.' I would sooner have blown my nose on a hedgehog.

I shook open the handkerchief, keeping it well away from my face, and tried to ignore the damp yellow lines spidered across it: 'Red Cow tonight'. As I had expected, there was writing on it; unfortunately, it left me none the wiser.

'What's the Red Cow?' I asked Isaac.

'It's a tavern.'

That sounded plausible. 'Whereabouts?'

'On Red Cow square.'

'Which is doubtless on Red Cow lane near the Red Cow river,' I snapped. 'How do I reach it from here?'

The Red Cow was built on the north-western corner of the town, right at its very edge, where the inland road came in, and doubtless it was meant primarily to lure the sort of traveller who falls upon the first hostelry he finds in his destination, without discernment or thought. I speak as one who knows. The ramparts of the heights behind loomed over it, and the adjoining houses were dark.

For all its lonely location, though, it attracted enough custom to make it an effort to reach the bar, and an even greater effort to catch the eye of the stout landlord behind it. I was just wondering how I would find Isobel, when I felt a tugging on the back of my coat; I turned to see her dark eyes staring up at me, a smile on her face.

'Hallo,' I said, more stiffly than I meant. It was, I realized, the first time we had met publicly since that first night in the Crown and Anchor, and I suddenly felt pressed for conversation.

'Over here,' she said, pulling me to a table by the wall which had just become vacant.

I put down the two glasses I carried, and sat on the wooden stool. It was lower than I expected, and I fell onto it, knocking into the table leg and splashing wine out of the glasses.

'How many have you had already?' asked Isobel, giggling at me. 'There's nothing improves with drink, you know, saving perhaps my face.'

'Absolutely not,' I said chivalrously.

She pulled a frown. 'You mean, even spirits won't make me look pretty?'

'I mean,' I floundered, 'that, er, nothing can improve your face.' No. 'Because, viewed in any state, it remains the picture of perfection.' That was better.

It was obviously what she wanted: she leaned across the table – dragging her sleeve through a puddle of wine, I noticed – and squeezed my arm.

'Anyway,' I said, my embarrassment calmed by her touch. 'Why did you insist on bringing me out here? There are any number of more convenient and more convivial places in town.'

'Further away from eyes that talk,' she said, lowering her voice.

'Cunningham and his agents, you mean?'

'Them too.' She shook her hair loose. 'Anyhow, I thought you came to see me, not to review the tavern for the *Gentleman's Magazine*.'

There was a pause in our conversation.

'I trust Sally hasn't said anything to Miss Hoare?'

Isobel grimaced. 'Not yet. She keeps on giggling over it though, and you never know what's coming out when she opens her mouth.' A look of concern passed her face. 'But we'll not talk of that. How was the ball? Better than the Red Cow?'

'The drink was better, but the company worse,' I said. 'And none of the girls could touch you.'

'Miss Hoare said there was a navy officer there who was ever so handsome. Not that she said that, mind, but she did praise his Christian virtue and manly bearing, which is what she means by it.'

'That was probably Davenant. She didn't say anything about a drunken lout of an officer who monopolized the punchbowl, insulted his superiors, and pinched the arses of a few too many young ladies?'

'She'd certainly have said if you'd pinched her arse.' Isobel's face was screwed up like a bulldog's. 'But I ought to be slapping yours, if that's what you were doing.'

'Only because yours wasn't there,' I consoled her.

'One day it will be. Will you take me to a ball?'

'Of course,' I said, straight off, though how she would pass in society I could not imagine. No worse than I, most likely.

Isobel treated me to an exposition of how she imagined the ball would be, from the diamonds at her throat to the gilded carriage that would collect her at the end, and I listened with good humour, enjoying the sound of her voice and the animation of her face as she described each detail. I did not share my own recollections of dismal food, ghastly conversation, and some idiot (commonly me) being ill in the drawing room; she could discover all that for herself, if she ever got there.

But while Isobel talked, and I sipped my drink, I had half an eye on the rest of the room. When I'd entered it had been doing brisk business, but now more of the tables than not were empty, and every few minutes another knot of people would shuffle out of the door. None entered. The landlord mopped forlornly at his counter, rarely troubled for another drink. And the general noise of the place had dwindled to bare whispers, with the exception of Isobel's clear running voice.

The landlord squeezed round the end of his bar and came to our table.

'The rest of that bottle of wine, thank you,' I said.

His square face creased with a frown. 'It's not that, sir,' he said reluctantly. 'But might I ask, would you be a naval gentleman?'

'Naval, yes; gentleman, sometimes. What the devil concern is it of yours?'

'I thought so.' The man rubbed his hands together. 'It's just that, as you is, I'll be askin' you to leave.'

'I beg your pardon? Here am I, braving the salty brine and manning the wooden walls that protect men like you, landlord, from the depredations of our enemies, and you tell me that I cannot even enjoy a drink with a girl in your house? What sort of gratitude is that, sir?'

'Oh, I appreciates what you does.' He wiped his hands on his smock. 'But you see, sir, you're worryin' the other customers. They're afraid you're on the press.'

'The press gang?' I could not help but laugh at him. 'Do you see a crew of doughty boatswains with cudgels and cutlasses about me? Do you not think that if I wanted to round up seamen, I could contrive a better place for it than the most landward tavern in Dover?'

'Well, yes, sir. But that don't stop you frightin' 'em.' He looked at Isobel. 'Please, Miss Isobel – Mrs Dawson, that is to say. You'd not want it said that you were 'ere either.'

It was a clumsy threat, but it served its purpose.

'All right.' Isobel stood. 'We'd best go, Mr Jerrold. Don't want to intrude.'

I found it offensive to surrender to his bluntness, but I could only follow her lead and get to my feet. Before I went, though, I put my face very close to the barman's.

'You may get your way frightening little girls,' I told him, far braver than I felt. 'But next time, I *will* come with a party of well-armed sailors, and stay here enjoying your hospitality until you can't get the rats under your counter to take your drink, and you're forced into the poorhouse.' I banged my glass down on the table and swept out. Before he could decide to take offence.

Isobel took my arm as we walked down the road. 'I'm sorry,' she said. 'We should've gone somewhere more private.' She paused, then tugged at my hand. 'Come on.'

She led me, almost at a run, to the end of the road, but instead of turning in towards the square, she continued a few paces and then ducked between two mournful-looking houses into the open space beyond. My knee banged into something hard and I cursed.

'What was that?'

'A gravestone, I think,' she answered lightly. Her breath came in small gasps after the exertion.

'A gravestone? Where the devil are we?'

She put a finger to her lips. 'Shhh,' she said. 'Not the devil. Jesus. We're in the burying ground.'

And before I could remonstrate with her about her curious notions of romance, she was skipping off through the headstones, leaving me no choice but to stumble after her as best I could.

Soon it began to seem that the stones were in a poor state of repair, but so intent was I on following Isobel – she had a cat's agility in the dark – that it was only when she at length stopped against an enormous pillar that I realized we were no longer among the graves, but surrounded by rubble. The ground was paved, though weeds and grasses had long since broken through the slabs, but there were no walls surrounding us, only a handful of monolithic pillars, upright fragments of some ancient building. They towered over us, and I could see where broken arches still vaulted out into nothingness from atop them. It did not look safe, nor did it feel romantic, though it was certainly private. The thin curve of the waning moon shone overhead, casting everything in a mysterious silver light, but I confess I found it more eerie than beautiful. Isobel, though, seemed quite at ease.

'I've seen this before,' I realized. 'From the market square. Those ruined arches protruding above the rooftops.'

For some reason best known to themselves, the people of Dover seemed to tolerate the fractured remains of a broken church just behind the centre of the town. Perhaps it appealed to their aesthetic.

'That's right,' said Isobel. 'But it's private enough for us.'

I could not disagree. Although the market square was barely a few yards away, in the darkness the ruins felt terribly remote.

Isobel stepped backwards into a corner formed by two of the uprights. 'And even if they did want us at the Red Cow, there's some things decent people can't do in a public house.' She placed her hand over mine, and pressed it against her chest.

It was not the venue I would have chosen for a seduction. For one thing, it was bitingly cold; for another, our ghoulish surroundings had me tense with anxiety. I could barely concentrate on Isobel, for I was perpetually straining my ears for any sign that we were not alone. The night was quiet, but not still, and every crack and creak from around us convinced me that a gang of robbers would be upon us in moments. Still, there was no denying the warmth of Isobel's hand on mine, nor mine on her. She tipped her mouth up, and I took it in my own, pressing her body against the stone as I did. She moaned softly, and wrapped her hands around my back to pull me yet harder onto her. I slid my hand down, squeezing her cold thigh through the thin wool of her dress.

There is little exaggerating how dangerous a ruined churchyard at night can feel when you are there alone, and by nature I was particularly sensitive to it, but Isobel's passion, and the sweet noises she made, blunted the edge of my fear, distracted my senses. Which is why the rough hands that suddenly seized my shoulders came as a complete surprise. They pulled me away from her and thrust me to the ground; I banged my head against a jagged piece of masonry, and yelped. Isobel screamed, but another hand covered her mouth and stifled it. I was almost insensible with pain and terror, but as I rolled over, jabbing myself in the side on another rock as I did so, I saw a gleam of steel caught in the moonlight. It was in the hand of a dark figure whose low hat and high collar admitted to no description other than stockiness, and it hung over Isobel's face with naked menace.

''E don't like yer nobbin' with the navy,' a thick voice was saying. 'An' 'e surely don't like yer whorin' with 'em.' The knife went up. 'An' yer knows what 'appens when 'e don't like somethin'.'

I seem to remember that I consciously decided I would do nothing, that I was best left out of whatever horrific entanglement Isobel had found herself in. Whether in the ensuing seconds I changed my opinion, or whether my body rebelled against the mind's natural cowardice, I do not know; but, without any intent, I found myself staggering to my feet, stumbling towards her assailant.

There was a grunt of surprise from behind Isobel. A second man, as anonymously dressed as his counterpart, was standing there holding her arms to her back. The sound must have alerted the one with the knife for he paused in his stroke and turned.

'Impatient, is yer?' he said nastily. 'I was goin' to see to yer next. But I ain't 'ticular, if yer not gentleman enough to let the lady go first.'

Reversing his wrist, he drove the pommel of his knife hard into my stomach; I folded like a bedsheet and fell back to the ground, managing to jar my elbow on the same sharp stone. Through mottled eyes I saw the man above me take a piece of sacking from his belt. Before I could react, he had pulled it open and wrestled it fiercely over my pounding head. Dust and chaff filled my eyes, clinging to the tears that had welled over my cheeks, and suddenly I was in a blind darkness. I could hear screams from Isobel, cut abruptly, terribly short; then there was a sharp pain in my ankles as a thick rope bit tightly into them.

'Yer seen what come to yer mate Webb,' said the voice, invisible but horribly near. 'And the same'll come to you if yer don't keep clear o' where you shouldn't. See?'

A booted toe crashed into my ribs to punctuate the threat. I tried to scream, but all I got was a mouthful of blood and dust. And another cracking blow.

'Maybe yer should take some sea air to make yer better,' came an unhelpful suggestion, coupled with a well-aimed punch to the side of my head which had me gagging into the sacking. 'That's 'ow yer supposed to 'unt the owlers. Not askin' questions o' them what's far too grand fer you.'

They continued in the same vein for some minutes, kicking me around that churchyard until I felt quite as broken as the stones about me. Then, through the pounding sickness in my head, I heard a low whistle; with a final onslaught of desperate threats, the blows stopped and the noise lapsed into silence. Of Isobel there was no sound, though that I realized only later. For the moment, I could feel nothing beyond my own agony.

They had not tied my hands – they had rightly surmised that once on the ground, blind and hobbled, my defences would be inconsequentially feeble – but I had neither the strength nor the will to move a single, screaming muscle. Even the sound of footsteps drawing near, the sense through the thick sack-cloth that there was a light approaching, could not inspire me to action. I lay there, prone and helpless before whatever new fate approached.

'Oh ho!' came a voice, a rough voice that betrayed little sympathy, but not, thank God, a voice I recognized from my ordeal. 'Been a disturbance 'ere, 'as there?'

I managed to muster an incomprehensible moan, and repeated it again as heavy fingers prised the sack from my head, carelessly rolling me this way and that. I took several long, gasping breaths of the sweet air that greeted me before opening my dust-clogged eyes.

I should have guessed sooner, of course, should have recognized the voice from the outset, but in my punished state it needed several moments emptily staring at my rescuer before I could focus my sight and my thoughts together to produce a name. Constable Stubb.

'I 'opes you've not been up to mischief,' he said sternly.

He held a stout pole bearing a lantern, and its light chiselled ghoulish, mocking shadows into the cracks in his face. But I was not looking at him. My gaze was transfixed by the grave opposite me, which also fell within the orb of his lantern. The carved inscription had weathered into illegibility, but a new name had been crudely daubed over it, the paint so fresh it still dribbled down to form spidery serifs under the letters. Letters which spelled out, with as much reverence for spelling as for the tomb's original occupant, 'Martin Jerald'.

At such moments, the mind can prove indecently trivial. 'The bastards,' I thought. 'They've misspelled it.'

16

I WAS RAISED UP, DANGLING BY MY ARMS AND LEGS LIKE A CHILD being swung into a pond. They were weak, these bearers, and I scraped the ground where I sagged between them, but I was past caring. Then there were stairs, ascending, but with more hands to help me up them. At last soft feathers under my head, and a warm caress enveloping me. I slept.

I awoke to find that I seemed to be lying on a slope, angling sharply away from the roof above me, and for a moment I wondered by what force I was held there. Was I tied down? No – an experimental twitch of my limbs proved them to be free. I rolled over into the slope, hugging myself against the soft ground beneath me. Not ground, though – mattress. And not angled, but flat; it was the roof that angled. A white roof. A roof that could well have been the pitched ceiling of my room at the inn. I rolled back over for a wider view.

The wider view was rather obstructed by the face peering closely over me. Isobel. Behind her I could discern, or thought I could discern, the grubby features of Isaac, his nose wrinkled in morbid fascination.

'Where . . .?' I began, and stopped as I realized how dry my mouth was. And how stiff.

'Back at the inn.' Isobel stroked a cool hand over my forehead, her fingers running through clotted hair. 'They found you in the churchyard and brought you here. You weren't very well.'

I coughed a little. 'I don't feel very well,' I agreed, although I could at least be thankful that Stubb hadn't thought the gaol a more suitable hospital.

I relaxed my head back into my pillow, closing my eyes. A harsh grey light was coming through the high window. It must be well past dawn.

I remembered something. 'Crawley,' I whispered. 'I need to see Crawley.'

Isobel turned to Isaac and murmured something to him; he rose and left the room, casting a lingering glance over my face before he closed the door.

'Is it so bad?' I asked, grimacing. Certainly my lips and chin could not move very far without sending a stabbing pain through my jaw.

'Better than your ribs,' said Isobel, trying to force some cheer. 'And your arse. It looks like they dragged a plough over you and then paddled you with an oar for good measure.'

'It feels much like that.'

I lay very still. The sheet seemed to be stuck to me, and I did not relish the idea of pulling off half my skin with any sudden motion. Isobel cupped a hand underneath my head and lifted it, using the other to guide a cup of cold water to my lips. I sucked at it noisily.

'Rest now,' she said, when she had wiped my mouth with a handkerchief. 'You look like you need it.'

'Crawley,' I said again, stronger now. 'Mazard. I need to tell him about Mazard.'

'Shhhh.' Isobel pressed a finger over my lips and stroked the side of my neck. 'Captain Crawley's coming. You can sleep until then.'

She stood, and pulled a thin curtain over the window. It did little to darken the room, but it did take the sting off the light. Enough, it seemed, to allow me to doze, for when I opened my eyes again Crawley was there. He looked angry.

'I trust these are not the fruits of some alehouse altercation.' His voice was stern, but I sensed concern beneath it. Or perhaps I suffered delusions.

'No, sir,' I croaked, lifting myself up on one elbow. 'Regrettably not.'

As swiftly as I could, with frequent recourse to the cup Isobel held for me, I explained the facts of what had happened. I also proffered a few opinions that had begun to form in my aching skull.

'I was warned off my investigations, sir, told to stay out at sea. But what investigations have I made in the last few days? On Monday I saw Mazard, the banker, and yesterday I helped Bingham search a carriage from London. A carriage with a small fortune in gold aboard, which I saw being personally delivered to that same Mr Mazard.'

Crawley scowled. 'You are weakened, Lieutenant, and in a parlous state of mind. I shall therefore do you the courtesy of ignoring your ravings.'

I lifted an arm weakly in protest. 'Someone is funding the smugglers' trade, sir – so much is obvious. Webb, the man Ducker hauled up from the seabed, was apparently involved with them and may indeed have lost his life because of that, as my assailants hinted last night. I know that Webb was with the dead man, Vitos, and his companion Laminak, and I know they intended to visit Mazard the day before Vitos died under the cliffs. Every trail involving smugglers, gold or murder seems to lead to Mr Mazard, and not two days after I have confronted him I am beaten within an inch of my life.' Although I still could not envision the shape of the maze I had uncovered, for the first time I sensed I knew who was at its centre. And not alone, I thought. 'And of course, everyone knows who Mazard takes as his partner in all his businesses.'

I had overstated my case. I saw it at once in the incredulous irritation that crossed Crawley's face.

'You are in no condition for uninformed speculation, Lieutenant. No man would be who had suffered your injuries. You have not a shred of evidence that Mr Mazard even knew Vitos or Webb, let alone had a hand in their deaths. Accusing him of such monstrous crimes, without the most overwhelming proof of guilt, would make your position in this town, as well as my own, wholly untenable.' He pursed his lips. 'As for Sir Lawrence, I understand well that you feel little charity towards the man, but that does not give you the right to slander him. Doing so will hardly improve relations between you, and you will forfeit much of the sympathy you are due. He is a hard man who has taken against you. Many would be pressed to fault that.'

I slumped back. I should have known my idea would find little support, though I was convinced of the truth of it.

'Whoever it was,' I said flatly, 'they sent their men after me. I do not know that they will be contented with what they have achieved thus far.'

'I have two of the crew guarding the door,' said Crawley. 'And Constable Stubb is downstairs.' If he purposed to reassure me, he had only partially succeeded.

He stood, and donned his hat.

'I shall leave you to the ministrations of Mrs Dawson here,' he said, a touch awkwardly. 'And send the surgeon from the seamen's hospital.'

As soon as he was gone, Isobel sat down beside me.

'Pig,' she said, looking at the door.

'He's not a bad man,' I told her. 'He still suffers from his past mistakes. I can understand his reluctance to tilt at the two most powerful men on this station.' Especially at the behest, and on behalf, of a junior officer with a taste for drink, a nose for trouble, and perhaps no more than four days of a naval career remaining.

'Well, I wouldn't blink once if you told me that Sir Lawrence was up to his neck in this. He was round to the laundry at dawn, full of news for Miss Hoare of where I'd been last night. Constable Stubb must have seen me there and peached me to him.'

It took me a second to remember that she had in fact been in the same danger as I had, and I offered a slew of apologies for having been so remiss in asking after her.

'Not to worry,' she said, though her tone suggested she had been waiting for a concerned enquiry. 'They didn't want much with me. I got away with this.'

She ran a finger over her right cheek. Propping myself up, with some difficulty, I saw a long, thin scab where a shallow cut had been made.

'But they turned to you first,' I remembered. 'And spoke to you at some length.'

'Only as a way to get to you, I'd think,' said Isobel quickly. She looked away, perhaps ashamed of her disfigurement, though I doubted it would scar. 'Anyhow, whatever they meant by it, they got me in the end. Once Sir Lawrence had Miss Hoare on to how I was with you in the churchyard last night, she called me down and threw me out for being a troublemaker and a danger. That, and some things that don't need repeating.'

'So you are homeless?'

I squinted at her. A mournful feeling of shamed impotence stabbed at me, but only after a moment did I recognize it as that favourite state of my father's: guilt. It was not something I often experienced.

'I'm sorry,' I said. 'I seem to have brought a great deal of distress on you.'

'Don't be simple. I knew from the go that a navy officer wouldn't sit too well with some people. Not in Dover. 'Specially not one like you.' Isobel coughed a little, and gulped down some of the water. 'Besides, it could be worse. I stayed at the parson's last night. He offered me a room 'til I could rearrange myself.'

I tried to make some sound approximating to sympathy, though it emerged more as a strangled gurgle, and when I tried to pat her knee consolingly my hand fell short and flapped in mid-air like a dying fish.

'You may stay here tonight, if you want.' I spoke more formally than I had intended – without liquor to erode my manners, I was conscious there was a certain impropriety in my suggestion. I tried a smile. 'You'll find it warm, at least. Although perhaps you do not want to give Miss Hoare the satisfaction of being proved right on the subject of your character.'

Her mouth turned up in a weak grin. 'If she's any conscience, she'll repent of the depths she's driven me to.'

'Certainly if she knows me.'

That brought a full smile to her face, and she pushed my shoulder playfully. I tried not to wince.

I remember little of that day. Sometimes I slept, and sometimes I thought I slept, and occasionally I would wake up and listen to Isobel's rambling chatter. A surgeon came, with much tutting and scolding, as if I had brought these afflictions upon myself. He cleaned my wounds and wrapped me in so many bandages I believe I could have leaped from the window and bounced off the ground, if I'd had the strength to leave my bed. Crawley did not return, but Isaac brought up a bottle of brandy, for the 'medicinal' price of four shillings, and Isobel allowed me a short draught before removing it beyond my abbreviated reach.

It was dark when I next awoke, inside the room as well as out: the candle was snuffed, and there was only a crack of orange light under the door sill to give me my bearings. I felt hot, swathed in bandages as I was, and I scrabbled on the floor for the water.

There was a knock. I tensed, the smuggler's warning driving through my brain, but almost immediately my fears were allayed by the sound of Ducker's voice announcing a visitor. Swinging my legs out of bed, I stumbled painfully to the door. The bolt, I saw, had been shut from the inside.

'Who is it?' I asked cautiously.

'Nevell.' He sounded far more awake than I.

I shot the bolt open.

'Were you asleep?' asked Nevell. 'I do apologize. But I wanted to talk to you. About Mazard.'

I groaned. 'I'm glad someone does.'

Nevell stepped into the room, holding his candle forward as he examined the bandages that served as my nightshirt.

'The man outside said you had been the victim of unfortunate circumstance. You look as though you've gone head-on against a chaise and four.'

'All it took was a pair of ruffians,' I explained. 'With a distaste for the enquiries I was making. Enquiries which curiously all seemed to be leading to that most respectable buttress of the Dover community, Mr Mazard.' I sank down onto the edge of my bed, and motioned Nevell to the adjacent stool. 'I'm ill equipped to receive at the moment, but there's brandy somewhere behind you.'

Nevell reached for the bottle and swigged it liberally.

'Much required,' he said with satisfaction. 'I've hardly been out of the saddle since I saw you two days ago.'

'Naturally you heard of my plight and raced to be at my bedside,' I suggested, taking my own draught from the bottle.

'Naturally,' said Nevell, with a rather more sardonic laugh than I felt strictly necessary. 'Actually, I was passing through on other business, but I thought as I was here I might convey a curious piece of information I have gleaned about Mr Mazard. But perhaps you are more intimately acquainted with his affairs?'

'Quite possibly. And if I am, I don't commend it to you.'

Speaking quickly, I repeated the well-rehearsed gist of what I had proposed to Crawley that morning. To my surprised satisfaction, it met with a far warmer reception from Nevell.

'Mazard and Cunningham,' he mused. 'An intriguing proposition. And, as you've discovered, a dangerous one. But how much more dangerous if behind them you have nobility coming down from London to personally invest in their scheme?'

I thought of Lord Arlington and his chest of golden guineas, and groaned. 'I hope not. I doubt I could survive much more danger. But for now it remains speculation, unless you've brought more decisive news.'

Nevell shook his head. 'Sadly not. My news is merely a titbit, a curiosity which drew my attention. It seems that Mazard has written to his broker in London—'

'Not by the public post?' I interrupted.

'Careless, I agree. But he has instructed this agent to sell large holdings of stock, and of the government's debt, even if it be at a loss.'

'Is that so curious?' I asked. 'Of all the activities that Mazard may dabble in, I should have thought stock trading to be the least reprehensible. Surely you are not so great a snob that you begrudge a man a merchant's profit?'

'Not at all. But it is strange that when the prospects for peace, and so for the stocks to soar in value, are stronger than they have been in ten years, when Mazard can see the correspondence being ferried across outside his very window, he should choose this moment to dispose of his holdings. Why would a man with a nose for investment do that?'

'Why indeed?'

'Who can say?' Once again, Nevell retreated into enigma. 'But your Lord Arlington obviously felt there was an opportunity for a large amount of his money to be well invested in Dover. Perhaps Mazard too thinks he can put his capital to better use.' He leaned forward earnestly. 'And if you are correct, and he is the smugglers' banker, then think how big a haul of contraband you'd see it buy.'

'I shall keep my eyes open,' I told him, and promptly belied that as a powerful yawn overtook me.

Between my aches and my fatigue, with perhaps a dash of the brandy thrown over them, I confess I had not understood all I might have in Nevell's tale, and my stiff limbs were starting to long for a return to the warm bed. Nevell must have seen as much.

'I may be back soon,' he said, adjusting his hat as he made for the door. 'I shall leave you to convalesce until then. But don't drop your guard. Particularly in dark churchyards late at night.'

I locked the door after him and returned to bed, pulling the covers over my shivering body.

'You're back, are you?' asked Isobel sleepily, wrapping an arm around me. 'Ooh, you are cold.'

'I had a visitor,' I said, letting her press against me. Her warmth was pleasant. 'Who may be able to tar Mazard with something more than suspicions and coincidences.' I grunted, remembering how meagre his information was. 'Or who may be unable to prove so much as the weather.'

'Still,' murmured Isobel, sliding a slender leg between my own, 'anything to get to that bastard.'

I was finding the heat against my thigh most distracting. 'Well, I hope it proves worth being tanned to a leather,' I said, 'because I shall be in no condition to undertake any more dangerous exploits in the immediate future.'

Isobel laughed lightly, and sat up. The covers cascaded off her back; she raised her arms, and pulled the thin shift over her head. She was naked beneath it. Her fingers trailed over my bandaged chest, down across my stomach, and onto my hips.

'Well,' she giggled. 'Let's see what exploits your condition does allow.'

Much to my surprise, no-one knocked on the door. No-one shouted from the hallway, and nobody leaped through the window brandishing a wicked knife. Maybe the guards outside heard something, but if so, they took it with discretion and kept silent. Even the cockerels seemed to delay their fanfare as late as was decent. For once, against all precedent, we were left to enjoy ourselves alone. In peace. And with only a little aching.

17

IT SEEMS FAIR TO SAY THAT MY WAKING THE NEXT MORNING WAS THE happiest of all my time in Dover. Isobel and I and the sheets were all tangled together, soft and warm and tousled, and when I made to extricate myself it took little more than the tightening of her thin arms about my chest to dissuade me. She kissed the nape of my neck and tickled me behind my ears, and I hugged myself back against her. The small swell of her breasts pushed at the bruises and bandages on my back, but I was happy to allow the dull throbbing they antagonized and let her nestle there in contented silence.

Inevitably, there came a knock on the door.

'Lieutenant Jerrold, sir.' It was Ducker. 'Cap'n Crawley's respects, and if you'd like to come down to the 'arbour we'll be away afore long. If you're feelin' well enough, 'e said.'

Miraculously, the gentle exertions of the night seemed to have teased out much of the pain, but I debated a moment whether this was my public position. The temptation to stay all morning in bed with Isobel was overwhelming, but I could not forget that it was Thursday, and by the Monday I would need to demonstrate to my uncle some evidence at least of my innocence. Evidence that might be found if we managed to bring some smugglers to account, if they and Mazard and Vitos proved to be all bound up together. And it would be pleasant, I thought, to play the role of the suffering hero with Crawley for once, rather than the wastrel, to reap some reward from my ordeal. Besides, I would be far safer at sea from the attentions of those who meant me harm.

'I shall be out presently,' I called. 'I suggest you wait downstairs. I shall of course require some protection for the journey.' I would leave nothing to chance. 'I recommend you avoid the coffee.'

Pulling free of Isobel, reluctantly, I tried to dress myself. It was an effort, for I could scarcely bend enough to look in the mirror, and after a few theatrical harumphs Isobel took mercy on me, and helped me into my shirt, breeches and coat. I doubt she would have made much of a valet, though, for her fingers had a pleasing tendency to stray from the buttons at hand; even allowing for my immobility, my toilet seemed to take far longer than was absolutely necessary. In my magnanimity, I made no complaint.

'And what does the day hold for you?' I asked, as she adjusted my neck-cloth. I had decided not to shave, for my face was still tender.

'I'll try to find some work.' She was still entirely naked, her small body drawn tighter than ever as she stretched up to reach my neck.

'You can hardly fail to impress if you go attired like that.' I gazed on her with frank admiration. 'But perhaps not for the sort of occupation you seek.'

'I'll wear my maid's dress,' she said wickedly. 'Most men seem to like it. And more, when I let the neck down just enough so they think they've a chance.'

'What an unprincipled little cat you are.' I affected righteous shock, then laughed. 'No wonder I'm so fond of you.'

'Better to allow men ideas for nothing that they'd probably have anyhow, than let them pay to put their hands on you,' retorted Isobel. She stepped back, squinting at my *tout ensemble*, and smiled. ''Specially when there's only one pair of hands I want about me for the moment.'

I took her meaning and was happy to indulge her, putting my arms about the curve of her waist and drawing her close. An involuntary grimace warned her not to reciprocate too enthusiastically.

‘Good luck,’ I said, pulling my lips away from hers. ‘I had better not delay Ducker any further. I do not know how long we will be at sea, but I suppose I may return this evening. Will you be here?’ To my surprise, I found it was suddenly very important to me that she should be.

‘Of course.’ She grinned. ‘If I can sneak past that Isaac. Wouldn’t want me costing you a shilling.’

‘For you, my dear, a guinea.’

In the taproom, Ducker had ignored my advice regarding the coffee, and looked as though he regretted it. With him before me, and flanked by two of the crew, I proceeded to the docks.

The smell of fresh tar and shaven wood was thick about *Orestes*, and the new mast and rigging looked sharp enough, if a little delicate against the weathered timbers of her hull. The shipshape atmosphere must have infused the men as well, for they worked with rather more exertion than I had noticed before.

Crawley seemed surprised to see me. ‘You’ve come,’ he said, restraining any pleasure he felt in the event. ‘I had thought – feared – your condition might preclude your joining us.’

‘I may not be patched up as well as *Orestes*,’ I said bluffly, ‘but the doctor’s jury-rig should serve. Where are we bound?’

‘Up the coast. And then back down the coast. And then we shall retrace that path, and repeat it again, until it brings us into action with a smuggler. Whatever it is that has cursed our efforts of late, it will not be want of trying this time. Mr Ducker! Stand ready to cast off.’

We must have made a fine sight sailing proudly out of the harbour, our new sail bellying out in the firm breeze and a thick foam surging off our bows as we drove through the water. I saw Crawley and Ducker giving frequent attention to the new spars, but they seemed to hold well enough, harnessing the beam wind to urge us ever forward. The air snapped and billowed around my ears, and I had to grip the rail with a tender arm to hold myself upright on the steeply heeling deck. As Dover shrank behind us, I experienced a rare joy in the sensations of the sea, of being on a small ship under full sail, alive to every gust and eddy of the wind.

Whatever pleasure it afforded me, though, there was little practical work for me to do, save perhaps repeat orders that could be heard as well from Crawley's mouth as from my own on that small deck. Thus, once we were some way away from shore, Crawley handed me a small glass and told me to watch the shore from the weather rail.

'But it's barely lunchtime,' I objected. 'Surely there is none who would be so bold as to run contraband on a clear day in broad daylight?'

'These are villains who will take their chances any hour God sends,' said Crawley sharply. 'Particularly if they think their enemies too laggard to watch for them. Be ready, Mr Jerrold. "In such an hour as ye think not, the smuggler cometh." '

The rest of the morning, and much of the afternoon, saw the dogged unfolding of Crawley's dogged plan. We sailed up the coast as far as Deal, then brought our bows around and sailed down again for Dover. I enjoyed the first leg more, for on the return the wind rose. Now the frothing sea was never far from the gunwales, and frequently spilled over the side to wash my shoes and chill my shivering feet. I began to regret leaving my bed behind, for Crawley was not the least impressed with my stoicism, and I had precious little service to offer aboard ship.

We were about halfway back from Deal, with the turrets of Walmer castle just slipping from view, when I saw it: a small boat, drawn up on the beach in a narrow cleft in the cliff-face. At first I supposed it to be a fisherman, and felt sufficiently wretched that I might not have looked any further had I not also been bored to distraction by the monotony of the day. With a tired sigh, I hauled a larger glass from the rack and, balancing precariously against the bulwark, trained it towards the shore. My gaze swung from side to side as I struggled to pinpoint what I had seen previously; then I found my bearings, and honed in on the small vessel.

She was a cutter, I decided, like ourselves – the tall mast and the long bowsprit identified her readily enough, though she was some length shorter than *Orestes*. A few small figures topped her deck; a few more were at work on the beach. The boat's rig obscured my view for the moment, but *Orestes* was making steady progress along the coast, and as we drew away I gained a clear line of sight through to the shore party. My hand clenched tight about the glass. There was no mistaking it now: they were offloading casks from their boat, and rolling them quickly, but unhurriedly, up the beach.

'Captain Crawley, sir,' I shouted in excitement. 'A landing! Broad on the starboard quarter.'

Crawley was beside me in an instant, a glass already in his hand and aimed where I had indicated.

'By the good Lord you're right, Mr Jerrold,' he muttered. 'Not much size to her, granted, but perhaps a beginning.'

'Long as they're not landin' salt water again,' mumbled one of the men.

Crawley ignored him. 'Steersman, put us about. Mr Jerrold, run up the signal: "Prepare to be boarded." Once we are about, clear for action. They may yet try to run for it.'

Though I saw no tell-tale flashes of a spyglass ashore, they must have been watching us. I had lost sight of them for a moment as we went about, and by the time I could make them out again the beach was cleared, and the boat well into the water. We would be hard pressed to cross her bows before she passed on to the seaward side of us.

'A point to leeward, if you please,' shouted Crawley. 'I want the gunner to put a shot in front of her, slow her down.' His face trembled with tension. 'I will not see her pass us.'

Ropes creaked as *Orestes* eased to starboard. We were aiming further out to sea now, on a course that would give us more time to intersect our quarry, more time for the advantage of our sail area to tell. But the smuggler, if smuggler she were, was fairly racing along, almost bursting out of her goose-winged canvas she moved so fast.

Our deck shook as the for'ard cannon fired, and I saw the bow slew round from the shock. The mainsail buckled and slapped, spilling out wind from the brief change of course, while a cloud of acrid smoke swept over us. Crawley was shouting at the steersman and the men on the halyards to get us back on our line, but we had lost precious speed and time before we managed it. And the shot had not shown the least effect on our opponents.

'She's laying off a bit,' shouted Ducker from amidships. 'Showing us her arse.'

Through my glass I could see the truth of what he said: she had now turned her bow away from us on to almost the same course as we held, though several cables ahead.

'That's a queer move,' said Crawley. 'They'll never beat us canvas to canvas. I'd have said their only chance was to outmanoeuvre us.'

'At least on our bow they know we can't get a cannon on to them,' I thought aloud.

I saw Ducker moving aft, his face grim. A creased chart was clasped in his fist.

'It ain't that,' he said shortly. He unfurled the paper, and jabbed his finger on it. 'They're aimin' to use their draught to see 'em over the sands.'

Crawley's face went grey and his shoulders slumped; without a word he turned his back on us, as if unable to meet our gaze, though we only looked for orders. Suddenly, and for wholly obvious reasons, I remembered Davenant's words at the assembly: *cracked her open like a walnut.* It was not a thought to inspire me to accompany Crawley over the Goodwin Sands, graveyard of unnumbered ships. And the tide was receding ever further.

Crawley turned back to face us, and I hastily tried to don the mask of confidence, though I fear it might have seemed more like sickly terror.

'We will continue with the chase.'

Though they were not the words I wished to hear, his determined tone at least fed me a little strength.

'And trust our lives to almighty God,' he added after a short pause.

'And a man with a lead?' asked Ducker, not missing a beat.

'No, Mr Ducker. We have no time for that. We cannot shorten sail while our quarry continues to spread hers.'

We moved apart, Ducker to oversee the steerage, Crawley to fix his stare on the boat ahead of us, and I to the rail. I looked down at the heaving water under our gunwale, trying desperately to see past the waves and foam to the hidden depths beneath. I felt almost ill with the effort, and with the thought of the doom which might be rising, *de profundis*, to snatch us.

With a shiver that might have been the chill but probably wasn't, I tore myself away. If I saw anything, after all, it would almost certainly be too late – not that that thought was any comfort. Looking forward, I could see that we were at least holding our own against our target, were in fact inching slowly closer. Though inches were little against the distance that still divided us, and less still against the shrinking fathoms below our keel.

'We're overhauling her,' said Ducker.

'We'll be at the hook of Holland before we catch her,' snapped Crawley. 'Look at that sail – it's loose as a Plymouth whore.'

I could not believe he spoke with authority, nor with accuracy, for the sail could not have slipped more than a fraction from its intended trim. Ducker, though, was all bustle, mustering men on the halyards and hauling on the mainsail with a great commotion until it was just to his liking. To my unexacting eye, he did not appear to have changed it a whit, but Crawley seemed happier. Or at any rate, not quite so sour.

'She'll be plumb over the worst of it now, I reckon,' said Ducker, watching our quarry with a measured gaze. 'An' still goin' strong.'

I followed his eyes. For all Crawley's hectoring – or perhaps because of Ducker's infinitesimal adjustments, I allowed – we had gained clear distance on her; had we a bow chaser mounted, we might well have chanced a shot. I could see the men on her deck now without a glass, could see them scurrying about with a firm purpose, as intent on escaping us as we were on capturing them. A couple were on her stern looking back, though whether with fear or defiance I could not tell.

And then I could not care, for suddenly I had been flung to the deck with the unflinching thud of complete surprise. My bandaged body screamed in agony, even as I registered that there had been a ghastly lurch in our momentum, accompanied, so I thought, by a deep rasping from our hull. I looked up wildly: half the crew at least were as prone, some shouting in alarm or pain, but the sails were still full and the boat still moving forward.

'The sandbar! Put her about!' roared Crawley from behind me.

I turned slowly to see him clutching at the bulwark; then, with no patience for the stunned steersman, he launched himself across the deck and wrapped himself around the tiller, pushing it over with all his strength. Even after our scrape we did not want for steerage way, and the response was immediate: *Orestes*' bow came up, and for a second time she shuddered as she came head on into the wind. I could hear cordage straining and popping all about me as our canvas bulged to its limit, then lost the wind and whipped back across the deck before beginning to luff. Crawley had stopped us almost dead but, I saw now, at a crippling cost to our new rigging. With a wrenching, tearing sound, a block aloft broke free of its line and tumbled to the deck; then the strains on the mast shifted yet again, and two stays snapped open.

'Ware heads on deck!' shouted Ducker. The falling block had struck home without hitting anyone, but the loose rope-ends dangling from the masthead bucked and writhed in the air with a fearsome violence, and I needed no warning as to what those could do to a man's head. 'And get that sail down!'

'Cap'n, sir,' yelled a man from the bow, 'man overboard from the owler, sir!'

'What?' Crawley was on his feet in a second, heedless of any danger from above. 'What's that?'

With an eye and a half on the rigging above, I raised myself to my knees and peered over the side. The sailor was right: although the boat we had pursued so recklessly was now fading fast into the distance, well clear of the sands, there was a small object floating above the waves a little way off. I might have mistaken it for a seal, or a fisherman's float, or merely some driftwood, were it not for the occasional arm that broke the surface to wave at us, and the intermittent sound of desperate shouting.

'Get the jollyboat in the water and bring him in, Mr Jerrold,' said Crawley. 'We shall salvage what we can from this incident.'

Getting the boat launched from under a tangle of fallen rigging proved no easy task, but after the shock of the chase, and our near wreck, I think the men were glad of any activity to turn their hands to. Certainly they rowed with alacrity, if a little raggedly.

The bobbing head was still above water as we drew near, but I began to wonder with mounting concern if he was not mortally wounded, for the sea around him was infused with a rusty brown cloud spreading from his body.

'Draw sharks, that,' offered one of the crew.

'Well, I have no intention of jumping overboard to rescue him. Give me that boat-hook.'

Crouching in the bows, I extended the pole to the buoyant smuggler. Wounded he might have been, but he latched onto it with vigour and was swiftly hauled, coughing and shivering, into our boat.

'You are under arrest,' I told him.

He was a broad-shouldered man, with a narrow, rat-like face that swept forward to his nose like a ship's prow, the effect accentuated by the way his wet hair was slicked tightly back in the opposite direction. He did not seem to be hurt, but his white shirt bore a dark, rosewood stain, which seemed neither the colour of blood nor of the weaver's original design.

'You can't arrest me,' he said, with astonishing presumption and not the least hint of remorse. 'What've I done?' It sounded more like a taunt than a plea for mercy.

'Participated in an unlawful landing of unaccustomed goods,' I began. 'Ignored an order from one of his Majesty's ships to heave to. Maliciously attempted to drive our ship aground.'

He spat out some sea-water, insolently close to my feet. 'Can't read signals,' he said. 'An' we didn't force you to come galloping after us over the sands. Dangerous, they is. You ought to be more careful, 'specially if you can't 'andle your boat proper.'

So confounded was I by his bravado in the face of all evidence that I sat there gaping for a moment, speechless. Ducker, though, was already moving forward, a knife in his hand.

'No, quartermaster,' I shouted feebly, raising my hand, but with a deft movement, which our captive had the wit not to resist, he sliced through the brown-stained smock and pulled it open.

'We'll do you for this, right enough,' he announced. 'Thought you looked too big for your trousers.'

I stared at the wet man's torso. He was not broad-shouldered at all, but had created the illusion with a pair of long, tubular sacks hanging on a short length of rope around his neck, like a yoke. They were swollen out, and stained an even darker shade of the colour that had permeated the smock. With the tip of his knife, Ducker made a small incision in one. The taut fabric spilled open, and a mass of soggy brown leaves oozed through the crack, dribbling into the bilge.

Ducker pinched out a small quantity, held them under his nose to sniff, then passed them to me.

'Tea, Lieutenant?' he offered.

We took our captive – the puffer, Ducker called him, from the way his cargo puffed up his physique – back to *Orestes*, and thence sailed slowly back to Dover. We had nowhere to keep the prisoner, who would say nothing once his guilt had been affirmed, and Crawley was eager to get us into harbour, where he could inspect the damage. I doubted the exertions we had placed on *Orestes*' canvas had left it wholly sound, and there was always the worry of what the sandbar might have done below the waterline.

'Take our prisoner to the gaol,' Crawley said as we nosed into the outer harbour. 'A night there may loosen his tongue.'

'With respect, sir, may I request permission to stay the night ashore. I fear for the effect of a hammock on these ribs, and the knocks I've had today will have done little to help them mend.' I also ached to see Isobel, but I did not think he would find so much merit in that argument.

Crawley assumed a pensive scowl. 'Very well, Lieutenant,' he allowed at length. 'Your eyes, after all, were first to catch the smugglers. You may as well rest them adequately, and your bones likewise. Come to the gaol tomorrow morning, and we shall see what this villain has to say for himself.'

18

I ARRIVED AT THE GAOL LATE, THOUGH SADLY NOT THROUGH ANY distraction of vice. Isobel had not been at the inn when I returned, and despite the long-drawn minutes, and then hours, I had spent staring at the ceiling, hoping that each creak on the stairwell might herald her arrival, she had not come. I had slept badly, my ribs aching more than ever and my mind tossing with thoughts of Isobel, and with the dread fear of what my uncle would do if I could not resolve my innocence to his satisfaction in the next three days. It was that thought which woke me, and which weighed on my awkward preparations as I slowly dressed, ate, shaved, and at length ventured reluctantly out to the prison. Walking under the arch between the two dangling manacles did little to improve my humour.

It must have been a peculiarly law-abiding fortnight in Dover, for the cell seemed as empty now as it had been during my last sojourn. Visiting custom, though, was much improved: Crawley, Sir Lawrence Cunningham and Constable Stubb were all there, as well as Captain Bingham, whom I had not seen since the roadblock. They stood in a loose crescent, with the hunched form of Gibble holding a lantern behind them so that the object of their attentions was masked in shadow.

'Ah, Jerrold.' Crawley turned to meet me; disconcertingly, one half of his face was shrouded in darkness. 'Is your health recovered?'

'Passably, sir,' I said, reluctant to show any enthusiasm.

'Excellent.' He swung an arm around, like a showman with his freaks. 'Behold, the fruit of our labours.'

I pushed in between Cunningham and Bingham, as far from Gibble as I could manage, and looked at the wall where the captive sat loaded with irons.

'This, Lieutenant, is one Daniel Squires.' Crawley did not bother to reciprocate the introduction. 'Sir Lawrence has just been putting some questions to him.'

'The pressing question, of course, being: what does he know?'

Cunningham's hissing tone, I realized, was highly suited to the business of interrogation. I had not appreciated it as much when I was on the end of it.

'Who arranged your landing yesterday?' He put his mouth close to the prisoner's ear. 'Who leads your little gang?'

Squires shook his head.

'Whoever he may be, is he truly worth ten feet of rope choking the life out of you?' There was an abrasive edge to Cunningham's words now. 'I can make you dance a merry jig on the gallows, smuggler, until you wonder that you have the strength in you to continue. Or . . .' He paused. 'I can be merciful.'

I looked about. There was revulsion in the faces around me, but none of us said a word or raised a finger to interrupt Cunningham. He had us mesmerized with his cruelty, and we all felt the urgency of the situation, the possibility that this could be our best chance of breaking the smugglers. If Crawley was right, that no man came to Dover save on the strictest probation, then nothing could be more important to us.

'I despise you,' Cunningham whispered. 'You flout the laws of the kingdom and threaten its ordained order. You would see it crumble into fire and blood and murder, and all to feed your monstrous wickedness, your libertine appetite for sin and evil.'

With his tea-stained trousers and loaded chains, our smuggler did not look the familiar picture of insatiate vice. Nor could I wholly concur with the opinion that feeding the market for cheap spirits and tobacco was the apogee of licentiousness. But Cunningham held the floor.

'In France, you know, they slice off men's heads like cabbages if they offend against the state. A quick and painless death, they say.' Clearly, in his mind, an opportunity wasted. 'But here in England a good hangman can wring you out slowly, will keep you strung up between hope and despair until you've not a drop of life left in you.' The relish in his voice was grotesque. 'The punishment will always suit the crime, smuggler, and silence before an officer of his Majesty's law is perhaps the very greatest crime. Certainly in my eyes, and they are the eyes that will see you hang.'

'I doesn't know.' We all started as Squires spoke for the first time. His voice was sullen, but he seemed to have shrugged off Cunningham's threats, for there was no fear evident. ''S all done with a nudge an' a tip o' the 'at, no-one knows no-one. You could 'ang us 'til the crows et us, an' we'd still not give you nothin'.'

'Then we may as well give the crows their breakfast,' said Cunningham. 'If you cannot be of any use to us.'

'Didn't say that, did I?' Insolence crept into Squires' voice. 'We doesn't know oo runs the gaff, but we still 'as to know where they wants us.' He leaned forward into the orange light. 'An' they wants us all there tomorrer night.'

'Where?' Crawley's voice was taut to breaking.

'Well, that's a question fer you, ain't it?' One that Squires seemed in no hurry to answer. 'I wonders 'ow you'd value it?'

'I wonder how you value your neck,' Cunningham retorted. 'Do you presume to *barter* with his Majesty's justice?'

'Never, sir,' said Squires plaintively. 'But the truth of it is, sir, that me neck's in a tight spot already. If I doesn't talk to you, you'll 'ang me, an' fair enough. But if I does talk to you, there's others oo'll be none too pleased, oo'll not be wantin' to vote me Lord Mayor o' Dover, if you takes my meanin'.'

'We've no need to waste time bribing this felon,' interrupted

Bingham. 'We can as easily mount patrols along every inch of the coast tomorrow night.'

''Ardly, sir,' grinned the smuggler. 'We's there near to every night, and there's no-one sees us most times.'

'We saw you yesterday,' I objected. 'That's why you're here.'

'So you did, sir, so you did. But I reckon you 'ad a stroke o' luck when me shipmates tipped me overboard to lose some weight.' He gave a rueful chuckle. 'All's I'm sayin',' he continued, 'is that you got me cos you got lucky. Now, you could run your luck some more, but it's not served you so well of late, and per'aps you'd not care to gamble on it with so much to be lost. But if you knowed somethin' privy, sirs, well, that might change the shine o' the odds for you, might mark the cards for you so to speak. An' you *could* be knowin' somethin' privy, somethin' to let you get all the rest o' them what plugged me tomorrer night, if you just treat with me like gen'lemen.'

'More like a gambler, I think,' said Cunningham coldly. 'And whatever you may tell us, why should we think to act on the word of a smuggler?'

'Cos you'll not find an honest gen'leman oo'll tell what I can tell you. An' cos you know I'd rather see someone else's neck bein' stretched on your gibbet for what I said than be there meself for what I'd not said. An' cos I reckon you'd do right by a man what proved 'imself a friend to you. You'd set me up right enough, somewhere where me face weren't known an' the gang couldn't get me. Send me to Bristol, per'aps. There's a lot o' ways a man can disappear in Bristol, I'm told. You might even see to givin' me a small slice o' the goods recovered, if you was feelin' generous.'

'I'll send you to Botany Bay if you don't watch your tongue,' snapped Cunningham, but I could see that he, like all of us, was beginning to come around to the smuggler's persuasion.

'If you have dealt honestly with us, we shall remember it,' said Crawley evenly. 'Lying lips are an abomination to the Lord, but they that deal truly are His delight.'

'Bless you, rev'rend,' said the smuggler. 'I'll be takin' that as your word on scripture, then.' He looked up, scanning our faces. Nobody contradicted him.

'Where is this landing to be?' asked Crawley.

Squires settled back against the wall. 'Saint Marg'ret's, your grace. Big landin'. Biggest since the *Cambridge* landin' three years back, though you'll not've 'eard o' that, of course.'

'Saint Margaret's?' Bingham was incredulous. 'But there's a village there. Hardly the spot for a secret landing.'

'The villagers'll all be indoors then, won't they?' said Squires. 'They doesn't need to be told to watch the wall when we're about.'

'And what's the cargo to be?' asked Crawley.

Squires shrugged. ''Ollands, calicoes, brandy, bacca, tubs o' this an' that comin' in. But goin' back out, that's the one you want. Fifty thousand golden portraits o' George, all goin' over to show the Frenchies what a proper king looks like. Now *that*'d be worth somethin' to you, sirs.'

For a moment there was silence in the gaol, all save a quiet wheezing from somewhere deeper in. Cunningham's face was seized with a naked hunger, Bingham looked astonished, while Crawley's habitually stern mouth dangled open.

'Fifty thousand guineas?' asked Crawley at last. 'You'd need half a fleet to transport so much brandy.'

'An' a few ships more to keep it comfortable on the voyage,' agreed Squires. 'An' a few more to carry the Froggy soldiers what's to guard the landin' an' loadin'. Oh yes.' He nodded. 'They says Boney don't want to risk no chances with this. For fifty thousand guineas, I'd not argue. 'E's sendin' 'alf a legion of 'is best to make sure nothin' falls in the water.'

Again the room was still, our group torn between those who clearly thought this a fantasy and those who deemed it possible. All of us, though, I think, wanted to believe it.

'So, tomorrow night Buonaparte is sending a battalion of his soldiers to Saint Margaret's bay to hand over fifty thousand guineas' worth of contraband, assisted by your colleagues?' Bingham tugged at a stray lock of his red hair, disbelief rampant on his face. 'Impossible.'

'Like I said, sir, we does it near to every night. Oo's to notice a few more tubs an' a few Froggies with us? Saint Marg'ret's, tomorrer night,' he repeated. 'Go there an' you'll see it. I'd not go alone, though.'

'And at what time?'

'Mercy, sir, it's a landin' not the mail coach. You can't set your clock to it. It'll be somewhere 'tween sundown an' sunup, but likely near the top o' the tide.'

Squires sat back, clearly convinced he had earned his freedom. Judging by the faces of my companions, he was probably justified in his confidence.

Cunningham cleared his throat. 'I think, gentlemen, that we might adjourn somewhere more salubrious to discuss this intelligence. Perhaps to the guildhall. Fewer ears to hear our secrets.'

I turned to Crawley. 'If I may, sir, I would like to remain here a few minutes. This man may know something concerning the death of Mr Vitos.'

The idea had been distracting me ever since I'd arrived. I half recollected that I'd heard the name Danny mentioned that night, and I was curious whether the Daniel Squires before me could shed any light on the matter. I was also wary of raising the name of Mazard before the suspicious ears of Sir Lawrence.

'Very well,' said Crawley, clearly keen to be away. 'I suppose the turnkey will let you out and lock the gate.'

I had forgotten Gibble, standing behind us with the lantern all this time in silence. Now, though, he moved.

'Glarch,' he mumbled. 'Vregh.'

'It is his lunch hour,' translated Cunningham. 'Keeping the gaol is hungry work.'

'He can give me the key, and I shall lock it after myself,' I said impatiently. 'Doubtless we shall be making sail soon, and I do not wish to lose this opportunity to establish my good name.'

Cunningham raised his hooded eyelids, eloquently speaking everything he thought about my good name. Then he shrugged.

'Give him the key, Gibble.'

With much fussing and tugging, the thick ring of keys came away from Gibble's belt. I managed to avoid the touch of his fingers as I took it from him, but I could not escape the stickiness on the cold iron which left me feeling immediately soiled. I might well require Crawley and his bucket of water again after this.

'Shall I have Stubb stay to protect you?' Cunningham asked solicitously.

'He's wearing enough chains to set an anchor. I believe I will be safe.'

'We shall see you shortly in the guildhall,' said Crawley.

Then he and the rest of them were gone, and I was left alone with the prisoner.

'So,' I said, a touch awkwardly. 'As you will know, a man named Vitos tragically fell off a cliff some eleven days ago, before dawn on a Monday morning. There were smugglers there. One of them was called Danny.'

Squires raised his eyes. 'Lots of us by the name o' Danny.'

'You were there,' I said, attempting a confrontational approach.

'Beggin' yer pardon, sir, but I weren't.'

'Yes you were.'

He opened his eyes wide as a child's. 'I weren't, sir. Otherwise, o' course, I'd be all quick to 'elp. Ain't never 'eard o' Mister Vatos neither, afore you asks.'

'Vitos. Nor Laminak nor Webb, I suppose?'

'Sorry, sir.' He affected genuine regret, though I did not believe it.

'How about these fifty thousand guineas, then?' I asked, changing tack. 'Where are they at the moment?'

Squires looked at me as though I were feeble. 'If I knowed that, sir, I'd not've been riskin' my life with 'alf a pound o' tea yesterday, would I? I'd be ridin' a carriage in St James's.'

'Flat on your back in an alehouse, more likely. So you wouldn't know whether Mr Mazard, the banker down on Strond Street, happens to have the gold locked in his vault right now?'

I was standing very close over him, staring into those deceitful eyes with uncompromising venom. And, for a second, I saw him drop his gaze, before he lifted it again with restored vigour.

'Mr Mazard's a gen'leman, and worse'n that, a friend o' Sir Lawrence Cunningham's. You'd sooner find 'im throwin' 'is money in the pent than 'avin' dealin's with the likes of us.'

I stepped back. There was no doubting the simple logic of Squires' words, and no crack in the impertinent calm with which he delivered them, yet they decided me once and for all that Mazard must be at the centre of this. There was the obvious question as to why an imprisoned smuggler, with little to lose, would pass up an opportunity to slander an eminent citizen, most especially one with close ties to the magistrate. But more than that there was the manner of his words, a manner I remembered well from my schooldays of boys with a ridiculous piece of poetic bombast committed to memory, trying to get it out without catching the master's eye and bursting into laughter.

'Asides,' added Squires, shifting his manacled weight into a more comfortable position, 'you might want to watch what good names you questions, Lieutenant. Just think what I could tell the magistrate if 'e comes askin' about what I knows about you.'

I resisted the impulse to kick him. If he lied, he would get his justice in time; if he told the truth, I might just snatch enough glory with the fifty thousand guineas to vindicate myself in my uncle's eyes. And if Mazard were involved, perhaps the truth of it would come out on the beach the following night, when we apprehended his associates. Boiling with frustration, and glaring as ferociously as I could, I marched out of that miserable place. For what it matters, I still believe I locked the gate behind me.

I made for the guildhall, but Crawley was already descending its steps.

'It is decided,' he said. 'Colonel Copthorne will lead a substantial force from the castle tomorrow night, and array his men and guns at the top of the slope leading down to the beach. It is the only way up. If the soldiers escorting the contraband choose to fight, they will, he assures me, be cut down in a cauldron of fire and death.'

'Bravo,' I said reflexively, and promptly flinched under Crawley's sceptical stare.

'We,' he continued, 'will take *Orestes* out immediately, so as to catch the smugglers unawares tomorrow night. We will attempt to make contact with *Lancelot* and persuade her to join us. Otherwise, the duty of cutting off the smugglers' retreat will be all our own.'

Even he, incorrigible gloom-monger that he was, could not hide his excitement at the prospect.

'If we are exceptionally lucky,' I observed, 'we may even catch the bullion on the ships. Add it to the prize money.'

Crawley gave me a disapproving look. 'You realize, of course, that if that were to happen, the dragoons would have failed to apprehend the smugglers ashore.'

Unlikely though it seemed, I thought I sensed a note of mischief in his voice.

'We can only prepare for the worst,' I said dutifully. 'Speaking of which, sir, I must repair to my inn for a moment to fetch my pistols. And my sword.'

'Mine is with the smith having an edge put on it,' said Crawley. 'I shall meet you back here presently.'

I crossed the square and turned down the lane to the inn. Wan sunlight was breaking through the clouds above, and I whistled an invented tune as I reflected on the course events had taken. Vitos's death seemed less important now. If the intelligence from the smugglers were true, then action the following night could make or mend many reputations, not least my own. If the army did their bit on land, it might even pass without subjecting me to mortal danger. And when the smoke had cleared and the smugglers been hanged, there would be no denying that the significant moment of the affair had come when I noticed the landing being made the day before. Even my uncle could not overlook that.

The stable yard at the inn was silent and empty, as was the house within; it took me but a little time to mount the stairs, buckle on my sword, check the flints in my pistols and go back down. For all my excitement, I could not shake a lingering regret that Isobel had not been there, impatient though Crawley would be. And why had she not come last night? I asked myself, tumbling through a mire of half-formed, unhappy thoughts. Had she tired of me? It would not be the first time a girl had done so, though on those past occasions it had merely saved me the embarrassment of having to end it myself. Or, I wondered, had the same ruffians who had assaulted us in the churchyard come for her again, alone this time and unprotected? That thought did not sit well with my squeamish sensibilities.

So advanced, in fact, had my contemplation of her fate become that I almost missed her; only the blue woollen dress, and the strands of dark hair escaping the modesty of her mobcap, caught the edge of my eye as I regained the street. She did not notice me, and I might well have passed her entirely had I not been drawn to a second casual glance by the dim tugging of memory.

As my interest firmed into recognition, all other thoughts fled my head; I crossed the road at an undignified run and laid my hand on her arm. She turned, and her worried smile checked me momentarily. In the pause, I noticed for the first time that she was pushing a small cart piled high with canvas sacks.

'Isobel,' I said, breathing hard. 'What are you doing here? Where were you last night?'

'I couldn't come,' she said nervously, looking about. 'Miss Hoare took me back in, said she'd turn the cheek one last time. Now she's got me delivering the laundry.' She waved at her barrow.

'That's good news, surely?' I struggled to understand her tentative, awkward manner. I looked closer. 'She didn't chastise you, did she?'

Isobel shook her head. 'No, nothing like that. It's . . . I'd better be going on, anyhow. Miss Hoare won't like it if the laundry goes late.' She lifted the handles of her cart.

'Damn the laundry,' I said angrily, and rather too audibly to spare the sensitivities of the passers-by. 'I lay awake half the night waiting for you, with not a note nor a handkerchief to allay my hopes – my concern – and now that I do find you, you cannot run away fast enough.' I became aware that the traffic in the street had paused, that I had become a spectacle. 'If you find me repellent, or inconstant, or . . . or anything, then tell me and have done. But don't come to my bed once and then cut me every time I try to see you.'

'You'd not understand,' said Isobel, looking mortified at having her affairs thus discussed in public. 'And if you thought for two seconds about what I've said and done, you'd see how wrong you're thinking. Believe me, Martin, there are reasons I can't—'

'Believe you?' I echoed. 'I'll believe you when I see you – and that, it seems, is something I should refrain from.'

In an instant, a rush of wounded frustration choked my capacity for speech, and from a deeper part of my being I kicked out with my foot. Not at Isobel, but at the nearest insensible object I could reach: her cart. For a weak man, in a weakened state, I managed to pack a fair charge into my blow (though my toes felt it afterwards). My foot connected with one of the wheels on her barrow, and with a protesting lurch it toppled onto its side. Someone in the crowd about us screamed, which I remember seemed a little much; perhaps she owned some of the laundry which now lay straggled out in the muddy street.

That thought drew my eyes away from Isobel and down to the havoc I had wrought on her wares. Among the scattered canvas sacks, some of them spilling open to reveal the fine underclothes of the Dover gentry, there seemed to be a splintered pile of broken wood. I looked closer. Surely I had not been so frenzied as to have kicked apart the barrow? But no, the cart was intact; the wreckage I could see was from something that had been carried on it, hidden under the bags of laundry, a wooden box or barrel that had cracked open with the fall. A wooden box or barrel that was now leaching out a rich, golden liquid which trickled over the cobblestones in rivulets. It seeped into the scattered petticoats and shirts and undid all the hard scrubbing Miss Hoare's young ladies had administered.

I bent over and sniffed it, though I knew it well enough.

'Brandy,' I said, my thoughts unravelling even as I tried to gather them together. 'A tub of brandy, hidden under your laundry.'

All anger had left Isobel's face; now she just looked terrified, vulnerable.

'Please, Martin,' she pleaded. 'You can't understand.'

'You're right, I cannot.'

All sense, all passion, had drained from my body like the brandy in the road before me. I noticed vaguely that the crowd which had been so enthralled to witness our dispute was now wholly gone. Of the few people who passed us now, none looked for a second at the tearful girl, the dazed officer, or the soiled laundry blocking their way.

'So did you betray me?' I asked, without emotion. 'Were you the reason the smugglers always knew our movements? The reason they knew to find me in the churchyard that night? Was that why you came to my bed, so you could pass on my secrets to your masters?'

Isobel shook her head fiercely. 'No,' she whispered. 'No – never that.' She touched her cheek, where the thin line of dried blood was still there. 'And this was real enough.' Her tiny bosom heaved under the neck of her dress. She seemed to want to speak further, but could not find the breath.

'I suppose it hardly matters.' I found it easier, safer, to allow cold flippancy to mask my anguish. 'But you had better get your wares off the street. Miss Hoare will not approve of her laundry being so carelessly abandoned. And Mr Stubb is surely never far off.'

I stepped away, the stabbing pain in my toe the least I had to contend with.

'Martin,' said Isobel plaintively, but I did not turn.

I pushed my way across the square, heedless of the offence I caused, under the arches of the guildhall to where Crawley's blue uniform stood outside the gaol. Through my consuming bitterness, I noticed he appeared very grim.

'Jerrold.' The coldness in his tone snapped my thoughts away from Isobel. 'Come with me.'

Without explanation, he crossed the threshold of the gaol.

Perplexed, I followed him, aware as I did so that there were others behind me.

Gibble was at the far end of the room on the wrong side of the bars, holding a lantern as high as his crooked frame would allow.

'What do you see, Jerrold?' asked Crawley tautly.

I looked into the yellow gloom around Gibble. The cell was empty.

'He is . . . gone,' I said, struggling to grasp this new turn of events.

'Indeed.' A harsh voice rang out behind me. 'Our indispensable witness, escaped. I told you, Crawley, that Jerrold's character would reveal itself in time; I am only sorry I did not condemn it when I had the chance, before he could work this mischief.'

I turned in shock to see Cunningham louring in the doorway.

'Do you imply that I had some part in this?' My legs were quivering.

'The gate was locked after he'd bolted, Jerrold, so he must have had the key.' Cunningham spat out his words like grape shot. 'The key that is still in your belt. You helped him escape, lest he betray you for the spy and traitor that you are.' There was a chill, unadulterated triumph in his voice. 'The traitor I always knew you to be. Mr Stubb!'

Stubb stepped out of the shadows and clamped his burly hands about my arms. Through my confusion and horror, I was aware enough to wince. Meanwhile, Gibble had emerged and was bending before me; cold iron snapped about my ankles as he shackled them together.

'No need to add weights, Gibble,' said Cunningham. 'You may save them in case he gives you trouble.'

I looked desperately to Crawley, but his face was a mask of anger. He pulled the sword and pistols from my belt, as well as the key, and handed them to Ducker in silence. He would not look at me.

'Now, gentlemen,' said Cunningham savagely. 'We ought perhaps to devote our attentions to more significant matters. Hunting down the fugitive, for example. We may even suppose that with this traitor out of our path we shall enjoy more success than we have lately been accustomed to.'

The room began to empty, though Stubb never relented an inch of his numbing grasp. When only Cunningham remained, he spun me about and pushed me forward through the cell gate. With my legs bound, I fell inevitably onto my face with a howl of agony.

'I shall see you presently,' said Cunningham.

The gate slammed shut.

19

IN THE PAST FORTNIGHT I HAD BEEN ACCUSED OF MURDER, subjected to constant gibes by my superiors, assaulted in a churchyard, knocked unconscious in battle, deceived by a woman and thrown in gaol – twice, now. I was becoming a true connoisseur of self-pity. Alone in that cell, with only the distant light of the outer doorway to break the darkness, I finally gave full voice to my accumulated sorrows. I wept; I trembled, first with fury and then with terror; I cursed everyone I had ever met in Dover, from the coachman who'd driven me there to the poltroon who'd fallen over the cliff to the sadist who'd kicked me into this foul hell of a prison. I spared some peculiarly vicious thoughts for Squires, for being so wicked as to escape our captivity and blame it on me. If I ever met the villain again, I promised myself, he would be sure to suffer for it. I cursed Isobel for lying to me, for manipulating me, and then I realized how much I wanted her, and felt even more wretched. I wondered what the morrow would bring, whether Crawley would win the triumph he so craved, and whether he would remember me when I was hanging from a gibbet and he on the quarterdeck of a frigate in the Mediterranean. I remembered my uncle's ultimatum, now only two clear days away, and shook with the chill knowledge of certain failure. I kicked the floor and beat the walls with my fists and wept again. None of it helped me feel remotely better.

The light in the doorway began to dim. The occasional sounds from the market square beyond became more sporadic, then ceased altogether. The last dregs of light vanished. Cocks crowed; a cart rumbled past. All my hatreds and regrets, bitternesses and recriminations swarmed about my head in a frenzy of pity. Perhaps I slept; in complete darkness, and alone, I could scarce tell whether my imaginings came with my eyes open or shut. I saw Isobel, arching her naked back as morning light fell on her through the window; I saw Crawley, shouting for more canvas on a heaving deck; I saw Vitos, leaping off a cliff and flying like a bird; and I saw Webb, walking out of the waves with seaweed for hair and cockle shells for eyes. I saw Mazard silhouetted against a blood-red sun in his glass cage, laughing, and I saw a strange, flickering face chanting dark incantations in my ear.

I shook, and started. This last vision, I saw, was no dream but reality, a soft face inches from my own, whispering urgently at me.

'Martin.'

The voice was insistent, but curiously pleasant for that. Not unlike—

'*Martin!* You've not got much time.'

My dazed eyes at last began to fathom my surroundings. The blackness of the dungeon around me had been rolled back by a candle, its flame sputtering as much from the unsteady hand which held it as from the shifting prison vapours. And the person attached to that hand, whom no amount of incredulous blinking could dismiss, was Isobel.

'Come on,' she whispered, her dark eyes cast even rounder by the erratic shadows.

'They caught you, did they?' I asked dully. 'Well, I had nothing to do with it.'

'I came by myself.'

I began to feel the urgency in her voice, the almost desperate impatience.

'I'd recommend the Crown and Anchor over this piss-hole,

actually, if it's amusement you're looking for. Or even the Red Cow.' Despite my straitened situation, or perhaps because of it, I had become strangely facetious. 'Or perhaps you have some work you should be doing on a dark, deserted beach this evening.'

Holding the candle deftly to one side, she leaned forward and smacked me hard across the face. With Stubb's grazes still fresh on my cheek, the brusque sting of it was agonizing – an agony to which I gave full, uninhibited voice.

'Be quiet!' said Isobel sharply. 'Do you want to escape or not?'

'Escape?' The impact of the word was almost as bewildering as her slap, but with an edge that at last began to clear my muddied consciousness. Hope welled within me, but as quickly hardened into brittle suspicion. 'And how do you propose that?' And, more to the question, why?

But Isobel had withdrawn from the conversation – in view of my boorish off-handedness, I supposed – and taken the circle of light that surrounded her across to the far corner of the cell. As the darkness covered me again, I lost all resistance. I suddenly felt, more desperately than ever, my overwhelming need to escape that gaol, and I suddenly recognized that Isobel, here and now, would likely be my best, perhaps only, chance. Limping and hobbling with the weight of my chains, I stumbled after her before the light vanished.

But the light was drawn to a halt in the corner. Isobel had set the candle down and was scrabbling about the floor with her fingers, like a dog hunting its bone.

'Help me,' she said hurriedly as her hands came to a pause. Astonishingly, she seemed to have levered them into the very fabric of the floor. 'In here.'

I went down on my knees beside her, and for a second glimpsed a strange image of us both in a pew in church together, my father preaching over us. Then she was whispering hurriedly, gesturing at the crack she had opened in the flagstones and urging me to get my fingers into it. Too dazed to resist, I did as she said, shuddering a little at the slime oozing against my skin.

'Now, lift.'

Isobel's thin arms went taut, straining upwards, and quickly I joined the effort. With a low, grating rumble, I felt the stone in my hands go loose, then lift out of the floor. We pulled it forward over the lip of the adjoining slab. Then, panting slightly, I looked down at the pool of darkness we had uncovered.

'Get in,' whispered Isobel. 'And fast. We've not been as quiet as we should have.'

I could not begin to understand what was happening, but I could see enough to realize that this must be the escape she had offered. Yet still I dallied. Until now I had at least had the comfort of my innocence to sustain me. If I lowered myself into that hole, I would be surrendering that advantage, and with it all hope of absolving myself.

Isobel, however, had no patience with such niceties. '*Come on!*' she hissed, sensing my hesitation. 'Sir Lawrence can only hang you once, and he's set to do that anyhow.'

She was, of course, entirely correct, though that was scant comfort.

'I'll fare little better with your smuggling friends,' I objected. 'We may share a common enemy, but they'll hardly clasp a naval officer to their bosom, no matter how disgraced he might be.'

I felt my spirit stutter as I contemplated the full hopelessness of my condition. To be stabbed by the smugglers or hanged by Sir Lawrence – who could make a choice like that? But Isobel would allow me no time for pity.

'We're not going to the smugglers,' she insisted. 'I'm here on my own, to help you escape, if only you'd let me.'

'Do you think I'll believe that? I saw the brandy, you may recall.'

'*No!*' Her black hair flashed in the candlelight as she tossed her head angrily. 'I carted round a few tubs for them, and snitched on what Sir Lawrence was up to, too, back when I worked for him, but you'll not find a man or woman or a child even in Dover who'd done less if it was asked of them.' She fingered the cut on her cheek. 'You know as well as I do, Martin, that they don't ask kindly, and they don't ask more than once when they want something. But I never snitched on you, and I never meant you harm. And now, if you'll let me, I'll risk a lot of trouble to save you. If you're not so set on going to the gallows an honest man.'

There was much I could have said, but before I could begin to find the words there came a loud thump from the far end of the gaol, as of a door or a window closing.

That was enough for Isobel. Despairing of my doubts, my indecision, she put a palm on my back and shoved me forward. I half fell, half jumped into the hole before me, banging my tender ribs on the edge, and landed in darkness again. Above me I could hear Isobel tugging the flagstone back into position. When it had half covered the opening she appeared above me, and handed down the candle.

'Get clear,' she hissed. 'Over there.'

I stumbled cautiously forward, keeping my head well down and my arms out in front of me. Everything around me was dark, but while I could feel stony walls to my left and right, ahead the way seemed clear.

Isobel slithered down behind me, reached for a ring in the underside of the stone above us and pulled it across what remained of the opening. The slab flopped into its groove, dislodging a cloud of dust and pebbles onto us. Then we were alone, in silence.

Isobel took back the candle, though there was no room for her to squeeze past.

'Straight on,' she whispered. 'I'll tell you when to turn.'

We walked a long time in darkness, my fingers trailing over the crumbling walls on either side to guide me. Sometimes my hand would lose the surface, presumably where side tunnels branched into our passage; in other places I saw thin beams of dusty light filtering through what must have been the floorboards of parlours or drawing rooms above. Always there was the sound of Isobel behind me, whispering to herself and counting off the turnings as we passed them.

'Here,' she said at last, tugging on the back of my coat. 'Left.'

I felt my way into a narrow side tunnel and almost immediately yelped as my shin encountered a solid barrier barring my way.

Fortunately, the eerie silence of the surroundings stifled my cry enough to draw only a half-hearted 'shhh' from Isobel.

She reached the candle past my waist so that I could see what was before me. A wooden ladder was propped against the rough wall that abbreviated this branch of the passage, leading up through the roof of the tunnel into a small stone box. In which there must have been a crack, for when Isobel pulled back the candle I could see a thin slice of light carving through it.

'Where are we?' I asked. 'And where am I expected to go from here?'

'Somewhere you've been before,' said Isobel briskly. 'Except you were six feet up then. Unlike most of them you get around here – they're all six feet under.'

With a shudder, I saw that our little candle did not just shine off rock and earth. There were bones embedded in the walls.

'We're under – within – a churchyard,' I hazarded. The air around me seemed suddenly much fouler, much thicker.

'St James's. Just around the corner from Miss Hoare's, and exactly under that big statue of bad old Cal Drake. Which, you'll find, isn't half so solid as it looks.'

I stared again at the stone box capping the ladder. It must be the plinth, I realized, the base of Cal Drake's whited monument.

'Dedicated to his memory by his loving brother, and all who knew him,' I recited, the words forming effortlessly in my mind.

'And used in his loving memory just the way he'd want it,' said Isobel. 'To get tubs of spirits clean into the middle of town.'

I frowned. 'Just around the corner from Miss Hoare's? Were you the only washergirl who delivered more than starched linens to the good folk of Dover?'

Isobel shook her head. 'It's not like one of your ships, Martin; you don't have officers shouting orders and every man knows his station. Someone asks you to do something and you do it, and you don't think to ask too much about it. Sometimes you'd see that we didn't have every tub in the laundry full of soap suds, and sometimes you wouldn't.' She shivered. 'But that's nothing to you now. We're at the edge of the town here. If you go north you'll be in the fields on the east side of the river, and there shouldn't be anyone to trouble you. The valley'll take you into the downs, then you'll have to run your luck.'

Luck was the last thing to which I wanted to entrust my life, especially in my new apparent profession as outlaw, but this was a mere distraction compared to the turmoil that flooded me as I listened to Isobel's brief words at the foot of that ladder. I had followed her blindly thus far, implicitly believing – convincing myself – that she had some plan to save me; now, the reality of my situation began to close in. There was no salvation, *could* be no salvation, no redemption, in my old society; I had put myself beyond all hope of that. But I could not live the rest of my days as a brigand, hunted and alone. I doubted I would survive a week – and if I did, to what end? A ghost's life, if I was lucky, haunting the fringes of my former existence in torment for what had been, and with the weight of my guilt always before me.

None of which I could begin to communicate to Isobel, for at that moment I heard the sound of voices from above, the clattering of iron and wood on stone. The crack of light in the plinth over my head grew brighter, began to widen.

'Quickly,' breathed Isobel, pulling me back, 'down the tunnel!' Then she lifted her skirts, threw down the candle, and vanished.

I could not see her, nor indeed anything, and I dared not call her for the noises above me seemed closer than ever. Instead, flailing with my arms in front of me and tearing my hands on the flint shards in the wall, I plunged after her. The chains were still wrapped around my feet, and I cursed them – for their treacherous rattle, as much as their hindrance – as much as I cursed the folly that had brought me down this hole. With every twist and bend I stumbled around I had to contemplate the prospect that I would be abandoned in this labyrinth; I actually began to regret not being back in the stinking gaol. I thought of the disgust on Crawley's face when he heard the news that I had fled; I wondered what my uncle would make of it, whether he would care for anything except that I was never found. I ached to turn back, but the vision of the smugglers catching me alone, shackled and helpless, spurred me on. Occasionally, I fancied I heard something of their progress behind me, and then I would redouble my faltering steps, but of Isobel I neither saw nor heard the least sign. Whether that was because she had betrayed me or because she had suffered some horrible fate, I was too tired and too frantic even to think.

After a time, the low ceiling began to rise. The air was fresher here, and I could feel the first stirrings of a cool breeze over my face. And there was a strange, dull roaring noise, like wind on a hilltop, sounding from some distant, yet not so far distant, place. More hopefully still, even without the candle, the darkness was not as complete as it had been, for a pale yellow light glinted off the walls. It too seemed to have its source somewhere ahead.

Promising myself that this was the last effort I would make in this futile quest, I hobbled the last hundred yards down the tunnel. The light and the breeze grew steadily stronger; then, supporting myself against the rock wall, I rounded the final corner and came out of the darkness. Straight into the presence of the last man I expected to see.

20

THE TUNNEL HAD WIDENED INTO A CAVE, LARGER THAN THE FOREST holes I played in as a child but still quite low: a long, narrow chamber whose white walls, hewn from the chalk, flickered with the reflected glow of the torches mounted on iron brackets around them. Oily smoke drifted through the space but did not choke it – there must, I thought absently, be a ventilation shaft bored somewhere. Gleaming black muskets were stacked crookedly around the room, while crates and barrels filled the corners. At the far end, perhaps fifty yards from where I stood, a low, round hole led into what seemed to be another cave beyond. There could not have been more than two dozen men present, carrying weapons or rolling barrels, but in the close space they seemed a veritable crowd.

The man before me did not notice me for some moments, which I suppose was only to be expected, but confronted with this extraordinary scene of subterranean industry, I had not the wit to move. Then the crew on the barrels caught sight of me; with shouting and scuffling they came running and took hold of my limp arms. More gently than Stubb ever did, to their credit. I did not resist.

Through all this, the figure in the middle of the cave stayed resolutely still, until one of his men muttered my name in his ear. It made little difference to my predicament, yet still I felt a further flash of disquiet that my name and face should be so well known among them.

'Lieutenant Jerrold.' The first man spoke the name thoughtfully, turning those glassy blue eyes on to me. Though I well knew they could see nothing, there was still power in their stare, and I shivered to meet it. 'I was expectin' you to be in the gaol.'

'I found a way out.'

'So you did. Found it yourself, did you?'

'I had plenty of time to explore.'

I had no idea what had befallen Isobel, whether she had escaped down the tunnel, been captured or even killed. For all I knew she could have been chained up in the next cave, but as long as there was hope, I would do nothing to bring more trouble on her. And perhaps it would make me look more resourceful, more formidable in the smugglers' eyes.

Perhaps it would not, for the eyes that looked emptily upon me betrayed not the least respect. It was extraordinary, I thought, the difference circumstances could make. Alone in his peculiar boathouse, with a mouse-eaten jersey and tangled hair, he had seemed the very picture of helpless eccentricity. Now, with his hair tied tight with a crimson ribbon, a fresh shirt, and an evilly curved dagger stuck in his belt, Simon John, the erstwhile fisherman, looked wholly, menacingly terrifying. There was nothing of the meek old cripple in the sneering laugh he gave now.

'I reckon you'd have kept safer in the gaol, myself. Lot safer'n down here.' He flashed his teeth at me. 'Gets dangerous down here, down in Drake's cave.'

'Drake's dead,' I said stupidly. It was the first thought in my mind, but it put an expected and ferocious scowl on his face.

'Caleb Drake's dead, God rest his soul.' I doubted the Almighty had much business with Caleb Drake's soul, though I refrained from saying so. 'But Simon Drake's not. And I've got a ways to live, I reckon, before they get to scragging me.'

'*Qui est-ce?*'

A new speaker. Through my confusion I looked at him, and was briefly glad of the restraining hands that steadied me. He no longer wore the black suit which I had heard described so often; now he was dressed in blue overalls with red facings, gold buttons, gold epaulettes and cavalry boots. There was a pistol in his belt and a straight sword at his side, but what struck me most was that black beard, the thickly knit black eyebrows, and the black, penetrating eyes looking quizzically at me. After much searching, and much endeavour, I was at last face to face with the elusive Mr Laminak. And there was nothing I could do about it.

'This is Lieutenant Jerrold, what found your friend Major Vitos and couldn't stop askin' questions about him,' said Drake. 'Asked questions right the way into the gaol. Only he got out, same way Danny did, and found his way down here.'

Laminak's hand moved to the butt of his pistol. 'Then he should stay here.'

'Aye,' said Drake. 'But maybe not the way you think. No need to kill a calf afore he's a cow, as they says. Mr Jerrold might maybe do us a few good turns yet.'

He reached out an arm and felt for Laminak's epauletted shoulder. Having found it, he leaned on it and whispered a few words in the Frenchman's ear. I saw Laminak give a grudging nod, presumably lost on Drake, and mutter something in French. Then Drake turned back to face me.

'Happy day for you, Lieutenant. Colonel Laminak here reckons you're safe enough for us.' He turned to his men. 'Make him fast somewhere out of the way. We'll think what to do with him after tonight's all seen to.'

I tried to hide the hope that surged within me, but Drake must somehow have sensed it.

'What's that, Lieutenant – reckon we'll all be takin' your place in the gaol by tomorrow mornin'? Reckon that Danny Squires peached me into the noose, do you?'

I meant to keep myself still, but there was no suppressing the confusion within me.

'Yes.' Drake nodded. 'We'll have all the King's horses and all the

King's men, and his ships and guns as well I don't wonder, all waitin' down at Saint Margaret's tonight to catch old Simon Drake landin' brandy on the beach.' He laughed. ''Cept Simon Drake won't be there. You see that passage, Lieutenant?' He pointed to the arch at the far end of the cave. 'Where d'you reckon that goes?'

'The drawing room?' I felt that as a gentleman before villains, I ought to be showing some defiance, however feeble.

Drake chuckled. 'Goes three hundred feet plumb through the rock, it does, and comes out inches short of the stair shaft which runs from the shore battery up into the middle of the castle. Somewhere near the kitchens, I think they said.'

'You're going to force your way into the castle?'

Spoken aloud, it sounded ridiculous. But Drake was smiling broadly and nodding, while Laminak shifted on his feet and scowled.

'Boney – apologies, Colonel. His excellence the Emperor of France sent us half a legion of his best to sort us out. It shouldn't take much more than that, cos everyone in the castle'll be down chasing shadows at Saint Margaret's. Take the castle and you've got the harbour; take the harbour and you can land an hundred thousand men if you can land a dozen. Get 'em ashore, and London's just a short walk through clover. Or leastways, that's what they'll all be thinkin'.'

He seemed to grow bored of the conversation. 'Get him bound up.'

For all his vicious methods – or perhaps, as in the navy, because of them – Drake ran a tight crew. Without further orders, I was led to an alcove where ropes were fastened about my hands and tied to an iron ring in the wall. They left enough slack to allow me to sit on the ground in some comfort.

'Now keep yerself quiet,' advised one of the smugglers, 'or we'll come back an' give you a bit more rope. Enough to 'ang yerself,' he added, to make his meaning quite plain. 'An' if yer good, we'll get Smithy to knock off those shackles where yer legs is bleedin'.'

I sat there many hours, I think, trapped in the timeless day that must have already turned into a Saturday. If I'd thought much about it, I suppose I would have found it inconceivable that they hoped to invade England with a battalion of Frenchmen and a few Kentish smugglers, but I did not think much about it. I was happy enough to sit and watch them work, stacking casks, whetting and oiling their blades, priming muskets and going through the hundred miniature routines of an army before battle. Once – it might have been around dinner time, for all I knew – someone did think to bring me a few lumps of salt pork and a mug of ale, and later a huge man with scorched hands came to break off my leg-irons, but otherwise they paid me not the least heed.

My mind felt numb, emptied. For all the monstrous things I had heard and seen that day, the outrageous plans that had been revealed, I had not the strength to care for them. I was happy to observe in peace, with the careless indifference of a child at a hanging. Certainly I noticed things: I noticed that there were other passages leading from my cave, all apparently giving on to other parts of the catacombs, and I noticed that many dozens of people moved like ants through them. I noticed that of these men, the vast majority were uniformed, and spoke in French. I noticed that Drake and Laminak spent many hours in a small chamber just visible from where I sat, poring over charts and conspiring quietly together. And I noticed, some time later – well past nightfall, no doubt – that the activity began to dwindle.

A man appeared from an entrance not far from where I sat; the movement caught my eye, and I craned my neck around to see him better. The lean face and darting eyes were instantly recognizable, though he wore fewer chains than when I had last seen him. Drake hurried to meet him.

'They've all gone from the castle,' Squires announced. 'Thousand of 'em, easy. Reckon there can't be more'n a skeleton crew left now.'

'Skeletons is all they'll be, right enough,' Drake chuckled. 'Well done. You must've spun them a right pretty story.'

He walked away, moving slowly towards the front of the cave.

Behind him, the white crossbelts and black boots which shone in the firelight slowly organized themselves into two clear lines. A hush filled the space. The distant roaring of the surf, which somehow managed to seep through the rock, was the only sound now.

'Right,' barked Drake, looking down the mingled files of soldiers and smugglers. 'You knows what to do, and you knows who to stick it to. None of us wants to be spendin' a life breakin' our backs with tubs of geneva: do this one right, an' you'll all be rich as kings. Don't spare them you can kill, cos it'll give us the castle a whole sight faster. And soon as that's done,' he added viciously, 'the first thing I'll be doin' is takin' Sir Lawrence bloody Cunningham and stringin' him up from his own gibbet.'

He stepped back into the shadows to approving murmurs of agreement. Now, Laminak took his place and made his own speech – longer than Drake's, and in French. I caught the occasional word – *la gloire* seemed a particular theme – but otherwise it made as much sense to me as to the smugglers, who stood there in obvious, ill-concealed boredom. At length Laminak finished, to a chorus of dutiful French cheers.

'*Alors – allez!*'

With a rattling and clattering the men vanished, two by two, pouring out of the cave and the chambers and passages adjoining it, under the dark doorway and down the tunnel. They might not have been enough to invade England, but it was a sobering length of time before the last man marched past my forgotten little crevice. There was a pounding and a banging in the distance – the last remnants of the wall to the castle stairs being staved in, I assumed – and then I was alone. And probably, I thought with surprise, the safest man in Dover at that moment.

With my distraction gone, my mind, which had lingered in a resigned torpor all day, began to work again. It was an almighty struggle, forcing my thoughts around all I had learned, but at length I reasoned out two choices. For one, I could sit out the battle where I was, as safe as the mercy of Simon Drake would keep me, but although there seemed little doubt he thought I might serve some later purpose, I very much doubted I would enjoy his use of me. But if I was to avoid that, and the prospect of living an abbreviated life as an outlaw and highwayman, I would need to rehabilitate myself with my country. And if I was to have any hope of doing that, I would need to act quickly.

Pushing my back against the wall – I could almost feel the blood squeezing into the bandages that still bound my ribs – I stiffened my legs and slowly squirmed myself upright. My wrists were tied behind me, but by manipulating the rope through my fingers I managed to follow it to the ring where it was fastened. I could bend my hands sufficiently far back to get my fingers onto the knot, and desperately I started picking at it. But it was too tight, and the rope too thick; after ten minutes I had succeeded in fraying only my fingers, and splitting open a nail. I tried for the ring itself. It was about an inch thick, and I could just get my palms wrapped around it, but though I tugged at it with all my strength, it gave nothing.

I was still standing there, sweating from the heat of the nearby flames and aching in my shoulders, summoning my strength for another, last effort, when a new sound intruded on my isolation. Suddenly I was slithering awkwardly back down onto the floor, trying to assume a limp, helpless pose – not hard, after my exertions – for I could hear footsteps running down the tunnel on my left and coming steadily nearer. I half closed my eyes. It would be a smuggler who'd forgotten his cutlass, I supposed, though it did not seem the right direction.

And then the new arrival was upon me, and I opened my eyes very wide indeed.

'Isobel?'

For the second time that day – or perhaps in two days: my reckoning had slipped during those hours in the dark – I saw Isobel hurrying towards me, her blue dress now covered in chalk dust but otherwise, apparently, unharmed.

'I thought you'd be here,' she said. 'And I hoped they'd kept you alive.'

'For the present. But I would not care to try their patience. Can you get me out?' Again.

Isobel looked at the rope that bound me, then reached a hand up her skirts in a wholly undignified motion that would have made my mother faint with shock. To the relief of my morals, and the confound of my imagination, the hand emerged clasping a small dagger.

'Always something up my skirt,' she said lewdly, crouching by me to saw through the rope on my hands.

I stiffened to be so close to the blade, but she was expert enough and soon I felt the bonds fall away from my wrists. Before she could move I indulged the new freedom of my limbs by wrapping an arm across her back and pulling her in to kiss her on the lips. Ignoring the dire emergency of the situation, I allowed myself to enjoy it for some moments. She did not rebuke me.

'Thank you,' I said, pulling back at last. 'For all you've done. You escaped the smugglers in the tunnel, I presume?'

'Yes. I've had time enough to learn these passages. It wasn't hard to skip out from Drake's gang, even in the dark.'

'Good.' I rubbed my wrists tenderly. 'So, do you know if any of them come out near Saint Margaret's?'

'That one there,' she said, quick as a cat, pointing to an anonymous side tunnel. 'But you'll run straight into half an army if you go down that way – half an army that thinks you're as treacherous as they come.'

'I know,' I said impatiently. 'Which is why I need you to go. Run as fast as you can down to Saint Margaret's and find Captain Bingham. You'd better make yourself plain to see or they might shoot you as a smuggler – knowing no better, obviously. When you reach him, tell him that the vanguard of a French invasion force has tunnelled into the castle and, most probably, seized it. Tell him he and Colonel Copthorne must come at once if they wish to avert a full-blown invasion.'

'Is that true?' she asked, her face wide with disbelief.

'Of course it's true,' I snapped. 'If he refuses to believe you, insist on it, but on no account mention my name. If he asks how you know, tell him . . . tell him a man named Nevell sent you.' I gave a brief description of Nevell, as well as I could remember him. I hoped it would be enigmatic enough to be plausible. 'Tell the captain,' I added, 'that there is a spy inside who will open the gates for him.'

Isobel nodded. 'And who's that, then?' she asked, one eyebrow raised.

'Me. But don't tell Captain Bingham that.'

'Why not?'

'Because,' I said honestly, 'he probably won't believe you.'

As I kissed her goodbye and started down thc tunncl Drake and Laminak had taken, I wasn't entirely sure I believed it myself.

21

IT WAS NOT FAR TO THE STAIRS, AND HAVING PROCURED MYSELF A pistol which the smugglers had left behind, I reached them quickly enough through a brief chain of caves. Thick dust still filled the air, and there was rubble spilled across the steps where the wall had been demolished, but once I had picked my way through the shattered opening I found the stairs smooth going, well lit by lanterns recessed regularly into the walls. It remained nonetheless a heart-pounding climb, and not merely from the exertion of it. My right arm – my pistol arm – was pressed against the central spindle, and my footsteps sounded horribly loud in the close space. The staircase had the unpleasant effect of being one protracted blind corner, and I climbed with the mounting terror that I would round a bend to find a sword in my guts or a gun in my face, my adversaries well warned by the noise of my feet, or my pained breathing.

So intent was I on thoughts of ambush that I very nearly missed the end of the staircase and was close to ramming my skull into the thick trapdoor that capped it. Fortunately, my much-abused head had at last begun to draw the lesson of its experiences, and seemed to have developed an effective sense of unseen hazards close above. I looked up just in time, and stopped within a literal hair's breadth of the ceiling.

I paused. Then, with my left hand, I pushed tentatively against the wood. It gave readily, and I inched it open a fraction, putting my pistol to the crack. There was no challenge, but I halted nonetheless as I heard voices filtering through and saw the muzzle-like ends of a pair of cavalry boots pointing straight at my face. In the distance I could hear much clamour mingled with occasional shots, and I had to concentrate hard to discern the words that were being spoken above me, all the while petrified that someone would notice that the trapdoor was not shut fast. The light in the room was mercifully faint, though, and the occupants too intent on their conversation to look down.

'We've got the keep locked tight.' I had not heard Drake's voice often, but I had heard it enough, and in sufficiently memorable circumstances, to recognize it at once. 'And Danny should have the outer walls broomed out by now. If our luck's on the up, there'll be none that got away.'

'And if they did?'

A second man spoke, and I felt a shiver of righteous vindication as I recalled hearing that dangerous condescension in the glass office above the harbour: Mazard. Though it remained to be seen whether I would live to remind Crawley and Bingham how they had scorned my intuition.

'Dawn's not long off anyways,' Drake was saying, unworried. 'We'll be expectin' the dragoons for breakfast. We can hold them if they get here early.'

'And you can keep them at bay for two days?' Mazard sounded quite insistent. 'It all hangs on that.'

'We'll hold 'em. Asides, once the colonel gets his men aloft they won't know which way to shoot.'

'And the gold?'

A French voice, Laminak's, directly above me.

'Already loaded aboard my ship,' answered Mazard. 'The *Navarre* will sail with the tide, before the navy have the wit to close the harbour. Fifty thousand guineas for his Majesty the emperor to do with as he will, provided it comes back at forty per cent. And much more to follow, if our plans go as they should.'

'You can watch from the top of the tower when the boat sails, Colonel,' said Drake moodily. 'Where I'll be stringin' up Sir Lawrence Cunningham, soon as there's light.'

Mazard chuckled. 'Poor Cunningham. A true zealot – how it blinded him to greater opportunities. Perhaps I will go and pay my last respects.'

'You do that,' said Drake. 'I'll see to the walls, so to speak. And you'd best make sure you gets your machine up,' he added, apparently to Laminak. 'Don't want hot lead flyin' too near it. And it'd spoil it if they saw it comin'.'

The toes in front of me swivelled left and moved away; from the tramping on the floor, I guessed Mazard and Drake followed. Still, I stayed motionless. I did not think there had been anyone else involved in their counsels, but I waited another five minutes, just to be sure. Of course I could not be sure – there was too much commotion outside for that – but it would not do to be found cowering here when Isobel led Bingham's men through.

I chanced it. Pushing hard on the wood above me, I leaped out, brandishing my pistol wildly in as many directions as I could manage and trying to keep my balance as I tripped on the lip of the floor. My luck held: no-one challenged me. I brushed the loose hair from my face and stood up, backing against the wall to be sure I was alone in the small guard room I had entered. Then, keeping as much in the shadow as I could, I looked through one of the narrow windows – such as an archer might have used in a previous century – to my left.

It opened on to a courtyard, lit by many fires, and by their light I could see scores of blue-coated soldiers moving purposefully about. Sergeants bellowed orders in French, and their men moved with urgency, but in strangely erratic patterns, as if following an invisible, meandering path. The reason, I saw soon enough, was the bodies – dozens of them strewn over the cobbles in dark pools, mostly still wearing their red coats. Behind them the sharp, square walls of the Norman keep rose into the night. And around its corner, I saw with bewilderment, there seemed to be many men putting up a tent.

Crouching to keep below the windows, I edged my way around

the room to the door. I was on the east side of the courtyard; the main, northern gate would be somewhere to my right. I waited for a lull in the activity I could see, then, praying that no-one was watching, I slipped out.

I had thought to find a dead Frenchman, drag him inside and commandeer his uniform, but the brutal efficiency of Drake's operation thwarted my intentions: all the bodies I passed seemed to be English. I moved from corpse to corpse, growing ever sicker at the sight of their wounds and ever more anxious that I was carried too far from safety. My eyes jerked desperately over the bodies as I carried on. In my mounting panic I could not even spare precious seconds to the few who were still dying, who moaned or cried as I passed, much though I hated myself for it.

I heard the measured tramp of marching soldiers rounding the corner behind me and froze. I was too far from the guardhouse to go back – probably they could see it already. Hardly able to think, I glimpsed a shadowy doorway in the wall to my right and fled inside, my heart pounding with the hope I had not been observed.

Keeping very still, I noticed that I had not entered another room, but was at the head of a descending shaft of stairs. The tread of the soldiers grew steadily nearer, and the darkness about me was not as complete as I should have liked. I dived down the steps just as the light of the soldiers' torches passed the threshold.

I was led further down than I had expected – two storeys at least, I guessed – and unthinkingly I followed the stairs to the bottom. The air was dank where they emerged, in a narrow, brick-vaulted passage whose only entrance was the stairs by which I had come. Three iron-studded doors were set into each wall, all with small barred windows in their centres; they looked like nothing so much as cells. I recalled Drake's exhortation to take no prisoners. Perhaps, if they had failed to be quite so ruthless, I might discover a company of soldiers and improve the small odds in favour of my improbable task.

A task I might never begin, for even as I considered it I heard footsteps once again, echoing off the stair shaft and descending ever closer. Someone must have seen me, must have followed me down into this rat-trap. I tugged desperately on one of the oaken doors, but it gave not an inch. The footsteps rang loud; in a moment they would be round the last corner and I would be caught.

I lifted my pistol, though it was scant consolation. I've met men who swore that as long as they took an enemy with them they would not die in vain, but that always seemed a poor bargain to me. Could I surrender? After I had escaped their captivity once that day, they might well conclude I would not profit them the trouble.

Almost too late, I saw my chance. There was a small, sloping alcove under the curve of the stairs where I would be hidden from the sight of anyone coming down. It was not much of an escape, but it would serve better than being found meekly waiting. I squeezed myself in and crouched on my haunches, thumbing back the lock of my pistol as the feet passed over my head and stepped into the passage.

Involuntarily, I had clenched my eyes shut, but I opened them again as my head calmed and I realized I could hear only one man's footsteps. And they were not bearing down upon my little hole, but had stopped by one of the walls. Was he listening for me?

A key snapped in a lock, and a door swung open. He must have stepped through it, for immediately the sounds became fainter. And then I heard voices.

'Come to gloat, have you, Henri?'

I tensed so tight I almost blasted off my pistol in my shock. I knew that voice, would have recognized its grating whine anywhere. The diction lacked a little of its habitual precision, and sounded more fatigued than usual, but I could not mistake it. Sir Lawrence Cunningham.

'To say *adieu*, Cunningham. I do not suppose we will meet again.'

Mazard! The new arrival. So here they were, the two traitors conspiring together, as I had so long suspected. Damn Crawley and Bingham and all the others for ever doubting me, for allowing the villain to throw me in gaol.

'I suppose I should have known better,' Cunningham spat. 'I

knew you'd sell your daughter to an Ottoman if you thought you could profit sixpence on her – that, after all, is why I chose to do business with you, but I never guessed you'd give over the country to rack and ruin. Not with the profits you were making on it.'

'Profits?' Mazard sniffed disparagingly. 'When were you ever acquainted with profit? Carrying beer and bread, landlording alehouses, forcing poor girls to scrub and sew petticoats? All the pursuits of a noble English gentleman.'

This did not sound like the conversation of conspirators. I shuffled out of my niche, the better to hear them, keeping close to the wall and ever alert for any sound from above.

'Why be a man of principle like you, Cunningham, if it blinds you to true opportunities, for true profits? All the world is at war, the most expensive war ever fought by men, and it is much in our greatest interest to keep it so.'

'You won't prolong the war by opening the door to Buonaparte's invasion fleet. However handsomely he pays you.'

'Invasion fleet?' Mazard echoed. 'Is that what you think this is? A hundred thousand Frenchmen swarming across the Channel to put England to the sword and complete the tyrant's mastery of Europe?'

That had certainly been my understanding, whatever Cunningham thought, but Mazard's derision was manifest as he continued his haughty lecture.

'Buonaparte has no army within five hundred miles of here, and could hardly bring them across the Channel even if he did. But a small detachment, a few hundred soldiers smuggled over by men who knew the coast, they could make a landing. Nothing serious, of course: a castle sacked, a garrison killed, a prominent local magistrate publicly murdered. Enough to put all thoughts of peace from the hearts of our leaders, to strengthen the feeble minds of a weak government.'

'And all so you can maintain your position as the smugglers' venturer, when we earn handsomely enough carrying the navy's provisions?' Cunningham sounded sickened.

'All so I can maintain my position as banker to the world,' Mazard corrected. Conceit filled his voice. 'A venture you'd never have undertaken, with your provincial way of thinking. A venture to supply the Emperor of France with enough golden guineas to maintain an empire.'

I heard a fumbling, and the clink of metal.

'You see this guinea, Cunningham? In this room it is worth twenty-one shillings, but take it to Paris and they will give you thirty shillings for it, so desperate are they for gold. *Thirty shillings*,' he repeated, almost in awe. 'Nine shillings on the guinea. You will not make that with your washerwomen.' There was no disguising the triumph in his voice, and he did not try.

So that was it. All those golden coins I had seen flowing into Dover, and doubtless many thousands I had not, were channelled through Mazard and carried to France by smugglers, to fund Buonaparte at usurious rates of return and prolong the war from which Mazard already reaped enormous profits. Amid all the confusion that besieged my thoughts, I wondered vaguely how long he had wanted to boast of this to Cunningham, to show his plodding, conservative partner what vast sums he, Mazard, could conjure up.

'And they pay you back in brandy?' Cunningham asked. 'And gin and tobacco and cloths?'

'Some of it. And some in coin, mostly to be repaid over many years. I find it tedious to have to swap gold for bulky goods, of which I must then dispose. Even a man such as Lieutenant Jerrold might find the crew who had to carry fifty thousand guineas' worth of brandy ashore. I am happy to cast my gold upon the water, and await my just returns.'

The insult stung. Rapt though I had been by this extraordinary tale of treason, I began to think again on the urgency of my predicament. Bingham and his soldiers would be arriving soon, perhaps into an ambush, and I had said I would have the gate open for them. But I had Mazard standing on the other side of the wall from me; it would be a useful piece of work to bind him up there, to await justice. And though it defied my every inclination, I could free the innocent Sir Lawrence as well. Mazard had come down alone, and I had heard no others either in the cell or on the stairs above. These were the sort of odds I favoured.

I lifted myself up, aching from having crouched so long, held my pistol before me and stepped briskly through the open door. Mazard had his back to me, while Cunningham sat on a wooden bench facing me, his arms chained to the walls behind him. His clothes and face were torn; he was bruised all over, and scabbed blood above his lip suggested they had paid particular attention to his nose. His hair was wild, streaked and caked with the powder he used, so that he looked like some deranged harlequin. None of it, though, had quite broken the bite in his voice as he looked up and recognized me.

'Come to taunt me too, have you? Now that you have *me* imprisoned. I should have had you shot weeks ago.'

Mazard spun around, checking himself abruptly as he caught sight of my gun. His shocked eyes flickered from my face to my weapon and back. I could almost see the calculations which creased those smooth, almond features.

'Lieutenant Jerrold,' he said. 'You are supposed to be imprisoned in the cliffs.'

'I left.' I tightened my grip on the pistol. 'Unchain Sir Lawrence.'

'What?' Cunningham stared at me. 'Have you come to take me to my doom, Jerrold?'

'I've come to free you,' I snapped. 'If you had devoted half the time you spent condemning me to investigating your erstwhile partner, you would know that you put the wrong man in your gaol. Now, unlock his chains, Mazard.'

'I do not have the keys.'

'They're on a nail, on the far wall.' Cunningham thrust his head forward so that his arms stretched behind him like wings. 'Over there.'

I jerked my gun at Mazard. 'Get them.'

Humiliated anger contorted the banker's face, but he had no choice. At last I was facing my enemies – one of them, at least – with the advantage, and confidence flowed through me. Nor, after my ordeals, would I be slow to use the weapon. My determination must have showed, for Mazard took the ring of keys, crossed to Cunningham, and sprang open the shackles that held him.

No sooner was Cunningham free than he ploughed his fist hard into Mazard's face. Blood rose from the banker's lip and he swayed, just as a second blow to his stomach splayed him backwards onto the bench. He gagged, his head fell forward, and I heard a sob. With brutal force, Cunningham clamped the chains about his wrists and stepped back.

'Lieutenant Jerrold.' Cunningham was breathing hard, but there was no hiding his uncertainty. 'The man I least expected to be my salvation. How, if you are truly not one of these blackguards, did you come to be here?'

'I escaped from your captivity into theirs. When I wriggled free, I came after them. I might as well ask how you are here.'

'This foul little Frenchman came calling at my door in the middle of the night.' Mazard took a vicious kick on his shin. 'Informed me there was an emergency at the castle and dragged me out here. As soon as we reached the gate there were ruffians all about me. They bridled me up and brought me down here. Mazard they left alone. Then I was introduced to that singular villain Simon Drake, who paid me the compliments you see.' He touched his swollen cheek. 'Abused me for some minutes before he was called upstairs – left swearing a thousand wicked vengeances to come. Then you found me.'

'With little time to spare.' I looked at Mazard, and suddenly recollected something. 'That dead man I found on the beach. I take it he played some part in this?'

'His name was Major Vitos,' said Mazard, broken. 'A French engineer. He helped extend the tunnels. And provided other technical expertise.'

'He ought to have been more careful about his steps on the cliff-top.' This would have been useful intelligence two weeks ago. 'How did he come to die?'

'He had a fight with the revenue man, Webb. Webb was supposed to be aiding us, but proved to be a traitor.'

'And when Webb showed his true allegiance, he was killed too?'

Mazard's slumped head twitched in the affirmative.

In the ensuing silence, I heard the rumble of gunfire rolling down the stairs. There were a host of other questions to ask Mazard, but I could not delay further.

'Whatever the truth of it all, this castle has been taken by the French, for the time being at least, and the sooner they are relieved of it the better. Captain Bingham and Colonel Copthorne should be counterattacking at any moment, Sir Lawrence, and I have promised that I will try to open the gate for them.'

'How wonderfully heroic,' applauded Cunningham, and for a moment I profoundly regretted setting him loose. 'Very well, Jerrold, lead on. Is your weapon loaded?'

'Of course.' I doubted I could have summoned the courage to defy Mazard with a Quaker gun.

'Good.'

Before I could move, Cunningham had pulled the pistol from my hand. He extended his arm towards Mazard and without hesitation pulled the trigger. The room exploded with smoke and flame, blood and bone. Mazard's shattered head fell forward; he dangled from his manacles like a murderer hung in chains at the roadside. My ears rang with the echoing blast.

'*Adieu*, Henri.'

'You killed him.' The shock of his action, and the horror of the corpse, sickened me; I struggled to keep upright. 'He was a witness, Cunningham. We needed his knowledge.'

'He confessed everything.' There was no remorse in Cunningham's voice. 'And he played me for a fool. He deserved it.'

That Mazard had had an evil soul and a black heart I had no doubt, and I knew full well he had happily delivered Cunningham to torture and death. But I could not escape the suspicion that he had died not for these misdeeds, nor for his treason, but for the unforgivable crime of wounding Sir Lawrence's pride.

There was not the time to dwell on it.

'We should go,' I said, desperate to be away from there. 'Will you come?'

'Of course.' Sir Lawrence handed back the pistol, though I had no more powder for it. 'I still have business with Simon Drake.'

We came into the courtyard and continued to edge our way around the perimeter, in the hope that if we were seen we would be taken for smugglers. With my notorious luck, I thought bitterly, this would prove the first time in Dover I had *not* been mistaken as such.

As we skirted the north-eastern corner, the tent I had noticed earlier came into clearer view. It seemed a most unnatural contraption, quite apart from the incongruity of a band of cut-throat marauders erecting a marquee on the castle lawn. It was fastened down on all sides by guy ropes but bulged upwards in its centre, an indecent tumescence that appeared, as I watched, to grow ever larger and rounder. The canvas carried many concentric seams, over-sewn with loops of rope, and astonishingly, to judge by the giant leaping shadows within, there seemed to be a bonfire alight inside it.

'Some piratical ritual?' I whispered to Cunningham.

'There,' he hissed, ignoring my question. 'Standing by the brazier.'

He pointed to a spot about a dozen yards ahead of us, close to the wall. I looked, and began to breathe faster as I saw the back of a familiar crimson-tied queue, and a curved sword stuck in a belt. Of course, even if Drake turned around we would be invisible to him, but I did not think he had forged so successful a career as a blind smuggler without handsome compensation from his other senses. For the moment, though, he was deep in conversation. With Laminak.

'Takin' shape, is it? How much longer, d'you think?'

'Ten minutes. Maybe it will be less. But it must be up before the English arrive, otherwise it will be seen.'

Drake nodded, then licked a finger and held it in front of him.

'Wind's changin' too. You'll not get it to Canterbury with it like this.'

'Deal or Folkestone, then. So long as they will drop the shells somewhere, *n'importe où*, and make resemblance of an army with artillery.'

'Not goin' yerself, then?' asked Drake with a chuckle.

'Not after my last journey, *non*.'

'Well, your lads better hurry. Even our good English dragoons won't be so dozy for long. They'll be comin' soon enough.'

'He's right,' I hissed to Cunningham. 'Bingham and Copthorne's men should be here soon. We need to get to that gate.'

'Shall we fly there?' asked Cunningham.

He had a point. There was no room for us to pass behind Drake, and any other path would take us clear across Laminak's line of sight. Then, as I considered this, a shout from the walls above drew all our eyes.

'Guns up!' yelled an unseen voice. 'The 'goons is comin'!'

A volley of musket fire spat out from beyond the walls in confirmation of his words, while other voices bellowed, '*Ils arrivent!*' Laminak ran across the courtyard to his mysterious tent; it was now raised so high that the edges lifted off the ground, revealing a wicker basket underneath it and the lower portion of the bonfire which, unaccountably, seemed to be burning in the basket. Drake, meanwhile, had climbed some stairs, stopping just below the lip of the rampart.

'Come on, lads,' he called. 'We'll let 'em get to the moat, and then lock 'em down. Get the guns down there loaded up with grape.'

This, I supposed reluctantly, was the moment to take the gate. Drake and Laminak were out of my path, and the rest of the courtyard was confused by the attack. I would have to run for it.

'Defend my approach.' I sounded far readier than I felt, but I found a musket by a dead soldier on the ground and passed it to Cunningham. 'If anyone nears me, shoot him down.'

He raised his eyebrows, and I tried not to think about the musket's notoriously poor accuracy, but there was no time for refinements to my plan. I ran forward, squeezed round the brazier and made my way along the northern wall towards the gatehouse. It was only some twenty yards away, and still no-one had noticed me amid the uproar. Everywhere muskets were rattling incessantly, their sharp cracks underpinned by the occasional roar of artillery. I remembered Copthorne's intention of taking cannon with him to Saint Margaret's, and wondered whether he had managed to bring any back to bear on the smugglers. And what of Isobel, and the message I had entrusted to her?

I was almost at the gatehouse when my luck broke. Just as I passed the last flight of stairs a man came careering down from the walls. We struck each other heavily and both of us went down, but he was quicker to his feet and as I rolled over I saw he had a bayonet angled at my throat.

'*Anglais?*' he said uncertainly.

Through my terror, I heard his words repeated; not from nearby, though, but from back by the eastern walls. Had they found Cunningham as well? But the cry was being taken up around the courtyard, and with ever greater urgency; I saw men leaping down from the ramparts and running to form a loose line behind me. My captor glanced uncertainly in their direction, and I needed no more invitation to act: I seized the barrel of his musket and dragged it to one side, at the same time kicking him hard in the crutch of his trousers. He staggered; I jammed the musket upwards and saw the butt collide with his chin. He dropped to the ground.

Keeping hold of the musket, I stood, my legs trembling from the fright I had had. The way to the gatehouse was clear, but I wondered whether it mattered now, for almost all the French soldiers I could see were desperately firing at some invisible enemy around the corner of the keep. Even in the few seconds I watched them, several fell screaming. It must be Isobel, I thought jubilantly, she must have led Bingham's men through the tunnels and brought them up inside the walls, even while others attacked from without. No wonder the invaders did not know where to turn.

I moved my gaze. Drake was frantically waving his sword and screaming to know what was happening. Where was Laminak? I could not see him in the French line. But then, there was so much darkness and confusion he could have been anywhere.

A rising light by the keep caught my attention; I turned, and stared. It was the most extraordinary thing, and for a second it transfixed me utterly. The tent I had seen earlier no longer sagged, but swelled taut and majestic, raising itself as if by a magical power into the night. It was a balloon, such as I had once read of in the newspapers, powered by some mysterious property of air or gas; suspended beneath it on ropes, being lifted swiftly upwards, hung a wicker basket. A fire blazed in its centre under the open mouth of the balloon, and by its flames I could see – quite clearly, for he was very close to it – the bearded figure of Laminak feverishly throwing fuel onto the blaze.

I put the musket to my shoulder and pulled the trigger. The recoil knocked me backwards, but either my aim was foul or the ball had rolled out, for nothing halted the balloon's progress. I looked again. Some of the ropes that had moored it still dangled down off the basket's edge, but they too were rising quickly away. This was my last chance to reach Laminak.

Launching myself across the courtyard, heedless of the gunfire that crackled around me, I reached for one of the lines and grabbed it. For a moment, nothing happened; then I felt a jerk on my arms and my feet left the ground. I think I may briefly have slowed the balloon's ascent, but Laminak must have thrown on more tinder, for the ground receded precipitately beneath me. I clung onto the rope with all my strength, the fibres digging into my hands; I twisted my arms through it so that I should not fall, but that cut them so tight I feared they would be severed through. I could not hang there for long. Even if I could, I realized, if Laminak saw me he would have little difficulty cutting me loose, leaving me to plummet to the ground. At that thought I trembled, and, against all training and reason, like a virgin midshipman sent for the first time to the masthead, I looked down.

So intent had I been on holding on that I had not realized how far we had risen. We were high up, inconceivably high, two or three times as far as you could climb on a ship, and still ascending. The castle below was like a child's plaything, the rows of men in the courtyard all but invisible, though it struck me that if I could see anything at all from this distance, the dawn must be coming. Not soon enough to warm me, though: the air was very cold, and the wind whipped at me, swinging me on my rope like an enormous pendulum. It was also, I saw with apprehension, blowing the whole contraption further up the coast.

I had never had a head for heights, and I had never had a taste for violent motion. High over England, I vomited my guts out, and immediately the wind blew half of it straight back over my coat. I convulsed, and it was as well I was so tightly wrapped through the rope or I would easily have fallen.

The fit passed. I shook myself, and started to climb. Laminak could not yet have seen me, for the horror I held that he would appear above and slice through the line had not yet been realized. The thought that he might, though, spurred me on as I inched ever further up that bucking rope, managing to refrain from looking down again.

By the time I reached the top my arms were so sore I was minded to snap them off and throw them away. Clutching the rope between my knees, I flexed my aching fingers; I still had the pistol, and I did not want to lose that precious advantage through a loose grip. The rim of the basket was only a foot or so above me now, tantalizingly close. Had it been a tree branch, and I an eight-year-old, I would have mounted it without a thought. Trying hard to imagine that that was the case, I locked my knees together more tightly than ever, lifted one hand after the other onto the wicker rim, offered a prayer to God – who, after all, could not be so far away up here – and heaved with all the strength I possessed.

It was not the most decorous entry I have ever made, but the ungainly manner of it was my salvation: I dropped over the rim with a flood of relief and in so doing rocked the basket so much that Laminak, opposite me, lost his balance and was pitched to his knees. As he regained his footing I sat back against the wall of the basket and raised my pistol, resting the barrel on my knee to keep it from shaking.

'You've done this before,' I shouted over the roar of fire and wind.

I saw now that he could not have cast my line loose, for the cockpit of this peculiar vessel was divided by bulwarks into three even compartments. Laminak was on one side, I on the other, and in the space between us the fire made an almost insuperable obstacle.

'*Oui*,' he shouted back, his bearded face twisted with shock. To my enormous relief, it seemed he was not carrying a weapon. 'An Englishman tried to sabotage that also.'

'Webb, I presume.'

He nodded angrily. 'He killed Major Vitos, before I gave him the same death.'

I gestured towards the side of my compartment, where sausage-like sacks of sand hung from ropes. 'With one of those to keep him down.' At long last, much was becoming clear. 'You've inflicted a great deal of trouble on me, Laminak.' Strictly speaking, of course, Webb had caused the trouble, but he had done it with the best of intentions. 'I would happily shoot you right now, if I did not require your skill to land this flying carriage before it blows us into the sea.' Already, I had noticed, we were beginning to sink, possibly because Laminak had ceased feeding the fire between us.

'I agree,' said Laminak. 'If you do not shoot me, I will bring us onto the land.' He bent down and I stiffened, but it was only to pick up a pile of straw from about his feet. 'We will need this.'

Everything after that happened quickly. I saw him raise the straw as if to feed the fire that drove this strange ship, but as it came up he flung it violently forward. It passed through the flames and scattered over me. The fire flared; then came a snapping sound, and suddenly the floor was falling away beneath me. The flames had licked through the ropes that suspended my half of it, and without support it had see-sawed down until it was almost perpendicular. It was as well I had already been braced against its side, for on its new angle that was become its base; had I not been nestled in its crook I would have fallen immediately. As it was, my left side was pressed tight into the wicker, while on my right was only empty space.

Coals and hot ash tumbled down over me. I shut my eyes and pressed my face into my shoulder to duck them, but still I could feel them burning into my hands and neck. The basket was rocking and shuddering; at any moment I might be tossed from its cradle.

Shielding my eyes with my fingers, I tried to peer up through the smoke and flame. I could scarcely see anything, but I had a sense of Laminak trying to stand on the inner bulwark of his compartment, his arms pushed against the edges to clamp himself in. But if he had hoped to topple me out and save himself, he had misjudged it badly. Though the embers from the fire were falling over me, its flames rose higher than ever, licking over his body and igniting his clothes, his hair, the basket and ropes about him. There was nowhere for him to go; already the fire was edging towards the envelope of the balloon above him. With a horrible, unforgettable scream, he leaped off his perch. Arms flailed and smoke poured off him as he fell past me, down into the same oblivion that had overtaken Webb and Vitos before him.

Even had I felt anything other than relief, I had no time to savour his passing. My own clothes were already beginning to smoulder, and though I knew little enough of the forces keeping the vessel aloft, I could guess that the flapping, billowing shreds of the canopy would not suit the purpose. I looked down, and saw only waves rushing ever closer.

When the sea beneath seemed close enough to offer less hazard than the rising heat around me, I closed my eyes and let go. Air rushed past, and I suddenly remembered once seeing a sailor fall from his yard, remembered wondering what he had felt in those few infinite moments between the heavens and the depths. Surprisingly little, I now found – only a tight pressure against my chest and a dizzying vortex of colour below, moving so fast I could not grasp it. I felt a fearsome punch. Then darkness.

The tide carried me ashore, half drowned, half charred, half dead and less than half alive. It rolled me up onto the beach, like any one of the ten thousand other pebbles it would pick up that day, and left me near the tidemark. Seaweed filled my nostrils and flies buzzed through my ears, but I gave them no thought. I had none left.

The ticklish stroking of water about my ankles woke me: the tide was coming back in. And not just the tide. If I concentrated, I could hear footsteps grinding over the shingle. I opened my eyes.

'Jerrold,' said Crawley disdainfully. 'I had not expected to see you again.'

'Nor I you, sir,' I replied after a moment. Nor, now I considered it, had I expected to see him half naked and soaking wet. 'Have you been swimming?'

Even as I shook my head in hopeless consternation, I saw Ducker arrive behind Crawley. He, too, was dripping everywhere, but he eyed me with an unmistakable satisfaction.

'Lieutenant Jerrold, sir,' he said triumphantly. 'I knowed it.'

'Knew what, Ducker?'

He waved at the beach. 'Scene o' the crime. Knowed the killer'd come back.'

I tried to laugh, but only coughed up a small trickle of sea-water. 'You may be right.' Through his legs, behind him and a little further up the beach, I thought I could see the twisted limbs of Laminak's broken body. 'But I am not he.' I choked a little. 'Sir Lawrence Cunningham will vouch for me.'

It seemed the funniest joke in the world. No wonder they looked at me as though I were a madman.

22

THE BELLS WERE TOLLING AND THE CHURCHES DISGORGING THEIR congregations as we passed the smoking castle walls and came into the town. I did not imagine the government would want it widely known that a French army had managed to invade the country, but I could see the rumours already beginning to spread over the passing faces, all of which steadfastly refused to look at the unlikely trio of naval officers – grimy and soaking wet, one of them supported by the others – who walked, ghost-like, through their midst.

We reached the square.

'I suppose I ought to return you to the gaol, Lieutenant,' said Crawley hesitantly. 'That, after all, is where you are expected to be.'

None of us had spoken a word on the walk back, so I had yet to apprise him of my curious adventures. I did not have the strength to tell him now. I feared I would need formidable powers of stamina to convince anyone of the truth of it.

'It's for Sir Lawrence to put people in the gaol,' I argued. 'And even if you did, we have established that I can walk out of it at my leisure. Why not keep me aboard *Orestes* until Sir Lawrence returns?'

'*Orestes* is still at sea,' said Crawley. 'And you know well enough that we have no brig.'

'Then send me to my room at the inn and put Constable Stubb on the door. I need a bed, and a clean pair of clothes. You can see I'm too feeble to trouble him.' I could barely stand upright. 'And I promise I will not fly away out of the window. I've had my fill of that for this day.'

Crawley, who clearly longed for a bed and bath of his own, assented. Ducker led me back, sending Isaac to fetch Stubb. In truth, they could have left a limbless dwarf to guard me and I would not have overcome him, but I suppose it made them feel safer.

I left Ducker with a sage piece of advice to take back to Crawley, and then, as I heard Stubb's tread on the stairs, swiftly sequestered myself in my room. Though I do not know why I persisted in calling it my room, for it seemed more often than not I was a visitor there.

'I don't recall that I invited you back.' I was immeasurably tired, and it told in my voice.

'I couldn't risk Miss Hoare, and the parson couldn't have me,' explained Isobel quietly. 'His aunt's visiting. And I heard you wouldn't be needing it. Isaac let me in. For a sixpence.'

There was an awkward silence. On the one hand, of course, there was the fact that she had twice rescued me from certain doom – thrice, if you counted the soldiers she must have led into the castle keep. But on the other hand, being back here in the mundane confines of Dover reminded me of her unsavoury past, and in this room, a world away from danger and heroics, the rights and wrongs seemed infinitely difficult, moral complexities far beyond my consideration and judgement. Retreat seemed the easiest solution.

'I shall be in the bar.' I pulled on the door, but it did not give. 'Let me out,' I shouted, banging loudly.

'You might've walked out o' Dover gaol, but you'll not get past Hezekiah Stubb so easy,' the constable yelled back.

I offered a few pointed words which, on reflection, I would not have said in front of a lady.

'Can I speak, Martin?' asked Isobel from the bed. 'As you've nowhere else to go.'

'Very well.' I shrugged. Even that was an effort. 'But at least allow me my own bed. It's been two nights since I saw one of those.'

'I've warmed it for you.'

She slid off and took the stool. I lay down and let myself sink into the blessed softness of the mattress.

'Now,' said Isobel earnestly, 'you can send me away if you want, and I'll go, but I do . . .'

I couldn't have sent her away on a mail coach. I was fast asleep.

I awoke in darkness. There were thin arms clutched about my chest, and a warm cheek against my neck. Somehow my clothes had vanished – as well, really, for they had been very damp.

'You incorrigible marauder,' I muttered. 'Keeping the French from our shores is nothing against trying to keep you out of my bed.' It suddenly seemed ridiculous that I should want to. 'Are you awake?'

She murmured some sort of assent.

'How much did you really do for the smugglers?' I wondered. 'Or, if you will, how much did they put you up to?'

She thought on it for a while, so long that I thought she had fallen back into sleep.

'I took up with you at the Crown and Anchor, if that's what you're asking, because I wanted some nonsense, like I said,' she said at last. 'And I kept coming back because I liked it, and I thought you did, too. But the Drake gang, they've got ears on every wall in Dover, and they've been into me since I was that small. When you started asking your questions, they asked some back, and you can't shut your mouth to the Drake gang. I never peached you though,' she added hastily. 'Whatever they knew about where you'd be, that was someone else.'

'A banker named Henry Mazard, I should think. Benefiting from his friendship with Sir Lawrence. But go on.'

'Not much else to go on about. I delivered the tubs, of course, but everyone does that. I told them little odds and ends about Sir Lawrence when I was working for him, but there wasn't much I could tell worth saying.' She propped herself up on a bare arm. 'That's my history, Martin, and if it's a stain then it's one you can't scrub off me. You might as well try to remove my arms.'

'I certainly would not want that.' I grunted, and rolled over to kiss the limbs in question. 'Such lovely arms.'

'Just my arms?' she asked, pressing forward other portions of her aspect for my consideration.

'No,' I conceded. 'Not just your arms.'

Tired though I was, she would not let me sleep again until I had satisfied her of my admiration for all her body. And indeed, there was much to admire.

My last morning in Dover commenced, predictably, with a thumping. I had forgotten that advantage to sleeping in caves and gaols. It was a wonder there was not a fist-sized hole in my door by now.

'Cap'n Crawley wants you at the guild'all, sir,' said Ducker's voice. Then, more quietly, 'Did 'e try an escape, Mr Stubb?'

'No.'

Stubb sounded disappointed. But then, I suspected I had passed a more enjoyable night than he.

'Mr Cunningham says you can go,' Ducker told him. 'There's no need for it.'

I dressed.

'Stay here,' I told Isobel, wondering if by the perversity of her nature she would take that instruction as a reason to go. It certainly was not my purpose.

She smiled cheekily from the bed. 'Don't have a place to go anyway.'

To an unschooled observer, the guildhall that morning might well have been mistaken for the seamen's hospital. Crawley sported an enormous bruise on his cheek, Cunningham's face was wrapped like a leper's, and Colonel Copthorne had his arm in a sling. All looked strained and haggard. The only man in the room looking acceptable was the one I least expected to see: Nevell.

'Good morning, Lieutenant,' said Copthorne warmly. 'Thank you for attending. I thought we ought to assemble here to discuss the events of Saturday night. I have dispatches to write for my superiors

– doubtless, Captain Crawley, you have too – and it seemed they would read considerably better if we were agreed on what had actually happened. Hence your invitation, Lieutenant. From my initial enquiries, your name appears to arise with alarming frequency.'

He must have seen the apprehension in my face, for he went on, 'Before we begin, I should add that Sir Lawrence has already provided me with his most forceful assurances that he witnessed your conduct in the battle at the castle and is satisfied that you acted in the best traditions of your service. He is convinced that any slanders which have been laid against you are utterly baseless and without merit. He also wishes me to convey his thanks to you for conducting an examination of the security of his gaol, which conclusions he looks forward to receiving.'

Perhaps Sir Lawrence feared I would accuse him of murdering a captive in chains, or perhaps Simon Drake pummelled him harder than I'd realized, but I would not argue it. I nodded my gracious agreement. Cunningham gave a sickly smile.

'Now,' said Copthorne. 'What precisely did we witness on Saturday?'

'A French landing,' began Nevell.

'Of course it was a French landing,' snapped Copthorne. 'Or at least, there were certainly Frenchmen there – I killed four of the bastards myself. But Buonaparte's not going to invade with a battalion. Even his arrogance has its bounds. And he's kept his army in the East, long may it stay there.'

'It was a ploy,' I said wearily. 'A ploy to convince us that there was an invasion, to stop the government negotiating its peace and allow Mazard and his confederates to keep up the lucrative businesses they had supplying our forces, bringing in contraband, and, far more profitably, playing the creditor to the French government.'

'Creditor?' repeated Copthorne, dumbfounded. 'An Englishman funding the French tyrant? I never heard anything half so preposterous.'

'He made forty per cent.' For me, that silenced any argument.

Now Crawley spoke. 'I can substantiate much of Lieutenant Jerrold's story, Colonel. Yesterday morning, acting on information he relayed, I impounded Mazard's brig *Navarre*. From her charts, and the testimony of her master, we believe she was bound for France. In her hold were fifty thousand guineas.'

Copthorne's bandaged arm lifted from his sling as he drew a deep, disbelieving breath. 'But surely, Captain, Lieutenant, a continental power cannot be financed by a single provincial banker. There must have been partners. Accomplices.'

'There were,' confirmed Nevell. 'A French colonel, found dead on the beach this morning, and at present with the coroner. Simon Drake, brother of the late, nefarious Caleb Drake, who took care of the more dubious arrangements. He is also, as it happens, with the coroner. Shot, I'm told. In the back.' He raised an eyebrow, and glanced significantly at Cunningham.

Sir Lawrence grunted. 'The man was blind, makes no difference which side he was shot in. But these are underlings, trifles. I worked long enough with Mazard, God knows, and I can scarce believe he could muster such sums alone. If he was backing Buonaparte, who were *his* backers?'

The question hung in the air, while I thought back on Lord Arlington and his fabulous chest of golden guineas. Perhaps, later, I would mention it to Nevell. For now, though, I left him to contend alone with the expectant eyes fixed on him.

'Their identities remain obscure,' he admitted. 'And with Mazard dead in the cells of the castle, he will sadly not be telling us.' The vivid image of Mazard's broken skull ebbing blood flared in my mind. 'Certainly these investors exist, probably in London. But they will not be the sort of men to be dallied with. They will command the most significant interest, and they will be well protected. By all manner of means. The rich,' Nevell concluded glumly, 'usually are.'

'You mean, you do not know who they might be.'

I marvelled that Sir Lawrence had the gall to make this gibe, for all that the coroner had blamed Mazard's death on a falling-out among the smugglers. In that moment I was almost tempted to raise the truth of the matter, but wisely I forbore. I had crossed swords with Cunningham often enough.

'There is also the stock issue,' added Nevell. 'Part of Mazard's plan, we suspect, was that the seizure of the castle would prompt an invasion scare to sweep the stock exchange. He had sold off vast holdings in London with a view to buying them back when their prices had collapsed, then realizing huge gains when it emerged that there was no invasion after all. If we can find others who liquidated their stock in the past week, we may have some names to start with.'

'Hence the flying balloon,' I thought aloud. 'How much stronger the rumours if shells from an invisible army were falling on inland towns.'

Copthorne fixed me with a wholly incredulous stare. 'Flying balloons, Lieutenant?' he asked severely. I remembered on what tenuous threads my credibility still hung. 'Perhaps we should unravel this scheme from its beginnings.'

The conversation lasted many hours, until my back ached from sitting in the chair and my stomach demanded sustenance. Often I found myself talking, filling in details or explaining certain points, but even then I had more than half my mind distracted by a desire to get back to the inn. Most of it I knew, or had guessed, or did not care about, though I was amused to hear how Crawley, in his enthusiasm, had capsized the jollyboat coming ashore at Saint Margaret's. Otherwise it was all overwhelmingly tedious. Only at long last did Copthorne dismiss us. God knew how his report would read.

But there was one thing that did still intrigue me, though it had no place in the dispatches, and my patience had been so sapped by the meeting that I had little appetite for tact. The story of the jollyboat had prompted the memory of Davenant's gibe at the ball, and I was curious. With my reputation temporarily in the ascendant, I felt I could risk a direct approach.

'Tell me, sir,' I asked Crawley as we descended the steps, 'did you really sink the *Glorious*?'

He scowled viciously. 'I was the officer of the watch on deck,' he said. 'It was therefore my responsibility.'

'Unless, of course, a senior officer had come on deck,' I mused. 'A captain, or first lieutenant.'

'It was a confused night. It would be hard to recollect who precisely was on deck. That is why they have enquiries and courts-martial to establish such things.'

'The conclusions of courts-martial cannot always be relied upon.' If they could, I'd have been staring at the point of my sword long ago.

'The justice of the Lord is infinite,' said Crawley inscrutably. 'A man who one day suffers for his superior's error may on another day find his fortunes reversed, his reputation restored by the gallantry of his subordinates. Especially,' he added, 'if that gallantry brings a haul of fifty thousand contraband guineas.'

And that, it seemed, was all the answer I would get from Crawley – though if I ever sailed with him again, I thought, I would feel a good deal safer in shallow waters.

We reached the corner of the square.

'Well, Jerrold,' said Crawley awkwardly. 'I hardly needed a surplus lieutenant for my crew when the coast was crawling with smugglers. Now that our enemies are fallen away, it seems callous to keep you in Dover. Unless you care to stay.'

'I can think of few places, sir, where I would rather not be,' I said honestly. 'And I would not feel entirely safe here.' I did not believe that we had accounted for all Drake's associates, or his relatives. 'So, if you have no more use for me . . .'

Alarmingly, Crawley laughed. 'I suppose I could always have a use for someone of your peculiar abilities, Lieutenant, but it is my prerogative to give you leave, and I suspect a week or two away would do you far more good than shipping barrels of biscuit about until the Admiralty decides what to do with us. Go home and recover yourself. Doubtless you will need your strength for another ship soon enough.'

'Actually, sir, I have a mind to quit the navy.' So far it had only been a half-formed thought, but the prospect of home and rest made it suddenly enormously tempting. 'I do not know that I am suited to it. Too many low ceilings.'

Crawley looked keenly into my eyes, and touched my shoulder. 'Think on it, Jerrold, think on it,' he said. '"The wisdom of the prudent is to understand his way, but the folly of fools is deceit."'

We parted with a handshake and I returned to the inn. A mail coach was in the courtyard, its driver swearing at the ostlers that one of his wheels had come loose, and he would not suffer the awful consequences if they could not mend it swiftly.

I interrupted the flow of his invective. 'Excuse me,' I asked, 'but when do you depart?'

Amid a continuing torrent of abuse for the stable hands, I gathered that it would be in about half an hour, if those miserable sons of whores, et cetera, could fasten his wheel on straight.

Was he bound for London?

He would be lucky to get anywhere, he explained, on account that what the grooms had done to his wheel was so abominable that he did not doubt the Almighty would take offence and destroy the coach with a well-aimed shaft of His lightning.

But if the good Lord took mercy, would he have space for a passenger?

He could not imagine that any gentleman would want to endure ten hours' riding over that wheel, but if the gentleman was possessed of a criminal disregard for his comfort and safety, he did have the seats.

'Excellent. I shall have my trunk with you directly.'

I went to my room. Isobel was still there.

'I have been released,' I told her quickly. 'And there is a coach in the yard. I am going home.'

Her dark eyes moistened. 'Of course you are,' she said softly. 'You were only here for your job.'

'I would very much enjoy your company.'

At that, she stopped short. A tear trickled down her nose, and she had to wipe it on her sleeve.

'What about the magistrate?' she asked. 'You spent the morning with him. Doesn't he want to speak to me?'

I paused.

'I fear, Isobel, that in the telling of my adventure to him, I may inadvertently have misrepresented your part, implied that you were an innocent captive with me and that I rescued us both before sending you for help.' I smiled. 'We will need similar feats of invention if we are to concoct a story to explain you to my mother. You may have to be my long-lost cousin.'

She flung herself about me and squeezed me so hard my back cracked. It took some moments to peel her off, to remind her that she had little enough time to fetch her possessions from the laundry, and that there would be many hours of intimacy to come.

'I'll go to the parson, and Miss Hoare, and be back before you can say "Uncle Jack",' she promised.

'I'll see you in the courtyard,' I said, kissing her goodbye.

I was not entirely sure that what I was doing was wise, but it felt satisfying, and for now, that would do.

It needed less than two minutes to pack my diminished stock of respectable shirts into my trunk. With time to dispose of, I went downstairs.

'A glass of brandy,' I told Isaac.

'That's a shillin',' he replied, holding the drink hostage.

'A shilling?' I exclaimed. 'It was sixpence last week, you usurer!'

'Problem with the supply,' said Isaac blithely. 'Prices goes up. Not to worry though,' he added consolingly. 'It'll be sorted in a week or two, go back down. Always does.'

Doubtless it would, though that would be of little use to me. For the moment I suffered the cost of my own success. I supposed I could pay an extra sixpence for that.

There was a commotion in the yard outside and I went to the door. It was the coachman, again: his wheel seemed mended, but now there was a new carriage in the archway blocking his path. He spat and swore and waved his arms at the driver, a sturdy man in blue trousers and a red checked shirt who ignored him completely as he leaped down to open the carriage door. As it swung open, I saw it was painted with the design of a bright gold anchor wound with rope.

A gilded shoe stepped delicately to the ground. Its wearer sniffed the air disapprovingly, then turned. He stiffened as he caught sight of me in the doorway.

'Jerrold!' he roared, in a voice that silenced the blaspheming coachman instantly. 'You despicable cur! Unblushed by your past notoriety, I am now brought tales of the utmost villainy, of misdeeds so vile I can disbelieve them only a fraction less than I must believe them. So repellent, indeed, that I have been compelled to come all the way from London to pass judgement on your execrable little life. Do not think you will survive the ordeal. Well? Do you dare defend yourself?'

I laughed. 'Hallo, Uncle,' I said.

Author's Note

MY OWN HABIT WHEN READING NOVELS WITH AN HISTORICAL NOTE IS to flip to it well before I finish the book. If any readers share this tendency, they should know that this one covers several matters central to the resolution of the story. You have been warned.

The idea of English bankers funding Napoleon's conquests, or of French soldiers making commando raids on the British coast, may seem fantastical, but both are based firmly in fact. A golden guinea worth twenty-one shillings in England could fetch thirty shillings in Paris, and in those days, as now, not all financial institutions and speculators were so squeamish that they would pass up such rates of return, even if it meant supporting Britain's ancient enemy. The trade was enormous: it is estimated that at its height some ten thousand guineas a week were being ferried across the Channel, and a whole new class of vessel, known as 'guinea boats', was purpose-built for the task. After his capture and imprisonment, Napoleon acknowledged that there were times when this cash-flow was vital in keeping his army paid and his power secure.

French soldiers actually landing on British soil during this period is also fact. In 1798, several hundred soldiers landed on the Pembrokeshire coast as a diversion, hoping to draw away attention from another, larger force sailing for rebellious Ireland. In the event, both expeditions failed, but the last French musket-balls fired in Britain can still be seen in Fishguard. Seven years later, Napoleon's desire to conquer Britain was undimmed: throughout the summer of 1805 he kept an army of some hundred thousand men stationed around Boulogne. Known as the Army of England, Napoleon felt he needed only a few hours' naval supremacy in the Channel to make its crossing. A commemorative obelisk was begun and a campaign medal struck in anticipation of the expected triumph, but French naval weakness, even before the battle of Trafalgar that October, forced Napoleon to abandon his plans, redesignate his forces 'la Grande Armée' and, like another despot after him, turn his attentions east. But although we know now that this was to prove the end of the matter, that Trafalgar would secure British naval supremacy for over a century, this was by no means obvious at the time.

The other element of the book which may need some comment is the hot-air balloon. Balloons had been around for over twenty years by 1806, and had successfully been used to cross the Channel as early as 1785 (when, with a claim to inventing first-class air travel, the aeronauts carried with them copious supplies of port, brandy and cigars, which unfortunately had to be jettisoned when the balloon started to lose altitude prematurely). If there is an anachronism, it is that the balloon Jerrold finally encounters is of a much older design than would have been prevalent in 1806. I attribute this to the difficulties Laminak would have faced transporting hydrogen to Dover.

For the rest of the book, I have embellished as little as possible on what we know. Smuggling in the eighteenth century was considered the 'national evil', and its central role in life on the south coast cannot be overstated. In 1773, there were an estimated fifteen thousand men involved in smuggling in Kent alone, and the new taxes demanded by the wars against Napoleon, the blockade of France and the secondment of many customs cutters to naval service provided few disincentives thereafter. The techniques described in the book are authentic, though far from exhaustive, as smugglers and preventivemen grew ever more ingenious in their methods.

Smuggling did decline after 1805 as more resources were available to combat it, but exploded again after 1815 when a general economic crisis precipitated by peace and demobilization left thousands of men with no alternative livelihood. It was not brought under control until an innovative naval officer, Captain William McCulloch, introduced regular cordons of naval personnel ashore, in a blockade line which eventually stretched from Sheerness to Chichester and employed some three thousand men. The complications of the anti-smuggling business are well illustrated by one struggle Captain McCulloch faced within his own ranks: how to compensate officers serving ashore for the loss of their duty-free allowance.

Anyone visiting Dover today is unlikely to find much of the Georgian town left: the onslaughts of Victorian improvers and German bombers have left little from Jerrold's day, although most of the street names remain the same. The Western Docks and marina still follow the pattern of 1806, but the Eastern ferry terminal and anchorage are far more modern. The guildhall on the market square has been demolished, and the gaol where Jerrold spent so much time was partially destroyed in 1820 when an angry mob of townsfolk came to free two smugglers imprisoned there. The site is, however, well worth a visit, as it now houses the excellent Dover Museum. Of the churches featured, St James's (home of Caleb Drake's memorial) was bombed in the war but has been kept as a picturesque, ruined monument; its graveyard is now a leisure-centre car park. St Martin-le-Grand, where Martin and Isobel were attacked, was a ruin even in 1806, and is now completely gone, but its stones can still be seen recycled into the wall of the NatWest bank. Dover castle is well known and worth seeing. There you can still visit the caves tunnelled deep into the chalk cliffs.

Many people helped in the writing of this book, far more than I have the space to thank properly. I'm particularly grateful to Brian Williams and the staff at the Dover Museum and Library, whose accessible resources should be an example to small museums everywhere; to Barbara Tomlinson, Arthur Janes and the staff of the National Maritime Museum in Greenwich; to Trina, Carl and Aaron at Mystic Seaport, Connecticut; and to Tim Carter, for supplying charts, books, an outlet for my frustrations and the odd piece of sailing advice. Sadly, all their knowledge combined couldn't protect me from myself, and any mistakes that remain are entirely my own.

Away from the libraries, Gary Heslop and Sean Elliot allowed me an enormous amount of latitude when I was supposed to be working for them. Mike Jecks, the Crime Writers' Association, and the judges of the Debut Dagger gave me the chance, and the confidence, to develop the story, and opened many doors. Jane Conway-Gordon showed faith at an early stage and has been irreplaceable ever since. Selina Walker and Simon Thorogood vastly improved the book, and taught me a lot about writing in the process.

Helen and George Hayios tirelessly read everything I produced and gave invaluable criticism. They, my parents, and friends, colleagues and family old and new were constantly generous in their support and encouragement.

There were days when I struggled with the book, and days when it came easily. What kept me going through them all was my wife Emma. This is for her.